THE

AMERICAN
LAWYER

JOHN MARTEL

THE — A NOVEL — AMERICAN LAWYER

Vantage Point Books and the Vantage Point Books colophon are registered trademarks of Vantage Press, Inc.

FIRST EDITION: October 2012

Published by Vantage Point Books
Vantage Press, Inc.
271 Main Street
Great Barrington, MA 01230
www.vantagepointbooks.com

Manufactured in the United States of America
ISBN: 978-1-936467-61-7

Library of Congress Cataloging-in-Publication data are on file.

9   8   7   6   5   4   3   2   1

COVER DESIGN BY Victor Mingovits

This one is for three women in my life:
Melissa, my inspirational and loving daughter;
Mary, my treasured friend and sister;
and Bonnie, my wife, my keeper, my heart of gold.

ACKNOWLEDGEMENTS

THIS BOOK WOULD not have been born but for the mid-wifery of my brother-in-law, Don Eggleston, who terrified us over dinner one night with stories about the ongoing violence in Guatemala. He had grown up there during a bloody, thirty-six-year revolution, in which 200,000 people were killed. I was immediately inspired to base a novel there, so Don accompanied my wife and me to Guatemala City and introduced me to a friend who also became essential to the writing of this book. I am disappointed not to be able to acknowledge this brave and generous Guatemalan and his incredible wife by name, but they prefer to remain anonymous and I don't blame them. They know who they are, however, and they have my eternal gratitude.

My new Guatamalan friend (I'll call him Jack) arranged many hours of interviews with locals on both sides of the political spectrum, got me into the dread Pavoncito Prison for several hours, escorted me all over his country, and once even used his .45 caliber automatic to thwart a kidnapping/car-jacking attempt while we were returning to Guatemala City from a research trip to the Bay of Honduras and the dangerous *Río Dulce* area. (We had been warned, of course. The current advisory from the U.S. State Department admonishes that, "Emboldened armed robbers have attacked vehicles on main roads in broad daylight. Travel on rural roads always increases the risk of a criminal roadblock or ambush." The Appendix at the end of this book offers additional excerpts from the current State Department Advisory.)

Guatemala is an incredibly beautiful, but also very dangerous, third world country, in which problems of violence and corruption have sadly survived the Peace Accords of 1996.

David Lamb and Vantage Point Books have provided incredible editing and marketing support, for which I also thank Laura Ross, Lindsey Catherine Cornum and Brenna Filipello. I am also indebted to Barbara McHugh, Joe Pittman, and my intrepid super-agent, Doug Grad, for their support and keen editorial insights, as well as to my friend Jim Haydel, who has been a dear friend, critic, and editorial advisor for four decades. I am also grateful to Randy Wulff, Doug Young, Jay Martel, Rick Van Duzer, Will James, and the late Fred Hill, for their comments and encouragement. Although I never met him except through email, Robert Bermijo, a Guatemala City lawyer, was invaluable in helping me understand Guatemalan law and trial procedure under the country's new constitution. Any errors in either legal substance or procedure are the author's, not his.

I am indebted to numerous treatises and historical writers for their research and insights, most notably Carlos Fuentes, *The Buried Mirror*, and the writings of Rigoberta Menchu. My year buried in research on Guatemala led me from the defeat of the Maya in the sixteenth century to the present day and I salute this brave nation, under attack by drugs, gangs, and corruption, as it continues its struggle to achieve a lasting democracy and internal security for its citizens.

I have taken literary license with the course of history in only two respects that I'm aware of. First, I've slightly altered the year of death of The Emperor Charles V of Spain and provided him with a fictitious confessor named Cardinal Vespucci and an imagined document. I believe that other historical references are reasonably accurate, and I hope that their discovery will be as exciting and interesting for the reader as they were for me.

Finally, thanks to Bonnie Martel, who once again served admirably as copy editor, typist, tolerant wife, critic, partner, best friend, and the love of my life.

—JSM

AUTHOR'S NOTE ON HISTORICAL CONTEXT

IN HIGH SCHOOL history, we learned about the famous explorer and conquistador, Hernán Cortéz, who, under the banner of Spanish colonialism, brought the Aztecs to their knees in 1521 and raised the flag of Spain over Mexico. Some of us might recall that Cortéz then sent Pedro de Alvarado—an even meaner killing machine than himself—to conquer the Maya in what is now the political tinderbox we call Guatemala, the third largest country in Central America.

What few of us learned in school (or have forgotten, along with various algebraic formulae and the second verse of *America the Beautiful*), was that Cortéz went a bit squirrely as he grew old, suffering wide mood swings, heavy guilt-tripping, and paranoid fantasies. History records that with victory secured in the New World, things quickly deteriorated for Spain's hero. By 1525, the Crown's bureaucrats had taken over the military government and had launched formal charges against Cortéz for atrocities committed against the Indians, for having stolen Montezuma's treasure, and for having murdered his then-current wife, Catalina Juarez.

The Conquistador was recalled to Spain to face the charges and immediately took the offensive, insisting that the Crown return him to the new colonies, where he hoped to regain the glory he had once enjoyed. The Holy Roman Emperor Carlos Quinto finally issued a pardon and granted Cortéz a fiefdom in Mexico between Cuernavaca and Oaxaca. There he died, embittered and alone, with nothing to show for his conquest of the New World but a few hectares of its soil.

These are recorded facts known to all students of New World history. Less known is what the Emperor ordered Cortéz to do upon his return—and what Cortéz did instead, which threatened to disrupt the course of Central American history.

And how Cortéz's actions affected the fortunes of a young San Francisco lawyer named Jesse Hall nearly five centuries later.

—JSM

"Guatemala mocks me: 'Just as you think you understand, we'll show you that you understand nothing at all.'"

—SUSANNE JONAS

PROLOGUE
Guatemala City

AS THE FINAL residuum of life leaked out of Marisa Andrade, shock mercifully muted the pain from her multiple knife wounds.

But not her despair.

Nobody would come home in time to save her, not now. Not in the middle of the day. And who would take her place as executive director of *La Causa*, just when they were so close?

Her thoughts drifted to Teo, her shaggy bear of a husband, who had pleaded with her to stop courting danger. Would he ever understand the importance of her work?

Her face clenched as waves of pain broke through the solace of shock, jarring her into anger. Anger at having to relinquish the dream of seeing her country returned to the people, anger at having to die so young, and, most of all, anger that the sonofabitch who had killed her would probably get away with it.

¡Bastardo! She forced one eye open and saw that she had fallen near the credenza behind Teo's desk. One end of the *mantón,* the shawl

that served as a runner covering the credenza, hung tantalizingly close to her outstretched left arm. The shawl, her most treasured possession, had been handwoven by her Mayan mother and bore her tribal colors. Marisa watched the red and gold threads of the fringe dance like fragile, beckoning fingers in the shaft of sunlight that pierced the study's beveled glass window. *Quizás*, she thought; perhaps I can do this one last thing.

She reached up, and a stab of pain pierced her side as she grabbed a corner of the shawl. She pulled hard, but her fingers were wet with blood and slipped away from the fringe. Her breathing was shallow and erratic and she felt cold. Something—blood or perspiration—was blurring her vision. She tried again, despite the excruciating pain, but this time her fingers failed to reach the fringe.

Let it go, came a distant sound, more like a cello than a voice. Was it her mother's voice? *You've earned your rest,* it seemed to say.

No! she said, and reached up again, seizing the corner of the *mantón*. This time, she pulled harder and held on. She heard a small glass vase shatter against the floor amidst a shower of pencils, a fountain pen and inkwell, assorted papers, and, yes, her cell phone! Then stillness again but for the ticking of the clock.

The phone was only inches out of reach of her left hand, but it might as well have been in another room. Also the pens, the pencils. She felt bits of glass near her right hand and something wet. Her own blood?

The cello sang, *Let it go.*

1
San Francisco

THERE ARE THREE ways a pissed-off senior law firm partner can get rid of an irritatingly bright and popular associate who's up for partnership. Two of them do not involve homicide.

Most common is the time-honored method of overwhelming the young lawyer with more work than can possibly be done well, then firing him or her for substandard performance. The second way is to find an ill-prepared case in the office and assign it to the hapless associate just two or three days before trial, then give him the shoe when he loses.

The pissed-off senior partner in this instance was Eric Driver, the brilliant, porcine chief of Caldwell and Shaw's securities group. Driver picked the second method and Jesse Hall (the popular associate whose penchant for *pro bono publico* work had turned the parsimonious Driver against him) soon found himself studying a jury—a collection of retirees, housewives, two postal workers, and one Burger King night manager—that would soon judge his client, defendant Ben Staley.

Jesse didn't like what he saw. The jurors—especially the women—had obviously been charmed by plaintiff Calvin "Cal" Covington's glib bullshit on direct examination. The big Texan's pale blue, heavily-lidded eyes had caressed the jurors as warmly as his embellished drawl. Jesse had to admit that despite being abundantly full of crap, the man was engaging. Over six feet four, three inches taller than Jesse, Covington's looks were otherwise ordinary, and his manner was disarmingly folksy, his rumpled brown suit looking as if it had been recently washed—with him in it. Covington—sophisticated billionaire CEO of CalCorp International—had reinvented himself as the perfect plaintiff.

"I might as well have invited a fox into my chicken house," said Covington, finishing up his testimony in a tone of perfectly blended disappointment and righteous indignation. "Ben Staley quit my company, took our proprietary and confidential customer list with him, then sold auto parts to my customers far below his own cost. This was clearly predatory pricing—temporarily selling cheap to put me out of business, so he could then have my customers all to himself."

Covington finished with the anguished sigh of a man betrayed, and then spread his hands, palms up. What more was there to say?

"That's all we have, Your Honor," announced Norman Crandell, CalCorp's lawyer, a suave, grey-haired litigator wearing a $2,000 suit and a supercilious smile.

"Do you wish to cross-examine, counsel?" said Judge Martha Berman, a bright young Schwarzenegger appointee, whose tone suggested that Jesse would be insane to try it.

Jesse groaned inwardly and raked his fingers through his straw-colored hair. He had always hated injustice in any form, and Covington was an obvious commercial bully who had wrapped himself in the gauzy protection of arcane laws, artfully tailored by the best lawyers money could buy.

A plaintiff's verdict would finish Ben Staley, financially and emotionally. Although Jesse had only known the old guy a few days, he liked Ben and didn't want to let him down. But the case had been ill-prepared and it was clear to Jesse why Eric Driver had fired the associate who had worked it up. There was no defense expert witness. No witnesses at all. The case was full of holes.

Jesse had a single ace he might be able to play, but knew it would not be enough unless he could first break the spell Covington had cast over the jury.

He glanced up at the witness and his heart pounded with mingled anxiety and frustration. Covington returned Jesse's gaze with a laser look that said he was ready for anything the kid might throw at him. This was a man who had created an automotive supply empire out of nothing, boasting over six thousand retail stores internationally and total domination of the Internet auto-parts market. Whether you recently replaced your windshield or just a wiper, you probably contributed to CalCorp's bottom line.

"*Cross-examine*, Mr. Hall?" asked the judge, impatiently fiddling with her gavel. "Preferably before the close of the current epoch?"

Jesse rose and glanced upward as if for guidance. He was once again struck by the grandeur of the venerable, high-ceilinged courtroom that seemed too large for a case so small, a case that only himself and his client seemed genuinely interested in. He was aware of an uncomfortable dampness across his back and a sound like a broken bicycle pump—his own breathing. He knew the jury was watching him, waiting to see what he would do. He resisted the urge to lick his dry lips, knowing it might betray his anxiety. And there on the witness stand, the big man waited, too, a broad harmonica smile on his own full lips that exposed two even rows of large white teeth set above a chin the size of a bucket. Everything about the man was big.

Not just big, but very big and *very* rich—which got Jesse thinking. The trick in trial work was to try to break the connection between the jury and your opponent. And didn't Covington's great wealth put him into a different universe from every juror in the box? He felt a chill. He had his theme. Now he just had to develop it into a killer cross and hope his ace would provide the Big Finish. If so, who knew what might happen? He approached the witness. "Mr. Covington—"

"Call me 'Cal,' son. Everybody does." Jesse heard the subtext: *I may be powerful and richer than God, but, hell, folks, I'm just one of you.*

"Sir, you—CalCorp—are a Fortune 500 Company, right?"

"Yep. The good Lord has been excessively good to me, undeserving though I may be." Another smile at the jurors and two of them smiled back! Jesse felt more dampness spreading across his back.

"Standard and Poors says your company had six and a half billion dollars in sales last year. Sound right?"

"Ballpark," Covington said.

"Are you aware that Ben Staley had only two hundred thousand dollars in sales in this region since leaving CalCorp, far less than one-tenth of a thousandth of your total sales?"

Jesse knew—and hoped the jury would soon see—that to Cal Covington, old Ben Staley was merely a fly on an elephant's ass. But if Ben could get away with this intransigence, employees all over the world might get it in their heads to go out on their own. So, in Covington's view, the fly had to be swatted.

"Well, young man," the witness said, "that just tells me old Ben shoulda stayed with me instead of going out on his own and bitin' the hand that's been feedin' him." One juror actually nodded in agreement, sending a rivulet of perspiration down Jesse's forehead and into his left eye. "And don't forget that every sale Ben's made has taken money straight out of my pocket. Don't also forget while you're at it, that this here region is where CalCorp was born."

"We'll come to that, Mr. Covington. I'm just saying that your pockets are pretty deep compared with Ben's. Or looking at it another way, if Ben's sales had been ten-thousand times bigger than they were, your revenue wouldn't be dented by so much as one percent. Am I right?"

"Objection," shouted Crandell. "Conjectural and irrelevant."

"Withdrawn, Your Honor," said Jesse, relieved to have provoked the objection he'd counted on. He didn't have a clue if his numbers were accurate, but knew the impression on the jury would stick. "Tell me, sir, do you claim that Ben's sales were all made to retailers named on your secret list of customers?"

"I do," Covington said, with the solemnity of a wedding vow, "and secret was your word, not mine. I'd call it 'proprietary.'"

"So," Jesse said, "the list isn't a secret after all?"

Covington's face reddened slightly at his misstep, and Jesse saw a faint sheen of sweat forming on the massive forehead and bare scalp. Progress.

"Doesn't matter what you call it, young man. They were *my* customers!"

"*Your* customers," Jesse echoed, nodding slowly, and facing the jury. "I'm beginning to see what happened here, sir. Ben Staley confused himself into thinking he was operating in a competitive free-enterprise system."

"*Objection*, Your Honor," whined Covington's attorney.

"Withdrawn," said Jesse, noticing that two of the jurors were scrutinizing the CEO, eyebrows angled in confusion. Jesse knew he had chipped away at the edifice, but would need the Big Finish to bring the building down.

Jesse walked closer, invading the man's space. "Mr. Covington, I want you to talk to the jury about what else Ben Staley has done that's got you so upset."

Every trial lawyer's objective is control—of the witness, the adversary, even the judge—and Jesse was feeling his way toward it. The witness flashed Jesse a look that said nobody tells Cal Covington whom to talk to or what to talk about, but he drew a deep breath and said, "Well, he was telling CalCorp customers he could sell them the identical product that CalCorp sold, but for much less money."

Jesse recoiled in mock surprise. "With the result that people like these jurors would be able to pay less for new tires and other auto parts, is that it? Gosh, Mr. Covington, no wonder you were disturbed."

"*Your Honor*," shouted Norman Crandell.

"Move on, Mr. Hall," the judge said.

"Listen here, Counselor," Covington bellowed, "we lost every one of those customers because the man was cutting his prices to the bone with the clear intention of putting us out of business!"

Jesse faced the jury. "Putting the world's largest supplier of auto parts out of business? Tell me, sir, was old Ben Staley using a sling and sharp rocks by any chance?"

Five jurors laughed out loud, and the judge, struggling to contain her own amusement, said, "Mr. Hall—"

"Sorry, Judge. I'll change the subject." The jury's reaction told Jesse it was time to set up his ace. "Let's go back, Mr. Covington, and talk about how you turned CalCorp from a local Bay Area wholesaler into a Fortune 500 company."

"Objection, Your Honor," said Crandell. "It's Ben Staley's history that is at issue in this trial, not the injured party's."

"No, no, Norman," said Covington, overruling his lawyer, "I'd like these good people to know what it was like building a company from scratch." Here came the teeth again, the good old boy back in his comfort zone.

"First thing I did," Covington continued, "was to surround myself with people smarter than me, which turned out to be easier than I had hoped." Jesse glanced at the stolid-faced jurors, who he hoped were no longer in the thrall of the big man's fake humility. "Good people, plus wise investments, prudent budgetary restraints, hard work, and, if I say so myself, some damned good decision making."

"But who gave you your start?"

"Nobody. Hell, I'm a self-starter. I worked twenty-four-seven startin' back thirty-five years ago, and I still do."

Jesse slowly shook his head, his eyes wide with feigned admiration. He had a glimpse of the Big Finish now and, if he could keep stoking the plaintiff's ego, maybe a way to get there.

"Impressive," Jesse said. "Give us a typical day. At the beginning, I mean."

"Typical day? No such thing. I was either borrowing money, making sales calls, down on my knees with suppliers and wholesalers, whatever I had to do to stay afloat." Covington threw his shoulders back and grinned at the jury.

"You did it all," Jesse said.

"Damned right. No sales force in those days."

"But how exactly did you build your business?"

"Burnin' up shoe leather and a seventy-two Ford. Cold calls eight hours a day."

"Trying to win new customers? Offering good service at a fair price?"

"Never be undersold was my motto," Covington said, smiling again.

"What's your motto now, Mr. Covington? 'Undersell *me* and I'll bury you in litigation?'"

"*Objection—*"

"Withdrawn," Jesse said. Time to play his ace. "Here's my problem, sir. When you started out, you didn't get your customers just by burning shoe leather and driving around in your seventy-two Ford, right? You looked in the Yellow Pages under 'auto parts dealers,' so you'd know where to go, who to call on?"

The witness straightened and narrowed his eyes. "I burned the midnight oil, is what I did, Counselor—studyin' industry magazines and looking at newspaper advertisements, that sort of thing. Wasn't just the Yellow Pages."

"Really? Let's go back to the secret customer list you claim Ben stole from you. What about AAA Auto Parts? It's the first dealer on your list. Is that company listed in the Yellow Pages?"

"How would I know?"

Jesse walked back to counsel table where he picked up a copy of the Yellow Pages and had the clerk mark it for identification. Jesse approached the witness and handed him the book along with his customer list. "Take a look, sir. Is AAA also listed there in the Yellow Pages?"

After a quick look, Covington agreed it was.

"How about the next one, Astro Auto? It's there, too, isn't it?"

"Appears to be," the witness grudgingly admitted, his hard eyes flickering with anger.

"Well, let's save some time. Is *any* company on your secret customer list not also listed in the local Yellow Pages?"

Covington said, "No, but so what? The important thing is that *my* list consists of the kind of companies a wholesaler wants to deal with."

"Really? Then tell the jury how many companies listed in the Yellow Pages were *not* 'the kind of companies a wholesaler wants to deal with?'"

Covington stared at both listings. He crossed and uncrossed his legs and then stared some more. His mouth opened and then closed again.

"Mr. Covington?" Jesse said gently. "Should I repeat the question?"

"I . . . don't see any," the witness said, at last, so quietly Jesse barely heard him. It's over, thought Jesse. The jury doesn't know it yet, but Cal Covington does.

"Did you say something, sir? We couldn't hear you."

Covington flared. "*I said I don't see any.*"

"That's better. Please tell the jury how many auto parts dealers are on your secret list in this region?"

"Forty-seven," Covington said, scanning it quickly with an impatience that said he just wanted it over with.

"The exact number of dealers listed in the Yellow Pages, right?"

"Hell, I don't know. I didn't count 'em."

"Maybe not," Jesse said, "but I did." He took the book away from Covington and handed it to his opponent. "The record will show it's forty-seven. The two listings are identical. Your so-called proprietary customer list is simply a list of auto parts companies that advertise in the Yellow Pages."

Jesse moved in for the kill. "So it wasn't shoe leather that built your list, was it, Mr. Covington? It was your fingers. You let your fingers do the walking through the Yellow Pages. *Just like Ben did.*"

Although the case continued, everyone in the courtroom knew it had ended during Jesse's cross-examination of Cal Covington. The jury only deliberated long enough to select a foreman—about twenty minutes—before returning with a defense verdict.

. . .

JESSE RETURNED TO the office, and his secretary handed him a message: *"Simon Bradshaw heard the news. Ten o'clock tomorrow morning. His office."* She winked and said, "And Jesse, he sounded *very* happy!" Jesse smiled. He had done everything they'd asked of him, and if Driver tried to stop his election to partnership now, he would be hooted down by other members of the executive committee.

Partnership. Seven years of hard work and sacrifice was about to pay off.

2

AFTER A FITFUL night's sleep, Jesse caught the elevator to the penthouse level and entered Bradshaw's office. Although Jesse liked and admired his mentor, he was always appalled by the sheer opulence of Simon's immense L-shaped office. A twelve-foot ceiling was broken by an enormous skylight through which sunlight slanted onto fine Persian rugs and a fortress of a desk made of flawless Brazilian rosewood. Jesse didn't hold Simon Bradshaw's inherited wealth and Brahmin manner against him, for Simon had revealed his empathetic side early on, standing firmly behind Jesse's *pro bono* commitment, even when it had earned him the enmity of his more conservative partners.

But as Jesse entered the lavish office this time, he was shocked to see his antagonist, Eric Driver—the man's bald, pit-bull head sunk into his narrow shoulders—sitting next to *Calvin fucking Covington*!

"I think," said Driver, flashing a malevolent smile, "you men have met?"

Heat spread through Jesse's body and his heart seemed to fly loose in his chest. Had Covington bitched about his tactics at trial? Was Jesse about to be sacked?

"Call me Cal," Covington said, with a wink.

"Because 'everybody does,' right?" Jesse said, determined to appear cool no matter what.

Covington let out a yelp and extended his hand to Jesse. "Damn! I love this kid," he said, wiping tears of laughter from his eyes. "He didn't buy my bullshit, and neither did the jury."

And I still don't, Jesse thought, but managed a smile as he shook a hand the size of a catcher's mitt. He glanced at Simon Bradshaw, hoping for a clue, but Bradshaw only smiled and wrapped an avuncular arm around Jesse's shoulder.

"Cal has retained C&S as his outside general counsel, Jesse," Bradshaw announced. "His CFO is next door meeting with the heads of our business department as we speak, working on the company's quarterly SEC report, which Eric will oversee. I will be supervising CalCorp's general litigation world-wide."

"If you can't beat 'em," mused Cal, "you'd best join 'em. I like the way you handled yourself, Hall. You ate my lawyer alive, and once I got done lickin' my wounds, I figured C&S was the place for me and CalCorp."

Jesse nodded, everything suddenly clear. Nothing was more seductive to a litigant than the lawyer who had just handed him his ass on a platter. It was also clear that this was not Jesse's welcome-to-partnership meeting.

"Let's move into my conference area," Bradshaw said, and Jesse awkwardly followed the three older men. Bradshaw led the way, stylish as usual, turned out today in a grey pinstripe suit, white shirt, and a pearl grey silk tie color-coordinated with his short-cropped hair. The senior partner's face was ordinary, but for the penetrating dark eyes that pulled you in and made you forget the rest. In any case, the way he carried himself said he didn't care much about how his face looked and you shouldn't, either. He knew, as did everybody else at C&S, that he was the smartest guy in any room he occupied.

Bradshaw seated himself at the head of an elegant, ten-foot-long Mediterranean table adjacent to a fully equipped wet bar, and beckoned Covington to a chair next to him. Jesse took a seat beside Driver on the other side of the table and mused at the contrast between Bradshaw and the stubby Driver, whose own suit was a hopelessly wrinkled brown herringbone that seemed to change colors when he turned sideways. He dressed as if he hated his clothes and the time it took to put them on. Jesse once speculated to a friend that Driver resented him not only because of his preoccupation with justice for the poor, but because he, Jesse, wore socks that matched. Yet despite his short stature and disheveled manner, Driver's encyclopedic mind and rainmaking skills made him indispensable to the firm.

"Something to drink, Cal?" Simon Bradshaw asked.

"Just a Coke if you got one," Cal said.

Bradshaw poured a Coke into a frosted glass and handed it to Covington. He then turned to Jesse. "Cal has a little favor, Jesse, one I'm sure you'll be happy to do for him."

Covington said, "Jesse, they got my boy Kevin in prison in Guatemala. Eric here tells me you're smart and studied the ol' Española in college, so I need you to run down there and check out the lawyer I've hired to defend him. Make sure he's the best."

Jesse blinked, glanced at Simon—who had shut down the firm's Central American branch because of the rampant violence and gang-slayings of American citizens—but Simon was nodding his agreement.

"I . . . I don't know, Mr. Cov—" Jesse began, but Driver cut him off.

"I was just telling Cal that you're the *perfect* man for this, Jesse!"

"And I agree," added Simon. "Here is what we know. Cal's son is accused of killing a popular freelance writer—a left-wing activist—who was accusing the Vice President of Guatemala of corruption. Woman named Marisa Andrade."

Marisa Andrade! Jesse had long admired the internationally famous human rights advocate. And these people expected him to travel to a dangerous third world country to help the son of a Texas bullshitter who might have *murdered* her?

"I'm swamped at the moment, Mr. Covington," Jesse said. "And my Spanish is rusty."

Simon pushed his glasses up on his nose. "This is no time for modesty, Jesse. The lawyer retained by Cal's old firm says most people think the Vice President—Carano is his name—had young Covington arrested to cover his own action in ordering her assassination."

Cal Covington added, "I'm concerned my son ain't gonna get a fair shake down there."

Eric Driver rose to leave. "I'd better go meet with your people, Cal, but like I said, if you're looking for a fair shake in court, Jesse's your man. His lust for justice is absolutely . . . rapacious." Only Jesse caught Driver's mocking grin, a grin that told Jesse the bastard had found yet another method for getting rid of an unwanted associate: send him on a fool's errand to an out-of-control country like Guatemala, and hope for the worst.

Covington beamed. "Well, thanks, Eric. Nobody is more deserving of justice than my son," he said, reaching for his wallet, "and he's the apple of his mother's eye. Here's a picture."

"Good," Bradshaw said, accepting the small photo sealed in yellowed plastic as Driver left the room, "let's have a look at him."

"Not him. Her. This here's a picture of his sainted mother, Blanche, the apple of *my* eye. Ain't she somethin'?"

Jesse stared at the unremarkable photo of a small, thin woman about Covington's age, with a beatific smile and lively eyes that nearly spared her from being hopelessly plain.

"She looks . . . very nice," Jesse managed. "Beautiful eyes."

"Married twenty-six years," Cal said, his eyes glistening as he put the photo back into his wallet. "We have two other sons, both adopted. Jay and Julian. They're both deaf, but smart as hell and great kids. Blanche has been deaf since birth, but I never notice it anymore. Hell, I can sign nearly as fast as she can, which is good 'cause my little gal will talk your leg off."

Maybe he had misjudged the man, Jesse thought, and decided he'd cut him some slack, at least for now.

Jesse nodded, but it was clear Covington would talk all day about his wife if they let him. "What do they claim Kevin's motive was?"

Covington finished off his Coke and wiped his mouth with the back of his hand. "My lawyer down there—a guy named Juan Domínguez—says the cops claim Kevin was sleeping with the victim. She was married to some big-shot law professor who they say must have found out about it. When she broke it off, Kevin got pissed and killed her. All of it pure horse shit, of course."

"Has Kevin had any previous trouble with the law?"

"Hell no. He's the sweetest, most honest kid in the world. Spends all his vacation time in New Orleans helping to rebuild houses. When he's at home, he spends weekends at Glide Memorial helpin' out in a soup kitchen. Takes after his mother, obviously."

"Did Kevin know Marisa Andrade?" Jesse asked.

"Domínguez says he might have met her once when she interviewed him."

"Why was the victim interviewing him and why was he in Guatemala?"

"Kevin works for CalCorp," Cal said. "We've got twelve stores scattered around Central America, two in Guatemala City. He was down there checkin' them out. I don't know why she would have interviewed him or even if she did."

Bradshaw rose, signaling the end of the meeting, and handed Jesse an envelope. "Inside is your first class ticket on American, leaving tomorrow with an open return. I can't imagine it will take more than a day or two to vet Kevin's local counsel, but if you decide he's not top of the line, spend another day and retain a lawyer who is."

"Money's no object, Jesse," Covington added. "If Domínguez ain't the big dog with the brass collar in Guatemala City, you dump him. Here's some clippings about the case and the victim, plus some legal-type info Domínguez sent me."

Jesse scanned the package and said, "I see from this article on top that the victim was reporting on the discovery of an ancient document purporting to grant half the country back to Guatemala's Mayan people. What's that about?"

"She supported the land grant's authenticity," Cal said, "but it's got nothin' to do with the case. Domínguez says it's all bullshit anyways."

Nothing to do with the case? "Maybe it's bullshit," Jesse said, "but if the victim was supporting a document that would split the country in two, she had to be making powerful enemies in the government."

Cal shrugged. Bradshaw nodded. Jesse smiled. He felt himself warming to the project. Driver may have put a monkey wrench in his rise to partnership and his *pro bono* activities, but if Covington and his local guy were even half right, this was a case screaming for justice.

. . .

"HEY THERE, JESSE," Megan Harris said, her voice gliding through the phone into his ear with the grace of a Diana Krall ballad, sending a shudder through his groin and his heart into free-fall as it always did. He had loved Megan Harris from the first time she glanced his way that day at Whole Foods, giving him that sideways smile and cool tilt of her head. Her large, pale-grey eyes, coppery brown hair, and long legs had his heart reeling. After stalking her through two aisles, he had finally managed to act as if he didn't know what hummus was and she had acted like she didn't know he knew. He found out she was a third grade teacher living in a basement apartment on Russian Hill with her "roommates," a three-year-old daughter named Melissa and two cats named Riley and Cleo. Megan also had a dream: scoring a recording contract with the country rock band she moonlighted with on weekends—if she could pull it off without taking quality time away from Melissa, the only positive aspect of a brief and disastrous marriage.

On their first date, they found out how different they were. Megan's mother was a high school music teacher; her father an upper-echelon exec with IBM. Jesse's parents were carnies, until his mother left the carnival and his alcoholic, sideshow, fire-eating dad, and upgraded herself and her young son to trailer-trash status.

"My dad wanted me to learn the fire-eating trade, but I was terrified to close my mouth around the flame. No matter how hard he whipped my ass, I just couldn't try it."

"But you were only six, Jesse, and besides, why exactly would *anybody* want to close their mouth around a flaming torch?"

Jesse smiled. "See, that's the secret. First, you make sure your mouth is moist, and then you quickly close it around the fire to shut off the oxygen. Presto, no flame, no pain. I just couldn't make myself do it that first time."

"No flame, no pain," Megan repeated, almost to herself, then brightened and added, "Well, at least you had the last laugh by becoming a trial lawyer and never closing your mouth again. And you probably breathe fire in the courtroom."

Jesse laughed. "I like trial work, but my real dream is to make partner, build a war chest for a year or two at an obscenely high income and then enter politics, where I hope to make a difference in people's lives."

Megan brightened. "Okay, I'm impressed, but watch out for the lure of Montgomery Street. When the Mongols invaded China, those who weren't driven back out had their culture assimilated into Chinese society. And from my experience, when you come out of an impoverished background like you did, it's harder to resist the siren call of sudden wealth and public recognition."

Jesse felt his face redden. "From your *experience?* Based on casual observation I'd say you've never been all that poor."

Megan held up her hands in mock surrender. "You're right, of course. I just meant that the quest for justice must look a little different once you're inside the halls of power, instead of outside looking in like most of us do."

Jesse hunched his shoulders, cooled down. "Not when you grew up in a traveling road-show, seeing immigrants stranded in some Podunk town with no job and no money after busting their asses for three bucks an hour, dumped simply because somebody stronger came along willing to work even cheaper. Or when you've been awakened by your mom's screams as rogue cops trashed your sleeping quarters and burned your tents."

He stopped, caught himself. "Look, Megan, I'm just saying that

I learned first-hand about injustice in ways that can't be taught in school."

Her eyes clouded up. "I'm an idiot," she said quietly. "And I talk too much. Is there a reset button I can push? Start the evening over?"

Relieved, he nodded and picked up his glass as in a toast. "Deal, and I promise to stop being a pontifical jerk, at least until after dessert."

She laughed and clinked her glass against his. Jesse smiled back.

At first, everything seemed to go well. The sex was incredible, and Jesse grew to love Megan both for her idealism and her wild side, which came out when she played her weekend gigs, long hair flying back over her shoulders, then back down again over her acoustic guitar strings—unlike any school teacher he'd ever known. She was a great singer, but it was clear to Jesse that Melissa would always come first; over everything and everyone.

And even as their love deepened, Jesse sensed Megan's increasing impatience with his seven-day, eighty-hour weeks. He missed a weekend trip to the Happy Hollow Park and Zoo in San Jose and several other planned "family outings," and finally, the last straw: Megan had been urging that they just pick up and fly somewhere— "on a lark" was the way she always put it—just the two of them. He had agreed, but after Megan's mother had flown west to take care of Melissa, Jesse had to forfeit their non-refundable tickets to Paris— because of work.

"I can't do this anymore, Jesse," she confessed one brilliant sunny day soon after. They were walking up Montgomery toward Coit Tower, one of their favorite lunchtime picnic spots. Her eyes glistened in the sun like melting ice-chips as she added, "Your strategy to save the world doesn't fit with the kind of family life I'm looking for. I admire your dream, your plan—I really do—but I see that we'd just be extra baggage, weighing you down. There's just no space for us in your life right now. You'll soon be thirty, Jesse, and I don't picture you changing."

Jesse felt a sharp pain in his gut. "Cut me some slack here, Megan. Once I'm a partner, I'll be a free agent and have a lot more time."

"I think you're kidding yourself about that, Jesse."

"Not really," he said, "The firm is just especially busy right now, and I can't let everyone down. Everyone's busting their asses, not just me."

"The partners, too?"

"Hell yes, they work right alongside us, some even harder than I do."

The moment the words were out of his mouth he realized he had been out-lawyered by a third-grade schoolteacher. Partnership would change nothing and they both knew it.

"You can't change, Jesse," she said, "and I can't, either. Remember, I had a father a lot like you that I wish I had known."

"Wait a minute. Your dad's still around."

"My point exactly. He was always around, but never there. I want someone to share my life with and you're already married to your firm, just as he was married to IBM."

Why, Jesse wondered, do women look for their father in a man, and then hate him for it? But later, he would see that Megan had ended it to head off what would have been an even more painful breakup later on. Better a quick shot through the heart than death by a thousand cuts.

They split after nearly a year together, and Jesse plunged himself even more manically into his law practice, filling the void she had left until late at night when it was time to turn out the lights. Then, in those naked midnight hours, he missed her with an unrelenting yearning. Sometimes he even welcomed the pain, telling himself that if he confronted the anguish of his burning desire for her head-on, it might eventually lose its oxygen and die out.

No flame, no pain.

· · ·

MEGAN'S VOICE PULLED him back to the present. "I called to thank you for remembering Melissa's birthday. She adores her American Girl Doll."

"That's great," Jesse said, trying to control his breathing. She still did that to him.

"How are you, Jesse?"

"If this day was a fish, I'd throw it back. I thought it was going to be my Big Day at C&S, but instead I'm off to Guatemala of all places."

"Guatemala? Why there? It's a disaster zone, run by drugs and gangs."

She sounded genuinely concerned. "Megan," he blurted, trying to sound normal, knowing his voice resembled a car's broken muffler, "can we talk when I get back? Maybe go off on a lark like you always wanted and just talk?"

An awkward silence, then finally, "Take care down there, Jesse."

He felt the heat of regret flooding his face. "I'm sorry, Megan. I didn't mean to put this on you again. And don't worry about Guatemala, I'll be fine." At least he would be, if someone would get the damned Buick off his chest. "I'll be careful. I won't drink the water. A few days, then for sure it's back to partnership for sure at C&S and—"

"The Golden Fleece," she said quietly.

"The *Odyssey*, right?"

"No. Jason and the Argonauts."

Jesse rubbed his eyes. "Sounds like a heavy metal band."

Why had he spoiled a perfectly decent conversation by begging like a goddamn poodle? Was it to provoke her into putting him out of his misery once and for all? Well, so be it. He'd been alone most of his life and he could get used to it again. He'd be fine, and maybe a trip like this would help. Yeah, that's it. Distance himself completely from her life for a few days and get on with his own. Isn't that what Dr. Phil would say?

If only her love hadn't wrecked him for anybody new. He felt anger rising in his chest again, but held it back as they said their goodbyes. He replaced the receiver, listened to the silence for a minute, and then fished an overnight bag out of his closet.

DAY ONE

3
Guatemala City

THE NEXT MORNING at 6:30 a.m., Jesse boarded an American flight to Miami, then on to Guatemala City. Twelve hours later, he stumbled bleary-eyed through immigration and customs, then gazed into the noisy and crowded, fluorescent-lit lobby of La Aurora International Airport. It was nearly 9:00 p.m. Guatemala time.

The first thing he saw were nine teenagers in ill-fitting black and olive camouflage uniforms holding machine guns and restraining two German Shepherds the size of small horses. Jesse passed uneasily through this unnerving platoon and scanned the eager, waiting faces of all ages standing behind a barrier. Mingled smells of urine, perspiration, and disinfectant assailed his nose as he continued to look for someone looking for him. Sounds of crying children rose above the general hum of anticipation in the lobby.

"Señor Hall?" came a voice from a short, bald man holding a fedora that orbited nervously in his hands. A fold of flesh at his neck pressed against a top shirt button begging to be released. The man clearly was not among the food-deprived of Guatemala. He wore a dark blue suit, white shirt, maroon tie, and alligator loafers, yet despite being immaculately attired, he managed to look generally unkempt. Dandruff lay like powdered milk across his shoulders. One end of his mustache was longer than the other, and his teeth were stained yellow. He sweated a sickening-sweet cologne.

"Señor Domínguez?" Jesse said, trying to overcome his first negative impression of the man. He had read Domínguez's impressive four-page *curriculum vitae*, which included being named by the current administration as one of the ten leading trial lawyers in Guatemala.

"*Sí, sí, Señor, a sus ordenes*," the lawyer said, and then in English, "I am Domínguez. Welcome to Guatemala City."

"*Mil gracias*," Jesse said, still eyeing the youths with the automatic weapons. "Are they there to protect us or shoot us?"

Domínguez smiled, causing his oversized mustache to twitch over a fleshy upper lip. "I assure you, Señor, they are there for our protection."

"Then I wish they looked older than the Vienna Boys Choir. Those kids couldn't buy cigarettes in the U.S. Are those machine guns loaded?"

The smile was less certain this time. "My English is not well, Señor. I understand you speak Spanish?"

Jesse nodded, swatted at a buzzing fly. "*Español es bueno.*"

"Good," said Domínguez in Spanish, obviously relieved, but still perspiring profusely. "We will go over here to await your baggage, Señor."

"This is it," Jesse said, indicating his carry-on and a thin briefcase. "I don't plan on being in Guatemala long."

Domínguez issued his first sincere smile, apparently relieved at Jesse's remark. He probably knows why I'm here, Jesse told himself, noting that the stubby lawyer continued to dab at his forehead with a handkerchief. Jesse was already registering impressions, wondering if all this perspiring meant the local lawyer lacked cool under pressure, a requisite for any good trial lawyer. Or maybe it was just the humidity, so thick you could chew on it. Probably the heat, Jesse concluded, wanting desperately to like the guy, so he could get back home.

A silver Mercedes sedan and the *abogado's* driver were waiting at the curb, where the streets were slick and shiny with rain.

"I apologize for the rain, Señor Hall. It is unusual weather for April."

Jesse looked around and wondered how these hordes of people avoided colliding with each other, yet the cacophony of shouting people and honking cars created a sense of excitement and vitality. Joyful family members embraced one another at curbside and helped with overstuffed suitcases and huge boxes tied together with string.

"Our rainy season usually starts in late May or June, but it may rain on and off now until November," Domínguez added. He explained that though Jesse would need an umbrella, he would not be cold; even though the city was at nearly 4,500 feet, the average temperature would hover between seventy and eighty degrees Fahrenheit.

Hard as the rain was falling, it failed to cleanse the heavy air that assailed Jesse's nostrils and burned his eyes. Domínguez apparently observed Jesse's discomfort and said, "Too many cars and people." Over two million souls, Jesse knew from his prep work on the plane, struggling to survive in the largest city in Central America, under the cloud of a thirty-six-year civil war that had taken over 200,000 lives. And although the Peace Accords of 1996 had stopped the war, it had not stopped the killing.

Jesse surrendered his carry-on to the driver, who started the car and shot through a stop sign into the darkening night, then blended

into the flow of vehicles. Jesse had been prepared by his guidebook
for traffic mania, but this was beyond description. Brightly colored
"chicken buses" and cars of every description flew through stop signs as
Policía Municipal de Tránsito and the PNC—*Policía Nacional Civíl*—
sat hunched in their small Opels watching the melee as apathetically
as if waiting for an egg to boil. Domínguez's driver wove in and out
of lanes, apparently oblivious to the honking horns and mechanical
madness around them. The limo passed through what appeared to
be a middle-class residential section, where Rottweilers and various
junkyard guard dogs prowled the well-lighted flat rooftops, behind
coils of razor wire.

"What are the dogs doing up on the roofs?"

Domínguez chuckled, not bothering to look. "We have rampant
lawlessness here, so people must protect themselves. Roofs are a
common entry point."

"*Es una situación lamentable,*" Jesse said.

"These are the lucky ones, Señor Hall. In truly poor sections, not
even the dogs are safe. You'll also need to watch out for street kids,
particularly in Zone One. They'll take your pants along with your
wallet and you won't even know it."

"We have that in San Francisco, too," Jesse said, attempting to
empathize.

Domínguez shook his head. "You don't understand, Señor Hall. In
addition to gangs, we have about five thousand punks on the loose—
glue sniffers—most without families. They live by theft and prostitution.
The police have to do a little social cleansing once in a while."

"Social cleansing?"

"The program is called *Mano Dura*—'Strong Hand'—though
most of us call it 'street cleaning,'" Domínguez said. "Next morning,
the vagrants have disappeared."

Jesse stared at the smiling lawyer. "Thrown in jail?"

"No, Señor. We use 'disappear' in Guatemala to mean 'never seen again.'"

"They're killed?" Jesse was beginning to think things were worse here than he had heard, even worse than the chilling U.S. State Department's warning on Guatemala he had read on the way down.

"It is not for me to say, Señor. There are rumors that many end up in a Mexican bordello. The lucky ones are exported north, or even to Europe."

Jesse groaned inwardly. "Like coffee beans," he said.

"Regrettable, I agree, but a political necessity. Vice President Carano is working hard to get our crime rate under control."

"It's particularly regrettable to the kids who are 'disappeared.' Makes you wonder if your Vice President is the right man for the job. Maybe Marisa Andrade was right. Wasn't she his most outspoken critic before she was killed?"

Domínguez's voice had an edge as he said, "She was very outspoken."

"So wasn't Carano angered by her criticism? And her support for that document that purported to grant half of Guatemala to the Maya?"

Domínguez shrugged, looked straight ahead, and said nothing. Jesse was beginning to have doubts about this guy.

"Come on, Juan," he persisted, "aren't you looking for suspects other than your client who had a motive to silence Marisa?"

"It is early in my investigation," Domínguez said, but his mood had turned sullen.

"I understand, but tell me more about this so-called land grant letter. Where did it come from?"

"In my opinion? From the vivid imagination of a con artist who is trying to sell it to radical Mayan human rights organizations such as *La Causa.*"

"All right, but who does this con artist claim wrote it?"

"A Spanish king who became an emperor and then supposedly became guilty over certain . . . collateral damage that occurred during Cortez's liberation of the heathen in the area that is presently Guatemala."

"Collateral damage?" Jesse said. "What's that, code for Mayan ethnic cleansing?" Although Jesse didn't know if Domínguez would be effective in court, he had certainly mastered the art of euphemism.

Domínguez's features seemed to tighten, but he said nothing.

Jesse said, "If Marisa Andrade supported *La Causa's* efforts to acquire the land grant letter, that would be yet another bone in Carano's throat, right?"

"Of course she supported *La Causa's* efforts."

"Why do you say 'of course?'"

"Because," Domínguez said, his head impatiently bobbing from side to side, "Marisa Andrade was the Executive Director of *La Causa.*"

Jesse's tired eyes popped open. "Jesus, Juan, the reasons Carano might have wanted Marisa Andrade dead are multiplying like rabbits."

Even in the partial darkness, Jesse could see that Domínguez was scowling.

"Are you suggesting our acting head of state is guilty of murder, sir?"

"I'm saying it would piss off any leader to have his country split in two while he's running it and, like you said, he's the current *de facto* boss, right?"

"Yes," Domínguez grudgingly admitted. "President Ruiz has Alzheimers."

"So doesn't Carano have the most to lose if the land grant letter turns out to be real?" Jesse noticed a barely perceptible nod from the driver. Maybe he should fire Domínguez and retain the driver.

The car whizzed under a streetlight and Jesse could see another scowl on Domínguez's briefly illuminated face. "Victor Carano knows the land grant letter is a joke," the *abogado* said, "merely a cruel exploitation of tribal superstitions."

"But what if it's not? I read you've got a presidential election coming up, with a Mayan in the race. If the letter is real, wouldn't that be a boost for him?"

Again, Domínguez grudgingly nodded and said, "It is true that hope has spread like fire ants among the Maya and has galvanized them behind his campaign."

"And don't the Indians make up a majority of the population?"

Domínguez shrugged dismissively. "It does not matter. They do not vote in great numbers. The numerous tribes cannot agree on anything and never will."

Unless the land grant was authentic and united them, Jesse thought.

The car braked suddenly and skidded, barely avoiding a van that had ignored a stop sign. Their driver showed neither surprise nor annoyance. After Jesse had started breathing again, he said, "Tell me about this interview Kevin gave the victim. I can't imagine a crusading journalist like Marisa getting wet over auto parts."

"She interviewed him in connection with a story she was doing on Arturo Gómez, a notorious guerrilla rebel chief and drug trafficker. Kevin was rumored to have met with him, but the article was never published. Perhaps they never even met."

Jesse was stunned. *Perhaps* Kevin never met with a notorious, drug-trafficking guerrilla chieftain? *Perhaps*? How could Cal Covington not have mentioned even the remote possibility of such a meeting? Why was there nothing about it in the file he had read on the way down?

"Tell me, Juan, why in the world would Kevin have met with Gómez?"

"He denies it, of course, and the fact he is still alive and intact suggests he didn't. Gómez hates Americans. He does things like offering the head of a kidnap victim's penis to the poor soul's wife as proof of life."

"Why isn't he in prison?"

"Half the population here would revolt. The poor think he's Robin Hood and buy into the propaganda about his agrarian land reform agenda. Also, the government can't pin anything on him. He wrote the book on plausible deniability."

"All right," Jesse said, "but is Kevin's father aware of this rumored meeting?"

"Of course, and he agreed with me that such a meeting would be unlikely. He dismisses the rumor as unimportant."

Unimportant? Very worried now, Jesse wondered what else Cal Covington had dismissed as too "unimportant" to bother sharing with him.

"What about the rumored affair between Kevin and the victim? Do the police have any evidence to support that?"

"Our client denies the affair, but the police are said to have witnesses."

"All right, but just for the record, Señor, he's not 'our client,' he's *your* client. My client is his father."

"His father is not on trial," Domínguez said, "yet you are here."

Jesse paused, measured his response. "I'm just here to size up the situation for an anxious parent."

"You mean," said Domínguez, wiping his hands with his handkerchief, "you are here to look me over."

Jesse hitched his shoulders, slipped into an uneasy silence, though he was pleased to see a sign of grit in a man he urgently wanted to respect.

"In fact," continued Domínguez, "the illicit relationship provided the police the motive they needed. The defendant was apparently unwilling to give her up."

Jesse spun on the local lawyer. "Let me ask you point blank, Señor Domínguez: Whose side are you on in this case?"

Domínguez shrugged. "I am on the side of justice, of course."

Jesse considered the ambiguity in the answer but let it go. He was a long way from home and he'd better take it slow.

. . .

THE CAR SPED on and Jesse spotted more vicious-looking canine sentries roaming on roofs. On one porch, musicians played and a middle-aged woman danced on the sidewalk below them, more signs of the dark, but compelling, vibrancy of this huge city.

"I want to see the prosecutor first thing in the morning. Can you arrange that?"

Domínguez pursed his lips. "You better leave Señorita Ruiz to me. She is a bitch, Señor." Then he added, in English, "A real ball-buster."

"Is that why you haven't met with her?"

"I am planning to do it soon."

"We'll do it tomorrow," said Jesse, his exasperation showing. "¿Comprende?"

The lawyer's eyebrows shot up and his asymmetric mustache twitched in response to a forced smile. "Of course, Señor. I will make the necessary arrangements."

As a silver crescent moon sought an opening in the clouds, Jesse thought he spied the glow of a seething volcano off to his left.

"That is Pacaya," Domínguez said, following Jesse's gaze. "It has been destructive. Guatemala City is surrounded by volcanoes."

"Incredible," Jesse said, thinking that Domínguez might make a better tour guide than trial lawyer. "Where are we now?"

"We are in Zone Fifteen, Señor Hall. Our citizens live in twenty-one separate and unique zones, like *arrondissements* in Paris."

Sure, Jesse thought. Just like Paris.

. . .

IT WAS NEARLY ten o'clock when their car approached Jesse's hotel. The rain had let up, but the wipers were still at work. Jesse was tired, but not ready to quit. "Where was Kevin at the time of the murder?" Jesse asked.

"He said he was sleeping in his hotel, the Marriott."

"Alone, of course."

"Yes. Nobody saw him."

Their driver parked in front of the Conquistador Ramada, and Domínguez escorted Jesse inside. The old hotel was immaculate, with a large lobby and a reception desk behind which was a restaurant and bar. Waiting to check in, Jesse pointed to a giant mural of a blue-armored soldier on the wall. "Who's the hero on the white horse?"

"That's Pedro de Alvarado, heroic conqueror of Guatemala," the lawyer said proudly. "His ferocity brought the Maya to their knees."

Jesse wondered how the indigenous housekeeping and kitchen staff felt about working in a place named after the man who had raped and plundered their ancestors. He also wondered how a trial lawyer as politically insensitive as Juan Domínguez could possibly be effective in a courtroom.

Domínguez offered Jesse a drink at *El Refugio*, the hotel bar, but Jesse wanted refuge mainly from Domínguez at this point. The local lawyer promised to arrange an appointment with the prosecutor,

Elena María Ruiz Madera, before meeting Kevin Covington. These two meetings would tell him all he needed to know about the case and, more important, about Juan Domínguez. Jesse, already eager to get out of town, prayed that his initial misgivings were wrong and that the man would prove to be as good as his ratings.

Alone at last, he scanned his ten-by-fifteen room. It would do for a day or two—a bed, two chairs around a small round table, a thirteen-inch TV atop a dresser, and a small private bathroom with a shower the size of a vertical coffin. Not a single photograph or print adorned the rust-painted stucco walls, and a faint odor of cigar smoke permeated the atmosphere. The mattress sank under the weight of his carry-on bag.

He reviewed his day, made some notes, and fell asleep with his clothes on.

. . .

IN SAN FRANCISCO, a grim Simon Bradshaw huddled in his office with Eric Driver and Jim Haydel, another senior C&S securities lawyer. Haydel had offered grave misgivings about their new client's murky financial records and Bradshaw was trying hard to appear unworried. His father had led the firm through wars and recessions and had never allowed his anxiety to show, and Simon was determined to prove himself as good a man.

"Have you spoken to CalCorp's CPA about these . . . financial ambiguities?" Bradshaw asked Driver, involuntarily fingering the perfect knot on his power-red, seven-fold silk necktie. He was beginning to wonder if CalCorp was another Enron, and the thought sent a fresh jolt of acid to his insipient ulcer.

"Covington just fired his accountants and switched to Wulff and

Van Duzer," said Driver, "as reputable as they come. They'll get the information they need to file the company's K-1. No problem."

"What do Cal's former CPAs say?" Simon asked.

"They won't even talk to us," said Haydel, tanned, lanky, and, like Simon, a physical opposite of Driver. "Their senior guy just said, 'Good luck finding the money.' They resigned from the engagement and won't say why. In my book, Simon, CalCorp doesn't pass the smell test."

"Christ, Jim," growled Driver, "stop being an old lady for once."

But Haydel persisted. "There is simply no explanation for how CalCorp could have financed its exponential international growth with hardly any debt and holding on to most of the corporate stock. No debt, very little outside equity. Something's wrong. Capital appears to be flowing into the company off the books from somewhere, but nobody can tell us where. That's trouble, Simon."

Simon swallowed hard. His decision to take on representation of CalCorp was not just Caldwell and Shaw's best option, it was the firm's *only* option. The firm had taken major hits from the recession, the loss of a huge contingent fee case in Federal Court, and the unexpected settlement of two major antitrust cases that had been generating millions in monthly billings. Only a handful of C&S partners were aware that the firm had been rescued from a financial precipice at the eleventh hour mainly by checks already pouring in from the various CalCorp entities.

"Hold on, Jim," Driver said. "Let's remember who we represent here and quit acting like we're the fucking SEC. The books do balance, right?"

Haydel was visibly fuming. "They appear to."

"Come now, gentlemen," Simon interrupted. "What does CalCorp's CFO say?"

"He's in Europe," Haydel said, "'negotiating new franchise relationships.' Nobody else in their shop can tell us where the capital is coming from. They act like we're crazy to even ask."

"And they're right, dammit!" Driver said. "Who are we to say that Covington isn't growing the company on a slim profit margin like he says he is? *Fortune* called him an entrepreneurial genius, and that should be good enough for us. Hell, Simon, I can keep ten new lawyers busy on CalCorp projects alone!"

And triple your own annual bonus, Bradshaw thought.

"You owe it to me, Simon," Driver said, as if he had read Bradshaw's thoughts. "*And* you owe it to the firm."

Bradshaw leaned back in his chair and closed his eyes. C&S lawyers were familiar with this trance-like state, and even Eric Driver knew better than to interrupt it.

"All right," he said at last. "We'll stay the course as long as Wulff and Van Duzer sign on as CPAs."

"Good as done," Driver said, and left the room. Haydel, with a worried look, did likewise. Simon reached into his lower left desk drawer and closed his fingers around a handful of anti-acid tablets.

DAY TWO

4

AT 10:00 A.M. the next day, Jesse and Juan Domínguez arrived for their meeting with the chief prosecutor. Her office was in a run-down building that had once been a beautiful Spanish-Colonial style villa in *Zona* 2. Domínguez explained that the property had been confiscated from a major drug dealer and, ironically, currently housed prosecutors. As they approached the building, Domínguez explained that Elena María Ruiz Madera was one of sixty prosecutors based in Guatemala City, an *Agente de la Fiscalía del Ministerio Público*.

"Elena Ruiz is the *Jefe de Fiscalía*, the chief of the department," he said in English, "and has not lost a single case."

"Sounds tough," Jesse said, sidestepping a chicken that had wandered across his path.

"Muy dura," Domínguez said.

"But is she *Jefe* on merit, or because her father is President?"

The little lawyer spread his hands. "Who is to say how one gets through a doorway, Señor Hall? I can only say that once inside, she has performed admirably."

"Is she close to her father?" Jesse had read that the president was not only ill, but widowed.

"She is totally devoted to *El Presidente*. She is daughter, wife, and mother to him."

"She's never married?"

"Once, as a very young girl, to an army officer killed in action during our thirty-six year war."

Jesse nodded and they entered a building full of cracked walls, uneven floors, and acoustic ceiling tiles badly stained from years of trapped smoke and auto emissions. He glanced through an open bathroom door and saw a shower stall that had been converted into a file room. Everything about the place was run-down—everything but Chief Prosecutor Elena Ruiz Madera, who glided into the room as if on ice skates. Señorita Ruiz was more striking than classically beautiful. Her swept-back hair was pulled back on the sides, a liquid black color that shone like obsidian. Her features seemed somewhat irregular, the mouth at an angle to the plane of her face. But her eyes were stunningly beautiful, cat's eyes, colored pale brown and flecked with turquoise, their radiance undiminished by horn-rimmed glasses. She was tall for a Guatemalan woman, about five foot six, Jesse guessed, and although she was thin, almost fragile-looking, there was nothing delicate about her firm handshake or her imperious bearing. Jesse resolved that he would not allow her beauty to hijack his strategy for the meeting, which was to get as much as he could out of her and to show her he hadn't come into town on the last load of coffee beans.

"I am always pleased to meet a lawyer from the United States," she said in excellent English. She was dressed in a plain, charcoal-brown skirt suit, and she wore no makeup, or wore it so well he couldn't detect any. A pair of elegant silver medallion earrings was her only concession to *haute couture.* "So, Señor Hall from California, what can we do for you?"

Her eyes bore into Jesse's, not so much looking at him, but targeting him.

"I need a few minutes of your time, Señorita. As you know, I'm here at the request of Kevin Covington's father."

She turned to take a seat behind her metal desk, and Jesse saw that her hair, tied at the crown of her head, cascaded halfway down her back. For an instant, she lost her impervious aura and seemed little more than a girl whom Jesse could picture sitting proudly astride a horse. "And you have come to assure me," she said, glancing at some documents in front of her, "that Kevin Covington is a gentle soul who could never have perpetrated such a vicious crime."

"I haven't met the man, Señorita Ruiz. I've just come to listen and learn."

She met his eyes then, reappraising him. "All right, Señor Hall, we will talk, but I only have a few minutes, as I must be in court soon." She offered them seats, but glanced again at her watch.

"I get the point that you're busy, Señorita, but a man's freedom is at stake."

"Oh, much more than his freedom, Señor Hall. The death penalty will be applicable to the crime with which Señor Domínguez's client is charged. The victim was admired by the public and this was a vicious slaying, involving six knife wounds. A textbook jilted-lover crime of passion."

Domínguez got out his handkerchief and wiped his palms. Christ, Jesse wondered, did he do that in a courtroom, too?

"Was the murder weapon found?" Jesse asked.

"No, although a carving knife was missing from a set of four

contained in a wooden block in the kitchen. And yes," she added
before he asked, "we exonerated the husband."

"So soon? Was he not a prime suspect?"

"Briefly, until we arrested the defendant. What else can I tell you,
Señor? As I said, I must get to court. I am in trial on a difficult murder
case at the moment, in which the victim was given a '*corte de pelo y
manicura.*'"

Domínguez said, "It is the way death squads inhibit identification
of their victims here. They remove the head and hands. That's why we
call it a haircut and a manicure."

Jesse nodded as casually as he could, knowing that Elena Ruiz was
testing him, taking control of the meeting, letting everyone know
who was boss. He had learned from Simon Bradshaw the importance
of taking charge, whether in a meeting or the courtroom. Wherever
trial lawyers could be found, there would always be this dance, verbally
jousting for respect, trying to gain some small advantage.

He scanned the wall behind her and could feel her eyes still tracking
him. Jesse figured Elena Ruiz for a girl who could read your thoughts
at twenty paces, then fuck with them just for the fun of it. He would
be careful. He saw that she had a degree from San Carlos University.
Maybe an opening?

"You graduated from the local school?" Jesse asked.

"After two years at Boalt Hall, University of California Law School,"
she said. "I had to return home for my final year, then started work."

Boalt Hall. Shit, one of the best law schools in the U.S. Try another
angle.

"So, you look barely thirty, yet you're running a criminal division
of sixty prosecutors. Impressive. A nice picture behind you of the
President."

"Subtle as the proverbial train wreck, Señor Hall," she said, following his gaze to the oil painting of her father. "But it's all right. I have to deal with claims of nepotism all the time from insecure men."

Jesse felt heat rising into his face. "I was just thinking that it must be tough for women lawyers in what I hear is a pretty macho world."

"Yes, Señor Hall, but women in Guatemala are prized in prosecution work, because they are less vulnerable to bribery and," she added with a smile, "far more courageous."

"I don't doubt it for a minute, Señorita," Jesse said, managing to return her smile. He found himself wanting to get close to this woman, yet feeling tension in her presence. He was becoming more sympathetic to Domínguez's obvious anxiety.

"This is why my section of criminal prosecution is composed mostly of women. My predecessor was male, but he only assigned cases, never tried them. You must be aware, Señor Hall, that trying the cases is where the danger lies. Of course, if it's an easy case, I may give it to a man."

Jesus, this girl must eat roofing nails for breakfast, thought Jesse, plus she's smarter than a box of foxes.

"So who will handle the Covington trial?"

"I will," she said.

"Then you must not think it's an easy case for the prosecution."

"Very clever, Señor," she said, her full lips widening into another smile, "but you see, the Covington case is so easy a male prosecutor might fall asleep in the middle of trial and embarrass my section."

Ruiz pronounced the meeting at an end with a casual glance at the wall clock. Point, game, and match. Jesse managed to smile in defeat, although he hated himself for wanting so much to have impressed this woman. At least he had learned something important. Señorita Ruiz would be formidable in court. Domínguez would have to start eating raw meat.

"If it's such an easy case," Jesse said, "I assume you're willing to disclose the evidence you've got against Señor Covington."

She rose and came around her desk. Did she want him to get another look at her incredible legs? Courtesy compelled Jesse to rise as well.

"That would be premature, Señor Hall. We haven't accepted all of your country's liberal notions about the sharing of evidence. Besides, here that evidence goes first to the *Departamento de Investigaciones.* Then anything requiring analysis goes to their *Departamento Técnico Científico.*"

"So you're telling me there's evidence from the crime scene requiring analysis?" This was bad news. "When can Señor Domínguez see the report?"

"When we decide what we're going to do about Señor Covington. Maybe tomorrow, maybe weeks from now. As you know, we have no writ of *habeas corpus* in Guatemala."

"I understand, but I assume you're at least required to share exculpatory evidence?" Jesse was referring to evidence known to the government that tended to prove the defendant's innocence. Domínguez had obviously not asked for it.

Señorita Ruiz flashed him a wry smile. "Exculpatory? I'm sorry, sir, but that word does not translate easily into Spanish."

Bullshit, he thought, thoroughly irritated. He turned to Domínguez. "Feel free to chime in anytime, Señor," but to Jesse's chagrin, the chubby *abogado* appeared to be in a state of shock. Jesse turned back to the CP. "Are we talking linguistics here or plain old stonewalling?"

"We're talking about law, Señor Jesse Hall," she said, her voice mocking in its gentleness, "and ours does not recognize that obligation."

"Will you at least tell me whether you *have* that kind of information?"

"If I have no duty to provide it, I have no duty to tell you whether I have it."

The woman was good, and Kevin Covington was in deep trouble. He said, "I'm not sure either the American Consulate or the judge on the case will agree with you on that."

A slight flicker of something behind her eyes. Jesse saw it, but she said nothing, just met his gaze. Absurdly, Jesse felt a stirring in his groin and he plowed on. "This will be a high-profile case, attracting world press, Señorita. How you handle it will be carefully scrutinized."

Domínguez broke out a fresh handkerchief.

"I am used to being scrutinized, counsel," she said, extending her hand in farewell. "As daughter of the president of this country, I've lived my whole life in a fish bowl."

Jesse took her warm, dry hand in his at the door. "I hear you. But will you reconsider—"

"I will look into your request for disclosure," she said, starting to withdraw her hand, but not her gaze, "but you will have to excuse me now."

Jesse met her eyes and tightened his grip on her hand. "You're sounding like a politician, Señorita. Nothing ever got done just by 'looking into it.'"

He dropped her hand and strode out of the room, Domínguez scuttling behind him on stubby legs.

. . .

"A CARVING KNIFE from the kitchen?" Jesse said as they walked back to their car. "Smells like a domestic passion slaying to me."

"Or made to look like one," Domínguez offered, suddenly capable of speech.

Thank you, Inspector Clouseau, Jesse thought, growing frustrated. "Isn't it clear to you that . . . ?" Jesse stopped himself. Standards of professional excellence varied geographically, even between large cities in the U.S. "Can't we agree that the best defense for a man without an alibi would be to launch an offense against other logical suspects?"

"The victim's husband is an honored professor of law at San Carlos University. He was a suspect, of course, but they decided on Señor Covington."

"*Decided* on him? Why on him? Why not 'decide' on the husband? Or Carano? Or a burglary gone wrong?"

Out came the handkerchief. "Time will tell," he said. "Justice moves slowly here, Señor."

Jesse struggled for patience. "I want to meet with the client."

"This would also take some time." Domínguez explained that to gain access to the dreaded *El Centro Preventivo para Hombres de Zona 18*—known to its guests and alumni as *Purgatorio*—they needed the permission of the prison system's Director General.

"So what do I do?"

"You thank God that the Director happens to be married to my wife's sister."

Ah, that was better. At least the man was connected. "Okay, Domínguez, cut through the red tape, but also prepare and file a motion for bail."

"That," Domínguez said, "will not be possible."

Jesse gave the little lawyer a hard look. "I'll argue it myself if I have to."

"That is also not possible. Foreign lawyers cannot argue cases in Guate."

"Guate?"

"Short for Guatemala we commonly use here. Anyway, one has to be a member in good standing of the *Colegio de Abogados* to argue cases here."

This fat little bastard was wearing him down. Was *anything* possible in this fucking country? "Okay, we'll deal with that tomorrow, but I want to see the prisoner today."

"We'll have to wait until nightfall. It's safer, then."

"What do you mean, 'safer?'"

"Did you not see the mobs at the *el Parque Central* on our way here? It's nearly as bad out at the prison. At night, however, the protestors thin out."

"Nothing wrong with demonstrations in a democracy. What's the big deal?"

"The demands are more specific here."

"Quick justice, right? They want Kevin Covington tried as soon as possible?"

"No, Señor. They want to see Kevin Covington hanging by his neck from a tree as soon as possible."

. . .

LATER THAT DAY, Jesse placed a call to Cal Covington, who picked up on the first ring. "Christ, Jesse, I've been goin' nuts. What's the situation down there?"

"Everything's fine," Jesse lied.

"Including the local lawyer?"

Jesse hesitated a split second. "He looks good to me. Seems well-connected. Great résumé."

"You don't sound very convinced and you're damned sure not very convincing."

There was an edge in Cal's voice Jesse had not heard since the big man had been on the witness stand. Jesse knew he'd better put some real enthusiasm behind his pitch if he was ever going to get out of this place. "Really? Guess I'm just tired. He looks great. Really great."

"It's your call. Just be sure he's the top mouth down there. Now tell me about the prosecutor we're up against."

"She's smart, she doesn't lose, and her reputation seems pretty much the way Reggie Jackson described Tom Seaver."

"Which was?"

"He said Seaver was so good blind people would come to the park just to hear him pitch."

"Okay, so she's good. How's Kevin?"

Jesse wondered when Cal was going to get around to asking about his son's welfare. "*Purgatorio* is my next stop," Jesse said, then added, "thanks to Domínguez's connections."

Cal sent love to his son and told Jesse to be sure the boy was protected. "His life is in your hands, Jesse," he added and they bid each other goodbye, Jesse feeling an unwelcome flutter in his stomach.

5

DRIVING TO THE notorious *Purgatorio* in a light rain, Jesse and Domínguez passed through a well-lighted, upscale neighborhood. Resuming his tour guide mode, Domínguez proudly pointed out some "typical Guatemala City homes," two-story structures with tiny upper-floor balconies boasting wrought iron rails with flower-box windows. The white or earth-tone stucco walls were freshly painted, though many were spider-webbed with cracks. Wood doors were edged with multi-colored tiles, and ornate wooden benches sat in front of most houses. No lawns, few front yards. Jesse noticed razor wire at roof levels, but few dogs.

The neighborhood worsened as they neared the prison. No dogs or razor wire above these random shacks, probably because there was nothing inside worth stealing. Domínguez pulled up in front of the prison at 8:30 p.m., and looked relieved that the protesters had thinned to a silent handful, huddled under umbrellas or torn-up plastic trash bags. He parked the car and the two men walked toward the main gate, past concession booths selling bananas, fast food, Pepsi-Cola, and Mayan trinkets to visitors and demonstrators. Jesse noted that his presence seemed to arouse more curiosity than animosity among those who remained. It seemed, at this hour at least, more like a vigil than a protest. The hangers-on were mainly young men, some holding signs proclaiming, *'¡Justicia Ahora!'* and *'¡Venganza para Marisa!'*

Waiting at the gate, Jesse took in the drab, yellowish, single-story exterior of the prison, the tall fence surrounding the sprawling compound, and the intermittently spaced guard towers. Relax, he told himself. He'd been in prisons before on *pro bono* visits. They were all alike.

Just as he was beginning to doubt whether Señor Sandoval was going to show, the main gate opened and spotlights blasted their eyes. Out of the glare, a ghostly apparition approached them, followed by two larger figures.

"*Juan,*" came a staccato voice from the man in front. "*¿Cómo estás?*" The security chief had arrived.

Domínguez made the introductions, and Jesse was relieved to see that Señor Sandoval appeared to be an affable man, with an outsized glittery smile. He spoke no English and was even shorter than Domínguez, a stature Jesse now realized was typical in Guatemala. Unlike Domínguez, however, everything about Sandoval was thin, his body, his pencil mustache, his hair, even his voice.

"I am very sorry to have kept you waiting, Señor Hall," Sandoval said, flashing rows of large uneven teeth. "Please be so good as to follow me."

Although most of the remaining demonstrators were hanging around the Pepsi and *Tu Naranja es Crush* stands, a few spotted Sandoval and hurried toward him. The two guards brandished their AK-47s and held them at bay, though they continued shouting slogans and epithets. Sandoval hustled the lawyers inside the gate.

"Don't worry, Señor," Sandoval said in Spanish, seeing Jesse's unease. "By the time you leave the prison, they will all be headed home to their beds." He offered another smile and ushered them toward the search area, swinging an arm in a sweeping gesture. "Look around you, Señor, at one of Central America's finest correctional institutions."

"It's . . . unique," Jesse managed, not wanting to piss the guy off, although he was nauseated from the pungent odor of feces and vomit, barely masked by heavy doses of disinfectant still shiny and wet on the floors and walls. Jesse pictured the guards splashing the stuff everywhere when they heard that a *gringo* was about to enter the prison.

"*Mil gracias*," Sandoval said, as if Jesse had complimented him.

They took a right turn into the security area, where two men and three women searched visitors. Sandoval joked with one of the men and none of them even approached Jesse or Domínguez. One of the women glanced at Jesse and whispered something to Sandoval. The security chief roared with laughter.

"She said she would like to give the handsome American a full body and cavity search," Sandoval said, and laughed again. Jesse laughed with him, but wondered how deep Señor Sandoval's affability ran. He doubted that someone got to be top dog of prison security in a country like this by being a benign jokester.

Purgatorio was laid out as a giant rectangle, with a wide corridor running lengthwise down the center. Sandoval pointed out a small recreation yard, where men sat in groups or stared morosely at the intruders. Jesse was surprised that the inmates were dressed in the clothes they had apparently arrived in: athletic shoes, jeans, and T-shirts. Many wore long-sleeved shirts to conceal gang tattoos, often a sufficient basis for arrest or even death without trial in Guate.

The first sector to Jesse's right was Sector 12, the hospital. Although the patients were in bed, they did not look ill. Nor did the hospital look much like a hospital. He made a mental note: this must be where prisoners with connections or bribe money were transferred for safety.

They approached Sector 11, the maximum-security ward, and tattooed arms and grasping fingers shot through a barred window in a huge metal door. Jesse danced out of the way, feeling a chill as a hand brushed his shoulder. He felt like a visitor to an asylum run by lunatics. Okay, so prisons were not all alike.

"Let's go this way," Sandoval said. The sounds died as soon as the men were out of visual range of the max-security prisoners.

"I've seen enough, Señor Sandoval, and I'd really like to visit Señor Covington now."

"Of course," he said and took them to the visitation area, where a young man in a soiled sport coat and torn slacks waited on a small wooden stool. He sat in an ill-lighted cave carved out of the earth, approximately five by fifteen feet. The space had wood plank flooring, but the walls were unfinished. Jesse half expected to see bats and stalagmites. A single light bulb hung down on a long cord from the invisible ceiling, casting eerie shadows of the prisoner and the two guards who stood at opposite ends of the chamber. A scratched and filthy plexiglass partition separated inmates from visitors. Small holes in the barrier allowed the passage of sound.

Domínguez and Jesse were told to sit in straight-back chairs facing the prisoner. Sandoval took a seat behind the lawyers. Spotlighted by the overhead bulb, the prisoner sat hunched over on his stool, holding his stomach with both hands. Beneath dirt smudges, Kevin Covington's facial skin was pallid, accenting a large greenish-yellow bruise on his face. Jesse felt his own gut roiling at the pitiable sight.

Covington's head came up and he blinked at the visitors. He

obviously hadn't shaved for weeks and his dark hair looked filthy and unkempt. He was probably handsome under better circumstances, but looked ill, and much older than his twenty-five years.

"Kevin?" Jesse said. "Can you hear me?"

Kevin Covington squinted, dull eyes straining through the cloudy plastic shield. Then the eyes came alive, flickering with hope.

"You've come to take me out of here?" Kevin said, his voice gritty.

"I'm afraid not, Kevin. My name is Jesse Hall. Your dad sent me to see how you are."

"I'm scared shitless is how I am," Kevin said. "Did Dad seem . . . worried about me?"

"Of course. That's why I'm here. He tried to get a call through to you, but they wouldn't allow it."

"Well, tell him I did what he asked me to do."

"What was that? He told me you worked for him."

"For CalCorp, not his . . . East Coast organization."

"What's the East Coast organization?"

"Never mind." He glanced at his jailers, then back at Jesse. "I'm sure Dad already has an angle working, right?"

"Mr. Domínguez is the only angle I know about at the moment, Kevin. Things are a little different in Guatemala. Take a look in a mirror."

Kevin involuntarily put a hand to his battered eye and jaw. He took a deep breath that seemed to hurt him. Jesse figured he'd been clubbed in the ribs with a padded bat, the weapon of choice in foreign prisons, along with electrodes. Leaves minimal visible scarring and bruising, yet puts the prisoner in a world of hurt.

"He'll free me."

Jesse didn't know what to say. He wanted to console the man, not dash his hopes.

Kevin leaned into the plexiglass, motioned Jesse closer, then spoke in a raspy whisper. "They're roughing me up in here. Can't you guys get me bail?"

"Who's throwing down on you," Jesse asked, "the guards or other cons?"

"Both. The fact that I'm innocent doesn't seem to count for much."

"That's because everybody's innocent in prison. Anything broken?"

"Maybe a rib or two," he said, "but tell Dad I'm not letting anyone get, you know . . . close to me. I don't want him to worry about that."

"I'll tell him," Jesse said, touched by Kevin's devotion to his father. Maybe the old con man really did have a good side. He turned around to face Sandoval.

"Your prisoner has been beaten, Señor."

Sandoval said, "That bruise on his face? We cannot control all the prisoners."

"If we lift his shirt," Jesse said, "maybe take some x-rays, we'll also see bruised or broken ribs."

Sandoval examined the back of his hand. "I am sure you are mistaken, Señor."

"Mistaken? Shall we take a look right now?"

Sandoval blanched, as if trying to decide whether to be indignant or maintain his convivial facade. "I am trying to be cooperative, Señor, but perhaps I am wasting my time."

"You've been very helpful, Señor Sandoval, but there seems to be a race between the people inside and the mob outside to see who can kill this man first."

Sandoval spread his hands, palms up. "We can only do so much."

Jesse moved in close to the little man. "I'll bet the Red Cross or Amnesty International will know how to find the bruises on this man, Señor. So what I'd like to be able to tell the U.S. Consulate tomorrow morning is that you will personally see to it that this young American citizen lives to see his trial. I'm thinking a transfer to the hospital ward would be a good start."

"I will do what I can."

"I'm grateful for your courtesy, sir. Now would you be so good as to excuse us for a moment so that we can have a private word with the prisoner?"

Sandoval hesitated, but again acceded. He motioned the guards to step back away from Kevin and then left the room. Kevin continued to stare at Jesse, coming close to one of the half-inch holes in the plexiglass. Jesse quickly ran through some background questions, and Kevin answered him. Yes, he was in Guatemala on business for his father; yes, he was interviewed by the victim; no, they did not become intimate; no, he had not met Gómez; and no, he certainly did not kill Marisa Andrade.

"What exactly do you do for your father? You mentioned some 'East Coast operations.'"

"Is that what this is all about? They think I'm racketeering down here? My God, I swear it's all a set-up. I've done nothing wrong."

Racketeering? Kevin was revealing more than he intended. "Are you saying that your father's East Coast operations involve racketeering?"

"I thought you were his lawyers."

"My law firm now represents him, yes."

Kevin rubbed his eyes, then looked at Jesse and Domínguez as if seeing them for the first time. "Well, I'd rather not get into it anyway, except to say I work for CalCorp and *only* for CalCorp. Period. I'm a field supervisor, strictly an auto-parts man."

"So you're telling me that if your dad is involved in illegal operations on the East Coast unrelated to CalCorp, you're not involved?"

"I'm not telling you anything about my dad," Kevin said, betraying irritation. "I'm just saying I've done nothing wrong."

Jesse's jaw clenched as he contemplated the conversation he would have to have with Simon Bradshaw about his treasured new client. And the consequences.

"Okay, Kevin. Who do you think is setting you up?"

Kevin just stared into his hands and shook his head.

"And you deny having had an affair with Marisa Andrade?"

"Absolutely. I barely knew her, met her once. She thought I was dealing with Arturo Gómez."

"The guerrilla chief. I heard about that."

"Yeah. They call him *El Cobra*. The government thinks he's also a big-time trafficker."

"You don't know where she got the impression you had met?"

"The police—the PNC—think Dad has been involved with Gómez and knew I was his son. Marisa Andrade told me that much."

"She heard your dad was involved with Gómez in what? A drug deal?"

Kevin threw both hands in the air. "Can we get back to my case?"

"We are talking about your case," Jesse said, but could see that Kevin would say no more on the subject.

"All right," Jesse said, "where were you the morning Marisa was killed?"

"I was tired from visiting our retail outlets and crashed early in my hotel room."

Jesse frowned. Domínguez had reported that nobody had seen Kevin the morning of April 1 between ten and noon. He made no phone calls, ordered no food, nothing.

"I have no alibi, Jesse, okay? I'm sorry, and wish I could be more helpful. If I had known the Andrade woman was going to be murdered, I would have had a massage somewhere or signed on with a golf foursome."

Jesse felt a twinge of despair as he stared into the prisoner's eyes. One of the key tools in the trial lawyer's bag was the ability to tell fact from fiction, and Jesse could tell Kevin was lying. And without an alibi, the young man was in deep trouble.

But so was Jesse. It seemed clear that Cal Covington was in the rackets, probably drugs, and once Jesse told Bradshaw what he had learned, C&S would have to dump CalCorp. And maybe Bradshaw would then shoot the messenger. Eric Driver's plan was working better than he could have imagined.

Be a lawyer, Jesse berated himself. This might be your last opportunity to work with this poor bastard. "Help me out, Kevin. Who do you think might have had reason to kill Marisa Andrade?"

Kevin tossed his head off to one side, blew air out of his lower lip. "I have no idea, but when she interviewed me at her home office that day—"

"What day?"

"I think it was a day or two before she was killed. She seemed nervous. Phone rings, she jumps. Someone knocks on the door, she's out of her skin. I think she was in danger and knew it."

"The police initially theorized that Señor Andrade found out you were sleeping with his wife and killed her in a rage."

"It's possible, I suppose."

"That you were sleeping with his wife?"

"That he killed her. Will you use that at my trial?"

"I won't be your lawyer. I can't be, but Señor Domínguez—"

Kevin's eyes darted between the two lawyers. "With all respect to the Señor, I'd feel more comfortable if you were involved."

"It's not possible," Jesse said. "Señor Domínguez, please explain to Kevin in English the law that precludes foreign lawyers from trying cases here."

Obviously disgruntled, Domínguez did so. Kevin's face seemed to crumple.

"I'm sorry," Jesse said, and he meant it. God knows he had his own misgivings about Domínguez. But he had some about Kevin, too. The kid had seemed decent enough, working for the poor and all that, but he was clearly lying about how well he knew the victim, and maybe had a crook for a father.

Sandoval approached. Their time was up, and Jesse rose. Kevin put his face and hands against the plexiglass. "So, Jesse. Will I stand a chance at trial?"

Jesse stared down at the filthy, beaten-down young man. "I won't bullshit you, Kevin. The victim was a great woman and the people want vengeance."

Jesse realized that Domínguez had risen, too, and was standing beside him. "Everybody in Guatemala," Domínguez said in English, "even us who are not agreeing with her politically, we admire the Señora Andrade. Everybody they admire her."

"Apparently not everybody," Jesse said.

DAY THREE

6

WHILE DOMÍNGUEZ PREPARED the bail application the next morning, Jesse grabbed a shower and put in the dreaded call to Simon Bradshaw. The senior partner was as angry as Jesse expected, but at him, not Cal Covington.

"You asked his son that? Are you aware that we are Cal Covington's lawyers, bound by the most sacrosanct of confidential privileges?"

"I haven't told anybody—"

"And you won't. Here's what you *will* do. You will forget whatever it is you think you deduced from the kid's reference to his father's possible racketeering. You will be certain the local lawyer down there—Domingo, or whatever the hell his name is—also forgets anything *he* thought he heard. You will do what you were sent to do down there and nothing more. CalCorp is an important client. You'll soon be a partner, Jesse, so start thinking about the firm's welfare!"

"Sir," Jesse managed, "that's exactly what I am thinking about. If there is any truth to this East Coast business, it could be very embarrassing for C&S."

"Embarrassing? We're *lawyers* for Christ's sake, not a bunch of self-anointed saints running for the school board. We are above embarrassment."

Or beneath it, Jesse thought.

Silence. All he could hear was Bradshaw's heavy breathing and his own heart pounding in his throat. Finally, Bradshaw spoke, sounding calmer.

"Listen, Jesse. Sorry I shouted at you. I . . . I'm under considerable pressure at the moment, and you're the last person I want to take out my frustration on."

"It's fine, Simon—"

"You must know, Jesse, that you're the man I intend to turn the keys over to eventually, and . . . well, on a personal level, my wife insists you're the son I wished I'd had, and she might be right. So circumstances now require that I burden you with information about C&S that only four partners are aware of."

Jesse held his breath.

"The firm has hit a financial wall, temporary, of course, and regrettably common for the profession these days. The recession has turned some of our blue-chip clients into deadbeats. Our business department's mortgage securities practice is dead. Our two biggest income-producing cases have settled. Worse, we've lost major clients—Northern Metrics and Synoptics—to cut-rate firms. So, bottom line? *We need CalCorp, okay?*"

Jesse's head was so overloaded, all he could think of to say was, "All right."

"Good man. This was a shock to me, too, and I share your concern about Cal, but with his projected five-to-seven million a month coming in, the bank will maintain our line of credit and we'll be fine." A pause and Jesse heard a match flare. He could picture the senior partner pushing his glasses back up on his aristocratic nose and taking a deep drag on his filtered Benson and Hedges, ignoring the local ordinances.

"Just be certain our client's son is well represented, Jesse, and we'll soon be popping the cork on some Cristal bubbly." Cristal was the firm's traditional welcome-to-partnership beverage of choice—a rap on your door, ExComm partners enter, beaming faces, fraternal handshakes. Bradshaw was the one partner with the clout to make good on a prediction like that. He had championed other dark-horse candidates and always prevailed.

"That . . . that would be terrific, Simon. Thank you."

. . .

JUAN DOMÍNGUEZ WAS clearly no Clarence Darrow, but if he performed well at the bail hearing, Jesse would reassess his talents and maybe would even be able to fly home the next day. Optimistic, he left early for their scheduled meeting, skipping the cab stand in front of the hotel in favor of a rickety, multi-colored *camioneta*, or "chicken bus." He wanted to see a little of the city. The rain had finally stopped, and sunlight bathed bright green vines climbing up brilliantly colored, tile-embroidered doorways. Bouncing along, he admired orchids hanging from small Crape Myrtle trees and lush ferns that seemed to spring up out of the steamy soil wherever they could find sunlight. High above the spires and crosses of the city's numerous churches, vanilla clouds crowned the smoldering volcanoes that surrounded the city like devoted sentinels. Jesse found himself surrendering to the troubled country's natural beauty.

Five blocks later, it was time to find a taxi, and Jesse leapt from the bus and into people jammed together on the busy sidewalk—street kids, cripples, Mayan women wearing *huilpiles* and bearing huge baskets on their heads, uniformed police with automatic weapons, and locals shopping at *tiendas*. He asked a PNC officer in Spanish where best to catch a cab and the wise ass responded, "I hear New York City is good."

Jesse resorted to renting a 2001 Suzuki and made it to Domínguez's office with only one near-collision and only a half-hour late, which qualified as being on time in Guate.

The lawyer's office was in a converted single-story suburban home, shared with two other *abogados*. The grounds were beautifully landscaped, and inside Domínguez's office numerous mounted certificates attested to his accreditation and various community activities. Domínguez proudly handed him the bail application, and Jesse was relieved to see it was a journeyman job, focusing on the circumstantial nature of the charges and the difficulty of flight considering the fact that Covington's passport would remain in government custody. Maybe there was hope for Domínguez.

"If you fail in this motion," he asked Domínguez, "when will he be tried?"

"Whenever they want to try him."

"But you saw the man. How long do you think he can stay alive there?"

"It is hard to say, Señor."

Jesse groaned. "Look, Juan, we have to win this bail motion. Won't the Court at least let us split the argument? You open, and I'll close."

"Not possible, and again, I must warn you: if you try that, you could be subject to prosecution for the felony of *Usurpación de Calidad,* the unauthorized practice of law."

"You're *warning* me?" Jesse had never smoked but he felt like starting. The man was acting more like a government toady than an advocate, and Jesse could only pray for a major metamorphosis at the hearing. He had never so much wanted to be proven wrong, but no longer felt optimistic.

"How about if Chief Prosecutor Ruiz stipulated to my appearance? She seemed to be an okay person, once she established that her *cojones* were bigger than mine."

"Don't expect any favors from the CP. She's tough, Señor Hall, a rabid reformer who cannot be bribed."

"I need you to understand that I didn't come to Guatemala to bribe people."

"I am only saying she is a very rigid about enforcing our laws."

"*Jesus*, man, that's what a prosecutor gets *paid* to do." The guy was hopeless. "All right, Juan, let's start over. There must be a way I can sit in."

"*Lo siento, Señor,*" Domínguez said, slipping between English and Spanish. "The only exception is *prueba de expertos*—expert testimony."

"You mean I could testify? Can I also sit at counsel table and advise you?"

"Yes. A foreigner can be admitted to offer expert testimony and advice."

"Fine," Jesse said, leaning down close into the lawyer's moon-shaped face and squeezing his arm hard. "I'm your expert, and here's my advice, *Amigo*: Be your best tomorrow, *comprende*? We get Kevin out on bail or you're finished."

. . .

SIMON BRADSHAW SAT at the head of his conference table, flanked by the grim faces of Eric Driver and Jim Haydel. They, and two others, were the only partners aware that before CalCorp dropped from heaven, the firm had been maintained on life support by an interest-free loan of seven million from Bradshaw's personal fortune.

"I still don't like it," Haydel said, "all our eggs in the CalCorp basket."

"Man-up, Jim!" Driver sneered. "If it wasn't for CalCorp's international presence, our overseas branch offices would be shut down by now. Better to be a captive firm than no firm at all."

"Maybe," Haydel countered, "but how the hell do we handle the workload?"

"With creativity, imagination, and some luck," said Bradshaw. "Most of the litigation and government contract work will be duplicative, so we'll apply templates. I've already set up a cookie-cutter operation for most of the work our various offices will be processing. I agree that we are taking on a massive amount of work, Jim, but it's auto parts for God's sake—simple contracts, liability insurance oversight, antitrust compliance counseling, and coordinating litigation around the world by a formula I've devised. Paralegals can do much of it, certainly the massive collection work."

Haydel shrugged. "Okay, but I think we should be more open with the other partners about the seriousness of our situation. And it's unseemly concealing your loan from them."

Driver snorted. "Brilliant, Jim. Let's tell them everything, and while we're at it, why not post it on *Facebook*? You think Chrysler selling automobiles out of bankruptcy was hard? Try selling legal services to a community that knows you're broke. Try holding on to our best people."

Bradshaw, obviously tired of the exchange, rose and, without a word, walked out of his own office, leaving the two partners staring at each other across the table.

DAY FOUR

7

THE NEXT DAY, Jesse and Domínguez walked up 7A *Avenida* in *Zona* 4 toward the *Centro Cívico*. Auto traffic was heavy, cars and buses speeding around the nearby rotunda, spewing carbon monoxide in their wakes. A high fence off to their left blocked the rusted railroad tracks, but not the odor of feces from the squatters' camp on the other side, near the abandoned station. At least the *Avenida* itself was free of beggars in this area and relatively clean. With obvious pride, the local lawyer pointed out the towering *Banco de Guatemala* off to his right, with its modern murals and exterior glyphs depicting the history of Guatemala and the bloody defeat of the "superstitious natives." Jesse tried not to listen.

They approached the *Centro Cívico,* where hundreds of demonstrators were noisily gathered in front of the *Torre de Tribunales,* the city's courthouse, a modern structure with graceful, slatted columns, fifteen stories high.

Jesse took in the sullen, ragtag crowd. "These are not happy people."

Domínguez spat on the ground. "They are mostly *indigos,* unemployed farmers from the highlands or former guerrillas. They worshiped Marisa and seek vengeance. I do not think we should try to go through there. People know I am representing her killer—"

"Her *what?*" Jesse said. "Jesus, man, are you Kevin's lawyer or his prosecutor?"

"I just mean that if they recognize me, it will be very bad for both of us."

"All right, so how do we get in?" The crowd was growing by the minute. Some people were scaling a fence and spilling over 10 *Avenida* from the abandoned railway station.

"We'll go back to my office and I'll phone the court clerk. I pay him well. He will explain our difficulty to the judges. Then, perhaps another day . . ."

Without a word, Jesse grabbed the portly little man by the arm and shoved him forward through the crowd. Domínguez had overestimated his fame, and the only complaints Jesse heard were when he pushed too hard. Once inside the courthouse door, Domínguez mopped his forehead and they quickly passed through security. The guard didn't even look inside Jesse's briefcase, nor did Jesse's cell phone set off the metal detector. It could have been a small automatic pistol.

"Interesting security system you have there," Jesse said to Domínguez, "Inspectors who don't inspect and metal detectors that don't detect."

The lawyer spread his hands. "It has a chilling effect on the guerrillas. You are white and perceived to be an American. They would not wish to offend you."

"I didn't think Americans were popular in Central America."

"But now there is Obama. And we always watched your TV shows."

And they still admire us? Jesse mused. They caught an elevator to the sixth floor, where the motion would be heard. Entering the courtroom, Jesse was surprised to see that it resembled those in America, with one major difference—there was no jury box, a distinction that could cost Kevin his life. Instead, there were three seats for the judges that served in Guatemala as both judge and jury. They sat on a raised dais, looking down on a small brown and white desk and a witness chair. Witnesses sat center stage, facing the judges, back against the rail that separated the court officers and attachés from the gallery. Jesse was also surprised to see so many people showing up for a bail hearing—over fifty already seated.

Elena Ruiz, *Jefe de Fiscalía,* sat to the gallery's right, against the interior wall. She looked stunning, despite her drab navy suit and apparent effort to look otherwise. Jesse and Domínguez took their seats next to the opposite wall, disquietingly marred by bullet holes. The court clerk sat to the left of the defense lawyers and the gallery sat in ochre-colored plastic cafeteria chairs. The blue and white flag of Guatemala hung to the Tribunal's right, just behind the clerk, and the state seal was planted on the wall above the presiding judge's seat.

Jesse felt the familiar fluttering in his stomach that always signaled an important court appearance. At 8:45 a.m., two young guards escorted the prisoner into the courtroom. Although Kevin's face was still deathly white, Jesse was relieved to see his bruises were healing and that he appeared free of new injuries.

"How's it going, Kevin?" Jesse said. "Are you in the hospital ward?"

Kevin gave his head a little hitch to one side and lowered his gaze. "Yes," he murmured, "I'm there."

"And you're okay?"

"Sure," he said through compressed lips. "I'm fine."

"Look at me, Kevin."

But Kevin's eyes had retreated inward, blurry and unfocused. He turned his head and, for a second, his vacant stare met Jesse's gaze. Kevin looked away and Jesse suspected he had been punked-out in the hospital ward. He felt heartsick, and to spare Kevin his dignity, Jesse said simply, "That's good. Now let's see if we can win this bail motion."

Kevin's composure broke and he seized Jesse's arm. "We've *got* to win. I can't go back there."

"We'll do our best," Jesse said, and turned to see that Elena Ruiz was watching him. She smiled and Jesse smiled back. What was there about this woman? Could it be the attraction was mutual? It made him feel good to think so, but then he slapped himself mentally. Wrong time for thoughts of sleeping with the enemy.

Behind him, the courtroom had filled with people, many of them Anglos with notebooks, undoubtedly reporters. Guatemala's "Flash Radio" was there, interviewing Domínguez right at the counsel table, but Jesse's attention was drawn to a huge, puffy-faced Guatemalan in his mid-fifties, seated Buddha-like in the rear of the courtroom. He seemed to be trying hard to remain unnoticed—tough for a man who looked to be six foot four and 280 pounds in a land of generally short people. Half the people in the courtroom were stealing glances at him. Who was this guy?

At nine, the three judges took their seats in the courtroom. A stern-looking woman was flanked by a chubby, middle-aged judge on one side and a man who seemed too young to be a judge on the other. All wore business attire.

The clerk, the person who seemed to do most of the work under the Guatemalan legal system, began reading the charges against Kevin. Judge Manuela Chavez, the presiding judge, seated in the middle, kept glancing at the defense lawyers as if they had somehow already offended her. Her grey, kinky hair was worn short and close to her head, accenting her elongated face. The other two judges carefully avoided any eye contact with Jesse, Domínguez, or the prisoner. Domínguez leaned across Kevin and whispered to Jesse that the oldest, dozing judge was Renaldo López, the only one not a known crony of Carano's. Swell, our one hope is a narcoleptic, thought Jesse.

When the clerk finished her endless commentary, the hearing got underway. Domínguez introduced Jesse as "an expert in court for the purpose of rendering advice, as permitted under Section 187." Judge Chavez scowled through her horn-rimmed glasses and equine face, but welcomed the visitor to the court in heavily accented English. Jesse thanked her in Spanish and Renaldo López awoke with a start, stroked his thin beard, and stared down at Jesse with apparent distaste. Domínguez had explained that Judge López suffered debilitating migraine headaches, and Jesse hoped this explained his hostile expression. If López was the one objective judge on the panel, they would need his support.

"Proceed, Counsel," said Judge Chavez.

Domínguez rose to his feet with the reluctance of a man being sentenced and briefly noted that the defendant's health was in jeopardy, pointing out the bruises. He added that the evidence disclosed by the prosecution appeared to be completely circumstantial and that the defendant could not flee without a passport. He then sat down.

Elena Ruiz rose and, with a lack of vigor that surprised Jesse, presented the evidence she expected to offer at trial: two witnesses who had observed Kevin and Marisa together in public; a witness who observed the defendant leaving the victim's house at or near the time of the murder; and a statement by the defendant in which he falsely denied all knowledge of the victim.

Jesse interpreted what had been said for Kevin's benefit and gave his arm an encouraging squeeze. "Her case sounds weak so far," he whispered.

But Kevin seemed unconsoled, and Jesse couldn't blame him. Domínguez's plea for his freedom had been devoid of passion.

"In addition," Señorita Ruiz concluded, "we will present an investigating officer who is our liaison to Interpol. He will testify concerning the Covington connection to a U.S. drug-racketeering ring."

Jesse felt himself flush with anger, and he elbowed Domínguez hard in the side, but the chubby *abogado* refused to object to Elena's patently prejudicial reference.

Jesse rose to his feet. "Your Honors," he said in Spanish and in an overly loud voice that came out a croak. "I wish to 'advise' my fellow counsel."

"You may do that," said Judge Chavez, "but you may not address the court or argue the case, Señor Hall."

"Well, *somebody* has to argue the case, Your Honors. For example, who are these so-called witnesses? Where's the investigating officer and the affidavits? The prosecutor can't just tell you what they're going to say without giving us an opportunity to confront them."

"*Sit down, Counselor,*" said the senior judge. "The request for bail is denied. This is a capital case in which the death sentence may be invoked. The possibilities of flight are obvious, given the character of the detainee."

"*Character*? Based on what?" Jesse said. "The prosecutor's blatantly improper hearsay claim that someone bearing his name is allegedly involved in racketeering?"

"*Siéntese*, Señor Hall!"

Instead, Jesse leaned down close to Domínguez and said, "This deck is stacked, *amigo*. Can you challenge judges in this country?"

"Yes," Domínguez whispered, refusing to look at Jesse. "Judges are subject to '*recusal*' by either the defense or prosecution."

"Good, then get your ass up there and *recusal* the hell out of all three of them."

"But they've done nothing," Domínguez said.

"That's my point, Juan, and so far you haven't, either. Can't you see that she just made a crucial ruling without even consulting the other two judges? The fix was in before we even started. *Challenge* them, dammit!"

"I *can't* do that, Señor Hall. I have a reputation in this city."

"For what? Getting along with judges?"

Domínguez was silent, his face frozen, and Jesse said, "Your Honor, I'd like to challenge you if you don't mind. All three of you, in fact."

He heard people gasping and snickering behind him.

"Sit down, Señor Hall," Judge Chavez said, speaking English, "or you will be removed from this court of law."

"You call this a court of law? Law implies justice, and justice allows a defendant to confront his accusers. Where are they?"

The gallery was growing noisier. Jesse saw expressions ranging from amusement to shock. He was glad to see more reporters had joined the onlookers.

"Señor Domínguez will have that right at the appropriate time, Señor Hall."

"That's nice, Your Honor, but by the time it gets around to being appropriate, my client could be dead. Have you ever been in that rat's nest you call a prison? Have you ever so much as—"

The senior judge nodded and Jesse was suddenly grabbed by both arms and jerked backward through the rail so hard it nearly dislocated his shoulders. Shocked by the assault, his instincts took over and he slammed both elbows into the solar plexuses of both bailiffs. Stunned and bent over, they released him, and Jesse took advantage of the confusion around him to stride out of the courtroom.

. . .

OUTSIDE IN THE elevator lobby minutes later, Jesse was getting his heart-rate under control, when a very angry Juan Domínguez charged toward him. "You should be grateful to me, Señor Hall," he snapped. "But for my apology and exemplary reputation, Judge Chavez would surely have charged you with contempt of court and assault on those officers."

"Really? Well, it appears to me, Juan, that you're a man in love with his own reputation. What you really are is a bag man who knows who to make payoffs to and a lawyer who's afraid to protect his client."

Domínguez moved into Jesse's face and said, "And what *you* are, Señor Hall, is a man who does not know what he is doing down here."

"Well, maybe I didn't, but I do now," Jesse said. "I'm down here to fire your incompetent ass."

Jesse looked over Domínguez's head and noticed the huge, bearded, red-faced man he had seen in the courtroom, now standing near the door and watching the exchange with obvious interest. Domínguez lifted his twin chins in defiance.

"You have no authority to terminate my services, and I remind you that this is, how you say, a high-profile case. I have my reputation in this city."

"I thought we had just covered the subject of your reputation. And don't worry about my authority. I'll have Kevin put your termination in writing before day's end."

Domínguez's face seemed ready to explode. "You do that, Señor," he shouted, "and I will tender my bill in the amount of fifty thousand U.S. dollars, which your client will pay within three days or I will sue you personally as his agent!"

Jesse smiled down at Domínguez and softly said, "You try that, Juan, and you'd better hire a real lawyer to represent you."

A new version of Juan Domínguez emerged, and this one poked a finger hard into Jesse's chest. "Listen to me, you *gringo* bastard. I have access to people who can make this city a very uncomfortable place for a visitor."

Jesse stared down at the red-faced man, picturing him as one of those chubby, unpopular kids in grade school, sucking up to a bully for protection, and now as a grownup, probably still doing it. Jesse leaned down close to the *abogado*. "Gosh, Juan, you're scaring me. But on that subject of 'access to people,' you might consider the possibility that those nasty mob connections you were afraid to object to just might be true. *Capice*?"

The local lawyer's eyes got as big as golf balls and his fat cheeks quivered as he spoke. "You dare threaten me?"

"I'm just saying we're at an impasse, *amigo*. Let's quietly go our separate ways."

Domínguez sputtered and wiped his face with a handkerchief before offering a grudging nod. "But remember," he said, "you have no lawyer and can only advise. So, Señor Tough Guy, what will you do now?"

"Well," Jesse said, "it's my fourth day in your fair city and it appears I'll be here a day or two more. So I guess what I'll do is go find a laundry."

Domínguez grunted something unintelligible and hurried down the stairs, not waiting for an elevator. Jesse smoothed his hair back and returned to the courtroom to find Kevin and make peace with anybody who would listen, wondering what in the hell he was going to do for a lawyer.

. . .

BACK AT THE Conquistador Ramada, Jesse called a law school classmate of Simon Bradshaw's, a local estate and tax lawyer, who Simon had provided in case some local help was needed. The classmate produced a list of the four best trial lawyers in town. Two were willing to meet with Jesse late that same afternoon. But when the first *abogado* connected Jesse's name with the Andrade murder case, he grimly proclaimed that his practice was now limited to real-estate law.

A half hour later, the second one shook his head sadly and offered to make Kevin Covington a will.

8

JESSE RETURNED TO *Purgatorio* later the same afternoon. But instead of going through the laborious process of seeking official permission again—this time without the benefit of Domínguez—Jesse simply handed the deputy warden a fifty at the front gate. He felt less guilty than he expected. When in Rome . . .

In less than an hour—including time spent listening to the deputy warden as he practiced his English—Jesse had secured Kevin's signature on a document firing Domínguez. He also managed to slip 2,000 *quetzales* to a guard who promised to see that Kevin was protected at night in the hospital ward. He then headed back to the Hotel Conquistador, where a message awaited him, nothing but a phone number. Jesse hoped that one of the lawyers from his earlier inquiries might have called back.

He punched the number, and on the first ring a man answered and identified himself as Professor Teodoro Andrade, Marisa's husband. His English was perfect. "I observed your 'conversation' with Señor Domínguez this morning after court," he said, "and I would like to assist you in finding competent counsel."

Jesse realized he was talking to the huge bearded man he had seen in court.

"If you're really Professor Andrade," Jesse said, "why would you want to help me?"

The voice said, "You mean, why should you trust me, yes?"

"That, too."

Jesse heard the rattle of ice in a glass in the background. "You may question me at length and draw your own conclusions about that, Señor. Your client needs competent counsel, and I know who they are. Indeed, I taught most of them."

"I'll be there in less than an hour."

Jesse phoned Simon Bradshaw and reported that he had fired Domínguez and that so far his attempts to replace him had failed. Simon, upset at first that Jesse had acted precipitously without first securing a new attorney, calmed down when Jesse assured him he would soon have a replacement, thanks to the proffered help of a respected local law professor. Jesse didn't bother to mention the professor was the victim's husband.

"Fine, Jesse, Cal will be pleased with himself that his instincts about Domínguez were correct. The only thing a client likes better than having a smart lawyer, is to think he is even smarter."

Jesse relaxed for the first time in days. He would soon be on his way home. He could already taste the Cristal and picture the smiling faces of the firm's executive committee as they welcomed him to partnership.

How could Eric Driver possibly block him now?

9

PROFESSOR ANDRADE'S HOME was in *Zona* 15, a world wholly apart from what Jesse had seen in *Zona* 1, or elsewhere in the city. Neat curbs and gutters. Clean, eight-foot white stucco walls. Razor wire, but no *perros* patrolling the roofs. It was by far the most attractive residential area Jesse had seen. He parked and started to lock his Suzuki, but heard a voice from behind the wrought-iron front entry gate. It belonged to a small, grey-haired woman who identified herself as Carmen, the housekeeper.

"You don't want to leave your car on the street," she said in Spanish, and directed him to a carport at the side of the house. A steel security gate slammed shut behind him.

Carmen met him at an open side door and led him into a small, dimly lit study. A single window opened out onto the side yard, but a curtain was drawn over it. There was a small fireplace, but it was not burning. Behind an ornate cherrywood desk, the giant, sad-faced man Jesse had seen in the rear of the courtroom sat in a high-backed leather swivel chair that groaned with relief as he lifted himself out of it. He was dressed in cream-colored slacks and a white, short-sleeved shirt, loafers, no socks. Grief was etched in dark depressions under each of his heavy-lidded dark eyes and in his pale, craggy face. He looked perilously unhealthy, like a man losing the fragile thread of his existence.

"Hello, Señor Hall," he said, in a hoarse whiskey voice. The professor's sparse grey hair was clipped short, as was his salt-and-pepper beard. His shoulders were rounded by time and sorrow, and his towering height seemed to burden him with an aura of apology to shorter people which, in Guatemala, included just about everyone. He looked neither flabby nor toned, just huge. His blue eyes suggested a Northern European mother or father. A delicate coffee cup was cradled in one of his large hands, and, although the cup appeared in jeopardy, Jesse could see the man possessed a certain grace of movement. The professor offered his other hand to Jesse and introduced himself.

"Have some coffee," he said, and Carmen instantly appeared bearing a tray. "You have met my warden?" he added, smiling with affection at Carmen.

Jesse said he had. He glanced around the study and realized he was standing in a crime scene. A pair of antique chairs faced the leather-topped desk, upon which sat an empty glass, an ashtray full of butts, and a burning cigarette. Behind the desk and swivel chair was a credenza covered by a beautiful, multi-colored *mantón* that appeared to be hand-woven. According to reports, the victim's body had been found near this credenza, which her husband had now converted into a makeshift bar. An ice bucket and half-full bottles stood among newspapers and a brass clock with exposed workings covered by a glass dome. Bookcases lined three of the walls, with framed photos in between books, one of them a picture of Teodoro, Marisa, and their daughter at an *al fresco* luncheon in happier days. Husband and daughter loomed on either side of the fragile-looking woman like bodyguards. Marisa had full lips and large, almond-shaped eyes. A natural beauty.

Teodoro Andrade's eyes followed Jesse's gaze, and he managed a plaintive smile, revealing large and even teeth, stained by coffee or nicotine, probably both. Jesse could see the man had been handsome once, before time and grief had dulled his countenance. Jesse smelled alcohol on his breath.

"I understand you're a law professor," Jesse said.

"I was."

"Will you return to teach at San Carlos University?"

"No. When the police named me as a suspect, my colleagues turned on me. After a week of accusatory stares, I quit showing up for classes. I had just lost my wife and needed more time. Then, just as I was 'pulling myself together,' as my daughter would say, they terminated me."

He turned toward the credenza and laced his coffee with brandy. "We export our best coffee beans, so we must fortify those we are left with." He held up the bottle, but Jesse declined.

"You didn't have tenure?" Jesse asked.

"Of course I did, but they terminated me anyway."

"But now that Kevin Covington has been charged—"

"The hell with all of them," he said, screwing the top back on the brandy bottle. "I have finished with teaching."

Could an entire faculty be wrong? Jesse resolved to tentatively accept the professor's help, but also to make sure that the big man shouldn't be the one occupying Kevin's cell.

"By the way, Señor Hall, both Domínguez and the prosecutor, Señorita Ruiz, were once my students. Ruiz was one of my best, and, you will not be surprised to hear that Domínguez—who maintains delusions of adequacy—was one of my worst."

Jesse smiled and said, "Elena Ruiz is very . . . impressive."

The professor scratched his beard, and said, "She has never lost a case. She also wins at cards. Do not play poker with her."

"I only gamble in court, and then only when I'm fairly sure I'll win."

Carmen entered, glared at the brandy bottle, and then at the professor, then went out.

"I saw you in court this morning," the professor said, a twinkle in his eye. "An interesting performance. Reminiscent of a World War Two kamikaze pilot."

Jesse smiled, nodded, and said, "I saw you as well, just after I flew down the smoke stack."

The professor's laugh came out more like a bronchial cough. "As you have undoubtedly discerned, Domínguez is a government lackey. I think he got off easy having his services terminated rather than his nose or jaw."

"I guess I'm lucky not to have ended up Kevin's roommate."

Andrade nodded. "Particularly with Elena Ruiz connecting the defendant with an American mob."

"Guilt by association," Jesse said, "but Kevin is not involved."

"Really? I hear his father has met with Arturo Gómez several times."

Jesse tried to show nothing on his face. "I doubt it," he said.

"Just a rumor," the big man agreed. "I take it you are searching for a new lawyer for young Covington?"

"I am, but I'm hoping you might tell me why the husband of a murder victim would be willing to help the accused killer?"

Andrade nodded and lit another cigarette, coughing as he exhaled. "Two reasons. First, the prosecutor claims the defendant's motive was that Marisa had broken off an adulterous affair with the suspect.

How can I allow that to stand? I will grant that there was much about my wife I did not understand, but the one thing I know is that she was not an adulteress. As a teacher grounded in the Socratic method, therefore, I ask myself why the police would slander her? The only plausible answer is that they needed a suspect to direct attention away from Carano, our ambitious Vice President. So, the most effective way for me to put this vicious rumor against my wife's virtue is to help you expose it. If that also happens to help young Covington, fine."

The men appraised each other, then the professor toasted Jesse with his cup and said "*salud.*" Jesse, drawn to the professor, reminded himself to be careful. If Andrade believed that Kevin had copulated with and/or murdered his wife, what better way to ensure a conviction than to select the lawyer who would present the defense in court?

Jesse said, "Okay, and for what it's worth, Professor Andrade, Kevin denies the relationship with your wife."

Andrade nodded and said, "I am an informal man. Please call me Teo."

"Thank you, and please call me Jesse."

"My second reason is that I do not want Carano to get away with it."

Jesse felt a rush of hope.

"Specifically," Andrade continued, "I think that her death was ordered by Vice President Victor Carano in order to silence her highly public attacks on him. In a recent *Guatemala Globe* Op-Ed piece, Marisa, in a rather shrill manner, detailed the way Carano has gradually usurped President Ruiz's power and co-opted key members of our congress. She also reported on 'mysterious transfers' from his discretionary offshore funds to 'persons unknown.' Marisa even indiscreetly hinted in *Hoy Revista* that Carano was head of a secret society called *La Cofradía* that runs crime and just about everything else here in Guate. "

Interesting information, thought Jesse, and he'd come back to it, but now he'd better be sure he wasn't being suckered-in by a wife-killer.

"I can't help but notice that you used words like 'shrill' and 'indiscreet' to characterize your wife's writing style. Did you have issues with your wife, Teo?"

Andrade scowled, and Jesse feared he had gone too far too fast. But the big man shrugged. "I concede that I disliked the virulence of her public attacks. I had a family to protect. She was the head of *La Causa,* a radical human rights organization with many enemies, mainly Carano's ARES brownshirts, para-military thugs. Death squads still operate here with impunity, and we were constantly hounded: stakeouts across the street, late-night phone calls with no one there, occasional rocks through a window."

"So naturally, you were critical of your wife's writings."

"Occasionally, especially when she suggested that Carano headed *La Cofradía.*"

"I can see that this would anger him, *La Cofradía* being a crime family."

"It is much more than that. The early *Cofradía* was a religious brotherhood, combining Catholic and pagan practices. This modern iteration is a shadow government consisting of high-ranking politicians, former military officers, and businessmen. It fixes elections and controls the five crime families in Guatemala."

"Aren't there laws against—"

"My dear young man, this secret society *makes* the laws, then appoints the judges to enforce them!"

Jesse made a mental note to learn more about *La Cofradía,* then said, "All right, but you did strongly disapprove of your wife's political positions?"

"I'm not a political person."

Jesse heard the evasion in the man's answer. "Still, it must have been hard being apolitical and living with Guatemala's foremost human rights activist."

The professor frowned. "I think it is bit late for marriage counseling, don't you agree?"

"Okay, I'll be blunt. It sounds to me as if the disagreements you had with your wife were serious, potentially incendiary."

The frown became a glare. "Let me be equally blunt with you, Señor Hall. I am offering you assistance in finding a defense lawyer in your murder case. You are free to take my help or leave it, but your insinuations are unwelcome."

"Sir, the victim in this case was your wife and you're a lawyer, so I hope you'll understand that I can't accept your assistance without first examining your motives in offering it."

The professor met Jesse's steady gaze and then shrugged. "All right, yes, we had 'issues.' She would call me a reactionary and a dilettante, forgetting that I was engaged in a worthy profession, teaching our youth. But she would say, 'We already have too many lawyers; what we need is *justice!*' And yes, sometimes I felt guilty that she was the more courageous of the two of us."

The big man rose, opened the curtain, and shifted his gaze outside, beyond the bougainvillea and purple *jacarandas*, out to the edge of his property, where the naked, glistening limbs of a fruit tree moved in the wind as if clawing the sky. "So yes, there were arguments," he added in a faltering, hoarse voice, "but I adored her." He grabbed the bottle of brandy and fell back into his chair, then added another splash into his cup and again held the bottle up to Jesse.

"I'll stick with the straight coffee for now, sir," Jesse said, realizing that the picture was getting clouded again. The one man in Guatemala who was offering help could be a wife-killer. The more brandy he drank, the more he seemed to be implicating himself. Where was a tape recorder when you needed one? Jesse decided to take the next step.

"Outside of the stress of Marisa's public activism, were you otherwise . . . close?"

"Were we 'romantically active?' That was Chief Inspector García's delicate phrasing. The assumption seems to be that this is impossible for a man of fifty-four and a woman of thirty-three."

Jesse felt his face heating up. "I don't mean to intrude, sir, I'm just wondering what you did together other than argue."

The professor lit his third cigarette in ten minutes with a quivering match and took a deep drag, then watched the smoke curl from his full lips and drift upward. Andrade again shifted his gaze back outside to the blood-red bougainvillea rimming the study's slightly opened window. Rain had begun to fall heavily on the leaves of two avocado trees just past the open window, producing an incessant, distracting sound, like sizzling bacon.

He took another drag, and then said, in a voice so faint Jesse wasn't sure he'd heard him right, "We danced."

"Sir?"

"That is what we did together," Teodoro said, his eyes suddenly misting as he continued to stare out through the window. "The girl loved to dance, and I am better at it than you would suppose. After dinner here at home, I would put on a Glenn Miller record—usually 'Moonlight Serenade'—and we would dance, Marissa's head warm against my chest. In good weather, we opened all the windows and let the breeze blow the curtains and we would drink champagne and dance some more. You see, Jesse, my age and poor health burdened me with certain . . . limitations, but Marisa and I found alternate paths to intimacy."

Jesse felt lost in the mood the professor had created. The big man continued to stare outside for a minute, then blinked and gave his head a quick shake. "That is what we did. You are too young to be familiar with Glenn Miller?"

"I've heard of him. Played trumpet, right?"

"Trombone. Slide trombone. But what was unique was the instantly recognizable sound of his orchestra. He had a clarinet and tenor saxophone play the same melodic line, with three other saxophones playing harmony against them."

"You sound like a musician yourself," Jesse said.

"I am a closet alto sax player, which is to say Marisa only allows me to play in a closet."

Jesse smiled, let the present-tense error pass.

"On the roof, actually."

"The roof?"

"That is where I play my saxophone," Teodoro said. Jesse, seeing that Teodoro Andrade's eyes were now moist with tears, wondered if his initial instincts, usually his most dependable method for appraising people, had been correct. The professor seemed to be a good and likeable man, thoroughly in love with his wife. On the other hand, Jesse knew that good and likeable men sometimes killed people they loved.

"Come, I'll show you my roof," the professor said, "and I promise I'll leave my saxophone in the closet. It has stopped raining, and there is no better view of the city anywhere."

Jesse followed the professor up to a flat roof, where he was greeted by blinding sunlight and a cacophony of bird sounds. Wind had scattered the dark cumulus rain clouds, and he had to shield his eyes to see a wired enclosure at least six feet high and ten feet long, which appeared to be full of doves. Beyond the cage sprawled Guatemala City, framed by its majestic volcanoes. Jesse heard the faint strum of a guitar.

"Meet my ladies," the professor said, wheezing from his climb. He reached into a bin and filled a utility scoop with feed. "I have raised them for years. Do not ask me why; they give me nothing but trouble."

"They're beautiful," Jesse said, looking at about thirty softly cooing doves, most of them staring back at him. They were generally grey—a few males, too, much lighter in color—with hints of purple coloring on their breasts and beautifully ribbed backs of light and dark shades of grey. Several of them fanned their tails in excitement, revealing white tips nearly an inch long.

"They provide comfort," the professor said, "and they never complain about my saxophone playing. I think Marisa was a little jealous of my ladies. 'You and your birds,' she would say. 'You and your precious birds.'"

Teodoro filled up feed cups with the scoop, but suddenly staggered and lurched into the side of the coop. The doves fluttered wildly, but he regained his balance and they quickly settled down again. "Look over there," he said. "The steeples of the *Catedral Metropolitana*, and there, westerly toward Antigua, is our highest active volcano, *Fuego*."

The smoldering, charcoal-grey mountain was both immense and ominous.

"It's . . . unreal," Jesse said, caught up in the awe-inspiring view.

"Yes," said Teodoro. "Guatemala is a country of illusion. Nothing is quite what it seems."

Including you, perhaps, Professor. "Tell me, sir, why do you think the police dismissed you as a suspect and charged Kevin instead?"

"Political expediency," he murmured. "Carano gains little by convicting me, but by publicizing the arrest of the son of a rumored U.S. racketeer, he scores points with the U.S. and its war on drugs, plus our citizens are reassured. But to answer your question, the police still think I killed her."

Once again, Jesse was stunned by the man's candor and jumped on it. "Did you?"

The professor responded with a wry smile that failed to conceal his obvious irritation. "Ah, the adversarial wolf again sheds his sheep's clothing. I must not forget you have a client to defend. You are thinking that maybe the old man heard all the gossip and went out of his head?"

"Many decent people kill their loved ones, Professor," he said. "Perhaps you're one of them."

Andrade's head jerked as if Jesse had shot him. "Well, young sir," Andrade said, staggering slightly, "you have found me out. I am, you see, guilty as charged."

Stunned, Jesse saw the professor's hand move toward a wood-handled knife stuck upright on a battered wooden table. The blade glistened hypnotically in the sun. "Yes, I killed her," he said, snatching it up.

Jesse tensed and backed away—this couldn't be happening—but the big man stayed at the table and began cutting up strips of leather. "Hole in the cage," he said, and began to repair the opening at one side of the cage. "Might lose another one of my ladies."

Still stunned, Jesse stared at the professor's back and saw him shudder. Was he weeping?

"I killed my wife with apathy, Jesse, just as you have suggested." He turned to look out toward the *Catedral*. "Maybe . . . maybe if I had been more open and shown interest, she might have listened to me.

And had she listened to me, she might be alive today." He savagely knotted the last leather strip in place, then slashed off the hanging end, jarring the cage in the process. "The bastard Carano must be brought to justice!" The birds again fluttered nervously, but he calmed them again with a falsetto crooning.

He turned to face Jesse. "You are very pale, Jesse. Are you ill?"

"Maybe a cold coming on," Jesse said, and Teo returned to his repair work, pointing to a larger, recently repaired hole in the mesh.

"One of my ladies is already gone."

Jesse said, "Will she come back?"

"No," Teodoro said quietly, his lips clamped together, working with surprisingly deft fingers, concentrating on the tear in the wire mesh, pulling it together with pieces of leather. "She is gone."

. . .

BACK DOWNSTAIRS, THEY reentered the study, where fading shafts of sunlight now pierced the stratus clouds and slanted through the western window. Jesse gratefully accepted a beer and realized his hand was still shaking. Teodoro poured himself two fingers of *Zacapa* rum, and their moods decompressed with some small talk. "You said earlier that you would not return to San Carlos. Will you teach law somewhere else?" Jesse asked.

"Never. It would be like someone teaching Hegelian idealism in the middle of a nuclear holocaust. Besides, I need, in some small way, to grant to my wife in death the attention I denied her in life." He paused, then slowly nodded his head as if he were agreeing with himself and added, "At the very least, that means ensuring the conviction of the man who ordered her death."

"Victor Carano?"

"*Exactamente.*"

Jesse nodded. There was no way to be sure about Teodoro Andrade, but Jesse decided that on balance, he would have to trust him, at least for now. "So, Professor, you'll help me find a trial lawyer for Kevin?"

Teodoro rummaged through papers on his desk. "Here are the three best in Guatemala."

Jesse took the paper. He looked at the three names, each followed by an address and phone number. None had been on his former list.

"You may use my name," Teodoro said. "The first two are former students. For background, you should also speak with my daughter, Anica. Regrettably, she was the one who found Marisa's . . . body. Marisa was her stepmother, actually, but Anica idolized her. Can you imagine the trauma?"

Jesse agreed it was hard to imagine.

"Well, she is getting better. She overheard Marisa's last conversation with Anastacia Ramírez, a fellow board member of *La Causa*. Marisa was close to tying Carano into some suspicious money transactions that might involve drug trafficking. Anica can also describe the enigmatic 'Carlos V' to you firsthand."

"I don't know what you mean."

Teodoro looked surprised. "Señorita Ruiz did not tell you about Marisa's dying message?"

"Message? What message?"

"Marisa managed to scrawl out some letters on the floor in mingled ink and blood. It appeared to read, 'Carlos V.'"

Jesse's eyes popped open. "The name of her killer?"

Teodoro casually resumed his search through the piles of papers scattered on his desk. "Obviously," the professor said. "Ah, here it is," he added, and handed Jesse a sheet of paper on which his daughter had sketched what she had seen scrawled on the floor. Jesse was jolted by the realization that the chief prosecutor had concealed this key clue to the murderer's identity, even when he had asked her straightaway about possible exculpatory evidence.

"What is wrong, Señor Hall? Is this not a good thing for your client?"

"It's a *very* good thing," Jesse said, barely containing his excitement, "Did Marisa know anyone named Carlos or Carl with a last name starting with a V?"

"No, but there was much about my wife I did not know."

A dog howled in the distance.

"Don't you see, Señor Andrade? We're talking silver bullet here."

"A silver bullet?"

"In the U.S., we'd say that this single clue could shoot holes in the case against Kevin. Your wife was obviously trying to reveal the identity of her killer and there's no way you can get Kevin or Covington out of 'Carlos V.'"

Jesse kept staring at the letters. Something was bothering him. He said, "How about someone whose name started with a W? Look at the shorter right side of the V. She might have been trying to complete a W when…"

"I don't know," said the professor, "I simply don't know," and fell into a large chair, obviously exhausted by drink and the trip to the roof. His cheeks sagged, and the pockets under his eyes bloomed darker. In the dim light of his study, he looked like an old man. Jesse said he could find his way out and thanked the professor for his help.

He drove to his hotel in an exhilarated mood. His suspicions of the professor had been largely allayed, and he had a list of the best advocates in the city. With "Carlos V"—or "W"—pointing away from Kevin, it should be easy to obtain competent counsel, and, with luck, he'd be on a flight to San Francisco the next night.

But first, he'd have another chat with the seductive, stonewalling prosecutor. And this time, he'd wear blinders.

DAY FIVE

10

AT NINE THE next morning, Jesse's euphoria gave way to anger as he approached the chief prosecutor's office. Elena Ruiz might call her concealment legitimate hardball, but to Jesse it was patently unethical. He had been reasonably detached up to now about this assignment, but no longer.

He stormed past the receptionist's desk and into Elena Ruiz's office. A well-dressed older man and a pretty young woman sat across from the chief prosecutor. They looked at him as if his head were on fire.

"Señor Hall?" Elena said, rising quickly. "As you can see, we are in a—"

"Who is Carlos?"

"Please, Señor, we—"

"Who is he?"

The prosecutor asked her wide-eyed guests if they would excuse her for a few minutes. They scuttled out the door, more than willing to give the crazy American a wide berth. The receptionist, hard on Jesse's heels, spun around and returned to the safety of her desk.

Jesse closed the door behind them, then advanced on Elena Ruiz's scarred metal desk and leaned across it. "Did it occur to your Nazi police force that the person you've arrested is named Kevin, not Carlos? What kind of tinhorn justice system are you running down here?"

Elena's eyes arrowed. "We have more laws in my country than we used to have." She removed a snub-nosed .38 revolver from her desk drawer and put it on her desk between them. "But regrettably, this is still what counts for justice in Guatemala."

"That's not justice, that's power."

"Perhaps, and what power I have will always be devoted to bringing about ultimate justice."

"A noble sentiment, but as a prosecutor, you're just one side of the coin."

She put the gun back in the drawer. "Really? You would do well, Señor, to be less vocal concerning things you know nothing about. You can be assured that all means available to me will be employed in the service of equality and justice. Now please leave my office."

"Or what? You'll shoot me full of justice? How about you take a break, go find a Scrabble game, and try to make 'Kevin' out of the letters, C-A-R-L-O-S."

"Get out, Señor Hall, or I will have you removed."

"Answer my question, Señorita, and I'm out of here. What kind of 'justice' excuses concealment of the identity of the real murderer from the defense?"

The prosecutor stared at Jesse for a full ten seconds, and then let her eyes soften. "Sit down, Señor Hall," she said, in a resigned tone. Jesse sat and she did, too. She began arranging the pencils, pens, and papers on her desk in an ordered symmetry. Buying time, Jesse knew. Trying to decide how far to go.

"As I told you, our law imposes no obligation to reveal exculpatory information," she began, "particularly to a lawyer who does not even represent the defendant. That aside, I will tell you that the police made an exhaustive search for anyone known to the victim named Carlos or Carl. They worked with the family and went through her address book and all her files. Nothing close. They searched her computer as well. Nothing. They interviewed twenty of her closest associates. There is simply no 'Carlos' among them and my conclusion is that this is what we call a false clue, proving nothing one way or the other. As it fails to point clearly to the victim's killer, therefore, it in no way exonerates your client."

"Then what harm would there have been in revealing it to the defense?"

"The evidence is being analyzed by the *Departamento Médico Forense*. Until forensics finishes their work, our policy is to regard the information as strictly confidential. As soon as they release their report, I will be free to turn it over to Mr. Covington's lawyer who, I repeat, Señor Hall, you are not."

Jesse stared into her unblinking eyes, then took a deep breath and rubbed his own. "That's true, but will you notify Kevin's lawyer when he can get the results from forensics?"

"Of course," she said. "Is it true you have terminated Juan Domínguez?"

"I felt like it, but I just fired him." Jesse saw that she was stifling a smile, and added, "That coffee smells good."

She followed his eyes to the urn on a credenza behind her. "Would you care for some coffee, Señor Hall?"

"Well, if you insist, and if you will call me Jesse."

"Sit down, Jesse."

Jesse sat back down and she poured them each a cup.

"I appreciate this," he said. "I haven't wasted many hours sleeping."

"You do look tired," she said, and her apparent sincerity combined with her good looks sounded an alarm bell. This wasn't the time for some damned mating dance. A man's life was at stake.

"I'll be gone as soon as I get Kevin a lawyer. Meanwhile, I'd be grateful if you'd give me a preview on what his lawyer is going to see—whenever you get around to letting him or her see it."

She considered his words for a minute, and then said, "What do you know about me?"

"I know your father is President and that you probably had to work harder than most people to prove you deserved your job. I've been told you've won all your cases and have improved the quality of prosecution in Guatemala City. I hear you play high-stakes poker with people on your staff and win at that, too. I know firsthand that you're damned attractive and smart as hell. I'm hoping you're also fair and open-minded."

She considered his words, her head tilted to one side. A river of hair shone like volcanic glass as it tumbled down over one shoulder. "I am some of those things," she said, smiling, "and I only win at poker most of the time." She smiled. "I've decided to reward your persistence. Do not presume too much from this rare act of benevolence."

Jesse bowed in mock gratitude, wondering if she meant he should not presume that his obvious attraction to her was mutual. The only thing he had figured out about Elena Ruiz was the futility of trying to figure her out. She was beginning to symbolize the enigmatic beauty and mystery of Guatemala.

"Out of respect for you as a fellow trial lawyer," she continued, "I will make certain concessions. First, this is not the strongest case I have had, though there is no doubt I shall win it."

She paused and scribbled something on a sheet of paper. "Second, here is the name of the witness who saw Señor Kevin Covington leaving the Andrade house around 11:45 the morning of the murder wearing a green jacket identical to the one he was arrested in. The defense would get her name eventually. Consider it a peace offering."

Jesse glanced at the name. "How does she know it was—"

"The witness is quite reliable. She selected the suspect from a picture gallery as well as a lineup.

"Third, here is a copy of the coroner's report, which puts the time of death between eleven and twelve on April the first, based on 'body temperature of 96.9 degrees, a purplish cast to the skin, pale lips and nails, and the absence of *rigor mortis* or even early non-fixed lividity.'"

Jesse scanned the report. He had second-chaired a murder trial under C&S's *pro bono publico* program during his second year and remembered more than he cared to about the impact of death on the human body. One thing he remembered was the eggs—flies, eggs, then maggots. He said, "I note that early traces of eggs were detected in the eyes, nose, and mouth."

Elena smiled. "You impress me, Jesse Hall. You are suggesting a much earlier time of death. A time, for example, when the defendant was not seen leaving the crime scene? Bravo, but I must disappoint you. In Guatemala, our flies lay eggs well within ten minutes."

Jesse nodded. "I see no mention of feces." If a few hours had passed before the victim's step-daughter discovered the body, there would have been no wind left in the lungs, so everything beneath the pallid skin would have collapsed, the eyes would be flat as blown-out tires as fluids leaked out, and the sphincter would have released.

"No, and our coroner always mentions it if it is present."

"When did he arrive?"

"Before one o'clock, a half-hour after the victim's daughter discovered the body."

Jesse had hit a dead end. He knew that the body cooled at about one and a half degrees for every hour that passed after death and that the hands and feet would indeed develop a bluish-purple cast. He was forced to conclude that the report was correct in estimating death at between eleven and twelve noon and that forensics in this country knew what they were doing. More bad news for Kevin.

Elena handed him another document. "I am also giving you an Interpol report indicating that the defendant's father indeed has connections with certain criminal elements based in the United States."

Jesse's stomach did a double-clutch, but he concealed his surprise and said, "Covington is the majority stockholder and CEO of the biggest auto parts retail operations in the world, a company he built from scratch. Does your report show that?"

"Yes, but it shows that the 'scratch' probably came from drug money and still does. Moreover, it is not a great leap of logic to infer 'like father, like son.'"

"That particular leap would never be allowed in a U.S. court, Elena, certainly not in a murder case."

The prosecutor flashed an ironic smile. "You must forgive us, Jesse. Here, in primitive Guatemala, we natives have not yet grasped the high moral concepts of a more modern culture."

"I understand, but I thought your judges looked very cool yesterday in their bone necklaces and traditional headdress."

"Thank you. We are elevating our cultural perspective constantly, aided by American television gems such as *Real Housewives* and *Wife Swap*."

Jesse smiled. "Part of our international exchange policy. You give us mind-numbing drugs, we give you mind-numbing entertainment."

"I'm not finished."

"You forgot *Biggest Loser* and *Trading Spouses*?"

"I'm not finished sharing information about the case. Fourth, Kevin Covington's fingerprint is on a glass found in the Andrade's bathroom."

"Fingerprint?"

"Eight points."

Jesse struggled to mask his astonishment and growing anger at Kevin. "In the U.S., you'd be lucky to even get an eight-point fingerprint into evidence. Besides, the victim conducted Kevin's interview at her home office." Jesse let that lie sink in then added, "Even the son of a Interpol racketeer washes his hands occasionally."

"Especially those with a guilty conscience," she said.

"Whatever. Anyway, the prosecution would learn about the home interview eventually. Consider it a peace offering."

Elena smiled wryly. "You are kind beyond words, but as it turns out, Señora Andrade conducted her regular interviews in an office lent to her by the *Globe*."

"That doesn't rule out the possibility that—"

"We also have witnesses who have attested to their 'close relationship.'"

Jesse shook his head. "She was too high-profile a person. She would not have risked a display of intimacy with an American in public any more than you would."

Jesse watched for her reaction to his choice of words.

"I have learned, Jesse, that caution is often victimized by passion."

Despite Jesse's despair over everything she was telling him, there was something in her last words that floated toward him like a promissory note. The girl was playing with him, but he felt heat spreading the length of his body. "I can think of worse things," he said.

"Fifth," Elena continued, "in case you are still counting: Mr. Covington has no alibi whatsoever."

Jesse took a deep breath and again reminded himself that he was the only advocate Kevin had at the moment. Kevin may have been lying about not knowing the victim, but with the mysterious Carlos in the picture, he could be innocent. These new facts were like neon arrows pointing in opposite directions.

"Okay, Elena, a couple of questions?"

"Certainly."

"This witness who allegedly saw Kevin leave near the coroner's time of death—did she see him from the front or the back?"

"The back."

"Walking away?"

"Yes."

"Thank you. Now, let's assume you can prove the two of them had an affair. That's not illegal in Guatemala, is it?" He ventured a smile.

"No, but if someone denies it to the police, it strongly suggests guilt."

"Not if someone denies it to protect the honor and reputation of a lady."

This drew an amused look from the chief prosecutor. "How gallant these American gangsters!"

"And what about the husband?" Jesse said. "Isn't he always the first suspect when an adulterous wife is found murdered? Especially when the multiple wounds suggest a passion killing and the weapon used was a convenient kitchen knife—which your police conveniently can't find."

Jesse felt bad about betraying the one man who had extended the hand of friendship and assistance. And Professor Andrade seemed sincere about wanting to find the real killer. But isn't that the first thing a charged wife-killer says? O.J. Simpson came to mind.

"Your premise is erroneous, Jesse. Professor Andrade rejects the notion of his wife's affair with Señor Covington, and he knows nothing yet about the defendant's fingerprints in his home or the witnesses who saw the couple engaged in public displays of affection."

"What about other suspects, such as Victor Carano? Have you considered that Marisa's public accusations against him and her support of the alleged land grant might have motivated him to silence her?"

She laughed. "Montezuma's final revenge? *¿Justicia último?* Nobody really takes that so-called land grant letter seriously. Indeed, some think that even Marisa Andrade was beginning to doubt its authenticity. Besides, a bilateral commission, including three Mayan legislators, is performing an independent audit of historic legislative and court records, looking for any trace of support for the alleged grant. They will find none. There *is* no land grant. Trust me."

Trust me. Jesse mentally put his hand over his wallet. "For something that doesn't exist, it's sure causing a lot of excitement. Where did the letter purportedly come from?"

Elena shrugged. "An ancient bible was stolen from an archeological dig near Antigua and the anonymous con artist trying to sell the letter claims it was found tucked in that bible. The original thief was murdered, which lends drama, if not authenticity, to the hoax."

"If Carano is so sure it's a hoax, why not just call a press conference?"

"In politics," she said, "timing is everything. He'll wait for the report."

"And tell the commission to issue it when he's ready to have it?"

"Exactly. I think he is enjoying the land grant hysteria. I have never seen him so happy. You'd think he had created the phony letter himself."

"How could Carano be happy about a rumor that says he's about to lose half of the country he controls? Unless, of course, he honestly knows it's a hoax."

She nodded. "I am not saying the man is capable of honesty, but he does know the letter is a hoax."

Jesse rubbed his eyes. "He *knows*? You're not telling me something."

"I'm not telling you a lot of things."

Jesse shook his head. The woman was talking in circles again.

"Now it's my turn," she said. "When can I expect the name of Señor Covington's new counsel?"

"I told you," he said, "I'm working on it."

"Work fast," she said. "I'm moving to expedite the trial. Here is a copy of my motion requesting a trial date in one week."

"One week? You can't do that. The defendant has no lawyer."

Her face hardened. "I've been ordered to do this by the Vice President, who fears that the protestors will riot, perhaps take the law into their own hands."

"Let me get this straight: you're railroading my client to death row next week for his own protection?"

"Do you want to see your client lynched?"

"Of course not, but you have to give me time to get the man a lawyer or the government will end up lynching him anyway."

"Take your time; take all week."

"Look, Elena, you can show Kevin's father hangs out with some bad guys and you may prove Kevin and the victim were lovers and that he lied about it, I get that. You may even have a witness who'll try to identify him—from the back. But that's not a murder case; it's mainly guilt by association. It's already obvious to me that the guy most motivated to silence Marisa's criticism currently heads your own government."

Elena's eyes darkened. "My father heads this country."

"You know who I'm talking about."

"Good day, Jesse, I really must—"

"I'll leave in a minute, but listen: Teodoro Andrade is convinced Marisa had the goods on Carano, that he was heading some kind of shadow government that drug cartels report to. I'm sure you've heard of *La Cofradía*?"

The usually cool Elena actually blinked. "I am certainly no fan of the Vice President," she said, "but that may be stretching things."

"How about the CIA? I assume it's still active here in Guatemala?"

"Do cancer cells still multiply?"

"Who is the station chief in Guatemala City?"

Her eyes widened, then went flat. He had struck a nerve. "What relevance could that possibly have?" she said, then rose. "You must excuse me."

"In a minute. Marisa Andrade also suggested in the *Globe* that money was flowing out of Carano's discretionary account to an offshore account, then back into Guatemala. This sounds like drugs to me, and whenever there's offshore accounts and drug trafficking in Central America, the CIA is never far away."

Elena nodded. "How could this most recent manifestation of your active imagination serve to shift guilt from Señor Kevin Covington?"

"What if Marisa was on to a Carano-CIA drug deal and they had to shut her up?"

Elena gave him an amused look and rose to her feet.

"What's so funny?"

"Your fantasy life. You've watched too many of your American movies."

"Maybe. Do you know the identity of the local station chief?"

She pressed her intercom button. "Rosa, please bring my guests back," she said, then turned to Jesse. "For what it's worth, we think his name is Webster."

"What's his cover?"

"A German construction company," she said. "Now leave, Jesse."

Jesse rose and headed for the door, "You've met this Webster?"

"Dammit, Jesse, no, I have never met him."

"Has Vice President Carano met him?"

"Undoubtedly, as *de facto* head of state owing to my father's illness. Now go!"

"Okay," Jesse said, turning at the door, "but if you found Marisa was right and that money from Carano's discretionary fund was coming back into Guatemala from offshore, would you tell me who it went to?"

"Why would that be relevant to the defense?"

"I'm not sure, Elena. But if Marisa was on to something fishy—"

"If it appears related to the case, I will tell you."

"Thank you."

Someone knocked on the door. Elena seemed startled, suddenly uneasy again. "I wish you well, Jesse, and hope to see you before you leave our city."

"I hope to see you whenever or wherever you'll let me," Jesse said, and the way her head swung around made him instantly regret it. They had been subtly dancing on the ethical edge of flirtation, and he had just stepped on her foot.

"Just one last thing. Tell me Webster's first name and where to find him, and I'm out of here," Jesse said, but Elena had turned away from him.

"Come in, Rosa," Elena said to the door, and the two earlier visitors cautiously reentered the room. Elena made no introductions.

. . .

JESSE WALKED BACK to the Suzuki and watched the sun break through the palms and mango trees that ringed the property. The air tasted fresh, but he felt like his head was swarming with bees. He couldn't believe the trial was about to start. And why had a cool customer like Elena gone batshit when he started talking about the CIA and *La Cofradía?* And what was going on with the land grant and this "Carlos V" guy? And Kevin's supposed romancing of the victim? Too damned many moving parts.

Jesse would send these questions to the part of his brain he had long ago dubbed "will-call," a place where they could percolate overnight. He had learned that he could check back into will-call the following morning and his brain, left to its own devices, would sometimes have sorted things out for him during his sleep.

Meanwhile, he felt he was catching on to Elena's game. Every time she told him something, there were ten other things she *didn't* tell him. Keeping her hole card close to her perfect chest. But at least he knew there might be other people out there with a motive to silence Marisa. This Webster character, for one. In addition, Elena didn't deny that money was flowing out of Carano's account, and even seemed to know about it. What if Marisa was right about a Carano-CIA drug connection, and what if the money coming back in from offshore could be traced to the CIA spook, Webster?

In law school, you got as much credit for spotting the issues as for knowing the applicable rule. Real life, however, exacted harsher demands. Real life wanted answers, and Kevin's new lawyer would have to come up with some soon with the trial starting in a week. After lunch he would meet with the three hot-shot lawyers on Teodoro's list and retain one of them, then say goodbye to Guatemala.

But something nagged at him, something about how she'd acted when he mentioned the CIA guy. For example, why hadn't she told him Webster's first name when he asked her? She must know it. Why the reluctance? It made no sense . . . unless . . . unlessss . . .

Wheels in his brain began to turn, then turn faster, cogs falling into place: CIA, drugs, the short right side of the V after CARLOS and... *holy shit!* Could it be? Jesse spun, ran back past Elena's receptionist, and reprised his barge-in routine. There sat the same two people, looking at him in the same surprised way.

"*Señor Hall?*" Elena said. Her eyes sparked as he approached her desk. "*Really!*"

"You never answered my question, Elena. *What is Webster's first-name?*"

Elena's full lips clamped together into a straight line. She looked at him as if he had tracked dog shit into the room. The seated couple began to rise again, but Elena motioned them to stay seated.

"His first name is Carl," she said, almost a whisper. "Now *get out.*"

"*Carl* Webster? Jesus, Elena, the victim's first language was Spanish! She would have called him Carlos! *Jesus Christ, Elena!*"

Elena sat without speaking, staring down at a pencil she twirled in her fingers.

11

JESSE'S BRIEF ELATION from having identified Carl Webster as "Carlos" was crushed by a succession of rejections by every lawyer on Teodoro's list. One wouldn't even let him past the receptionist; the other two cited "conflicts." Then he got a call from Cal.

"I just talked to Cy!" Covington shouted. "He said you fired Kevin's lawyer without a new one set up to take his place. Is that true?"

"I'm working on finding—"

"That's like starting a fuckin' liver transplant before you've found a donor! Are you *trying* to get my son killed?"

"Hold on, sir," Jesse said. "In the first place, Señor Domínguez couldn't lead flies to a feed lot." When dealing with an angry man, Jesse believed it best to talk to him in his own idiom. Jesse also believed that the best defense was a good offense, especially when no defense was readily available. "In the second place, the prosecutor is claiming you and your son are connected with a drug racketeering outfit trafficking in Guatemala. So what is it exactly you sent Kevin here to do?"

Silence, then the tinkling of ice in a glass and a change in tone.

"All right, Hall, but you're my lawyer, and don't forget it, because here comes a privileged communication." Another pause and Jesse pictured the man taking a heavy pull on his drink. "I haven't always been a straight arrow, okay? But I am now, and the kid's never had anything to do with my past . . . activities."

"He's certainly aware of them."

"He's my son."

Jesse wiped sweat off his brow, tried to dampen his skepticism. "Is there anything else your lawyer should know?"

"No, I swear, that's it. I'm squeaky clean. The past is past." The sound of a match striking, air expelled. Jesse tried to put his disgust aside.

"I'll keep trying to find him another lawyer," he said, then told Cal about the "Carlos V" clue left by the victim.

"What's with the V?" Cal asked.

"I'm working on it." Jesse didn't mention Carl Webster and wasn't sure why. Probably because with Cal Covington, Jesse was never sure whether Dr. Jekyll or Mr. Hyde was on the line. Cal was also one of those clients you didn't want to encourage too much at the beginning because it could create expectations you might not be able to deliver on. When that happens, the lawyer ends up contending with his own client as much as with his adversary.

"All right," Covington said, seemingly mollified. "Call me back tomorrow when you've hired the new mouth, okay? Sorry I blew off a minute ago. I appreciate what you're doin' there. Give my kid a hug from his Big Daddy. Tell him his mother and I love him with all our hearts and he's gonna be okay."

Jesse dressed and drove his little rental car toward the Andrade property for the second time in two days. He had called Teo to report the bad news about the lawyers and learned that his daughter was home and might be willing to speak about the conversation she overheard between her mother and Anastacia Ramírez the morning she was murdered. Teo also promised to supply Jesse with a new list of lawyers and a package of additional notes and articles by Marisa that he had discovered the homicide investigators had missed.

Although highly conjectural, a defense was beginning to take shape in Jesse's mind. It went like this: Marisa may have told her *La Causa* friend, Anastacia, that she was suspicious Carano might be involved with drug trafficking, which would explain why money was flowing into an offshore bank account out of his discretionary fund, then back into Guatemala. After the elder Bush's El Salvatore disaster, you could look up "drugs" in a Central American dictionary and you'd find the CIA in bold type. As for who murdered Marisa, look in that same dictionary under "assassination" and the same acronym would pop up, probably under a picture of the station chief, who happened in this instance to be one Carl Webster. Marisa had also hinted that she was close to exposing high-ranking officials, so the defense could claim that some of Carano's offshore money came back into Guate to Carl Webster for services rendered in silencing her. Throw in the Carlos message scrawled by the dying victim and it's a slam-dunk for the defendant. How could any lawyer in any country resist stepping into such a high profile, career-making case?

Elena must have known she had a weak case, which might explain her somewhat casual attitude, her occasional out-of-the-blue revelations and concessions. Could it be she had known all along Kevin was innocent? If so, why wouldn't she want to try to nail Carano as the guy ordering the hit? Hadn't Carano usurped her father's standing as head of state? Maybe Jesse could convince her they had a common interest in shifting the attack toward the Vice President.

Anyway, his best hope for ultimately getting Kevin a decent lawyer

and a fair trial would be to get as close as he could to Elena Ruiz
and, like Br'er Rabbit getting tossed into the briar patch, he'd happily
make the best of it.

. . .

TEO LED JESSE into his book-lined study. "I should have called
the lawyers myself. I meant to."

But got drunk instead, Jesse thought, eyeing one of those fragile cups
that always appeared in jeopardy in Teo's huge hand. The small room
was lit as before, by just one lamp and the glow of the study's small
gas-burning fireplace. The men took their usual chairs, surrounded by
books, plaques, and photographs. Jesse glanced again at pictures of Teo
with Marisa and Anica, Teo in cap and gown presiding at a graduation
ceremony, Teo up on the roof with his birds, Sonny Stitt holding an
alto sax, and Teo shaking hands with equally distinguished-looking
men in dark suits, all considerably shorter than he.

"All three lawyers spoke highly of you," Jesse said, "and this group
at least seemed competent."

Teo stared into his small fireplace. "Competent cowards," he said,
"afraid of being caught between the wrath of Carano and the mob
hysteria in the streets." He sipped from his cup, then added, "Do not
worry, my friend, I have a new list, and this time I will call each of
them myself in advance."

"Good," Jesse said, though again nursing doubts about both Teo's
motives and sincerity. But where else could he turn?

Teo handed him a large envelope. "Here are Marisa's notes, articles,
drafts, and research materials I found out on a garage shelf. The PNC
either didn't look there or just missed it."

Jesse took the package and perused the contents. After two minutes, he felt an electrical power surge up his spine. Under Marisa's list of "Things to Do," midway down the page, there it was: "5. Check out Webster—query possible CIA connections?"

"Teo," he said, trying to control the excitement in his voice, "did your wife ever mention interviewing Carl Webster?"

Teo gave him a blank look, and then brightened and said, "Yes, I believe so. I heard her talking to her editor about him once. Apparently, he wanted her to track a rumor that Webster was a CIA station chief. Yes, I remember now. She got nowhere with him. By the way, she referred to him as Carlos—"

Teo froze, dumbstruck by his own words. "Oh, good Lord, Jesse. Carlos W!"

"Exactly," Jesse said, and heard the front door open and close.

"It's Anica, just back from a date with her dear boyfriend, Julio."

"You don't seem to approve."

Teo frowned. "She's impressed that he is Gómez's nephew—one of forty or so—but related nonetheless. The boy lives on a soapbox, constantly haranguing against the government, and Anica is nearly as bad. Even with Marisa gone, I have no peace." Teo rose and shuffled to his makeshift bar. "Come on, Jesse, join me."

"I'll take a beer if you've got one."

Teo went to the kitchen and returned with a cold *Moza*. He sat and lit a cigarette, unaware that he already had one burning in the ashtray.

"It's not my place, Teo, but shouldn't you be taking better care of yourself? You're all that girl has now."

"Not really," Teo said. "I suspect she will marry Julio when she graduates. She has no interest in going on to the University.

"Anica!" he shouted, and, seconds later, Anica Andrade flew into the study, apparently unaware Jesse was there. She was a long-legged, round-faced girl, who managed to look attractive despite her chopped hair and garish attire. She wore giant hoop earrings and too much makeup. Her tight Che Guevara T-shirt prominently displayed her nipples. Her hands were stuffed into the pockets of faded jeans that hung stylishly low on her hips.

"Come, dear, and meet Señor Hall."

The first thing Jesse noticed as the voluptuous young girl approached him—well, the second thing—was the sadness in her eyes. Was that so surprising?

Teo said, "Anica, Señor Hall is a lawyer from San Francisco."

"I know who he is," she said, spitting out the words through tight lips. "He is one of the ninety-eight percent."

"Ninety-eight percent?" Jesse said.

"Yes, the ninety-eight percent of lawyers who give the rest a bad name."

Teo glowered at her. "Show some courtesy to our guest, Anica. Señor Hall would like to hear firsthand what your mother said on the phone to Anastacia Ramirez the morning she was killed."

"I have nothing to say to a man who would aid my mother's killer."

"He is simply doing his job, Anica. Señor Hall is trying to establish that Marisa's death was politically motivated, probably by Carano. We share a common interest in this endeavor, Anica, do we not?"

"Well, I suppose that any enemy of Carano is a friend of mine. 'Entre abogados te veas.'"

Teo glanced at Jesse and said, "It's a curse people here put on their enemies."

Jesse smiled and said, "Yo entiendo. Loosely, it means, 'May you be surrounded by lawyers.' 'Rodeado por los abogados.'"

"Exactamente," Teo said. "She is needling you, Jesse. Again, I apologize."

"I don't mind, Teo," Jesse said, "though I've noticed the minute people find themselves in serious trouble, they *want* to be 'surrounded by lawyers.'"

Anica said, "Okay, *gringo*, what do you want to know?"

"You were the one who found your stepmother, right?"

The girl looked into her clasped hands and nodded.

"As I understand it," Jesse continued, "you were attending classes earlier in the day and decided to come home for lunch."

"Yes," she said, and closed her eyes for a few seconds, as if putting herself back in the moment, then told him in a new, quieter voice how she had discovered her mother's body twenty or thirty minutes after noon on April 1.

"What did you do?"

"Nothing. I just stood there. There was blood all around her. I guess I was in some kind of shock, like my mind was denying what my eyes were seeing."

"What did you do next?"

The girl's eyes softened, then filled with tears. "Like I said, I did . . . *nothing*. Just stood there—like some retard."

"There was nothing you could do," Jesse said, touched by her tears of shame. "Tell me about that conversation you overheard your mother having before you left for school."

The girl straightened her shoulders. "She was talking to Anastacia Ramirez. They talked often, even though they openly disagreed about the validity of the land grant."

"Often at a high pitch," Teodoro injected, turning toward Jesse. "Anastacia was the leader of *La Causa,* until Marisa defeated her recently in a hotly contested election."

"Did that cause additional tension between them?" Jesse asked.

"For awhile," Anica said, "but I think they got past it."

"Tell me exactly what she said, as best as you can recall."

Anica recounted how Marisa had said she had found a way to confirm that money was flowing from Carano's account to an offshore account, and then coming back into a different account in Guate. Also her suspicion that trafficking was involved, her doubts about the "old mail"—their code for the supposed ancient land grant letter—and Marisa's discovery that someone they always called their "secret friend" was probably high up in *La Cofradía*.

"I didn't say anything about this to the PNC, but after telling Papa what I'd heard, he told me to write it all down while it was fresh in my mind."

"You did well," Jesse said. "Did Marisa mention to either of you that she was interviewing Kevin Covington?"

"No," Teo said, "but I knew she was talking to people who either knew or had met Arturo Gómez."

The guerrilla leader, Jesse remembered. "What's he like?"

"He is a psychopath," Teo said. "Tortures victims and likes young girls. *Very* young girls."

Anica frowned, but said nothing.

"Do you think," Jesse said, "he might try to start another revolution?"

"I am not so sure," Teo said. "He strikes me as more a rebel than a revolutionary."

"I'm not sure I know the difference."

Teodoro Andrade looked at Jesse over the lip of his cup, which he raised to his lips with both hands. "Jean-Paul Sartre said it most clearly: 'A rebel wants to go on being a rebel, while the revolutionary wants to change things.' *El Cobra*—which is what his men call him—is content with the *status quo* and the money he makes off drug trafficking and occasional insurgencies into Guatemala City. Still, many people idealize him and believe that if Miguel Aguilera, the

Mayan candidate, loses the upcoming Presidential election to the pig Carano, there will be such discontent that Gómez may simply elect himself and kill anyone who disagrees with him."

"Is Aguilera a serious candidate?"

"Very much so."

Jesse made a note.

"Does Gómez actively attack the army here in the city?"

"Constantly," Teo said.

"That's ridiculous, Papa," Anica said. She turned toward Jesse and said, "Julio says the stories about Gómez raping young girls and torturing victims are government distortions intended to discredit him. Julio says Gómez only attacks corrupt enemies of the people."

"'Julio says, Julio says,'" Teo echoed. "Rubbish! Gómez's Livingston guerrillas not only attack the army, they have set off bombs in the *Plaza Mayor* and *Centro Cívico*. Civilians, not just soldiers, have been killed. His sexual proclivities have been documented by parents who have lost their children. Most of us," Teo added with a sideways glance at Anica, "know that all Gómez really wants is to control all drug trafficking in Guatemala."

Jesse intervened, saying, "Could Miguel Aguilera defeat Carano?"

"Not now," Anica said, "although he could have won if Mother had been able to acquire the land grant letter she wrote about."

Teo groaned. "Please, Anica. There *is* no such letter. You cannot continue to ignore the truth."

"Why not, Papa?" she said, her tone as cold as a metal slab. "Mother spoke the truth for years and you completely ignored *her!*"

Teo winced, and Jesse stepped in again. "Teo, you think Carano is responsible for Marisa's death, in part because of her advocacy for the land grant letter. But she had begun to have doubts about it herself, didn't she?"

Teo said, "Possibly, if Anica heard correctly, and the tragic irony is that Carano didn't know it. All he knew was that the people who claim to have the letter had sent her purported excerpts from it and she had dutifully published a few of them in the *Guatemala Globe*. Anastacia, incidentally, never trusted the land grant and still doesn't."

Anica said, "Will you at least admit that many people disagree with you about the land grant, Papa, and that the Mayan could beat Carano if it is proven to be authentic?"

Teo paused, considered her words. "All right, I will concede that *if* the land grant letter were acquired *and* authenticated, both very unlikely, it would be huge for Aguilera. It would give him and *La Causa*, with whose values I wholly agree, a major bargaining chip in pushing for land reform. All very nice, but the letter is too good to be true and not legally binding anyway."

Anica's expression softened. "All right, Papa, and I concede there may be legal problems with the land grant. It's just that we younger people are more unwilling to give up hope. Our future is at stake."

Father and daughter exchanged a look and Jesse realized a kind of rapprochement had been achieved. He could see that there was love between these two survivors, struggling to find its way.

"Could I have a look at the notes you made of the conversation you overheard and your drawing?" Jesse asked.

Teodoro nodded to her and she produced two sheets of paper, along with the original of her sketch of upper-case letters scrawled by her mother in blood. The letters clearly spelled out CARLOS V, although the right side of the V was indeed only half the length of the left side. The police would have actual photos from which the defense could draw an inference that Marisa had died before she could complete a W. Kevin was probably innocent, and there was hope for him.

"Will the police investigate Carano?" she asked.

This inspired a cough of laughter from Teo, who said, "Surely you know the police *work* for Carano, my dear." His laughter suddenly turned to choking and his face contorted in pain. He put his glass down and began to furiously rub his temples.

"Papa? Are you all right?"

"I'm fine, dear. Just tired, I guess."

"It's your drinking, Papa. You are killing yourself. Have you had another blackout?"

"Blackout?" Jesse asked. "Have you been having blackouts, Teo?"

The professor flushed with embarrassment, then broke out in loud laughter and said, "How would I know?"

"That is not funny, Papa," Anica said, her eyebrows angled with concern.

"Why don't you see what Carmen is cooking for us," Teo said.

After she had left the room, Jesse said, "Is it true?"

"Only one time that I am aware of. I was eating breakfast early one morning a month ago and the next thing I knew it was noon. It appears I had delivered a passable lecture at the law school and was never aware I had even left home."

Jesse was suddenly suspicious again, wondering what else Teo might have done during a blackout. "What does the doc say?"

Teo sipped his drink. "He wants a brain scan to rule out a possible tumor."

"And?"

"I have not had one. My doctor admits that if surgery were indicated, my heart could not endure it anyway. He has been after me for years to exercise."

"But you don't?"

"I stand with Mozart. When his doctor advised exercise, he purchased a pool table." He smiled. "Fortunately, my doctor is a friend and promised me he would not notify the *Municipal de Tránsito*. I'd be doomed without my driver's license."

Jesse concealed his renewed uneasiness and resumed perusing the materials Teo had given him. Some pages appeared to be excerpts from the land grant letter and copies of her articles on the subject. "I'll take a look at her articles and pass the package on to Kevin's new lawyer," Jesse said. "He or she will eventually have to disclose all this to the prosecution."

"I understand, and here is my new list of possible lawyers. I will personally make appointments for you in the morning. They will not like it that Elena is trying to advance the trial date, but perhaps we should consider that a blessing. The mobs are getting bigger and more violent every day at the courthouse and *El Centro Preventivo para Hombres*."

"They'll probably calm down once the trial starts."

"You still do not understand, Jesse. If they have their way, there will be no need for a trial."

. . .

IN SAN FRANCISCO, Cal Covington strode into Simon Bradshaw's office as if it were his own. Unbidden, he walked straight into the dimly-lit conference area and took a seat at the head of the large table, bare but for a conference telephone in the center. Simon clapped his hands once and overhead lights flooded the area. He hated leaving his favored position behind his desk, where he would have enjoyed a height advantage while seated. Simon, no stranger to power gamesmanship, was frequently finding himself captive to Covington's superior leverage. Did Cal know the firm was in trouble? Was he letting Bradshaw know who was in control? Had he intuited Bradshaw's agenda?

"Okay, Cy, I'm here. What's the problem, other than the fact that your lawyer down in Guatemala can't scratch his ass with a handful of fishhooks?"

"Not to worry. Jesse is one of our best young lawyers, and he probably has already retained a good replacement for your son. Your usual Coke?"

Drinks poured, Bradshaw went straight to the point. "I understand from my securities group that CalCorp's new CPA firm has already backed out."

"Wulff and Van Duzer? Fuck 'em. I've already got another new outfit with balls. They'll call you later today. No problem."

"I think there *is* a problem, Cal," Bradshaw said in a tone as casual as he could muster. He sipped his drink, steadied his eyes on the glass in his hand. "A financial problem."

"Meet with my CFO about it."

"He's still in Europe, Cal, as you must know. The problem is that your CPA firm quit because they could find neither debt nor equity to support your growth. CalCorp in India, for example, was capitalized by a Liberian company that was funded by an investment company called Crescent Financial that was funded, in turn, through an offshore bank in the Netherlands Antilles. All CalCorp expansions were capitalized in roughly the same way."

Bradshaw paused, giving Cal an opportunity to explain and sweep away his worst imaginings.

But what Covington said was, "So?"

"Well," Bradshaw said, pushing his glasses up on his nose. "I was hoping you could . . . explain how all this phenomenal growth is being funded."

"Sounds to me like you just explained it."

Bradshaw took a deep breath. "Look, Cal. You're a public company. The SEC and Wall Street analysts will eventually want to know who is providing money to those offshore banks that are funding the investment companies that fund the companies that capitalize CalCorp's expansion."

Flashing a smile, Covington held up his glass in a mock toast. "I like the way you think, Cy. Comforts me that you're lookin' out for my best interests. But what you need to understand is I ain't one bit afraid of those Wall Street piss-ants or the SEC bean-counters neither. So you fellas just cool your engines."

Simon Bradshaw tried to put aside his disgust at being called "Cy." Nobody had ever called him that, except for this illiterate cowpoke who didn't know a Simon from a Cyrus. But he also realized that lurking behind his growing disdain for Covington was something else, something that was making his palms sweat.

"Try to understand, Cal. The 'bean-counters' may decide to follow the money, track it downstream until the trail runs out at some offshore bank. Everybody's on edge after Enron."

Cal exhaled loudly, put his Coke down with an audible *thunk,* and fixed Simon with a hard look. "Are you one of those people who are 'on edge,' Cy?"

Bradshaw quickly averted his eyes. Hell yes, he was on edge— anxious about Cal's rumored racketeering connection, about the possibility of C&S failing on his watch, about losing the seven million he'd lent the firm, about his two daughters at Stanford at 100K a year, about his new 150-foot cabin cruiser that slept twelve . . .

"Well, no, I'm just trying to ask the questions that—"

But Cal Covington was on his feet, and Bradshaw felt an avuncular hand on his shoulder. "The only relevant question is whether I can count on you, Cy."

Bradshaw felt a touch of vertigo. Damned high blood pressure. He blinked his eyes, swallowed hard, and then slowly rose and took Cal Covington's extended hand, cursing the dampness of his own.

"Of course you can, Cal," he said at last, "no problem."

12

JESSE POUNDED DOWN a Whopper and fries at Burger King for dinner without pleasure or even much consciousness. He just needed food, and he needed it fast, so he didn't take time to find a more traditional *comida corriente*—a daily special at two bucks American, usually involving tortillas and beans with some *yucca* and *qüisqúil,* a local squash famous for containing all the nutrients of a rubber doorstop.

Jesse was surprised to see so many Pizza Huts, Burger Kings, Wendy's, and McDonald's, most of them protected by AK-47-wielding kids called *Guachiman.* The assumption was that folks should feel secure when enjoying a relaxing, extravagant meal. Domínguez had told him that American fast food joints are considered upscale eating in Guatemala City, beyond the reach of a vast majority of the citizens.

Jesse walked back to the hotel in a light drizzle under Crape Myrtle trees bursting with flaming-red blossoms. He watched kids begging and dodging cars in the middle of the street, others kicking a beat-up soccer ball shiny with gutter water. Traffic tore past in both directions, belching noxious fumes and honking for no apparent reason. The blanket of mist in the air seemed to trap and magnify the smells and street sounds.

He entered the Conquistador Ramada lobby and shook the moisture off his jacket. He caught a nasty look from the usually friendly desk clerk, a stump of a middle-aged man named Santos, who had a perpetually florid face and two ill-fitting suits which he seemed to alternate daily. The clerk shoved a message from Teo across the desk toward Jesse and walked away without so much as a smile. What was that about?

At the newsstand on his way to the elevator, he grabbed a copy of the afternoon newspaper. In his room, he scanned the news. The front page story covering the imminent trial sent a gentle strum up his spine that turned into a heavy metal concert when he turned to the second page and spotted a five-by-seven photo of himself leaving the courthouse and staring into a camera, his eyes as big as pheasant eggs. Beneath the shot was an unflattering editorial about his "unwanted presence in our city, representing U.S. mob interests." Furious, he called Teo.

"I've seen it, Jesse, and so have others. I am sorry to tell you that not one lawyer on my new list will even agree to meet with you."

Jesse felt dampness inside his clothing, his shirt suddenly glued to his back. Could Teo be conning him?

"Keep trying," Jesse said, intending to call some of the lawyers himself. "I'm going to visit Carl Webster."

"Ah, Carlos W," Teo said. "I will go with you. I would like to confront this man, face to face."

Jesse heard the hostility. "That's not the way to play this, Teo. I'll go alone and do the old Yankee Doodle with him. Just find me the German construction company he works for."

"Going alone is no longer a safe option for you, Jesse," Teo added, a true sadness in his voice. "You are quite recognizable now."

Jesse tried to swallow his suspicions. "Thank you, Teo. I'll be very careful from this time forward. But I need to come up with something that makes Kevin's case more appealing to your courageous Guatemalan advocates, and it will only work one-on-one."

"If you insist," Teo said, "but you had better acquire a handgun."

"I don't know how to find one, and if I did, I wouldn't know how to use it."

"If I had one, I'd give it to you," Teo said. "I'll look into the matter."

Jesse signed off and took three aspirin for a developing headache, feeling more and more like a bird being drawn into a jet engine.

DAY SIX

13

TEO QUICKLY RESPONDED with the location of Webster's current construction site, and Jesse hit the road for Antigua, forty-five kilometers southwest of Guatemala City on CA1, at 6:30 a.m. Forty-five minutes later, he entered the eastern outskirts of the "Paris of Central America," renowned for its language schools, fine Mayan arts, crafts, and natural beauty.

Jesse turned his rented Suzuki down the *Calle del Arco* under the archway clock tower toward Webster's construction site at the south end of town. He gazed upward, stunned by the majesty of the volcanoes that surrounded the small city, one of them still active, ringed by a halo of white clouds and aptly named *Fuego*. Teo had described Antigua as a spotless oasis in a desert of turmoil, and he was right. The ambiance of the city washed over Jesse like a warm, soothing bath. He felt freedom from anxiety for the first time since wheels-up in San Francisco.

It was still early, so he walked the few quiet blocks to the *Parque Central*, surrounded by boutiques and sidewalk vendors. Megan—a decent photographer with an eye for authentic beauty—would love the ironwork that decorated the heavy wooden doors and the colorful shop windows along the cobblestoned streets that surrounded the square. Pottery, turquoise jewelry, and colorful *serapes* abounded. He pictured her aiming her camera at the cottages along the street, painted earth tones of yellow, brown, orange, and green, with red and blue shutters decorating the windows. He glanced at his watch. Time to go to work.

Jesse drove to the construction site, a half acre of land under attack by noisy, heavy equipment. On the perimeter, men scurried like ants, setting wooden forms for cement foundations and nailing them into place by hand. Few of the men wore hard hats. American hip-hop and traditional Latin music filled the air, as did the stench of standing water surrounding the site.

Jesse found Carl Webster in the superintendent's shack. The man's sun-mottled forearms and bulging shoulders lent credence to his cover. As tall as Jesse, in his late forties or early fifties, Webster offered a wary smile and a firm handshake, with calluses that hadn't come from central casting. He didn't much look like a killer for hire, or an undercover CIA station chief, either. He looked like a construction superintendent. Jesse handed Webster a business card and said he represented the father of defendant Kevin Covington.

"I know who you are," Webster said. "I saw it in the *Globe*."

A worried-looking man whom Jesse took to be the foreman flew through the door and spoke to Webster, his arms gesturing wildly.

"We got a problem, Mr. Hall," Webster said. "Follow us if you want to."

"Sure, I'll tag along if you don't mind."

Jesse followed the men to the northeast corner of the site.

"We can't see how to set the rebar on this corner," the foreman told Webster. "The architect's plans show the plumbing, electrical, and A/C coming through here, straight into the swimming pool. His plans are wrong."

Webster studied the situation for a minute and then deftly unrolled the plans and went directly to a sheet halfway down. "Shut off the goddamn boom box," he shouted over his shoulder, then lowered himself into the trench and began cutting and twisting the reinforcing steel bars with hand tools. After fifteen minutes of this, Jesse wondered if Webster had forgotten him, but made use of the time to refine his strategy. First, flush the CIA station chief out of his impressive cover, and then use the threat of exposure to keep him talking.

"Let's go back to the shack," Webster said when finished, wiping perspiration from his forehead with a bandana. "I'll clean up and we'll have some coffee. That'll hold 'em for a while."

"You seem to know what you're doing," Jesse admitted.

Webster, still panting from the exertion, gave Jesse an amused look. "I wish I could say the same for you."

"Meaning?"

"Like I said, I read the *Globe*."

"Then you've probably guessed why I've come to see you."

"I have no fucking idea."

"There's talk that you're connected with the CIA."

Webster gazed straight into Jesse's eyes and said, "That's bullshit. I've been in construction all my life. Got on with Amis Construction in Oklahoma City when I was twenty, building roads and tarmac for airfields. After two years with Amis, I got on with Coats International and they sent me to Egypt. Maybe that's how I got the spook reputation."

No, thought Jesse, that's maybe where the CIA recruited you. "What did you do there?"

"We were constructing a power plant in the mid-1980s. I was an assistant construction project supervisor, the guy who rats out foot-dragging subcontractors."

Jesse asked Webster how long he had been in Guatemala, and Webster told him it had been two years. He loved the people from the start, fell in love with a *Ladino* girl he now lived with, and had never been happier in his life.

"But I'm busy, Mr. Hall, as you can see, so tell me what I can do for you."

Jesse took a quick glance around, and then decided to go for it. "I'm busy, too, sir, so you don't have to admit you're in the Company, but *gringo*-to-*gringo*, I need *you* to know that *I* know. Are you with me?"

Webster managed an amused smile. "You been watching too many movies, young man."

"Funny, I was told the same thing yesterday by the top enforcement officer in Guatemala City before she confirmed that you're CIA. Look, Webster, just give me a little background information and I'm gone, okay? Satisfy my curiosity?"

Webster flashed a menacing look, then turned away and poured himself, but not Jesse, a cup of coffee. He took a seat behind his plywood desk and sipped from his cup with a steady hand. The guy was cool.

"You want information," he said, "go to the Chamber of Commerce."

"Is that what you told Marisa Andrade when she interviewed you?"

Webster said nothing.

"Called you Carlos, right? Is that what the locals call you down here?"

Webster slowly rose. "I know where you're headed with this. The police already visited with me about that 'Carlos V' thing, and if you know the 'top enforcement officer' here, you also know Carano's boys cleared me."

"How well do you know Carano?"

"I've seen his name in the paper, that's it. Look, kid, I'm the job super, and that's all I do. I don't socialize with heads of state." Webster started to move around his desk toward the door.

"Mr. Webster, I'm at sea here and—"

"No, Mr. Hall, you're at around four thousand five hundred feet above sea level, so maybe you're suffering from hypoxia. Gotta go now. You, too."

But the phone rang, and Webster sat down again and dealt with a cement delivery problem for ten minutes. The man was a spook, all right, and a damned good one. Clear blue eyes under that shaved head, taking Jesse in with a kind of casual surveillance. All innocence. But maybe he'd play the game as long as he didn't have to show all his cards. When Webster hung up, he continued to stare at the phone, as if hoping it would ring again and this damned lawyer would get tired and leave. But the lawyer wasn't leaving.

"I'm sure keeping your cover is important," Jesse said, "so why not give me two minutes of your time? That way we both get what we want."

Carl Webster poured more coffee, considered the veiled threat, and exhaled loudly in resignation. "Okay, you're wrong about me, but you've got two minutes, then you're gone, deal?"

"Deal," Jesse lied. "What do you know about the Vice President?"

"Alls I know is that he's a hard worker, a political animal like all of 'em, a compromiser. Big *cojones* for a little shit, but no touch with the people. Still, he'll easily win the election."

"So you've had experience with him?"

"Hell, it's my business to know about the people who can hand out government contracts. My company can't make money without 'em."

"So you've met him?"

"Sure, around a thirty-foot conference table and in a room with a thousand other people."

"Is that the only basis of your experience with him?"

Webster squinted a little, but said, "That's what I'm sayin'."

"I hear he's a heartbeat away from the presidency right now with President Ruiz ill."

"It's a race between bad health and his enemies as to which gets Ruiz first."

"With Carano at the head of the line?"

Webster nodded, glanced at his watch. "Some of Ruiz's friends aren't so friendly, either."

"Meaning?"

"I've heard they are afraid he might blab something now he's got the Alzheimer's. Probably why his daughter guards him like a lioness protecting a cub."

"What would he blab?"

"Time's up, Counselor."

Jesse didn't budge. "What will happen when Ruiz dies?"

"Simple," Webster said, sipping from his cup. "Elena Ruiz will flee into exile and Carano will crown himself King Shit."

Elena. Jesse felt a twinge. "Have you heard the rumors that Carano heads *La Cofradía?*"

Webster rose again and walked to the door of the shack and shoved it open with his free hand. "Goodbye, Mr. Hall."

But Jesse had drawn blood and wasn't about to quit. "I'm not interested in blowing your cover, Mr. Webster. I'm just trying to protect an innocent fellow American. You could help me."

"'Innocent fellow American?' Him and his father are probably drug-dealing vermin like people are sayin'. Traffickers like them feed terrorism and waste people's lives."

"For a construction superintendent, you seem to know a lot about my client."

Webster shrugged. "Calvin Covington's drug involvement in Guate ain't a secret. Like I said, I read the *Globe*. I got work to do, so please go through that door, or I'll have to help you."

"Help is what I'm looking for, sir."

"You won't find it. There's too much evidence Kevin Covington killed Marisa Andrade and that he might be connected with a pinko, drug-dealing guerrilla the government fears more than anything."

"Arturo Gómez."

Webster nodded and finished off his coffee. His hand, Jesse noticed, was still rock-steady. "As for the Indians," he said, "don't look for support from them, neither. Shit man, your client killed their most respected hero. So like it's writ on walls around the world: 'Yankee Go Home.'"

Jesse watched Webster walk out, leaving the door open and him standing there alone. Webster may or may not be CIA, but he damned sure knew Carano better than he was admitting. Proving he was Carlos V and Marisa's assassin, however, remained in the realm of wishful thinking.

14

BY NOON, JESSE had reached *Purgatorio*, only to learn after an hour of throwing *quetzales* around that Kevin had been transferred to a temporary holding cell at the *Centro Cívico,* where the *Torre de Tribunales* was located. He had been moved because the trial was "starting next week." *Shit.* Things were moving too fast.

Jesse raced to the *Centro Cívico*, pulled a ball cap low down over his eyes, and eased through the sixty or seventy rag-tag protestors in front of the *Torre de Tribunales.* He proceeded to the back entrance to the holding cells and presented his identification.

"What is your business here, Señor?" the guard inquired in Spanish.

"Soy abogado y quiero visitar al Señor Kevin Covington," Jesse said.

The guard denied any knowledge of a Señor Covington, and after five minutes of frustration, Jesse demanded to speak to his superior. When the stone-faced lieutenant in charge arrived at the gate, he admitted Kevin was being held there, but denied Jesse access on the grounds that he was neither a Guatemalan lawyer nor Kevin's counsel of record.

"All right, but allow me to make a phone call," he told the lieutenant in Spanish, showing his cell phone. "*Momentito, por favor.*"

Within seconds, he was connected to Elena Ruiz's annex office on the second floor of the *Torre de Tribunales*. She had been in a staff meeting upstairs.

"Elena, I'm downstairs at the jail's back entrance trying to visit Kevin Covington. Can you help or do I have to get myself thrown into prison to talk to him?"

"It is lunch hour, Señor Hall. It is not convenient."

"Yeah? Well, the trial date next week is not convenient, either, considering the defendant isn't even lawyered-up yet. The press will kill you."

"Perhaps your termination of Señor Domínguez was a bit hasty?"

"Doesn't matter. I know you can't prosecute an American citizen *in propria persona* with all those reporters watching."

"Carano is adamant, Jesse, desperate to appease the mob. I am sorry."

"Then show it. Get the date continued and let me talk to the defendant!"

. . .

TWENTY MINUTES LATER, Jesse was sitting across from the prisoner, whose newly bruised face and vacant eyes stabbed at Jesse's stomach.

"What did you do to this man?" Jesse shouted at one of the guards in Spanish.

"He fall down," another guard said in English.

"Looks like he fell down about fifteen times, *cabrón.*"

The guard gave his shoulders a non-committal hitch and looked away.

A scarred wooden table separated the lawyer and prisoner. They sat on yellow molded plastic chairs with rusted chrome legs in a tiny room with pale-grey, scarred plastered walls. The place reeked of sweat, feces, stale smoke, and Lysol. But it wasn't just the dismal environment, or even the sight of the prisoner, that had Jesse's brain reeling, but the image of himself sinking deeper into the quicksand of the prisoner's fate.

Kevin stared down at the floor between his manacled ankles.

"What happened to you, Kevin?"

The prisoner wiped his face with a forearm, spreading blood from his broken lip across the yellow bruises on his face. He winced when he lowered his arm. Even worse than the blood and bruising was the fear in his eyes.

"I'll talk to the prosecutor," Jesse said. "Get you some protection."

The prisoner nodded again and said, in a slurred whisper, "When . . . will they let me go?"

Jesse steeled himself. He felt bad kicking a man when he was down, but it was time to lower the hammer—before it was too late.

"I know you're hurting, Kevin, but we need to talk."

Kevin nodded.

"A couple of things aren't adding up, and if I'm going to be able to get you a lawyer, your story has to be straight and true. You follow me?"

"I think so, but I've told you the truth."

"Bullshit, and if you lie to your new lawyer the way you've lied to me, those lies will come back at you during the trial when it's too late for him or her to do anything about them."

"I don't know what you're—"

"Hold on, Kevin." Jesse leaned in close to Kevin and managed to fix him with a hard gaze despite his conflicting emotions. "Don't say one more word unless it's the truth. You tell me everything right now or you'll be coming home in a plastic bag. I'm sorry, but that's the way it is."

"Dad will help me," Kevin muttered.

Jesse rubbed his face again with both hands. "That's your plan? Dad pulling a bunny out of his hat at the last minute? Well, let me tell you one last time, Kevin, Cal's strings don't stretch to Guatemala."

The smile on Kevin's face died and he turned away from Jesse's hot eyes. "He'll come when he has to," he murmured at last. "People are counting on it."

"What do you mean by that? What people?"

"Nothing. Forget about it."

Jesse rose. This wasn't working. "Goodbye, Kevin. I can't help you." To enhance the bluff, Jesse shook his head sadly, patted Kevin on the shoulder and headed for the door. Kevin staggered to his feet, and then yelped with pain as the manacles dug into his ankles. He staggered around the table and tried to grab Jesse's sleeve, but tripped on his leg chains.

"Don't leave me here, Jesse! These bastards will kill me."

The guard grabbed Kevin and slammed him back in his chair. Jesse paused.

Kevin gasped, "All right, I stretched things a little. I'm just scared."

Jesse leaned over, put his mouth close to Kevin's ear and said, "Tell me everything. *Now.*"

Kevin nodded so hard his manacles clanked together. "Okay."

"Start with the basics. Why did you tell the cops you didn't even know the victim?

"I guess I . . . panicked, which was pretty stupid."

"Agreed. Were you at her house on the day of the murder?"

"No. I hadn't seen her for days."

"Were you having an affair with her?"

Kevin hesitated, then came to a decision and nodded his head slowly.

"Oh, Christ," Jesse said. "I cannot fucking believe it."

"You mean because she had brains and beauty and I'm just an ordinary—"

"No," Jesse said. "I mean I can't believe what this does to your case. It also complicates retaining new lead counsel."

"Sorry, but you wanted the truth." The prisoner's face brightened. "You should have seen her, Jesse. She was . . . awesome."

"How did it start between you?"

"She heard the government was watching me as an undesirable alien, probably because Dad had allegedly met with Gómez. She thought I might have met Gómez, too, and wanted to interview me. She was pretty, Jesse, and the next day we met again and, well . . . you know. The thing is, the woman was lonely, Jesse, and scared, too. She knew I was someone who would be here today and gone tomorrow— safe, you know?—and I think she was trying to cram a little life into whatever time she had left. So it just happened. The funny thing is, I fell hard. I'd never met anyone like her."

"Go on."

"Her husband was a decent guy, I guess, but he hadn't slept with Marisa in years. He was older and in bad health. And even though I think she liked me, she quickly broke it off; said she felt guilty about feeling so good. But it was incredible while it lasted, Jesse. I mean we breathed real life into each other!"

"Not for long."

Kevin's eyes clamped shut in misery and he dug the knuckles of one hand against his cut mouth. He seemed to be intentionally inflicting pain on himself.

"And you didn't actually meet Gómez?" Jesse said.

"No. I was supposed to meet him to give him a message from Dad and his associates withdrawing from the drug consortium. My dad wanted out of . . . unlawful activities altogether. But the meet never happened. All I did here was work with our two local CalCorp retailers, and then I got arrested."

Jesse said, "You know what happens to you if you're lying to me again?"

"I'm finished with that. I was just afraid you'd walk away if you found out about my father's past . . . activities in this region."

"Let's get back to Marisa. Exactly how long did it last between you?"

"We slept together twice, then she broke it off."

"Were you angry?"

Kevin managed a smile. "I hope you're more subtle in court. Okay, I was hurt and disappointed, maybe even a little mad, but not mad enough to want to hurt her. Shit, man, I was in love with her. Still am, God help me."

"Go on."

Jesse saw tears welling up in Kevin's eyes. He leaned close to Jesse and said, "Do you believe I'm innocent? I need to know."

Jesse was surprised to hear the question and the emotion behind it. He was even more surprised at his answer. "I do, not that it matters."

"It matters to me. A lot."

"Let me ask you again. Did Professor Andrade find out about you and his wife? Could he have killed her?"

Kevin slowly shook his head. "It's possible, I guess, but I honestly don't think he has it in him. She said he didn't support her work, but otherwise treated her well and totally loved her."

Interesting, thought Jesse. Give the defendant a chance to hang the weight on the cuckold and he defends him instead. But Jesse felt conflicted again, thinking of Teo's boozing, blackouts, a missing kitchen knife, and wounds consistent with a passion slaying.

Chanting broke out from below on the *Centro Cívico*, syncopated by the beat of a drum. Kevin clamped his eyes shut and covered his ears. Jesse felt clammy and nauseous. "*¡Denos el gringo! ¡Denos el gringo!*"

"It's nice to be wanted," Kevin said with a wry smile. The forced effort caused him to wince with pain again. "You should hear it later on when the crowd maxes out."

"The police are out there, too. Don't worry."

Kevin half-smiled at the absurdity of the advice. "So what now?"

"We keep you here where it's safer, while I keep trying to get you a competent lawyer. I have to say that part isn't looking good. Everybody's afraid."

The prisoner glumly took in the words, elbows propped on knees, chin resting on clasped hands, eyes cast downward. Jesse added, "Anything I can get for you?"

The prisoner gave his head a little self-conscious jerk to one side. "I've had the shits for days now. Do they have Pepto-Bismol down here? Maybe some ear plugs?"

Jesse nodded, stood up, and managed a reassuring smile, hoping he had heard the last of Kevin's lies. The guards came and jerked the prisoner to his feet, but Kevin seized Jesse's hand and held on with surprising strength. The guards roughly pulled him away and shoved him through the door.

A ghost-like chill passed through Jesse, leaving behind a message that told him it would be a long time before he saw the Golden Gate Bridge again.

. . .

JESSE FEARED THAT leaving the *Centro Cívico* would prove more difficult than entering. There appeared to be over a hundred people milling about now—led by a man with a bullhorn—chanting and waving homemade signs with familiar anti-American slogans.

Jesse donned his cap, swallowed his anxiety, and headed straight through them. Anonymous, just one of them. But thirty paces outside the building, a small, short-haired woman carrying a baby recognized him from the newspaper photo and jammed a finger at him.

"¡Allí es el abogado Americano del narco!" she screamed, and the crowd's rumble of protest was suddenly a deafening roar. His path was blocked and menacing faces circled him. He started to push his way through the demonstrators, but found himself up against an unyielding wall of rage. Hands reached out to grab him and a blow out of nowhere hit him in the ear.

He shot a look back at the guards inside the large glass entrance doors of the *Torre de Tribunales* and saw only expressionless faces—except for one who was smiling. He was hit by something hard. Pain shot through his head and he lost his balance as callused hands wrestled him to the ground. Uneven cobblestone pavers dug into his back and he tried to sit up but both of his arms were pinned to the pavement. Fear had shut off his oxygen and he was losing awareness. The blurred figure of the woman who had identified him spat in his face but he felt nothing. A new chant broke out: *"!Mátelo! ¡Mátelo!"* A kid with an aluminum baseball bat broke through the crowd and swung it at Jesse's head, but missed—too many people in his way. Jesse vaguely registered that the kid was no more than twelve, though his face seemed distorted by centuries of hatred. The bat came up again, cheered on by the crowd. Jesse clamped his eyes shut.

"*Wait!*" shouted the man with a bullhorn in Spanish. "*We'll hold the lawyer hostage until they give us Covington!*" The crowd roared its approval, and a man kicked Jesse in the side for good measure before jerking him to his feet.

"The defendant is innocent!" Jesse croaked. "Give him a chance to prove it!"

He couldn't tell if he was even heard. Another blow came from somewhere behind him but was deflected by his shoulder. He braced for the next assault, but a new set of strong hands suddenly grabbed him by the arms and began dragging him back toward the front entrance to the courthouse, their night sticks slashing through the mob like scythes through a field of wheat.

Police! PNC! Jesse had never been so happy to see cops.

"Relax, Señor," came a rough but reassuring voice in Spanish from beside Jesse, "you are safe."

Dazed, Jesse's eyes were drawn upward to a second-story window and he felt a frisson of relief and gratitude. Elena's face, his shining angel of mercy, gazed down on him as if from heaven.

. . .

LATER, A PNC matron roughly applied an antibiotic to Jesse's abrasions. "No stitches needed," she grunted in Spanish, and led him to a small but immaculate conference room where Elena sat waiting under a large poster of Vice President Carano. Jesse's legs were rubbery, and he gratefully fell into a chair next to her.

"I assume the cavalry was your doing," Jesse said, pouring himself some water from a pitcher in the center of a four-by-eight foot wooden table.

"Cavalry?"

"It appears lawyers are even less popular here than in the U.S."

He tried not to wince when she gently touched a bruised area on the back of his neck. "I apologize for the enthusiasm of my people," she said, and a look of surprising tenderness passed behind her eyes. "They want justice."

He put a hand on hers and said, "Thank you for helping me."

Their eyes were locked together as before, and although she did not respond to his touch, Jesse thought he could feel something like warm, static electricity in her hand. He leaned so close that only inches separated their faces. The smell of soap and lilac in her hair assuaged his pain. He saw her parted lips and moved in to kiss her.

Jesse heard voices approaching the door and she moved back. He wondered if her resistance was motivated by the imminent interruption or disapproval of his recklessness. Or if she had simply lost whatever interest he fantasized she had in him. A loud double-rap on the door preceded the head of courthouse security—the *Policía de Presidios*—a small man with large boots and a perpetual expression of amusement.

"How is our American visitor?" he said in Spanish, after bowing to acknowledge the President's daughter.

"I'm fine, Captain, thanks to your capable men," Jesse said, also in Spanish. Then, seeing that the Captain was not leaving, Jesse turned back to Elena. "So what about my request to delay the trial, Chief Prosecutor?"

"Have you found counsel?" she asked.

"I think you already know the answer to that," Jesse said.

"All right," she said. The Captain turned away for an instant, and she gave Jesse an amused smile. "File your request, Señor Hall. It would be useless to oppose it under the circumstances."

"You are very kind, Señorita Ruiz," he said, then thanked the Captain again and rose.

After the Captain escorted him out a back security gate of the *Torre de Tribunales,* Jesse stepped into a sudden downpour and felt a jolt of elation that would have inspired a Gene Kelly routine if there had been a lamppost handy. Being with Elena was a balm for his wounds, and she had taken her sweet time moving back from his effort to kiss her, hadn't she? It could come to nothing, of course, probably just an itch he'd never be able to scratch.

But it was good to know he could still itch.

. . .

AFTER JESSE HAD cleaned himself up in his hotel room, he gritted his teeth and returned a call to Cal Covington.

"Did you hire a new lawyer?"

"Not yet," Jesse said. "Sir, I just talked to you yesterday."

"Well, hell, Jesse, ain't you been down there what, five, six days already?"

"Look, Cal, lawyers won't touch the case, and I'm not sure I blame them. Hordes of protesters surround the courthouse and prison, and the judges have thrown an impossible trial schedule at us. Also, Kevin keeps lying. Good lawyers avoid a client they can't work with."

"Kevin's doin' his best in a bad situation. Try walkin' a mile in his moccasins. Besides, with that new clue left by the dying victim, the local piranha should be fightin' to get this case."

"It's different here. The local bar doesn't whore after publicity like some of our U.S. criminal defense lawyers do. In Guatemala, it's dangerous to call attention to yourself."

"Buncha chicken-shits. Okay, Hall, let me put it to you this way. You get Kevin good representation in the next twenty-four hours or you can kiss your ass goodbye at C&S."

. . .

LATER AT TEO'S house, Carmen took in Jesse's bruises. He watched shock register on her face, but she said nothing, just led him past a dining room table still littered with lunch leftovers.

"Something to eat, Señor?" she said, and he thanked her but declined, saying that he needed to see the professor right away.

The tiny, slightly bent housekeeper hustled ahead of him and then gestured toward the study. Passing the family room, Jesse saw Anica, twirling her hair with her fingers, watching a *Friends* rerun on TV. She glanced at Jesse, seemingly torn between disdain and a habit of flirtatiousness. "I have heard that trial work is rough," she said, "but the way you look right now, maybe you should switch to probate law."

"My worshiping fans mobbed me at the *Centro Cívico*."

The mellow tones of an alto sax could be heard from up on the roof, a melancholy melody that drifted down the staircase as softly as a chiffon veil.

"I'll get him," Anica said, reluctantly unfolding her long legs. "Otherwise, you'll have to wait until he either runs out of rum or his 'ladies' complain."

Minutes later, the melody was bitten off in mid-chorus, and Teo came pounding down the stairs, a half-empty glass in his hand. "My God," he exclaimed, halfway down, "what happened to you?"

Jesse told him.

"Lawless bastards in a lawless country," Teo said. "Come, have a rum, excellent for headaches. Until the next day, of course."

"I enjoyed your playing."

Teo actually blushed. "I didn't hear you come in. Well, how about that drink?"

"Rum and soda sounds good. We have cause for celebration."

"Wonderful," he said. He poured rum for Jesse and another for himself. "What shall we drink to, your survival at the hands of a vengeful mob?"

"Something even better. I've found Kevin's lawyer."

Teo looked perplexed. "Wonderful, but who?"

Jesse touched glasses with the professor and said, "It's you, Teo."

Teo looked surprised, then barked out a laugh that led to a coughing spasm.

"*What?*" exclaimed Anica.

"And me," added Jesse, smiling to hide his own trepidation.

Teo sipped his drink and turned to Anica. "These Americans revel in gallows humor."

"I'm serious, Teo. You can bring me in as advisor, and I'll stay here as long as it takes. I think Kevin's innocent, and together we can show it. I don't like it any better than you do, but there's no other way."

Teo stared at Jesse, his eyes narrowing. "Anica, please give us some privacy," he said. The girl crinkled her nose in annoyance, but complied.

The professor collapsed into his favorite chair and stared into the fireplace. "You are a bright young man, Jesse, and presumably a decent lawyer. You are not, however, in touch with reality at the moment. Further, you display little understanding of my situation."

Jesse sat across from Teo, meeting his hard gaze, and said, "I am young, sir, I'll grant you. But our 'situations' aren't so different. We're both highly motivated."

"How so?"

"You want to clear Marisa's name, avenge her death, and reveal Carano as her killer."

Teo nodded and said, "And you want to make partnership in that blue-stocking law firm and make a lot of money."

"Right now it's enough that I stand with an innocent man whose life and freedom are at stake."

Teo lit a cigarette. "Because you do appear to be serious about this, I must remind you that I have never stood for anything and certainly never stood before a judge. I was Marisa's ivory tower egghead, remember? Hardly a qualified trial lawyer."

"Don't worry about that. We can pull it off together."

The older man shook his head. "You want another reason?" He held up his rum on ice. "My health."

"That's the best you can do?"

"My heart is bad," Teo said, his voice lowered to a whisper. "In addition, Anica has already disclosed that I have a rather serious memory problem, hardly a felicitous attribute for a trial lawyer to possess."

"Mine is good enough for both of us."

"No doubt, but in addition to being neither competent, experienced, physically capable, nor emotionally willing, I lack the objectivity to serve as counsel in this case. Have you forgotten that the prosecution's motive is that Covington was having an affair with my wife?"

"Which you do not believe," Jesse said, experiencing a shiver of guilt. How long could he lie to this man? As long as it took, he decided.

"Of course not," Teo agreed, "but even apart from the murder charge, can you not see the absurd irony in the alleged cuckold defending the man accused of adultery with his wife?"

"I can't think of a better way to show your contempt for the rumor. And as a former law professor, wouldn't you like to see some justice done here in Guatemala?"

"Justice is a rare commodity in Guate, my young friend. When it does occur, it is quite by accident, I assure you. If I really had courage, I would inflict 'justice' on Carano with my own bare hands."

"Violence was not Marisa's way."

"She *courted* violence, and it led to her death."

"But her *life* had value, you see that now. Because of what she made of it."

Teo nodded. "You are being unintentionally cruel, Jesse. Marisa was indeed a saint, while I was a bag of lifeless bones rattling around in a crumbling ivory tower, hermetically sealed in my own hot air. She was right about that, too. But there is yet another irony: one murder suspect defending another."

"You were cleared when they arrested Kevin."

"Cleared?" Teo said, and placed his glass down, rose to his feet, and stared out the window of his study, muscles twitching in his lantern jaw. Jesse followed the professor's gaze to a flame tree in full bloom. Its bright red colors seemed to mock the sullen mood within the house. "Cleared for now, at least," he conceded, and collapsed in a chair, head forward, supported by his right hand. "Jesse, look at me. I drink too much, and my heart is not only broken, but diseased."

"You could quit drinking."

"I drink for the courage to get up in the morning and get dressed. You see, Jesse, life is either worth living or it isn't. With Marisa, it was worth it. Without her, the jury is out."

Jesse waited then, the silence broken only by the tinkling of ice in Teo's glass. "Ever hear of Yogi Berra?" Jesse said at last. "He was a baseball player-philosopher who said, 'When you get to a fork in the road, take it.'"

"I get your point, and fully intend to make some changes. When I am up to it."

"When you're up to it?" Jesse said. "Would that be before or after you drink yourself to death?"

Teo glared at Jesse, his face flushed with sudden anger. Jesse knew he was overstepping, but he could not leave the house without Teo's agreement. Kevin was dead without it.

"Look, Teo, changes are tough to make, and from what I've seen, are only made when a person has hit bottom, not when he's 'up to it.' Ever hear of a happy person going through the pain of change or even *wanting* to change?"

Teo said nothing.

"Come on, Teo, wouldn't you like to make your life count for something?"

Teo stared at the tip of his cigarette for a minute, and said, "Would I like to have left my mark? Would I have wanted my life to have been . . . *significant*? Well, who would *not* wish that? But alas, to paraphrase your American actor John Barrrymore, regrets have replaced my dreams."

"It's not too late, Teo. Help me expose Carano. *Finish what Marisa started.*"

Teo stared at him with eyes so full of pain that Jesse could barely return his gaze. The big man turned away and began to pace. Jesse waited, held his breath, said nothing. He had pled his case, and there was nothing more to say.

Teo rose and picked up a photo of Marisa. He stood looking at it for a full minute, tilting his head, solemnly taking her in from different angles. Then he placed the photograph back on the table and turned toward Jesse.

"All right," he said, exhaling loudly. "I shall endeavor to assist you. Just do not look for me to be like one of your American movie characters, suddenly clean-shaven, giving up the booze. I will do what I can. I will try to get you accredited to go into court with me. But do not count on me for much once we get there."

He held out his hand.

Jesse met the red-rimmed eyes of his new co-counsel, physically and emotionally unstable, a self-described drunk, and a man who just might have killed his wife.

He reached out and took the man's hand.

DAY SEVEN

15

JESSE AND TEO worked on the case at Teo's dining room table from 8:30 the next morning until lunchtime. Midway through the session, Jesse had an idea, and persuaded Teo to call a friend he had mentioned, an expatriate Israeli who was a private investigator. Within hours, the Israeli reported back that Carl Webster frequented a bar and grill nearly every weeknight called Guate Mollie's. Jesse's plan was to casually encounter Webster at Mollie's cocktail hour, buy him some drinks, try to get him to admit Marisa called him Carlos, then hit him with a biggest bluff he had ever tried.

Teo listened skeptically. "You're going to tell him you have proof he's been receiving money from Carano's unlisted account? He'll know you are on a fishing expedition and deny it."

"Maybe, but I'll know if he's lying. And if he tries to explain that it's government contract money, I'll know he's our killer."

"And you'll know this because?"

"Because governments don't pay their private companies by sending money offshore and then back to one of the company's employees."

Teo considered Jesse's logic, cocked his head to one side.

"Besides, Teo, what's to lose by trying it?"

"Plenty," Teo said. "If you are wrong, you've gained nothing but Webster's heightened emnity. If you are right, *he* has nothing to lose by killing again."

Jesse felt a twinge in his stomach.

. . .

AT ONE-THIRTY, CARMEN set the table as if they weren't there. Ten minutes later, Anica and her boyfriend arrived, taking in Jesse's bruised face, but saying nothing. Anica embraced her father, then Teo introduced Jesse to Julio, a scholarly-looking young man in his early twenties, lean to the point of fragility, with piercing dark eyes behind thick, round glasses, and a sensitive, wide-angled gaze that seemed to take in everything and search for meaning in the slightest gesture. Jesse was pleased to meet him, hoping to learn more about the young man's distant uncle, the mysterious Arturo Gómez.

Carmen's luncheon spread included corn bread, *chojin*—a popular pork rind and radish salad—chicken *quesadillas*, and stuffed maize dumplings called *chuchitos*. Jesse greeted the home-cooked meal with enthusiasm, and every time Carmen came out of the kitchen, she urged Jesse to take another portion. Anica and Julio ate in silence, dampening the otherwise upbeat mood of the table.

Teo cleared his throat. "The children are unhappy with me, Jesse, for taking on the defense of a man accused of killing Marisa. Although they believe me that Carano is the true enemy here, Julio thinks I should become an active revolutionary rather than a practicing trial attorney."

Julio gestured awkwardly, his thin arms almost knocking over a glass, and directed his gaze at Jesse. "I am merely saying that as

Marisa's husband, the professor has tremendous moral authority and should support *La Causa's* effort to reach the goal shared by my uncle: equality for the people."

"So," Teo said, his tone less friendly, "you embrace *El Cobra* as 'my uncle' now?"

Julio smoothed back his shoulder-length hair. "My uncle has excellent ideas for agrarian reform, public health, and education."

"You mean after he has taken over by force," Teo said, "and bankrupted the government by destroying efficient coffee, sugar, and corn *fincas*. That's his idea of 'agrarian reform.' And his idea of an education program will come through the barrel of a gun."

Jesse felt sorry for everyone in the room. Julio desperately wanting Teo to support *La Causa* and going about it all wrong. Anica wanting peace between her lover and her father. Teo wanting Julio out of their lives.

Jesse looked at Julio, an outrageous idea forming in his mind. "Kevin told me that Marisa interviewed him because she thought he had met your uncle."

"What has that to do with anything?" Julio said.

"I'm just thinking, what if he did meet your uncle and won't admit it? He claims he came down here to unwind a drug syndicate with Gómez, but says they never connected."

"My uncle is not in any drug deals with the mafia or anyone else." Teo audibly snickered.

"I've heard his headquarters is somewhere north of Livingston, Julio," Jesse said, "in the *Río Dulce* area?"

"Yes. So what? Everybody knows that."

"It just seems to be an interesting coincidence that his camp is in the center of the largest drug distribution center in Central America and the subject of a U.S. State Department's warning to travelers."

"Okay," Julio said, "maybe my uncle has to do a few drug deals to raise money for the greater good. That is more than I can say about your client's incentive in meeting with my uncle."

"So Kevin did meet with your uncle? It's a long shot, but ever since I got here I've been wondering why Kevin has no alibi."

"Your point," Teo said, "is that the mere fact he is without an alibi suggests he has one he cannot admit to? Like being with Gómez, talking drugs? That is reaching, my friend."

"How about this for a reason he has no alibi?" Anica said. "He's *guilty*."

Jesse shook his head. "If a smart young man like Kevin Covington were going to murder somebody, he'd prepare himself a rock-solid alibi."

"But even if you are right," Teo said, "do you think Gómez would just fly one of his helicopters into town and admit he was discussing a drug deal with the son of a *gringo* mobster? Gómez cannot exonerate Kevin without implicating himself. Elena Ruiz would like hanging him even more than hanging Kevin."

Jesse said, "The *topic* of their conversation would be hearsay and irrelevant in court. The only relevance to the conversation is simply that one took place—and maybe took place at the very time Marisa Andrade was being murdered, hundreds of miles away."

"And I'm sure they were discussing world peace," said Anica, rolling her eyes. "Or chatting about next year's corn crop."

Jesse pressed on. "I need to think more about it, but if our theory is that Marisa's death was a political assassination sponsored by Carano, wouldn't Gómez love to help us destroy Carano by supporting our theory? Hell, Teo, that's what motivated you to help me, isn't it?"

"Largely, yes, but I will not be arrested for helping you. Gómez could be."

"But I've done some checking on the Internet and with Elena," Jesse said. "Despite Gómez's history of crime, there are currently no actual charges pending against him. The government can't pin anything on him."

"It is common knowledge that he runs drugs and is behind the attacks in the city," Teo said.

"My uncle only fights fire with fire when necessary," Julio said.

"The ends justifying the means, Julio?" Teo added in a sarcastic tone. "With Gómez prescribing both?"

"Well, why not? Could life here be any worse than under Carano?"

"*Much* worse, if your uncle triggers a revolution," Teo said. "And his style of takeover will not follow the Egyptian model. Blood will run in the streets."

"I disagree, but with Marisa gone, he may have to act."

"Sorry, Julio," Jesse said, "but I'm missing the connection."

"It is simple," Julio said. "If *La Causa* had been able to acquire and authenticate the original of the land grant, it would have united twenty Mayan dialects into one resounding voice. Aguilera would have defeated Carano and we'd have had a peaceful transition, an end to corruption."

"Ah yes, the mythical land grant," Teo said, rolling his eyes, "about which, by the way, Anica heard her mother expressing doubts to Anastacia."

"Anica heard it wrong!" Julio said. "Marisa had no doubts."

Anica stared silently into her coffee cup.

Jesse steered the conversation back to Gómez. "Tell me straight out, Julio. Do you think your uncle would come into town and testify if he were subpoenaed?"

Julio shook his head, and said, "I seriously doubt it."

"But Gómez hasn't been formally charged with anything," Jesse said, "so he'd be keeping himself technically straight with the law if he honored the subpoena. But if he ignored the court's subpoena, he'd be in contempt, and Carano's PNC could arrest and hold him on that alone, am I right?"

Julio nodded. "I suppose that's true, but I would not want to be the poor soul who shows up in his camp with a subpoena."

Poor soul. Jesse felt as if an icy hand had been laid on his bare shoulder.

· · ·

JESSE WOVE THROUGH traffic toward Guate Mollie's, haunted by an urge to call Megan, to hear her voice. He dialed the first four numbers on his cell—nearly running into a chicken bus—then put the phone down. Why burden her with his anxiety and loneliness? Let it be.

He turned his thoughts to the immediate tasks ahead. The Gómez-as-alibi notion was a pipe dream he'd better shelve; focus on building a defense around Marisa's dying message and the Carano money trail—if he could find evidence to support it. Then all he'd have to do at trial would be to control the brilliant and enigmatic Elena Ruiz, a hostile panel of judges, an adulterous client, and, of course, his drunken co-counsel.

Guate Mollie's was not a typical Guatemalan bar and grill. Owner Molly Hoffman was a 200-pound expatriate from New Jersey with a flare for irony, who had affected a '70s hip American bar motif, down to the last hanging fern. Disparate artifacts hung from the ceiling between the ferns—a broken umbrella, an ancient Schwinn bicycle, assorted hockey sticks, and three automobile grills. Old '70s album covers and signed minor-celebrity photos adorned the walls. The bar was thirty feet of artistry in oak, which Molly shipped from New Orleans when the old Metronome Bar shut down. "Cost more to ship it than I paid for it," she volunteered, rapturously running chubby fingers along the solid, curved railing. "But ain't it somethin'?" Jesse agreed it was.

Half the stools at the old bar had already been filled by an affluent mix of mainly white men and women, some laughing, others staring vacantly at themselves in the mirror behind the bar. A smoky haze hung over their heads and a pungent aroma of grilled chicken beckoned from the kitchen.

Jesse sipped a beer and waited. At 7:40, two beers later, he was about to give up for the night when Webster came in and took a seat at the end of the bar nearest the door. The bartender greeted him warmly, as did several other regulars, but nobody ventured to join him.

It didn't take long for Webster's laser-blue eyes to sweep the room and land hard on Jesse, who tried to look as surprised as his quarry obviously was. Jesse picked up his beer and sauntered down to where Webster had seated himself.

"Come here often?" Jesse said, smiling. Webster ignored the quip, so Jesse added, "Should I be worried about you being here, or is this just a coincidence?"

"I'm not following you, Hall, so you can stop playing cops and robbers. For the last time, I'm in construction, and that's all. I also happen to be a regular here. What's your story? Slumming, or trying to get laid?"

"Just looking for a little English-speaking company," Jesse said, noticing that Webster was wearing well-made shoes and an elegant silk sport coat. If Jesse had not been with the man the day before, he'd never have recognized him. "Mind if I join you?"

Webster hitched his shoulders to indicate his indifference.

"We got off on the wrong foot yesterday, Carl. Buy you a drink?"

Webster shrugged again, signaled the bartender with two fingers, and soon had another glass half-filled with Tequila and a second Monte Carlo beer in front of him. Jesse tossed out twenty dollars worth of *quetzales* and ordered a fresh beer for himself.

Webster sipped from the beer and said, "You look like shit, Hall."

"I've been told," Jessed said. "Minor scuffle with some locals."

Twenty minutes and yet another Tequila with a beer back produced nothing more than information about recent climate changes, new construction techniques, and Webster's love affair with a beautiful country he would never leave. He also mentioned his recent forty-eighth birthday, two divorces, and the joy of living with a young local girl he called Pearl. As the liquor finally took hold, he produced a colored photo from his wallet. Perlita Ramos was pretty, but a melancholy in her friendly brown eyes seemed to recognize the futility of her relationship with the man behind the camera.

"Fine looking woman," Jesse said, handing it back.

Webster stared lovingly at the photo, then replaced it in his wallet and nodded agreement. "I understand Marisa Andrade was also a beauty," Jesse added.

Webster said nothing.

"How many times did she interview you, Carl?"

Unblinking, Webster stared into his beer glass. For an instant, Jesse thought his question hadn't been heard over the din of the bar. Then, without moving his eyes, Webster said, "Señora Andrade was on the wrong track, just as you are, Hall. Difference between you is, she realized it and stopped pestering me."

"So she did interview you?"

"Once, which is also the only time you'll ask me about her. Clear?"

"Her husband says she called you Carlos."

Webster didn't flinch. Not even the movement of an eyelash. Finally he turned and focused hard on Jesse's eyes. "Just how bad," he said, "are you trying to fuck me up here in Guate? And don't tell me you being in Mollie's place tonight is a coincidence."

Jesse waited, said nothing.

Webster betrayed a nervous glance down the bar and ground out the stub of a cigarette. "I told you before; the PNC asked me about that 'Carlos V' bullshit and accepted my alibi. So how about getting off my back. Starting now." His gaze returned to his near-empty glass.

"But did the PNC ask you," Jesse said, scrutinizing Webster's granite profile, "whether you've received money from Victor Carano's offshore account?"

Jesse saw a flicker of movement invade the cool blue eyes. "Where the fuck would you get an idea like that?"

Jesse looked the man squarely in the eye. "I've got sources, too, Carl."

Webster stared into his glass.

"Nothing to say, Carl?"

Webster slowly rose from his stool, polished off his drink, and said, "Looks like I've got to find me a new watering hole." He spoke in a tone more resigned than angry.

"I'm not trying to blow your cover, Carl. I just want some answers."

"My 'cover,'" he whispered in disgust, and stole another glance around the suddenly crowded room. He reached into his pocket and threw some quetzales on the bar, then leaned in close to Jesse and said, "Look, Hall, if you were right about me being with the CIA—which you are not—and if you were a decent, law-abiding U.S. citizen—which I assume you are—you'd get the hell out of Guatemala and keep your mouth shut about rumors of my involvement with the CIA. And you'd do it quicker than a cat jumping off a hot stove."

"And if I won't jump off that hot stove, you'll push me off?"

"Somebody will," Webster snarled and stormed out of the bar.

Despite the threat, Jesse looked at himself in the mirror behind the bar and realized he was smiling. Webster hadn't given him a flat-out admission, but neither had he mustered a credible denial about the money or about Marisa calling him "Carlos." And Webster had not become merely nervous toward the end, he had seemed afraid. But of whom? And what? There was vulnerability there, if only he could find a way to exploit it.

Then it hit him, an idea so outrageous it might work. He called Teo on his cell phone, asked him if he still wanted to meet Carl Webster.

"Of course I do."

"Good. I've got an idea."

Jesse clicked off, glanced at his watch, pushed away his unfinished beer, and strode out of Guate Mollie's.

DAY EIGHT

16

IN COURT THE next morning, the judges and members of the press were visibly stunned by Teo's application to represent a man accused of his wife's murder. After recovering her composure, however, Judge Chavez admitted him as counsel for Kevin Covington. Teo then made his pitch to allow Jesse to participate in the trial as his "adviser of record," and Chief Prosecutor Elena Ruiz was so complaisant as to render it difficult for the judges to reject the requests. Jesse was gratified to see things going smoothly in court for once—the judges hadn't even expressed annoyance over his previous behavior—and he dared to hope that justice might actually prevail for Kevin. He remained worried, however, about his dissembling to Teo concerning Kevin's affair with Marisa. He hoped—rationalized?—that Teo already knew the truth in his heart and that he would deal with the issue impassively when it became too obvious to ignore.

Jesse worried about something else, too. What was Juan Domínguez doing in court, the little shit, smiling and staring at him through narrowed eyes?

Jesse felt the hearing was a success, although the Tribunal balked when Teo moved for a two-week delay of trial, also apathetically opposed by Elena. "The people demand prompt justice," Judge Chavez said.

"Your Honors," Teo said, "I joined the case just today. I have not even met my client. To start this trial in seven days would deny the defendant that very justice the people seek."

Jesse noted with approval that Teo made a point of glancing at the reporters, who had taken over a full row of the gallery.

Judge Chavez's bloodless lips hinted at a sardonic smile. "In that case, Professor, we will commence trial in *eight* days."

After court was recessed, Teo warned Jesse not to take too much comfort in the ruling that would permit him to participate. The judges were probably instructed by Carano to go along, reasoning that convicting and executing a U.S. citizen would attract less negative scrutiny by Washington if a U.S. lawyer were involved in the defense.

"You seem to think we're playing against a stacked deck."

Teo shrugged. "In Guate, when the government prosecutes, the government wins."

"How about Judge Renaldo López?" López had made Jesse nervous from the start, the way he gazed down at the lawyers through slack-lidded eyes, rarely speaking, just observing. "Domínguez said he was independent."

Teo lit a cigarette, exhaled a blast of smoke. "It's true. López is a cousin of President Ruiz and too popular with the people to be ignored or sent out to pasture. But Chavez is an FRG hack, Guatemala's ruling party."

"How about Guzmán, the young one who sits on the right side?"

"Ambitious, wealthy, and conservative. His parents are big FRG supporters and have one of the biggest coffee *fincas* in Guatemala."

"So how does Kevin win in a situation like this?"

"His lawyer will have to do a Perry Mason."

"You still get that here? So yeah, we just expose the real guilty party, bring him to his knees blubbering a confession and pleading for mercy."

The professor nodded, but Jesse added, "That doesn't happen in real life."

Teo let out a sardonic chuckle. "But this is not real life. This is Guatemala."

. . .

JESSE TRIED FOR the third time to contact Anastacia Ramirez on his cell phone, eager to explore the phone call Marisa made to her the morning of her murder. Her husband answered the phone each time, reporting that his wife was away indefinitely on holiday, then hanging up. Teo said he would attempt to talk his way into the Ramirez house, but reminded Jesse that with Marisa gone, Anastacia was finally in possession of what she had always coveted—the presidency of *La Causa*—and might not be willing to cooperate.

"Fine, but try," Jesse said, "and then check with all utilities or sales people who might have had reps in the area on April first. See what kind of uniforms they wear. The witness saw a man in a green coat leaving the front of the house, and Kevin was arrested in a green jacket."

In need of a break, Jesse headed back to the hotel to make some phone calls. As he walked down the threadbare carpet to his room, he saw that his door was ajar. The maid? No cart. Slowly, carefully he eased the door open.

"Come in, Señor," said a short, pasty-faced man in a seedy-looking plaid sport coat, "come in and close the door."

"I don't intend to do that," said Jesse, and started to back away before he felt a firm push from behind. Where did that guy come from? This other man was tall, with an alarmingly pockmarked face and a receding chin unconcealed by a spiritless goatee.

The short one eyed his wristwatch. "Come, Señor, we must go."

"I won't be doing that, either," Jesse said, glancing at the tall, skinny man behind him. "Who the hell are you?"

"ARES," the fat man said, producing an ID card. "We just need to ask you some questions down at the courthouse."

Jesse knew that ARES, Carano's private Gestapo, was an internal security force known for brutality and skill in disappearing "enemies of the new democracy." He felt the raw edge of fear buzzing in his head. He said, "Is this where I ask you if I have a choice?"

"Sure," said the tall man. "Easy way or hard way."

"I want to call the American Consulate first."

The shorter man laughed and delivered a solid punch to Jesse's left kidney.

. . .

ALONE IN THE back seat of an ARES car, Jesse felt it was safe to renew his request to contact the Consulate. "There is no need for that," said the tall one riding in the front passenger seat. "We are merely having a sociable visit, a friendly exchange."

"You hit me and I didn't hit you. That's not an exchange, and it's damned sure not friendly."

The man ignored the remark. "You were sent here to fire Kevin Covington's lawyer, were you not?"

"No," Jesse said. "I just came down to check his competence."

"And?"

"It was nowhere to be found. I had no choice but to replace him."

"With yourself?" the driver said. "How convenient. And because of this clever maneuver, you are now allowed private conversations with the defendant in connection with your international trafficking conspiracy. We have a witness, a respected professional, who overheard some of those early conversations."

Jesse flared. *Fucking Domínguez!* The moon-faced little shit-head was having his revenge. What was next? More kidney punches? Electrodes to his testicles? Nonstop Justin Bieber videos?

Carano's office occupied the southwest corner of the third floor of *El Palacio Nacional de la Cultura,* a national museum located across from *El Parque Centra.* Jesse was amused at the grand appellation, *El Palacio Nacional,* for the gigantic edifice seemed less a palace than an architectural nightmare, a hodge-podge of Spanish Renaissance and neo-classical influence. The building consisted of an enormous and unimaginative rectangular cement block with a facade of ornamental fake stone outside, with frescoed arches and bland murals proclaiming Guatemala's troubled pre-Columbian and colonial history.

By contrast, Victor Carano's remodeled ballroom of an office boasted elegant furnishings and oil paintings by F. Luis Mora and Diego Velásquez. Two ARES plainclothes escorted Jesse inside, their footsteps echoing like pistol-shots on the marble floor.

Carano remained seated at this desk in a high-backed chair covered with hand-tooled antique leather. The chair and desk were so huge they made the Vice President look unnaturally small, surely not the impression he intended to create. His light-skinned, aristocratic face was round as a pumpkin, but his eyes were dark and intense. Without speaking, he exuded an arrogant authority that sent Jesse's pulse racing again.

"Hello, Señor Hall," he said at last, his eyes continuing to take

Jesse's measure. Carano wore his power like a tailored suit, conveying the presence of a man never plagued by self-doubt. "I understand there was a misunderstanding as my men detained you. I apologize."

The man was a master of euphemism. "They 'detained' me the way DeMarcus Ware detains quarterbacks."

Carano issued a fake smile, as if he knew who the Cowboys pass rusher was. Jesse noticed that unlike all other government offices he had been in, there was no portrait of President Ruiz. Instead, a life-sized photo of Carano himself graced the wall behind his desk.

"Yes, well, our ARES agents were trained here by U.S. Special Forces personnel," Carano said, signaling the two escorts to leave the room. "They sometimes become a bit . . . overzealous." He then motioned Jesse to sit, watching him like a snake viewing a mouse. "That said, it is time we met, Señor Hall. Since you seem to be showing interest in me—I hear you intend to make me a suspect in the Andrade case—I'll now show more interest in you."

"Don't be put off by being a suspect," Jesse said. "I consider everybody a suspect, including Teo Andrade, my only friend here. And if kidnapping a U.S. citizen is your idea of showing interest, I'd prefer to be ignored."

Jesse saw a spark behind Carano's black eyes, a warning flare. "You are becoming a difficult man to ignore, Señor Hall. I hear disturbing reports that you are an agent for an American mob, sent to hinder my humble efforts to stop the very drug trafficking your client embraces."

"I am hardly a criminal," Jesse said, curbing his anger, "nor is my client a trafficker or a mobster. I was sent to help see justice done. I hope you, as *de facto* head of state, would support that effort."

"We have many good *abogados* in Guatemala already," Carano said, still smiling, but not with his eyes. "We do not need another one."

Jesse's head was spinning. In trial, he was always prepared, but now his mind was a blur. What were they going to do to him? *Think*. Goal *número uno*, get out of this alive. Goal *número dos*, try to stay calm and learn something that might help the case if you do.

"I respectfully disagree, Señor Carano," Jesse said. "It seems to me that wherever an innocent man is confined against his will, there's need for another lawyer. Mind telling me why *I* am here?"

"That's what I want to know."

"I mean here in this office."

"You are here in this office for instruction. People like you are disrupting our efforts to make a success of our fledgling democracy."

"Really? Somebody once said that a democracy has to be more than two wolves and a sheep voting on what to have for dinner. If you are serious about a democracy, I'd suggest you start with a workable justice system."

"We have an excellent legal system, Señor Hall, although it may not be your brand of Western justice."

"With all respect, sir, I doubt you are familiar with our brand of justice."

"To the contrary, Señor Hall," Carano said. "It happens I was born in your country—Arlington, Virginia, to be exact—while my father was serving as Ambassador to the Organization of American States. I returned to Georgetown for my freshman and sophomore years to study political science. Are you surprised?"

Jesse nodded to concede that he was.

"I was eight when President Kennedy was killed. Kennedy was an inspiration to my father, who was a gentle man and a true patriot, beloved by the people of Guatemala. He instilled in me a desire to devote my life to creating a true democracy here in Guatemala, thanks in no small part to the generous assistance of your country."

"Really. How are you doing that?" The man was vain and he was onstage, so keep him talking long enough, he might reveal something useful.

Carano smiled broadly. "It is simple. Politics, like sex, is all about presentation, and success in politics is measured in dollars. So you want to know why I am succeeding where others have failed in Latin America? De Lozada and Morales in Bolivia, Correa in Ecuador, Kirchner and his runaway inflation in Argentina?"

"Please tell me," Jesse said, trying to convey an obsequious sincerity.

"Simple. They all lacked my political acumen. I am succeeding by maintaining a constant flow of aid from the U.S.A., currently spread too thin to adequately assist its friends in Latin America. You see, U.S. foreign aid is based on its national security interests, and lately, Guatemala has not been perceived to be as threatening to your security as North Korea or current disturbances in the Middle East."

Jesse said, "I hardly see Guatemala as a threat to the United States."

Carano's eyes sparked. He was obviously not a man used to being challenged. "That, Señor Gringo, is because you are either blind or stupid. I have loosened your government's purse strings by demonstrating that our trafficking and terrorism present a threat to your country."

"But all Central American countries are awash in drugs. As for terrorists, you do not appear to have any."

"Oh?" Carano said, taking his seat and steepling his fingers. "Wrong again, Señor. Have you not been here long enough to see the devastation wrought on our poor country by the revolutionary terrorist Arturo Gómez? He is the Che Guevera of Guatemala, and I want you to tell that to everyone in your country!"

Was that why he brought him here? If so, maybe a deal could be cut. "I'd be happy to," Jesse said, "but I hear that Gómez is more drug lord than terrorist."

"Wrong. Drugs are not a serious problem in my country, but Gómez is a very real threat to Guatemala and the entire hemisphere."

"As real as the land grant letter?"

The shift seemed to throw Carano off balance. "Land grant? I cannot speak to that until the Special Commission renders its decision."

"When will that be?"

"When they have completed their work." Abruptly, he stood. "I will detain you no longer, Señor Hall. You must begin packing for your trip home tomorrow."

"Tomorrow?"

"Yes. My car will pick you up at eight in the morning. Your flight to San Francisco is already arranged. At our expense. Are there any more questions?"

Jesse's eyes popped. "You're *deporting* me? *Tomorrow?*"

"You have become a nuisance, Señor Hall. I can no longer protect you."

Salvage what you can, Jesse told himself. "You ask me if I had any more questions. Just one. Would you describe your contacts with Mr. Carl Webster?"

"Webster? I do not believe I know the man," said Carano. "An American?"

"An American to whom you gave substantial amounts of money."

Jesse's trial lawyer's eyes probed for a sign, a twitch of the lips, a blink of the eyes. Nothing. He was as inscrutable as Webster had been at first.

"Why in the world would I give my money to someone I don't know?"

Jesse hesitated. His next words could get him disappeared, not merely deported. "In the first place, it's not your money. It's the people's money, sent offshore from your discretionary account."

Carano said, "I suppose that is why it's called a discretionary account, my young friend. I assure you that your president has the same kind of account. It allows chiefs of state to direct funds without bureaucratic delays when needed to protect the national interest."

Jesse looked straight into Carano's eyes. "I think you directed those funds to be laundered offshore, then sent back into Guatemala to the personal account of Mr. Carl Webster."

Bingo! There was the tell, a reddening in his upper cheeks. Could just be anger at Jesse's audacity. Or it could be a four bagger.

"I know of no such payments, although it's conceivable that some construction contract has slipped my mind."

Jesse smiled. "I didn't mention he was in construction, which tells me you *do* know Mr. Webster. Perhaps you know him as *Carlos Webster*?"

Carano tried to cover the slip. "I must have read his name in the newspaper. Or perhaps on a construction contract."

"If your discretionary fund was used for a construction project, the money would go to the company rather than to a job superintendent, right?"

Carano's entire face turned red. "I've reconsidered. You are not going to the airport tomorrow. You are going today. My men will accompany you."

Don't tempt me, Jesse thought, but said, "I won't be leaving for a while, sir, but thanks for the offer."

Carano pursed his red lips and put some steel in his voice. "Staying here would be a mistake, Señor Hall."

"Well, sir, you made one yourself today by showing so much 'interest' in me. It tells me I must be doing something right."

But Carano resumed his seat and pressed a button near his phone. Two brownshirts entered soundlessly. Jesse remained seated. His bluff had produced two results, one good, one bad. Now he had to run a bigger one to avoid deportation.

"Given the fact that you know so much about how Washington works, Señor Vice President, I don't have to tell you that they don't take kindly to kangaroo courts back home. And they don't like financing countries that do."

The remarks seemed to start wheels turning behind Carano's outwardly calm eyes. He seemed a little off balance. Push him harder. More bluff and bull.

"Are you aware that the *Boston Globe*, the Associated Press, and the *Washington Post* were all in court this morning? If you want to see Uncle Sam's purse strings tighten up quickly, just keep threatening one American citizen trying to defend another."

Carano carefully removed a cigarette from an elegant box and lit it.

"By the way," Jesse continued, "are you also aware that my client, Calvin Covington, has an army of lobbyists in Washington D.C. roughly the size of your entire legislature? Let's see how long your foreign aid flows when they're done with you."

Carano drew heavily on his cigarette, and then inhaled again. Otherwise, he appeared calm, except for that residual flush in his upper cheeks. "You misunderstand me, Señor. I simply need you to know that you must be very careful. We are in crisis here, as you can see. Let us agree that you take one week to find someone else to assist Professor Andrade."

"One week?"

Carano crushed his cigarette into an ashtray, then stared down at the mangled butt, held between thumb and forefinger. "One week. After that, I can no longer guarantee your safety in Guatemala. *¿Entendido?*"

Without awaiting a response, Carano nodded to the goons, who escorted Jesse down the elevator and out into the blinding light of the *Palacio's* huge, open concrete plaza, where a flock of *paraulatas* warbled their gentle birdsong from their perches in surrounding trees. The men offered Jesse no ride back to the hotel.

Time to switch tactics. Carano would invite a storm of criticism if he deported a lawyer once the trial was actually underway, so ready or not, it had better get started.

· · ·

JESSE GRABBED A quick lunch at *Pollo Campero*, Guatemala's improved, spicier version of Colonel Sanders, and walked back to the Conquistador Hotel. He smiled with relief to see the door securely locked this time, but the smile faded when he opened it and entered his room. The mattress had been overturned, all drawers pulled out and dumped on the floor, his files scattered everywhere, his cell phone crushed to fragments. The television was on.

All his case notes were gone, even his laptop. That left only the notes from Marisa's files Teo had given him, which Jesse had fortuitously left in the trunk of his rental car. Heartsick, he fell onto the edge of his bed. The *bastards*. After two of them kidnapped him, others moved in to sack his room.

In his bathroom, nothing had been disturbed, except that a bar of soap from the basin had been used to write the single word "*VAYA*" on his mirror. Go.

He went downstairs to a pay phone and called Teo to tell him everything that had happened. "Marisa was right about the money, Teo. I think it went to the CIA guy."

"Be careful, Jesse. If they are in it together, Webster will be dangerous."

"I'll watch myself."

"Good."

"We also have to go along with the expedited trial date, get the press corps up and running, and stay alert at all times for another ambush."

"Circle the wagons?"

"Good one, Teo."

"How about lunch, Jesse? Meet me at Europa? We need to talk."

"I've eaten, sort of, but I'll come have some coffee with you."

Jesse hung up and returned to his room to begin putting his things back together, trying to snap out of his dejection. His ears were still ringing, his kidney still ached. He thought about home, about Megan. He pictured her at school, buried in kids. He was tempted again to call her, but knew it would be a bridge to nowhere.

17

THE EUROPA BAR was a popular mezzanine watering hole in the Old City, founded by an Oregonian and famous for its hamburgers, chili, and used books in English. Its halcyon days were the 1970s and '80s during the civil war, when English-speaking residents and foreign correspondents gathered to exchange information. Jesse hurried past the bright posters and European Union flags adorning the drab white concrete walls toward a U-shaped bar at the far corner, where Teo sat sipping a Gallo beer. Jesse figured he had been waiting for at least twenty minutes, judging by the cigarette butts in the ashtray.

"So when do we see this Webster?" Teo asked, once they had a table.

"Tomorrow morning at his construction site in Antigua. I think Carano's money went straight to the guy who killed Marisa, and I think that guy was Carl Webster. I've set up a meet with Elena to try to urge her to move faster to confirm the money trail. If we get it in time, we'll have Webster singing like a toucan. If not, we'll wing it."

"Why would she help you?" Teo said.

Jesse shrugged. "She's a professional."

Teo said, "A professional *prosecutor*. You would do well to remember that. She is also said to be the kind of woman who knows that the way to a man's heart is through his chest with a stiletto."

"I'll be careful," Jesse said. "Remember, she hates Carano as much as you do. If he becomes President, she's dead meat and her father, too."

A pert young woman took their order, then poured coffee for a tall English woman sitting at the table next to them, eating the diner-style bacon, eggs, and hash browns, for which Europa was famous. Jesse noticed that Teo seemed in good spirits and was drinking beer instead of rum. Was he straightening himself out after all?

"When is your meeting?" Teo said.

"Tonight, at a little bistro outside of town."

"At night?" Teo said, raising an eyebrow. "Just the two of you? Of course. Makes perfect sense."

Jesse blushed. "I told her I'd been ordered out of Guatemala and that my room had been tossed. It was her idea to keep the meet private and off the record."

Teo winked and smiled. "Of *course*."

Jesse ignored him. "So, what did you want to tell me?"

Teo's eyes were typically red, but sparkling with enthusiasm. "Some good news for once. I checked all services coming and going from our house on April first and found that our electric meter was checked that day. The City records show he checked our meter at 11:46 a.m., which is when the witness claims she saw Kevin leaving the house."

"Tell me he was wearing a green jacket."

Teo laughed. "As green as your eyes, Jesse. Charcoal green, actually, which did not appear green at first, but outside, in the bright sunlight, the jacket was indeed green, with a logo on the front the witness couldn't have seen."

"Not to quibble Teo, but I haven't seen many bright sunlit days since I've been here."

Teo smiled proudly and handed Jesse a printout of the weather on April 1 that read, "Clear skies and sunshine."

"You're getting good at this," Jesse said.

Teo bowed in mock modesty.

"This eliminates their key witness," Jesse said.

"But they've still got the claimed affair, the absence of an alibi, and guilt by association."

"And maybe more," said Jesse, hating himself for not telling Teo about Kevin's fingerprints in his house. What would happen when he found out about it? Would he remain in denial and accept the version that Marisa had simply interviewed Kevin in her home office? Would he see the truth and turn on his own client? Strangle his co-counsel?

Teo said nothing, so Jesse gratefully changed the subject. "What did you learn from Anastacia Ramirez?"

"I couldn't get past her husband at the door. He slammed it in my face, said he would shoot me next time."

"Why are they angry with you?"

Teo's euphoria vanished. "They think I am a turncoat for representing my wife's accused murderer. And, of course, they all think I failed to support her crusade."

"What do *you* think, Teo?"

Teo took a long pull on his beer and looked at Jesse with heavily hooded eyes. "I should have been more patient with Marisa. I wish that I had . . . listened . . . really *listened* to her."

Jesse nodded. *I wish I had listened.* A universal lament.

Lunch was served. Teo had fish, and Jesse picked at a local side dish of nearly raw *qüisqúil* that would serve as excellent mortar if one happened to have some bricks around that needed laying.

They ate in silence. Jesse wished that he could come up with something consoling to say. But all he could hear in his head was a loud echo from his own failed relationship with Megan Harris. *I wish I had listened.*

.   .   .

LATE THAT AFTERNOON, alone in his hotel room, Jesse gave in to the need to talk to Megan. If he got her voice mail, he'd at least get to hear her voice. If she picked up and the mood seemed right, maybe he'd tell her the good news about his imminent partnership, then dust off the old things-will-be-different campaign. See if it would fly better when launched from afar. He knew there wasn't much reason for hope, but maybe he'd suggest they get together for dinner when he got back. Old times. He checked his watch and grabbed his new cellphone. She might be home by now.

"Jess?" Her voice sounded surprised and pleased.

"It's me. How are you?"

"I'm . . . fine. Are you back?" She seemed excited that he might be.

"No. Still in Guatemala."

"Oh, well, are you all right?"

His stomach clutched, and he considered exploiting her apparent concern by telling her the reason he had called was because he was being held for ransom by vicious guerrilla psychopaths after having been savaged by wild dogs. Instead, he asked about her students, her music, and Melissa. Then he told her about his new involvement in the case.

"I'm so glad to hear from you. You're really okay?"

Jesse felt a tightening in his throat. "I'm fine, Megan."

"How is the trial going? Have you been the bug or the windshield?"

"A little of both. It's been dicey, but things are coming together."

"Do you think you can get him off?"

"Believe it or not, the alleged murderer is innocent for once."

"Not."

"What?"

"You gave me an option: 'believe it or not.' Based on the news we're getting up here, I pick 'not.'"

"The case is making the news in San Francisco?"

"Sure. Daily reports on the AP wire, plus the *Chronicle* did a feature on you and the case this morning. The article reported on your client's lies to the police, his rumored mob connections, and the witness who spotted him. So I'm sticking with 'not,' though I'm proud of you anyway and know you'll get him off, even though he's guilty."

Jesse smiled. "Afraid you've got it backwards, Megan. He's *not* guilty, and I might *not* get him off. The case is a slow-motion train wreck."

"So I shouldn't change my bet in the teachers' pool?"

Jesse laughed. The girl could still lighten him up, even when the flood waters had risen to his nose. He pictured her beautiful face, holding her close.

"I can't offer information on betting. Might keep me out of the Hall of Fame. Anyway, I'll give it my best shot."

"I know you will. Twenty-five hours a day, right?"

"I can't help the way I am, any more than I can help loving you, Megan."

A painful silence ensued, interrupted by a horn honking below Jesse's room. He had no choice now but to plow on. "I want us to get back together. I want another chance." There it was. He heard the words at the same time Megan did and was nearly as shocked by them as she apparently was. He used the sleeve of his shirt to wipe beads of sweat off his forehead. Then waited. And waited some more. He heard her loudly exhale.

"Oh, Jess . . . "

Jesse could hear the frustration in her voice and knew she was fighting tears.

"I'm sorry, Jess," she said into the silence. "I loved you with all my heart and maybe still do. But I need a reliable partner and Melissa needs a real father, not someone wearing a hair shirt who pops in at midnight and is gone by six a.m. before she's awake."

"I wanted to be that real father," Jesse said.

"But not right now, isn't that it?"

His mouth opened, then closed. "I shouldn't have called," he whispered. "I'm sorry."

Out of nowhere, the green serpent intruded, wanting to ask if she was seeing anyone. He'd better say goodbye before he sank to even lower depths.

"Don't feel that way, Jess," she said at last. "It's just that I thought things were settled between us. I can't go through all that again."

"I understand."

"Goodbye, Jess. Please take care of yourself."

He stared at the dead phone. He walked over to the washbasin, twisted the corroded chrome handle, heard the grating sound of metal on metal, let the rust clear out, then splashed cold water on his face. What a fool he had been to shoot off his mouth. But at least he knew where he stood. The last bridge between them was burned now, ashes in the water.

He slapped himself lightly a few times on both cheeks. Get a grip, he told the guy in the mirror, there was always the work. And with a capital murder trial set to start in eight days, he'd better get to it.

18

THAT EVENING, JESSE drove his Suzuki north of the city on the road to Tikal. He had just purchased a new, inexpensive laptop and some additional clothing: a lightweight suit, two dress-shirts, extra socks and underwear. He had agonized like a teenager over what to wear for his imminent meeting with Elena.

He parked the car in front of *Paradiso*, a small café bistro with a curved entry wall of limestone slabs, on which skittered a pair of *gorrobos,* larger than most American lizards. Beautiful fork-tailed *Golondrinas* were nesting up in the eaves of the roof and took wing when they saw him.

Inside the restaurant, a low bamboo ceiling and a stone- and stucco-walled interior provided a pleasant escape from the humidity outside. He chose a table in a dark corner, far from the curved bar, so that he and the chief prosecutor could speak privately. A lone guitarist strummed a *bossa nova* song at the end of the bar, next to a huge stone fireplace. A voluptuous, barefoot, dark-skinned woman with hair down to her waist, clad in a red and yellow *huilpile,* swayed in front of the guitar player. She could have been a body double for

Megan, but he didn't want to think of her now. That was in the past.

He still wasn't sure what to make of Elena Ruiz, but he looked forward to seeing her with unnerving anticipation. Teo was right: she was their adversary and probably had an agenda Jesse would never understand. But Elena hated Carano—had reason to fear him, too—and might relish the opportunity to help Jesse prove he had sent money to a CIA operative.

He looked at his watch, feeling a little on edge, thinking he should go ahead and order a beer. But his gaze drifted back to the entrance, and there she was, coming through the door. His intention of maintaining a professional distance faltered as he watched her eyes straining in the darkness, looking even more stunning than he remembered. She surveyed the room, unable to spot him, a rare lack of certainty in her dark eyes. He remained unseen a minute longer in order to enjoy this rare trace of vulnerability.

Then she was coming toward him, a sudden smile on her face. "I am sorry to be late, Señor Hall."

"What happened to 'Jesse?'" he said.

"Hello, Jesse," she said, extending her hand. Was it the accent that infused her voice with the sound of violins?

Jesse looked into her large dark eyes. She had changed from her office gear into a simple black dress with spaghetti shoulder straps, revealing a hint of décolleté. Got to be a message there. A simple chain-medallion hung from her graceful neck, ending between her high breasts. A black and gold Pashmina shawl covered her shoulders, and a touch of blush highlighted her prominent cheekbones. The guitarist began to play *The Girl From Ipanema*. Give me a break, thought Jesse.

"I wish it were not so humid," she said, apparently unaware of his scrutiny. "The patio is so beautiful this time of year. How did you know about this place?"

"I'm a trained professional," Jesse said with a smile, "an investigative trial lawyer highly skilled in research." He signaled to an old man with a tray coming toward them and added, "That, plus the Ramada's concierge told me about it when I first arrived. I'm going to have a beer. What would you like?"

"A vacation," she said, and began to remove her shawl. Jesse helped her, gently grazing her hair with the back of his hand. A wave of excitement passed through him and he reminded himself to be careful.

"Lacking that, a rum and soda would be nice. It's been a difficult day."

"I have an idea how you could reduce your case load."

"Let me guess," she said, and they settled into a comfort zone, discussing the weather, the latest news, and a White Stripes CD she had just picked up.

"Are you ready for trial, Elena?" Working his way in.

"Yes, of course. It's a simple enough case."

"Then you won't do anything to delay it?"

"Ah, Jesse, first the trial date is too soon, now you want to finish your work and go home. You do not like us here in Guatemala?"

The innuendo did not go unnoticed by Jesse. "I like you a whole lot, Elena, but as I told you on the phone, Carano has ordered me out of town."

Elena waved a dismissive hand in the air. "The man is an idiot."

"Not according to him. He claims he's saving Guatemala single-handedly by extracting maximum aid from the U.S. to ward off a left-wing revolution."

Elena broke out in a genuine and spontaneous laugh. "What makes it hilarious is that his strategy is working! Despite the Great Recession, U.S. aid is still flowing into Guatemala faster than he can steal it."

Jesse nodded, but couldn't manage a smile and Elena added, "I am being insensitive about your country. I am sorry. So what will you do?"

Jesse shrugged. "I'll stay, unless his ARES thugs disappear me or he simply deports me as an 'undesirable.'"

Elena fingered the clasp on her purse, then smiled and said, "I don't think 'undesirable' is an apt description for the person under scrutiny here."

There it was again, the come-on. No doubt about it. Playing him like a fiddle, but he felt his heart move anyway. The romantic guitar strains floated toward them and she met his gaze. He felt something else move.

"But, yes," she added, as the drinks arrived, "he could deport you. I'm afraid the tyrant's power is becoming somewhat unchecked."

"I hear your father's illness gave him a chance to fill the vacuum."

"True, although our Vice President is not above creating his own vacuums, sometimes with bullets."

Jesse nodded, sipped his beer, lowered his voice. "Listen Elena, I have reason to believe that Carano created a vacuum in the field of critical journalism."

"Marisa Andrade."

"Yep. And I think he paid Webster to do the kill."

"If you have proof of that allegation, Jesse, I'm listening."

"I was hoping *you'd* have it by now. I think the offshore money from Carano's discretionary fund came back to Carl Webster for killing Marisa. I ran bluffs on Carano and Webster and they each looked guilty as hell. Worried, too, in Webster's case."

"You were being provocative, Jesse, so of course you got a rise out of them."

"But neither one clearly denied it. Carano danced around some about maybe doing government construction work with Webster's German firm. But Webster's just an employee there."

"I said I would try to track the money, Jesse, and I will. But it will take time, and I cannot guarantee success."

"Okay, but I know you hate Carano. Remember the Arab proverb that says 'The enemy of my enemy is my friend?' Well, that makes us buddies, Elena."

She gazed into her glass. "All right, but let's not ruin a perfectly good cocktail hour by talking about Carano."

An old man came by to light a candle at their table, then hurried off.

"What do you make of Miguel Aguilera's chances in the election?" Jesse asked, slipping back onto neutral ground.

"Not good. A Mayan has never been elected and he is investing too much of his political capital on a land grant that doesn't grant land."

"You don't think there's any possibility—"

She gave her head an impatient shake. "The Bilateral Commission I told you about has found nothing, and this is where Carano's impeccable timing will come in. He has ordered the Commission's report to be released a week before the fall election."

"Timing the exposure for maximum political advantage. Smart. I've also heard that Marisa was losing faith in the letter's authenticity just before she was killed. Any idea what she might have learned?"

Elena stared off toward the fireplace, her gaze captured by the fire. "A Mayan woman on the Commission was one of Marisa's closest friends. She might have leaked to Marisa that they had found nothing." She paused then, gazed into his eyes, and said, "If your agenda was to talk about the case, Jesse, why this romantic setting?"

Jesse felt his cheeks burning. "I think you know why, but I notice you came anyway."

"Curiosity," she said, and tapped her fingernails against her glass, "so tell me about yourself, Jesse Hall, and your life in San Francisco."

Jesse gave Elena the short-form version of his life—his early poverty, the scholarships, his hope for partnership and his aspirations beyond. She listened, asked whether he was married, and he heard himself saying he had thought seriously about it, but it hadn't worked out.

She hesitated, and then said, "This is a personal question, but why did it end?"

"She'd say my ambition didn't allow time for a decent relationship."

"So you love your work?"

Did he? The geographical distance from the office was providing space for a new assessment. "It's hard sometimes. At first, you're trying dog-shit cases against a weak adversary, but the more you win, the bigger the cases get. There's more at stake, with tougher lawyers on the other side. Soon, you're on a platform diving into a tank that gets smaller with every victory. You must know what I mean."

She nodded. "And the platform keeps getting higher with each case."

Jesse nodded. "So it's stressful working at C&S, and though it's also often rewarding, I don't see myself committing a hell of a lot of justice along the way. I'll be glad to move on after a couple of years as a partner."

The *camarero* returned and offered them another round. Elena declined, reminded Jesse of her dinner meeting. Jesse wondered if there really was a dinner meeting or if he had just failed her first-date test.

"How about you, Elena?" he asked, as if he didn't know the answer, "Have you been married?"

She said nothing at first, and then surprised him by taking a cigarette out of a case and lighting it herself before Jesse could grab the candle. She glanced at him through a cloud of exhaled smoke, then began speaking about her marriage as a teenage military brat to a handsome young army lieutenant, an ambitious soldier with crystal blue eyes and an innocent face she later learned masked the heart of a true killer.

"He soon began beating me, and when it got so bad I had to go to the hospital, my father forced the truth out of me. He handpicked Raul a week later for a battle against a guerrilla uprising from which no one returned."

Jesse said nothing.

"You are wondering how that made me feel?" she said softly, staring into the candlelight. "Well, it must have been what I wanted or I wouldn't have let my father know that it was Raul who assaulted me. I knew that my father would protect me."

"The way you protect him now," Jesse said. "Will you marry again?"

Elena rose and reached for her shawl.

"Wait, Elena," he said. "I presume too much sometimes—"

"It's quite all right, but I really must go. I told you . . ."

"I know," Jesse said. "Your dinner." He rose reluctantly and left money on the table for the drinks.

"Yes, well, goodnight," she said, and held out her hand. "Until next time."

Next time. That was something, at least.

When he took her hand, he felt that electric charge again. He put his other hand on hers, surrounding it. Her eyes told him what he wanted to know.

"So how about we meet here," he said, "same time, day after tomorrow?"

She smiled, but shook her head. "Professionally, that would not be a good idea. You can see that."

Jesse knew she was right. She turned toward the entrance. Jesse followed.

"I'll try to hold the trial date, Jesse, and I won't object too much to you speaking up in court. Your client deserves a fair trial and, well, the professor is drinking and everybody knows it."

"I appreciate that."

"But you realize I will fight you in this case?"

"I know. But if I bring you hard evidence, I know you'll do the right thing."

"Perhaps. Meanwhile, you've got to take care of yourself. Anyone who confronts Carano and Carl Webster within the same forty-eight hour period has put his life in jeopardy."

"How about yourself? The way Carano is usurping power, you and your father would be safer elsewhere."

"This is my country, Jesse. I am a public servant. My home number and address are publicly listed. I will not cower in a secret location, nor will I run off to Switzerland in exile. My job is to stay and use all means at my disposal to protect Guatemala, and hopefully, to change it."

"You don't think your country is on the right path to a new democracy?"

"Generally, but there are obstacles in the path that must first be removed."

"Such as?"

"Goodnight, Jesse."

Jesse realized he was still holding her hand. "You say you will use whatever means at your disposal to remove these obstacles," he said. "Did you mean the power of your office? Your father's office? No offense, but it looks to me that his time has passed."

"I must go."

"I know," Jesse said, but didn't let go of her hand.

"Jesse?"

"Yes."

"Please stop looking at me that way."

"Cuff me and read me my rights. I can't help it."

"I must go," she said. They were almost to the door, but when they reached an alcove leading to restrooms, Jesse gently took her arm, guided her inside, next to an old phone booth, and turned her toward him.

"Jesse ..."

He kissed her gently, tentatively. She didn't respond, so he backed off and met her questioning eyes. Then she came to him, her lips demanding, their mouths welded together, lips, tongues, teeth, inhaling each other's breath. Jesse pressed the full length of his body against hers and she returned the pressure. Seconds, minutes, all sense of time lost.

Elena broke away. "We can't—"

"I know." He kissed her again and felt her arms tighten around him, drawing his body even tighter into hers, pushing hard against him, moving her hips into his. But then her head pulled back, and Jesse saw that her eyes were opened wide, as if in disbelief at what was happening.

Someone was behind them, an elderly woman passing by. She gave them a smile, and they looked at each other self-consciously. Elena broke the tension. "Is this what you meant by 'hard evidence?'"

Jesse smiled, held up both hands. "Just glad to see you," he quipped, and saw that for better or for worse, rationality was returning.

"Goodnight, Jesse," she said, smoothing her dress with long, graceful fingers. Jesse nodded, but when she turned away, he grabbed her hand, pulled it to his lips, and kissed it.

She smiled at this and kissed him on the cheek. "This was a mistake, Jesse, but no harm done. Tomorrow, it's back to business as usual."

Jesse nodded, though he knew nothing between them would be "business as usual" again. He managed a grin, saying, "Sure. See you in court, Counselor." In the darkness of the parking lot he watched her drive off. He opened his car door, and a sedan started up near the place Elena had been parked and took off without its headlights on. Had the driver forgotten his lights? A few hundred yards down the road, the headlights came on. He hadn't seen anybody walk to that car. Should he be worried about her?

Then he thought he caught movement in the front seat of a black Mercedes off to his left. Chill out, he told himself, you're seeing things, getting the pretrial jitters, over-dramatizing everything. Still, he hurried into his car, and quickly locked the door. He started the engine and sped off after the second car. He kept one eye in the rear view, but saw no one behind him.

He raced along, not sure what he would do if he caught up with the car that might or might not be following Elena. Slowly, the twin dots that had been the car's taillights disappeared into the hazy night. He floored the Suzuki, but it was no match for any of the cars ahead of him. He was alone on the road.

He mused at his paranoia and headed for home, thinking about what had just happened between the two of them. He believed she would help him with the money trail. But there was something else he wanted from her that filled him with excitement. Something that had nothing to do with the case.

· · ·

AFTER THREE HOURS of battling with himself over a lonely dinner and a mediocre bottle of wine, Jesse found himself pacing back and forth in front of Elena's front door with the frustration of a caged animal, his head a supernova of torment, an aching profusion of lust, loneliness, and fatigue. He stopped, glared at the door as if at an enemy, then rang her bell, having rehearsed a bullshit story based on seeing the car pull out behind her at the restaurant. But when she opened the door and met his eyes, he could find no words.

She wore a white bathrobe, slightly open between her pale breasts. Her hair, the color of polished ebony, now released from all restraint, flowed down over them.

There was no surprise in her expression and he saw that her eyes were glistening in the overhead porch light. Was it joy he saw? Sadness? Both?

They didn't make it to the bedroom. His lips burned into hers as before, but with more urgency now. His feverish hands were inside the robe, caressing her hard nipples while pushing his instant erection hard against her. She returned his passion, her hands fumbling to release his belt. His slacks and underwear dropped to the floor and he lifted her off the floor. She locked her perfect legs around his hips and guided him deep into her instant wetness and groaned softy as he entered her. To Jesse, the sensation was less of penetration than being enveloped in a feeling of oneness with her. He was so hard into her tightness he was afraid he would hurt her.

They writhed against each other with an animal-like aggression, her heels digging into his buttocks, pulling him ever deeper. Their lips remained savagely locked together, each unable to get enough of the other. She began to shudder and within seconds, their mingled cries of ecstasy filled the night.

. . .

JESSE AWOKE EARLY the next morning and soundlessly eased himself out of Elena's bed. In the semi-darkness, her hair was a dark halo against a white pillow, and Jesse paused to study the perfect line of her nose, her throat, and the swell of her small breasts. He could tell by her rhythmic deep breathing that she was asleep. He longed to touch her, to awaken her, to kiss her, to be inside her once more, but he quietly began to dress.

He remembered being half-awake sometime in the early morning hours and feeling her hand gently caressing his face. Her exploring fingers were warm and gentle, but had penetrated his skin like ultrasound. There was an intimacy in her touch that somehow exceeded their earlier frantic couplings, that was even greater than the comfort they had reached with each other between passionate flare-ups, when they either talked or rested in a silent embrace. But her touch! Her touch was more than the sum of all these earlier parts. It was a caress offering love.

And he had feigned sleep.

He had intended to leave the house earlier. Exposure would be bad for the case, but it would be disastrous for her career.

Dressed but for his shoes, he stole through the living room toward the front door. He paused midway, noticing an old framed photograph of an awkward-looking, teenage Elena with her parents—her handsome father in full-dress military attire—and another recent shot of the *Jefe de Fiscalía*, surrounded by her staff. Jesse mused at how little you can tell about how a kid is going to turn out by early appearances. Time and responsibility had etched fine lines around her mouth and eyes, but the older Elena in the current photo was nothing short of magnificent.

Except for one wall occupied entirely by books—philosophy, political theory, and literary fiction—the room was sparsely furnished: IKEA-type furniture and a twelve-inch TV in the corner, probably serving only to provide news. This was a woman without time for frivolity.

The sound of a door opening caused him to spin around.

"Good morning, Elena," he said. "I didn't want to wake—"

She stared at him as if he were an intruder. He took a step toward her, but she stopped him with an extended hand. "This never happened, Jesse."

Jesse smiled. "Oh, it happened all right, and it was wonderful. I was thinking we might make it happen again tonight."

Elena shook her head, pulled the robe tighter around her throat. "I don't wish to presume too much, but I must tell you that I am . . . unavailable."

"What the hell does that mean?"

She turned abruptly and said, "Goodbye, Jesse," and walked quickly back into her bedroom and softly closed the door.

DAY NINE

19

THE NEXT MORNING brought another muggy day, trying hard to rain. Teo picked Jesse up outside his hotel, and they headed to Antigua for another confrontation with Webster.

Jesse's head was still whirling from the night before. What was the incredible appeal of this woman? Though uniquely attractive, she was not the most beautiful woman he had known. He concluded it was her unknowableness—much like the dark intensity of Guatemala—and, of course, the wholly unprofessional nature of what they had done; the seductive wrongness of it all, turning his blood to fire.

Teo and Jesse traveled in silence for the first ten kilometers before Teo said, "Well? What did you get out of your meeting last night that will make this trip worth the doing?"

Jesse stirred from his reflections. "Nothing new, so we'll run a bluff."

"Do you ever tire of bluffing?"

"It's what you do when you have nothing else, Teo. I'll start by telling him I had a secret meeting with the chief prosecutor last night. He won't believe me, so then I'll suggest he use the CIA resources he denies he has to confirm that we were in fact together last night. Or he could just call the *Paradiso*. We were seen there by all the staff."

"All right so far," Teo said, but his tone still skeptical. "Then what?"

Jesse smiled. "I'll tell him the 'agenda' for my meeting with the prosecutor was a plan to grant Webster full immunity in exchange for ratting out Carano. I'll claim that Elena now realizes that Kevin is innocent."

"But if Webster is who you think he is, he knows Carano has more power than Elena Ruiz."

"But not more than President Eduardo Ruiz. I will tell him the army remains loyal to Ruiz, which you've told me is the case."

"But even if he goes for that much, why would he think she would grant him immunity if he *is* the actual killer?"

"Elementary, my dear Professor. I'll explain that this is the price Elena is willing to pay to get Carano before Carano gets her—and her father. Then I'll tell Webster it's his only way to escape lethal injection."

"And after he laughs at you?" Teo said. "As I am trying hard not to do now?"

"I'll say that if he rejects the offer, she will officially and publicly blow his CIA cover in a way that will wreck his career, and then she'll charge him with Marisa's murder. She'll charge him as Carl Webster, aka Carlos Webster. She will do all this within twenty-four hours." Teo seemed interested now, so Jesse kept talking. "Even if he thinks he's got a solid alibi, he will fear losing his job here. He's a man in love with a girl and a country. So it might work. Your presence, honored sir, will lend a touch of credibility, as well as providing a witness to any admissions if he takes the bait. You'll agree it's worth a try?"

"I concede you have thought this through—to a point. But won't he want to know the evidence the CP has against him? This is not a naïve schoolboy you are dealing with."

"I'll tell him she did not disclose this to me, other than confirming my suspicions about the money trail between Carano and himself and, of course, the Carlos V death clue."

Teo rubbed his temples, as if all this thinking was making his brain hurt. "All right, but why would you be the one making the offer instead of Elena Ruiz?"

"Politics. She has to have deniability."

The devil's advocate was quiet for a minute, then, "Aren't you risking embarrassment to Elena? Have you considered how she will react if it works? Or even if it doesn't and she finds out how you used her office to attempt this stunt?"

"I've thought a lot about it, and it's a win-win for her. If it doesn't work he won't raise it with her and she'd deny it anyway. If it does work, she'll deny she authorized it, but then proceed to nail Webster *and* Carano. If it all blows up—if I'm missing something—I'll come forward and take the hit."

"All right, but what about Webster? What if he believes you and accepts the deal, then later finds out you made it up and there's no immunity?"

"He'll be complaining to me through prison bars. The bastard murdered your wife, Teo. Am I supposed to feel bad about this?"

"You will get no argument from me."

The two men rode in silence for the next ten minutes, then Teo, with a straight face, asked, "So what else did you get from Elena last night?"

. . .

FORTY MINUTES LATER, Jesse knocked on the metal door of the construction trailer. There was no response. He rapped again, harder this time. Nothing. He stepped back, noticed that no smoke was coming out of the roof's heater vent. They peeked through all the windows and saw that the trailer was empty. They wandered out to the building site, where a cement truck's barrel was turning, but nothing was flowing into the forms for the exterior walls. Jesse spotted the foreman he had seen on his earlier visit and told him he was looking for Señor Webster.

"So am I," said the disgruntled-looking foreman. "We've got flooding in the subterranean area and two of our pumps are out. We are totally stalled."

"He hasn't been here? Did you call him at home?"

"Three times," the foreman said, hands on hips. "I left two messages, hung up the last time. He unplugs his phone when he's sleeping one off. I'd go get him out of bed, but I can't leave with all this water."

"I'll do it," said Jesse. "Give me his address."

The foreman hesitated, his eyes narrowed.

"You remember me from before, right?" said Jesse. "Carl is a friend of mine from the States."

Shouts of frustration came from the excavation. Webster's crew was arguing with the cement truck driver, who kept looking at his watch. "Okay," the foreman said, wiping a sleeve across his forehead, "but tell him to get his ass out here quick. We need two new pumps by noon or we're going to be screwed with our foundation pours. He lives in the city at 2244 *Calle Sandova*. That's in Zone Ten."

"No problem," Jesse said, and the two lawyers headed for their car.

. . .

WEBSTER'S HOUSE WAS impressive by Guatemala City standards: white stucco, a beautiful garden, and a sign warning of electronic surveillance instead of dogs on the roof. No cars on the street. Money, thought Jesse. Lots of money.

"He is not home," said Teo, after ringing the security gate bell for the third time.

"I hear the TV all the way out here," Jesse said. "The alarm is probably off because he's in there, maybe in the shower so he can't hear the bell." Jesse opened the gate. No alarm.

Growing bolder, Jesse walked around to the side of the house and found an iron gate ajar. Teo followed and they entered a backyard lush with fern, *ceiba*, and a large *araucaria* tree. Jesse approached a window and stretched to peer inside. He was startled by a face staring back at him, then realized he was looking into a large vanity mirror over a dresser in what must be the master bedroom.

He braced one foot on a two-by-two inch wooden ledge around the lower perimeter of the house, then applied his fingers to the windowsill and pulled himself higher.

What he saw caused his breath to rush out like air from a blown tire.

What he saw was a hand and blood, blood everywhere. The shock of it weakened his fragile purchase on the sill and he found himself on the ground, gasping for air.

"What is it, Jesse?" said Teo. "Are you injured?"

"Somebody . . . is either dead or dying in there, Teo. The bed sheets are drenched in blood."

"Webster?"

"I don't know. Whoever it is was too close to the wall. I just saw the fingers of one hand. We've got to get in there, Teo. Use your cell phone and call the police, I'll try the back door."

"Maybe we should just . . ."

"Call them now, Teo!"

Jesse leapt up the three steps up to the back porch. He knocked loudly, then found a rock and broke the glass in the door. Inside the house, he walked down a hallway and found himself in a living room. Sunlight streamed through a window, illuminating thousands of dancing dust motes and an eclectic array of furnishings covered in plaids and leather, including a large sofa, book-ended by hand-hewn end tables. Above a blackened stone fireplace mantle hung a large framed oil painting depicting plump angelic children in togas pouring water out of urns into a Roman bath. Jesse wiped sweat from his forehead. He felt dizzy.

Disoriented, he retraced his steps down the hall and glanced into a room with a desk, two chairs, a fake palm, and a television, apparently Webster's office. He went another ten feet down a hallway and saw the bedroom and the bloodstained sheets. He steeled himself, then slowly walked around the bed and saw, not Webster, but a woman with short dark hair, lying face up on the floor, covered in blood and wearing nothing but a laced thong. Webster's girlfriend? The room smelled of urine and feces, and Jesse knew she had been dead for several hours. He opened a window, and then cursed himself for not using a towel. What the fuck was he thinking? He swiped at the sill with a small pillow. Where else had he left prints?

He felt woozy, listened to Teo outside the window calmly talking to the police on his cell. He took a deep breath, forced his eyes back on the woman. Her face was so bloody it was hard to judge her age.

Early thirties? Three bullet wounds were clearly visible—head, neck, and stomach. A reddish brown crust surrounded each hole.

This had to be Webster's girlfriend. Had Webster killed her? He closed her vacant eyes and nausea overcame him. He hurried into the nearest bathroom but nothing came up. On rubber legs, he returned to Webster's office and searched for a computer, but only a monitor stood on the desk and no computer. Webster—or someone—must have taken it. There were no signs of a struggle anywhere, or even disorder. If the place had been tossed, Martha Stewart must have done it. Bet they wore gloves. Jesse wished he had some as his trembling fingers rifled through files, finding nothing but construction documents: specifications, change-order files, contracts, typical project documentation. One security file cabinet was unlocked, open, and nearly empty. Was that where Webster had kept his CIA stuff? Or might he have a secure office somewhere else? A station chief didn't just leave secret shit lying around, did he?

Frustrated and still woozy, Jesse let himself out onto the front porch, just as the first PNC car pulled up and discharged three men: two plainclothes and one wearing a typically ill-fitting and threadbare blue PNC uniform. Teo was halfway down the walkway, motioning the men toward the front door. He spotted Jesse coming out the front door and hurried up the stairs, which groaned under his weight. When he reached the top, he was wheezing like a punctured bagpipe. Jesse eyed the PNC coming through the gate and quickly updated Teo on what he had found.

"Three shots?" Teo said. "Webster must have been in a rage."

"Or in the darkness of night, someone thought they were killing Webster."

"But where is Webster?"

A small man with rigid features and sunken eyes set in a pallid face charged up the walkway toward the front stairs, leading the other two PNC men. Teo told Jesse that the small man was Chief Inspector Antonio García. "He interrogated Anica and me the day Marisa was killed. The man has the sensitivity of a fence post."

"I assume they know who Webster is, so they sent their top dog."

"They will never catch Webster," Teo said, his face grim. "A CIA station chief can arrange things."

"Don't jump to conclusions, Teo. I don't know much about the man, but he sounded like he loved the girl."

"He did not love her much last night," said Teo.

"It's a little early to be convicting him," Jesse said, but his trial lawyer's mind had already begun to calculate the advantageous consequences of this slaying. A murder charge against Webster would make it impossible for the judges to ignore the Carlos V clue, especially if Elena's people could trace money coming to him from Carano's discretionary account.

Inspector García danced up the front steps like a man about to receive an Oscar. "Well, Professor Andrade," he said, his dark, accusing eyes flickering between Jesse and Teo. "We meet again, under similar circumstances."

Almost everything about the inspector was dark. He wore a navy blue suit, dark grey shirt, and shiny black shoes. When he spoke, his chin jutted forward, exposing a row of small, nicotine-stained lower teeth.

"Perhaps if your people did your job," Teo said, "these 'meetings' would not be necessary. Carl Webster should have been locked up weeks ago. My wife provided you with everything but a video of Webster in the act of killing her."

"Patience, Professor," Inspector García said, his hard features working themselves into a condescending smile. "We will do our job, wherever it might lead us."

García's cold eyes rested on Jesse, who described what he had seen. He tentatively identified the victim, leaving out his unsuccessful search of Webster's home office.

"Please wait here," García said, "while we investigate. You, too, Señor Hall, if you please."

Jesse nodded, and he and Teo waited for at least a half hour in the living room, while the chief inspector officiously ordered his men here and there, apparently having forgotten Jesse and Teo. But García's revenge for Teo's earlier sarcasm came swiftly when Teo's request to use the bathroom was denied by a PNC cop. "Orders, sir."

After another fifteen minutes, the chief inspector reentered the room and told Jesse he could leave, but that he had some questions for the professor.

"We're in the same car, so I'll stay, thank you," Jesse said.

"I am told, Señor," the inspector said through his tight-lipped smile, "that you speak excellent Spanish. Am I not making myself clear? You will be so good as to leave now."

"It's all right, Jesse," said Teo. "Go ahead. They will take me home." Teo then headed for the bathroom. "But first, Chief Inspector, I must urinate, and if your man feels compelled to shoot me for that, he will have to do so."

When Teo returned, Jesse was still defiantly waiting.

García said, "I asked you to leave us, Señor Hall, and will have you escorted down the stairs if you require assistance."

"If you are implying that Professor Andrade is a suspect," Jesse said, "I insist on staying."

"As his lawyer?"

"Yes."

Teo watched the back-and-forth exchange as if at a tennis match, saying nothing.

"My understanding is that you are not qualified to practice here in my country, Señor," said the little inspector. "Under our Constitution."

"Isn't that for a judge to decide?"

"At this moment, and in this place, I am the judge," García said, his eyes sparking. "Concerning whether the professor is a suspect, are you not curious why he was observed sitting in his car across the street from this house for the last three days in a row?"

"You must be mistaken—"

"And why he went to so much trouble to obtain Mr. Webster's address from the U.S. Consulate. We have you on tape, Professor."

Jesse stole a quick look at Teo, who averted his eyes. Jesse tried to digest the information, but could feel his stomach rebelling. "What are you suggesting, Chief Inspector?" he said, in the coolest voice he could manage.

"Is it not clear to you, Señor Hall? The professor's wife, she is murdered. He is distraught, fired from his job, drinking heavily, and angry about being cuckolded."

Jesse reached a restraining hand toward his friend, but it was unnecessary. Teo looked utterly defeated. "She is dying," García continued, his tone growing even more pontifical, "but she forms the letters 'Carlos V,' which leads the grieving husband to the mistaken conclusion that Carl Webster was the murderer. The grieving husband obtains Señor Webster's address, stakes out the house for three days, then last night, he makes yet another mistake and . . .well, here we are."

"You are the one mistaken, Chief Inspector," Jesse said, managing some conviction in his voice. "Professor Andrade and I are, as you know, defending the man you have charged with murder. You are correct that one of our defense theories is that it was Webster, not Kevin Covington, who murdered Marisa Andrade. This is not rationalization, but a probability." Jesse managed to look García squarely in the eye. "I asked the professor to obtain his address so that we could observe his movements before interviewing him here today."

The inspector frowned, appearing to see through the lie, but unclear what to do about it. He aimed a skeptical glance at Teo. "I suppose that you concur with your friend's creative narrative?"

Teo, who had been earnestly studying his cuticles, managed a credible-sounding yes and Jesse added, "If you wish further confirmation, please contact the chief prosecutor. I have revealed our defense theory to her."

"I assure you that I will do that, Señor Hall."

"Fine, then may we leave?"

"Of course, Señor Hall, but with your permission, I would like to hear all this from the professor himself. If you will excuse us, we will return him to his home the minute we are finished. Please do not require me to have you . . . escorted out."

"It's all right, Jesse," Teo whispered to Jesse, "you know he is right that you are not qualified to practice alone in Guate. But do not worry. I am quite capable of handling this idiot. Here are my car keys. Have some lunch, and I will call you later at the hotel."

Jesse nodded, too tired and distraught to argue or concoct more lies. With a last glance at his forlorn friend, Jesse left the house, his heart heavy with despair.

20

JESSE PUNCHED IN the number of Elena's direct line from his cell phone—he had promised to use it only in emergencies—in the lobby of the Conquistador. A noisy lunch-hour crowd had filled up the popular hotel restaurant, and Jesse could barely hear. He slipped into an alcove, which neither dampened the din from the restaurant nor dulled the aroma of *jacon*—a popular cilantro chicken dish—drifting out from the kitchen. Jesse realized that it was 1:30 p.m. and, despite the turmoil in his heart, he was starving.

Elena picked up on the second ring. Her voice sounded as it had on their first meeting: more professionally courteous than friendly. Jesse said, "I assume you know Webster's girlfriend was killed and that Webster's missing." He decided not to mention the Teo-García dust-up.

"I know. Her name was Perlita Ramos. But that's all I know so far."

"Any news for me on tracking the money?"

"Patience, Jesse. I know what you are thinking—that Webster's disappearance points more strongly to him as an assassin in the employ of Carano."

"That's how I see it."

"Well, we know that Carano's money came back into banks, but I don't have the accounts yet. We should know more by tomorrow."

"And you'll tell me?"

"If it is relevant to your client's case, yes."

"I don't want to get you in trouble, Elena. It won't come back at you."

"I was appointed by the President" she said, "not by Victor Carano. My duty is solely to do justice, and if we've got the wrong man, so be it. This is my standard *modus operandi*."

"You keep telling me there's nothing personal in any help you give me. I accept that, but I need to see you again."

"You will, Jesse. I think our next scheduled court appearance is—"

"You know what I mean."

"You will be going home soon, Jesse, win or lose. My life is here."

"I understand completely. You've made it clear that I'm nothing but a boy-toy you can discard like a used match when you've had your way with me. Now, when can I see you again?"

He heard stifled laughter and she said, "How about tonight?"

. . .

FATIGUE CAUGHT UP with Jesse in his room after lunch, and despite his new concerns about Teo, and against all odds, he fell into a deep sleep for two hours. He was half awakened by the insistent ring of the room telephone. He put a pillow over his head, but the ringing continued. Jesse opened one eye and glared at the black receiver. He glared it into silence, but it started again. He picked it up.

"They have him!" It was Anica Andrade and she was screaming.

"They have Papa!" When Jesse calmed her down, she told him that Teo had been taken away in handcuffs and was being held as a "material witness" in the slaying of Perlita Ramos.

"*¡Eso es mierda, Jesse!*" she screamed, then, in English, "First they kill my mother, now they take Papa, too?"

Fucking García, Jesse thought. Got me out of the way, then nailed Teo. Jesse reached for a reassuring tone he didn't feel. "I'm sure they're just holding him temporarily, Anica. I'll make some calls and go see him. Don't worry, okay?"

"Not worry? You know nothing about how things work in Guate. Carano and ARES have him and will never let him go. People disappear here all the time. They are also frequently shot trying to escape."

"Teo would not try to escape."

She groaned. "Oh Jesus, you *are* an idiot!"

Jesse felt embarrassment creeping in around the edges of his desperation. "Let me see what I can do."

"You'd better do something quick. This is all your fault. Why couldn't you have just stayed in the United States?"

Jesse was stung by her hostility, but understood it. "Be calm. You may be questioned yourself. Was your father home last night?"

"Yes. We watched TV until I went to bed around ten. I'm sure he must have gone to bed, too. Or maybe he stayed up to watch the news or maybe . . ."

Jesse called Elena back and left a message, feeling himself sinking ever deeper into the quagmire of this Guatemalan legal jungle. One thing was clear: Teo had nothing resembling a credible alibi.

. . .

MINUTES LATER AS Jesse was dressing, his room phone rang
again.

"Hello, Hot-Shot. I've been trying to reach you—"

"Hang up, Cal, and call me back on my new cell." Jesse gave him
the number and disconnected. His phone rang in seconds.

"So what's goin' on down there, Jesse? Why the cloak and dagger
crap?"

"What's going on?" Jesse said. "Well, let's see. I've been kidnapped
and my laptop and files were stolen. I've been ordered by the guy
who runs Guatemala to leave the country. There's been another
murder and Kevin's lead lawyer has just been jailed for it. And then
there's—"

"You *are* bullshitting me, right? Who's this new lawyer?"

Jesse cursed himself for having answered the phone. "Professor
Andrade."

"The victim's *husband*? You hired the victim's fuckin' *husband*?"

"He's highly respected, Cal, and—"

"You mean he *was* highly respected . . . . before he started *killin'*
people?"

"It's all a mistake, and I'm going to get him out."

Jesse felt a headache coming on. "And by the way, Cal, Kevin says
he did what you wanted him to do. Mind telling me what that was?"

"Tendin' to business is what it was." After a beat he added, "Have
I made a mistake puttin' my trust in you, kid? You sound like a man
with two wheels in a ditch. You got any good news for me? Or do I
have to pay more for good news?"

Jesse summoned patience, remembered Simon Bradshaw telling
him once that a good trial lawyer had to be able to pick the fly shit

out of the pepper, know what's important, what isn't, always make the best of things. So Jesse patiently told Covington that the trial would be starting in seven days and about how they had learned that the man leaving the scene of the murder was actually a utilities worker, not Kevin. He threw in how clearly the Carlos V clue pointed to the fugitive Carl Webster, thus away from Kevin, and that he, Jesse, would be able to stay on the case as an adviser.

"That's all real nice, kid," Cal said, "but now that your local lawyer is in the hoosegow, it seems to me we're back where we started about ten days ago?" Cal Covington was a man who knew fly shit from pepper, too. "What kind of Chinese fire drill are you runnin' down there, Jesse? What's next, they toss you in jail, too?"

"It may be the safest place to be."

"Save your jokes for someone with a sense of humor. I want Kevin out of there, so he can go finish dealing with Gómez."

Jesse froze. Go *finish*? There was the answer to his question, the implications of which were too large to fit into his small room, let alone his aching head.

"Are you telling me they *met*?" Jesse had forgotten the most basic tenet of trial work: *everybody lies.* Some young trial lawyers had trouble grasping this essential truth about lying, and they never amounted to much. Jesse, however, was raised in the Church of Chicanery on fast food and deception with bunco artists for parents, so he knew better. Clients render up truth to their lawyer like a rich man parts with money—in bits and pieces, and only when forced to. Why waste the truth on someone who doesn't want it?

"Didn't Cy tell you that's why I sent him down there?"

Jesse smiled. *Cy*? I bet Simon loves that one. "You and Kevin both told me that Kevin was in Guatemala on CalCorp business. And Kevin denies ever connecting with Gómez."

"It's all just business, kid, and it's *my* business, not yours. Far as you're concerned, it don't matter if he did or he didn't talk to Gómez."

"Listen, Cal, it matters a lot. I've suspected they might have hooked up, and it might provide Kevin with a bullet-proof alibi if they were together on April first."

"I'll only say this once more: *it don't matter*. Stay away from Gómez."

"I can't do that, Cal. If the Carlos V clue incriminating Webster doesn't wash, I need a backup, and that means getting Gómez in as an alibi witness. To win, we've got to give these hostile judges either the real killer—Webster—or an ironclad alibi from the lips of a man without motive to lie: Arturo Gómez."

"Pin it on Webster then, and as for your dumb-ass move in hiring Andrade, forget about him. Go out and buy me a real goddam lawyer."

"We've been through this, Cal. There's no time and nobody else to do it. Sorry, but I have to go get the professor out of jail now. I'll call you—"

"Hold on. The professor didn't really commit that new murder, did he?"

Jesse stared out his window, down at the teeming street.

"Well, did he?"

"I don't know," Jesse said, tired of lying, even to himself. He officially now distrusted everyone, including his co-counsel, who may have killed Webster's girlfriend and maybe Webster, too. Most of all, he distrusted his client, who was at best a drug trafficker, and maybe a killer as well.

. . .

JESSE HAD BEEN pacing for hours, waiting for Elena to answer his message, and didn't try to control his frustration when she finally did. "What have the police done with the professor?" he shouted.

His outburst was greeted by silence and Jesse tried to relax his white-knuckled hold on his cell phone.

"And hello to you, Jesse," she said at last.

He closed his eyes, blew air out of his tightened lips, trying to program the frenzy out of his voice. But he *was* frenzied. He had to get Teo out, and not just because of the imminent trial. Jail was no place for a man with a bad heart to go cold turkey. Jesse could picture him, probably already sweating and shaking.

"Have you heard where they're holding him, Elena?"

"I have. I am sorry to tell you he was taken to *Purgatorio.*"

"Come on, Elena, he can't survive an hour in that snake pit! Why are they holding him at all? What can you tell me?"

"Here's what I know," she said, her voice irritatingly calm. "The professor was on a three-day stakeout of Webster's house before the girl was killed there."

"I heard this from García. He was alone?"

"Except for a flask from which he was seen liberally partaking."

Jesse swallowed, wondering how the sandpaper had entered his throat. "Yeah, yeah," he croaked. "Go on."

"She had been dead for several hours when you found her, plenty of time for him to join you for the ride to Antigua and then back to the City. As you must know, the professor has been telling anybody who would listen that Carano arranged his wife's death and that Webster was his hired assassin. It doesn't look good for Andrade: motive, means, and opportunity."

"But what motive would he have for killing an innocent girl?" Jesse asked, though he knew what her answer would be. He had that sinking feeling again, slogging downward into a dark, fetid lostness. Alone again, not only separated from his co-counsel, but from Elena as well, whose voice seemed cold and distant, as if speaking to an adversary. Well, whom was he kidding? That's exactly what he was, and probably all he'd ever been. There would be no date tonight.

"A distinguished professor of law," he continued, trying to recover some initiative, putting a little sizzle into it, "does not suddenly break through a security system into a house and shoot a young woman he doesn't know, with a gun he doesn't own."

"The theory is that he went in before sunrise, undoubtedly drunk, and killed the girl thinking he was killing Webster."

"But they don't have the weapon, right?"

"No, they don't," she said. "And another point in his favor is that Webster is missing. I suspect that Inspector García really thinks Webster may have killed Perlita Ramos himself. Neighbors have heard arguments."

"Does García think Webster has left the country?"

"Probably. According to forensics, he'd have a six- to eight-hour jump on us. The PNC has put out an Interpol alert on him. If they find him, he will become the leading suspect. Obviously, that would be good for Professor Andrade."

"Finding him could be tough."

"Don't underestimate Interpol."

"He's got a big start, and he's CIA. And whether he did it or somebody else did, you find out who killed Perlita Ramos, and you'll have the murderer of Marisa Andrade." Jesse didn't have to mention where Kevin was at the time of Perlita's murder.

"They didn't teach clairvoyance at Boalt Hall, Jesse. I must have picked the wrong school."

"This isn't mysticism, just common sense. Marisa was overheard telling Anastacia Ramirez she had the goods on Carano. So Carano pays Webster to kill Marisa, then has Webster killed to avoid blackmail or loose lips."

"But Webster was not killed," Elena countered. "The only body is the woman's."

"So far. Look, Elena, I was on my way to see Kevin this afternoon. Would you get Teo out of *Purgatorio* and have him brought into a holding cell at the *Torre de la Tribunales?* Maybe arrange for me to see him, too?"

"I will try, but you'll have to come in at night, when the crowd thins out. They're getting nasty. I'll have someone meet you at the back entrance."

"Thank you, Elena. I appreciate it."

"I would do the same for anyone in your situation."

"I know you would, but you don't have to be so damned touchy about everything you do for me."

"Yes, I do."

Because you care about me, Jesse thought, a half smile crossing his haggard face despite his desolation. You do. You fucking care about me.

True to Elena's word, Jesse was met that night by a plainclothes cop who swiftly steered him through a gate at the rear of the *Torre de la Tribunales*. Once inside, however, Jesse was taken to a desk on the third floor, where a captain in charge informed him that Teo Andrade was still imprisoned at *Purgatorio*. He would, however, be allowed to see his client of record, Kevin Covington.

Elena was not in her office, and his protests about Teo got him nowhere. Jesse swallowed his frustration and went to interview Kevin.

As usual, the sight of his despondent client momentarily quelled Jesse's anger at the man's continuing mendacity. He started by breaking the news about Teo.

"Did he do it?" Kevin said. "Another one of those blackouts Marisa told me about?"

"I don't think so," Jesse said, and took note that the bruising on the defendant's face was clearing up, and there were no fresh cuts or scrapes. "You're looking better, Kevin."

"I can survive here in the courthouse holding cell, but I can't go back to *Purgatorio*."

"You may have to," Jesse said.

Kevin lowered his head and whispered, with utter conviction, "I'll kill myself. I'll skip purgatory and go straight to hell."

"Don't talk like that, Kevin. You gotta stay tough, not let them break you."

"You don't know what it's like."

Jesse nodded.

"And isn't the trial supposed to start?"

"It is," Jesse said, "but that's not necessarily good news. Not without an alibi."

"I wish to God I had one."

Kevin glanced away from Jesse's penetrating gaze, but not before Jesse saw something pass across the prisoner's eyes, giving him away. Jesse had the trial lawyer's ability to go from a guess to a feeling to near-certainty all in a split second, based on nothing but his gut and physical cues: the slightest tremor in the subject's voice, a hand gesture, an averted gaze.

"Oh, you've got one, all right," Jesse said.

"I don't know what you mean."

"I mean you were with Gómez at the exact time the murder was committed, six hours away from the crime scene. That's called an alibi."

Kevin managed an incredulous look, but his eyes avoided Jesse's. "I don't understand."

Jesse exhaled loudly. "You keep this up, Kevin, and you'll be going back to *Purgatorio* for a short stay before they bring you back, convict you, then strap you onto a gurney and stick the needle in."

Kevin started to rise, but lost his balance and fell back. "Bullshit, Jesse! Their case is all circumstantial, you told me so yourself."

Jesse exhaled, leaned back in his chair, feeling his way in. "See, Kevin, that's a mistake a lot of people make. Live witnesses come to court with their own motivations—fear, anger, prejudice, a desire for attention—and their own limitations, bad eyesight, hearing, I.Q., whatever. But circumstantial evidence doesn't lie. It just *is*. It comes into court without prejudice and tells its own quiet truth."

"This lecture is leading somewhere, teacher?"

"Okay, you want an example? A defendant denies being in a certain house, but his fingerprints are there in the bathroom. Who does the judge believe, the defendant or his fingerprints?"

Kevin lifted his hands to rub his eyes, rattling the chains that hung from his wrists down to a strap around his waist. He said nothing.

"You get the point, Kevin? If this defendant had told his lawyer the truth from the get-go, he and his lawyer could have talked about an innocent reason for his being in that room. Like maybe he had to use the facilities while being interviewed."

"I get the point."

"Really? What is the point, Kevin?"

"I should have admitted I was in her house."

"That's part of it," Jesse said, leaning into the prisoner. "The rest is that the truth will always come out, and when it does, it'll always bite you in the ass. But in this particular case, the truth can also set you free. Remember that one?"

"Of course I do. But in 'this particular case,' it can also get you killed."

Jesse stared at him until Kevin averted his eyes. "Gómez?" he said. "You're afraid Gómez will have you killed?"

Kevin threw out his hands in frustration and hunched over in his chair, his head in his hands. In a barely audible whisper, he said, "I can't say any more. There are too many people involved in this."

"Like who?"

Kevin just gave his head a little shake, and the room went silent but for an occasional wheezing sound from the guard at the door and the ticking of a large wall clock that was about seven hours slow. After a few minutes of this, Kevin looked up and said, "Well, *say* something, Jesse."

Jesse rose to his feet and stuffed his hands into his pockets. "I'm still trying to gain information, Kevin, and I've observed that people don't learn much while their lips are moving."

"I've told you all I can."

"Then you are seriously fucked, Kevin. If you won't admit you were with Gómez on April first, you are a dead man walking. I guarantee it."

Kevin looked down at his hands clutching one another. His mind seemed to be grappling with how much he should say. Finally, he leaned across the table as close to Jesse as he could get and lowered his voice. "All right, yes, Dad pressured me into going out there to hand Gómez a letter pulling out of the syndicate. Dad's associates had originally planned to take over the Central American drug market.

Gómez would cut out the Estevez cartel in Colombia and Dad was supposed to hold the line against the Italians based in the U.S."

"So you *are* in your father's organization?"

"God no! He's been saying he wants to get out of his . . . irregular activities now that CalCorp has taken off. But he couldn't come down himself and didn't trust anybody else to do it. Plus, Gómez wouldn't trust just anybody, either, but he would trust blood. So yes, I met with him and gave him a sealed envelope. That was all I did. I heard the news about Marisa's murder while I was with him."

Jesse stared at him. There it was. But was it all?

"I know I should have told you all this at the start, but I knew you'd want to try to bring him in if I did. Dad would never allow that."

"You'd rather die in Guatemala than disobey your father?"

"I owe him. Everything I have and am is because he's always stood by me."

"Okay, Kevin, but tell me this: why wouldn't Cal allow Gómez to testify if it would save your life, *if* he's really out of the drug business anyway? What would be left to hide? You see my logic?"

Kevin shook his head more violently. "I've said too much already. You don't know Gómez. He's got people everywhere, and he kills and tortures for the pure pleasure it gives him. He will kill me before the government can get around to it—and he won't use a sterilized needle."

Kevin buried his face in his hands. Silence. Abruptly, Jesse rose and said, "I can't help you if you keep lying to me, Kevin. Nobody can."

Kevin stared at his hands and, again, his head rolled from side to side on sagging shoulders. Jesse had never admired the kind of lawyer who shoots the dead, but he forced himself to keep applying pressure. "*Answer me, Kevin!*"

Kevin squirmed in his chair, rubbed his eyes again, and Jesse could see the internal battle raging inside his head. When he began speaking, the words came at first as if yanked out with pliers, then in a torrent.

"All right. Yes . . . you're right. Dad . . . wasn't backing out of the deal. I thought he was, and that's the truth. But the envelope I hand-delivered to Gómez turned out to contain the names of U.S. distributors—proof that Dad's group could deal five times what he'd been doing before and ten times what the Italians could."

"The Italian mafia is in Guate?"

"The mafia's in trouble, looking for ways to survive, and they were trying to muscle in on Dad's deal. The Chinese, too. Anyway, the risks are high, but this new deal will be huge. Gómez likes Dad and it's all going to work out."

"It sounds like you might be in it, too, Kevin."

"*No way!*" Kevin said with such intensity that Jesse somehow believed him. "I did this one thing, because he asked me to. I hate what he's been doing, but he's my father, dammit! He swore this would be his last caper and once he struck the deal, he'd sell out his interest, run his company, and build more schools for people with hearing disabilities. And I believe him!"

Cal. What a bastard. He had everybody fooled, his own son, even Simon Bradshaw. Kevin was just another victim, possibly going to his death for a murder he didn't commit. Jesse shuddered, contemplating the conversation he would have to have with Simon.

"Okay," Jesse said, putting aside his frustration. "How were they going to pull it off? Taking out the Estevez cartel *and* keeping the Italian mafia at bay is a tall order, even for Gómez and your father's organization."

"Trust me, Jesse, you don't need to know any of this. It could get you killed."

"I'll be the judge of what I need to know. Who else is Gómez dealing with? Anyone in government?"

Kevin looked down and said nothing. Jesse waited, staring at the top of his client's head. Finally the young man began to speak again, but in that maddeningly slow, whisper of a voice. "I think someone pretty high up."

"Who?" Jesse asked, thinking *La Cofradía*. Or maybe Carano? Or the CIA? Or maybe the whole stinking rat pack in it together?

"I swear to God I don't know. What's more, I don't *want* to know."

Jesse looked at him and Kevin looked back. He was telling the truth at last, the whole truth, Jesse felt sure of it. "All right, Kevin."

The prisoner's shoulders dropped and he seemed to start breathing again. He rubbed his face hard. His chains rattled. "Well, Counselor?" he said, looking up at Jesse. "You know it all now, but I won't betray my father by involving Gómez. Isn't there some way we can win without him?"

Jesse frowned. Without the client's cooperation, the defense would fail. "I'll do my best, but it won't be easy. It's a different game here."

"You have no other strategy?"

Jesse shrugged. "Strategy? Defending a case like this is like trying to get into a locked building without a key. You push hard on the door, then you look for a window to climb in. No window? You make one, or you dig a trench under the foundation. Get me? You try everything, until you find what works. But without the alibi, I'll need your hands on the shovel from now on, okay? I can't do this alone."

Kevin nodded, his eyes alive again. "There'll be no more lies, because I have no more secrets. But what have we got to go on?"

"Well, thanks to Teo, we can neutralize the witness who claimed to see you leaving the house. And we've got Marisa's message pointing to Carl Webster, as well as his sudden disappearance. And maybe we can trace money from Carano to Webster. None of these separately will do the job, but together? Maybe. The problem is we've got a Carano-picked panel that can do what they want in the absence of an alibi."

Kevin nodded again, his eyes coming back alive. "But we do have a shot?"

"A shot, if we can get your lead lawyer out of jail."

Jesse felt tired to the bone. He had a killer headache that had spread to his teeth. His legs felt encased in iron. Everything seemed upside down in Guatemala City. He felt like Alice, litigating in Wonderland from the bottom of the rabbit hole, about to stand before a corrupt panel of judges, laboring under a threat by the head of government. He was miles from home, representing an innocent messenger for a gangster who happened to be his law firm's White Knight and savior. On top of that, his co-counsel was in custody, suspected of murder, and he was getting no help from anybody except his adversary.

Beam me the hell out of here, Scotty, he thought, and walked as fast as he could toward the fresh, clear air outside.

DAY TEN

21

JESSE AWOKE EARLY and called Simon Bradshaw, trying to keep the desperation out of his voice. "I'm telling you, Simon, the rumors about Cal are true! Kevin met with a drug lord near here to confirm Cal's participation in a huge new syndicate."

"And I told you to ignore those rumors. Covington is aggressive, but he's not a criminal. You must have misunderstood the boy."

"It's the truth, Simon, from Kevin's own lips. He didn't realize the message he was delivering until Gómez opened the letter in front of him."

"Kevin handed over the letter himself? He told you this?"

"Reluctantly. He loves the old fraud. I'm sorry about this, Simon. I know you'll have to get rid of Covington and CalCorp now, but the lying sack of shit took us all for a ride. I'm as upset about it as you are, but I'd like to see this through. The kid is innocent. Can we continue on a *pro bono* basis?"

The silence from the other end was so prolonged Jesse thought he'd been disconnected. Then he heard breathing. Jesse knew he was asking a lot, especially having just burst Simon's bubble. And maybe his own dream of making partner.

"I'll take it up with ExComm tomorrow," came the voice from the other end. "Meanwhile, keep all this new information to yourself. I'll deal with it."

Jesse could hear the frustration in the senior partner's voice and tried to keep his own anger in check. "I really am sorry about CalCorp, Simon. I realize this puts the firm in a bind."

But Bradshaw had hung up.

. . .

IN SAN FRANCISCO, as Simon Bradshaw clicked the speaker phone off, the man across from him calmly sipped a Coca-Cola.

"Good Lord, Calvin," Bradshaw said. "Is he right? A *drug* syndicate?"

"It don't matter what Jesse Hall thinks he heard," said Covington. "His hands are tied, bound by silence. He's my lawyer, just like you are."

Simon noted that Cal hadn't answered his question. Careful, he warned himself. "Not necessarily, Cal. Technically, lawyers are not barred from revealing client information when necessary to prevent the commission of a new crime."

"Present company excluded, right, Cy ol' buddy?"

Bradshaw felt himself turn pale. The firm's life flashed before his eyes; everything he and his father had accomplished was suddenly an unendurable weight resting on his shoulders. What to do? If he could somehow hang on for just two more months, attract some new clients, cut some costs, and then cut CalCorp, too?

"Yes . . . yes, of course, Cal. Present company excluded." But Simon couldn't let it rest this way. "But Jesse has . . . heard things. So, well, uhh . . . hypothetically . . . and just assuming for sake of argument that there was, say, a grain of truth in what your son told Jesse, perhaps it might not be too late for you to . . . well, unwind any such hypothetical operation down there?"

Cal gently placed the empty Coke bottle down on Bradshaw's desk. He rose to his feet and brushed some wayward cracker crumbs from his trousers. He then hitched his massive shoulders and smiled down at the still-seated Bradshaw.

"That boy of yours has become a liability, Cy. He's a loose cannon, a threat to all of us. He's been nosing around in my personal business like a dog chasing a meat wagon. I need you to make him stop. Now!"

"It's just his nature, Cal. Jesse's always been . . . obsessively thorough."

The smile disappeared, replaced by a cold glare. "Bull*shit*, Cy. He's an obsessively thorough *problem* is what he is. I heard you tell him you would 'deal with it,' so get off your ass and goddam deal with it, with *him!* If you won't, by God, *I* will."

.   .   .

JESSE ENTERED THE courtroom for a crucial procedural hearing he would be allowed to argue in Teo's absence and exchanged with Elena a look that evinced both their attraction and inner conflict. Jesse asked about Teo's status, and Elena assured him he had been transferred to the courthouse and that Jesse could see him after court. Just then, the judges marched in, and the spectators, fewer than before, were quickly subdued into silence by a hard look from Judge Chavez. Kevin was brought in and pushed into a seat. He managed a wan smile and Jesse smiled back. Chavez told them to proceed, and from that point on, Jesse felt like Alice again, right back in Wonderland.

Most bizarre was Elena's performance. Even the judges were

giving her looks. She seemed to be tanking the motions; total rollover. She had previously thrown him an occasional bone, but this was a whole side of beef. Yes, they had been intimate, but Elena was too professional to allow that to influence her. Something was up.

The hearing resulted in several orders, all favorable to the defense, including one permitting Jesse a continuation of full standing at the bar so long as Teo Andrade remained in custody. This was an unprecedented waiver of a Constitutional provision, but with no objection by the prosecution and with the press watching, Judge Chavez had no choice but to go along with Jesse's motion.

Yeah, something was definitely wrong. In fact, the whole situation was getting nuttier by the minute. Kevin was rejecting a valid alibi that could free him and Elena was taking a dive on issues that could convict him. *Both Kevin and his prosecutor seemed bent on losing their cases!*

What was he missing? It was like a dream in which he was in the backseat of a speeding car, with Elena and his client taking turns at the wheel.

Afterward, Jesse came up behind Elena as she was leaving the courtroom and took her firmly by the arm. She turned, smiled, and said, "Good job in there."

Jesse said, "I appreciate the compliment, Elena, but Donald Duck could have won those motions the way you were rolling over. What's going on?"

Elena's smile faded and color rose in her cheeks, but a man was passing by, so she hesitated before speaking, briefcase in one hand, the other on her hip. When the stranger was a safe distance away, she turned on Jesse, her dark eyes popping. "*Rolling over?* What are you suggesting, Counselor? That I'm sacrificing my career and principles on the altar of your dazzling personality? You obviously have a low opinion of me, and an inflated opinion of yourself."

"Hold on, Elena. I just wanted to be sure nobody had, well, threatened you into going easy on me. Kevin's father wields considerable power."

But she had stormed off toward the elevator.

One thing was certain: his ability to alienate women he cared about knew neither geographical nor ethnic boundaries.

22

JESSE RETURNED TO his room and busied himself with appeals to the police on Teo's behalf that went unheeded, attempts to speak with Anastacia Ramirez that were rebuffed, and calls to Elena Ruiz that went unanswered. In between, he drank Pepsi and nibbled at a dry *casadilla* he had picked up on the way back from court. He had never felt so lonely, but he resolved to back off from Elena. He'd be leaving Guate soon and, for better or for worse, his heart still belonged—would always belong—to Megan Harris, even if she was finished with him. Then he put thoughts of both women aside; there wasn't enough time to try a tough case and engage in unrequited love affairs with two women at the same time.

The phone rang. It was Elena, telling him he could see Teo at 1:15.

"Thanks, Elena, and I'm sorry about irritating you earlier today."

"Irritating me? I don't know what you mean. That must have been my bitchy twin, Irma."

Jesse laughed. "Which one am I talking to now?"

"The one who is always apologizing for the other one's defensive outburst. I've been . . . under pressure lately and sometimes bite the hand that is extended in friendship."

"Glad we're friends again, because I need a huge favor."

"Let me guess. You want me to intercede in your co-counsel's behalf."

"Always a step ahead. Look, Elena. It's not because Kevin needs him. You and I know that Kevin is probably better off with me defending him alone now that I've been allowed to. But Teo will die if we don't get him out. How about bail? You know he won't run."

Jesse heard the rustling of papers, could feel her discomfort. "We do not like to encroach on the province of the police."

"I'm *begging* you, Elena. I think his heart will fail him."

"I will think about it, Jesse," she said, "but I must go."

. . .

LATER, WITH THE hood of a sweatshirt covering his head, Jesse reached the *Torre de Tribunales*, unrecognized by the protestors. He presented his card to the guard at the back entrance and was again escorted to a small prisoner interview room smelling of stale tobacco and Lysol. Fluorescent lighting contributed to the room's bleak mood.

After two loud raps on the door, a guard entered with Teo Andrade in tow. He was handcuffed, but his legs were not manacled.

"Jesse, is that you? Thank God you've come. May I go home? How is Anica? Have they found Webster? What day is today?"

The older man's skin was the same dull vanilla color as the walls that surrounded them. He looked ill and shaky, and Jesse suspected he was indeed going through cold-turkey detox. His beard, usually neatly trimmed, was scraggy, and his eyes were a hazy rainbow of yellowish-white, rimmed in red. They seemed to have been sucked back into his skull, leaving black pockets that hung in folds over his cheeks. He smelled of perspiration and old booze.

"Slow down, Teo. Anica is fine, no sign of Webster, and you won't have to go back to *Purgatorio*. But I'm afraid you won't be released today."

The glimmer of hope in Teo's eyes faded, and Jesse reflected on how quickly prison could drain the life out of a man without actually killing him. They sat in silence, Jesse letting Teo shape the direction of their conversation. "Unspeakable horrors," the older man murmured, then appeared to drift off.

"Come again?" Jesse said. Teo seemed to have forgotten he was there.

"*Purgatorio!*" He shouted. "The rotten bastards!" Then, abruptly changing course, he said, "I'm sorry I didn't tell you about watching Webster." He stared angrily at his hands as if they had been responsible for the concealment. "I knew you would be worried about what I might do."

Teo seemed confused and disoriented. Jesse said, "Which was?"

Teo's eyes met Jesse's, then he lowered them again into his clenched hands. "Depending on what I learned and, eventually, what Webster had to say for himself, I suppose I could envision a circumstance that might have involved some sort of . . . physical retribution." He paused before continuing. "For God's sake, Jesse, Webster killed my wife! He must have killed his girl, too. Why the hell would *I* kill her?"

"Mistakes happen," Jesse said, and instantly regretted it.

Teo shook his head violently. "I swear, Jesse. I was as stunned as you by what we found. I thought at first it *was* Webster in the bedroom, so did you. And yes, I will admit I *hoped* it was Webster. *But I didn't kill that girl.*"

He met Jesse's eyes with an unwavering gaze and leaned in closer.

"I am one of the few people in Guatemala City who does not carry a gun. I've never fired or even owned one. The police won't find one unless they plant it."

Jesse nodded.

"It is unbecoming to admit it, Jesse, but I am . . . afraid. Afraid that such evil I've seen exists! These men in authority are capable of demonic cruelty. *Christ*, my head is, uh . . . oh, God. How is Anica . . . does the evidence look bad for me?"

"Anica is fine, and the evidence is weak. All they have are your suspicious stakeouts of Webster's house. Carano is just putting another obstacle in our path."

Teo agreed and they sat in silence for a minute before he spoke again.

"Are you ever afraid, Jesse?"

"Me? Sure. Megan used to say that anyone who runs as fast as I do all day and night must be afraid of something."

"Well, I'm afraid of what Carano is going to do to me and Anica. The man is a contagion, a cancer cell that has proliferated throughout the body of our country. I had no idea how far it had spread. I have seen horrors in *Purgatorio* I never dreamed could exist. My head is . . . is . . . am I making any sense?"

"Yes, of course you are, and I know what you mean. To know a country, you've got to know its prisons."

"What they do to people, to fellow human beings . . . it *must* not be allowed to stand. If Aguilera fails, maybe Gómez is the answer after all."

"Are you serious?"

"I met many of his followers in prison. They admit he's a savage, but claim he is also a saint, that his intentions are to rescue and reform our poor country."

"Okay, but let's take things a step at a time."

"Can you get me out?"

"You know Guate has no *habeas corpus*, Teo. But I'm talking to Elena."

"What's going to happen with the case in the meantime?"

"It's going as scheduled. I could get a delay, but Carano might deport me at any time, plus Kevin can't take much more abuse in prison. Elena and the Tribunal have agreed under the circumstance to let me be standup until you get out."

Teo managed a self-deprecating smile. "Maybe it's best for Kevin's case if I stay right here. You decide."

23

JESSE HEADED BACK to his room to check for messages and to continue his preparation for trial. At 4:15 in the afternoon, his phone rang.

"Jesse? It is me, Teo."

"Teo!" Jesse could hear the slurring in Teo's speech. He had been drinking, but that meant he had been released. "You're *out?*"

"Yes, I am temporarily free, but is it not wonderful what has happened? Perhaps there is hope for our country yet."

"Teo, slow down. What are you talking about?"

"You obviously have not seen the afternoon newspaper. Go downstairs and get a copy, then call me. And Jesse, I regret the consequences to the case."

Teo hung up before Jesse could ask him what he meant. Jesse hurried downstairs to the gift shop and saw the *Globe's* headline even before he could grab a copy off the rack.

LOCAL PROFESSOR VALIDATES RUMORS

OF ANCIENT LAND GRANT TO MAYAN DESCENDANTS

Jesse ran back upstairs to his room and scanned to the end of the story.

> *"Professor José Linares Cruz, who is head of the history department at San Carlos University, added, 'It reflects an intention by the Emperor Charles V to dedicate all land in Guatemalan—land located west of what we now know as longitude 90°40' West—to the indigenous people of this country. This includes Antigua.'"*

Antigua and nearly half the country! Christ, no wonder the upper-crust were upset by the rumor.

> *"Linares added that the signature and seal appeared to be that of Charles V."*

Jesse paused to consider the consequences of this claim and concluded that Teo had been wrong in thinking it would screw up their case. In fact, this authentication would strengthen Jesse's argument that Carano had needed to stop Marisa Andrade before she and *La Causa* could raise the money to buy the document and make it public. Throw in the Carlos V clue pointing to Carl Webster and the money trail from Carano to Webster, and not even these three judges would be able to ignore the Vice President's complicity—particularly with the world press looking on.

Jesse's phone kept ringing, but he kept reading. Professor Linares Cruz opined that the emperor's motivation in granting the land was guilt for the atrocities that Hernán Cortéz had perpetrated against the Maya, that having charged Cortéz with murder and genocide was insufficient to expiate his, the emperor's, guilt. Then Jesse read the last line of the article:

> *"Many will now justifiably conclude that there is no reason why the order from Carlos V should not now belatedly be carried out."*

The Emperor-King's name—Carlos V—was like a rope that someone had jerked, starting a motor that sent his mind roaring out to sea, carrying Kevin's defense with it. Now he knew why Teo had expressed regrets. The phone was still ringing. He knew it was Teo.

"Well?" came the cautious voice. "What do you think?"

"I'll be there in fifteen minutes," Jesse said. "We need to talk."

. . .

JULIO AND ANICA disappeared up the stairs as Jesse passed through Teo's front door, his thoughts still tumbling one into the other. Carmen greeted him, and Teo motioned him into his study. The older man's face was glowing, but he managed to give Jesse a sympathetic look.

"Tell me you're not thinking that Marisa was referring to the Emperor Charles the Fifth?" Jesse said.

Teo nodded. "In her last moments, she indeed affirmed the authenticity of the land grant, signed by the Emperor Carlos Quinto. Carlos V."

"*Jesus*, Teo, that's not what people do when they're dying. They name their killer if they can and she *did!* Besides, both Anica and Anastacia say that Marisa had cooled to the land grant the morning she died, remember?"

Teo shook his head. "Anica misunderstood her mother and Anastacia is untrustworthy on this issue. She has opposed the land grant from the beginning."

"As have most rational people."

"You are wrong. Face it, Jesse, she spelled out 'Carlos V'—not 'Carl W.'"

"Yes, Teo, but why not stick with the Carl Webster interpretation so that we can win our case, and let Linares Cruz fight the authentication battle later?"

"No, Jesse. The land grant is too important to the upcoming election and to my country. Marisa's courageous dying declaration will now be seen as corroborating Linares Cruz, *La Causa* will acquire the original letter, and Aguilera will be able to unite the Mayan majority. We will finally be rid of Carano! Short of killing him myself, I could have no sweeter revenge."

Jesse paced over to the window, striving for clarity. He couldn't let this happen. "What's going on, Teo? Did you drink the *La Causa* Kool-Aid while you were in prison? What happened to the logical lawyer who once proclaimed the land grant to be a hoax?"

"Call it a foxhole conversion," Teo said, offering an ironic smile. "Although I was imprisoned for but a short time, I saw Carano's ARES thugs do things I did not know humans were capable of doing. The scales fell from my eyes. I was Paul on the road to Damascus." Teo carefully placed his glass on the small chest next to his chair. He lit a cigarette, then watched the flame of the match snake up the wood all the way to his fingers before blowing it out. "Marisa knew all this and wrote about it, while her husband crouched like a frightened child at recess with a class bully on the prowl."

Teo's brow furrowed and he took a deep drag on his smoke. "After her funeral, I sat that night on the edge of my cold coffin of a bed and wished I had been buried with her. I would have welcomed the cold earth in my mouth and ears, the worms feeding on my flesh."

Jesse could think of nothing to say.

"What I am trying to tell you, Jesse, is that I may have found a reason to live. Linares's authentication of the land grant has provided me a chance for redemption."

"Redemption," Jesse whispered, seeing their defense slipping away. He felt he had been racing a few yards ahead of an avalanche and had just lost a ski.

The phone rang and Teo took it in the kitchen. Jesse's joy over Teo's release had evaporated, and when Teo returned and offered him a drink, he readily accepted it. The phone kept ringing and Jesse saw that despite Teo's obvious fatigue, his eyes glowed with a new light.

"What's with all the phone calls?" Jesse said.

Teo leaned forward and hunched his shoulders. "It seems that my status as Marisa's widower, followed by my recent imprisonment, has conferred on me the imprimatur of minor martyrdom. I have accepted a seat on the governing board of *La Causa*. I intend to assist them in raising the money to acquire the land grant."

Jesse managed an encouraging smile, toasted his friend, but remembered why he drank so little. The depressive effect of the alcohol on top of the King Charles revelation was already bringing him down.

"That's a mighty weak basket for *La Causa* to put all its eggs in, Teo."

"Meaning?"

"Elena told me a while ago that Carano was happy about the land grant. I remember her exact words. She said, 'You'd think he had created the phony letter himself.' What if Aguilar and the reformers go ahead and bet everything on the land grant and Carano reveals it to be a fake just before the election? Aguilera would be dead in the water."

"But that was before Linares Cruz's opinion. He is an authority of great repute."

"Okay. What if he's right, but then the land grant is deemed unenforceable by the courts under existing Guatemalan law?"

Teo hitched his shoulders. "Constitutional law is not my forte and I suppose that is a possibility. On the other hand, Charles as former King of Spain, and then Holy Roman Emperor, certainly had the power to return the land to the Indians at the time he wrote the document and he obviously intended to do so."

"Jesus, Teo, that was five hundred years ago!"

"You are missing the point, Jesse. Whether our Constitutional Court accepts the document or not, it will serve as a dramatic symbol and rallying point for the Mayan candidate's followers. He can use it as a bargaining chip to promote his reforms. The Ladinos *Congreso* will accept them to avoid division of the country. And to think we owe it all to Linares Cruz, an arrogant anti-Catholic agnostic, a scoundrel and a liar with a gambling problem."

Jesse stared at him. "A scoundrel and a *liar*? Then why—"

"Do not misunderstand me. Professor Linares Cruz is highly regarded, the top man in his field in all of Central America. My assessment of his integrity is purely personal, and I don't care to revisit it."

Jesse slapped the arms of his chair in frustration. "Look, Teo. We're *lawyers,* remember? There is no higher duty on earth than that owed by a lawyer to his client and our main hope for winning this case has been the money trail plus tying the Carlos V clue to Webster! You're ready to piss it all away?"

Teo applied a hand to his forehead. "Now I know how my poor students felt. Must I endure a lecture on legal ethics?"

"You apparently need one. I understand what this land grant could mean to your country if it's real, but are you ready to sacrifice our client's life because a guy you describe as a 'scoundrel' and a 'liar' talked to a reporter about some dead king who might or might not have written a letter in Spain five hundred years ago dug up under mysterious circumstances near Antigua that you admit might or might not even be adopted by the courts even if it is real? *Jesus*, listen to yourself!"

His inhibitions loosened by rum, Jesse ended his peroration by slamming his hand down on Teo's desk, upending a clock and an ashtray full of butts. "Sorry," he said.

Teo slumped forward in his chair, elbows on knees. He looked up and gazed at Jesse with red-rimmed eyes filled with anguish.

"Tell me, my young friend, how I am to balance the life of one American mobster's son against the killing fields of the past and a renewed civil war if Carano is not deposed? Isn't thirty-six years of death and destruction enough?"

Julio, whom Jesse assumed had been eavesdropping on the staircase, entered the room, barely suppressing a smile. Jesse took the kid in, all pumped up like a gamecock. Probably just got laid upstairs and then heard that Teo was seeing things his way downstairs. His buoyancy made Jesse feel suddenly older than his twenty-nine years.

"Am I interrupting something?" Julio asked.

"No, no, Julio, come in," Teo said, straightening his shoulders. Jesse sensed an improved relationship between Julio and the older man. "I believe that our American guest was about to answer a question I put to him."

Jesse felt himself succumbing to despair. The case, and Kevin's life, would be lost now, as would CalCorp's business and his partnership. A no-win situation for everybody except, perhaps, Victor Carano. "I don't know how to deal with that kind of question, Teo," he said, "but I do think you're getting sucked in. Will you at least schedule a meeting with Linares Cruz? Give me a chance to quiz him a little."

Teo frowned. "I will do it, but as you know, he and I are not on the best of terms."

"Yet you say you respect him professionally? What happened between you?"

"Again, I'd rather not say."

"Will you say whether you're still on the case with me?"

"Of course. I still think Carano ordered Marisa's murder. Moreover, I gave you my word, did I not? I know this damages our defense, but there are other things we can do."

Other things we can do. Jesse had been thinking about that, but didn't like where it was taking him. Still, he couldn't let Kevin be victimized by Carano's thugs in judicial gowns, so when the phone rang again, he said, "Go ahead and take the call, Teo, I need to talk to Julio about something."

"I will be brief."

Jesse opened his briefcase and took out a map of eastern Guatemala.

"Point out where your uncle's encampment is, Julio."

"Why would you want to know that and why would I tell you?"

"Look, Julio. Maybe we got off on the wrong foot, but help me out here, okay? I just want to meet him."

Julio shrugged, studied the map, and indicated a general area. "It's public knowledge that his farm headquarters is generally northwest of a tiny town called Livingston, home of the *Garífuna*. But it is accessible only by air or water."

"Would you be willing to take me there?"

Julio shook his head furiously. "I could not do that."

"All right, then, how would I go about getting there?"

"I cannot tell you that, either, but I ask you again, why would you want to? A few days ago you were reading me your own State Department's warning about the extreme danger in *Río Dulce*."

"I know, and it's not that I want to go there, but that I may have to. It seems Señor Gómez could give Kevin Covington an alibi. Now that we've got this Spanish king in the picture, Kevin's as good as dead if he doesn't have one."

Julio said nothing, just stared at Jesse as if he were crazy.

"Just give me a rough map, Julio, and maybe smooth the way a little with your uncle; you know, the old 'he comes in peace' routine. Think about it, Julio. If Kevin loses, it's a victory for Victor Carano, which could hurt Miguel Aguilera."

Julio shook his head. "In the first place, *El Cobra* would never come in to testify."

"Just get me in to see him."

"You would be wasting your time and risking your life."

"Maybe, but I have to try. How do I see him?"

Julio stroked his incipient mustache and stared outside. "By invitation," he said at last. "If he wants to see you, he will send someone for you. If you insist, I will get word to him of your desire, but he will want to know why you want to talk with him."

Jesse thought for a minute. "Tell him I am the personal lawyer for Señor Cal Covington, and am coming owing to the unfortunate circumstances that have inconvenienced his son. Tell him it's a business meeting. Can you do that?"

"I think you would be more effective staying right here, Jesse. Anica is afraid the PNC could take Teo away again at any minute. It's the way they do things in Guatemala—take you, let you go, take you."

"I'll keep working on his problem. Will you help me with mine?"

Julio glanced toward the kitchen, from which they could hear Teo on the phone and whispered, "Teo really didn't kill anybody, did he?"

Jesse paused, sipped the coffee he had switched to. "I don't think so. I'm not sure of anything right now. But he's my friend and I won't leave Guatemala until we get things sorted out."

"We need him, Jesse. All of Guatemala needs him. *La Causa* has been failing since Marisa's murder and Miguel Aguilera is trailing badly at the polls. But with this new endorsement by Professor Linares, and Teo willing to speak out, we will surely be able to raise enough money to acquire the land grant, and with it, victory."

Jesse said, "I'm sorry, Julio, but I'm more suspicious than ever that the whole thing is a con. I can't prove the letter's a phony, however, any more than you can prove it's real. Anyway, I'd like to visit with your uncle and try to persuade him to come in and testify. It's all Kevin's got left."

Julio considered this, reached for his coffee cup. "I must warn you, Jesse," he said, lowering his voice, "my uncle can be . . . moody."

"I'd be careful not to push him."

"You aren't thinking of subpoenaing him are you?"

"No," Jesse lied. "We'll reason together. I'll use logic."

"What possible logic would compel Arturo Gómez to come into court?"

"I'll try to persuade him that the trial, with the world press present, would provide him the perfect forum to show the world he is a true revolutionary, not just a drug thug. He can exploit the opportunity to push his program for reform. While he's at it, he could sling a few barbs at Victor Carano, which would help your guy, Aguilera. If none of that works, I'd have to dazzle him with wit and charm."

Julio smiled. "I've been meaning to tell you your Spanish sucks."

"Worse than my English?"

"I'm serious, Jesse, he can be . . . impulsive."

"I'll tell him I have told the police and the American Consulate that I've gone to see him. If something would happen to me, everybody would know why."

Julio laughed. "You can't deal logically with *El Cobra*. And if you upset him, particularly in the presence of his men, it could be bad for you. He hates *gringos,* and draws a parallel between Cortéz's atrocities and your CIA's invasion in 1954."

Jesse started to reply, but Anica shouted to Julio from upstairs. "Okay," Julio told Jesse while pulling a cell phone from his pocket, "I'll give it a try."

Julio headed upstairs and Jesse tried to calm himself by picking up a book and not reading it. Ten minutes later, Julio returned with a look of surprise, a thumbs-up, and instructions on how the meeting would come about. He then went back upstairs.

Teo returned to his study, glowing with excitement. He clapped a hand on Jesse's shoulder. "We were about to discuss what we should do next."

Jesse laid the book back on Teo's desk. "I've been thinking about that. Let's meet with Professor Linares Cruz day after tomorrow so I can see if he really believes the things I read in the article. Meanwhile, Julio has set me up to see our alibi witness tomorrow morning, but I should be back by nightfall."

Teo blinked. "*Gómez?* I'll arrange the interview with Linares, but attempting to reason with Gómez would be madness. You would be in great danger."

"I don't have a whole lot of choices here, Teo, not if I can't match Carl Webster to Carlos V. We need an alibi. Julio says that Gómez's man will pick me up tomorrow and fly me out of a private airport into an airstrip at *Río Dulce.* I'll go upriver from there."

Jesse suddenly felt overcome by a deep fatigue and anxiety. But there was anger, too. Anger at Cal Covington, at Simon Bradshaw, at his lying client, at Teo, at the judges, and most of all, anger at himself for his own hubris and naiveté.

"The man cannot be trusted, Jesse. They call him *El Cobra* because he's such a snake."

"I've heard," Jesse said, sounding more courageous than he felt. "So I suppose I'll have to be *El Mongoose.*"

DAY ELEVEN

24

AT 5:30 IN the morning, Jesse waited in a small fluorescent-lit shack at a private landing strip located at the back of *La Aurora* International Airport. Julio had dropped him there at five without cell phone, recording device, or day pack, as instructed.

He was alone in the tiny, windowless office. On the walls were reassuring weather maps and flight schedules, but a part of him questioned his judgment in coming. He had arranged to have a sealed letter delivered to Teo noting his intentions with directions to deliver a copy to Elena Ruiz if he did not return in thirty-six hours. He included a separate letter to *La Prensa* and the *Guatemala Globe*. It wasn't much, but a poor backup plan was better than none.

Jesse walked outside and gazed skyward. Despite everything, this crazy, beautiful, war-scarred country was growing on him. He stood transfixed, watching the first gauzy light ease up over the eastern horizon, backlighting the surrounding volcanoes in stark profile. Jesse stared in awe as these craggy borders began to turn a dull yellow-orange, then a glowing gold. Then the sun rose, flaming red, subjugating a line of low stratus clouds that blanketed its path. He shivered, contemplating the danger that lurked below the surreal beauty of that horizon.

A mechanic shambled into a corrugated steel hanger off to his right and slammed the door shut. A metallic echo, then silence reigned again, broken only by the high-pitched roar of a commercial jet taxiing for takeoff.

Another five minutes passed, and just as he was thinking about looking for a pay phone and calling Julio, he heard a car pull up outside. The office door opened, revealing a small black man with a skull-like face and eyes like bottomless pits, who entered and identified himself, in English, as "the one you wait for." Jesse knew that the wiry little man was probably a *Garífuna*, one of the black Caribs whose descendants had escaped slave boats shipwrecked in the 1600s. The survivors had intermarried with local *Kalipuna* natives and set up a community in Livingston, near where Gómez's camp was rumored to be.

The *Garífuna* entered the office, slithered soundlessly into a plastic seat next to Jesse, and lapsed into silence. His clothes reeked of body odor and tobacco smoke. A fan rotated lazily overhead. Jesse's efforts to elicit the plan for the day went nowhere.

After nearly thirty minutes of maddening silence, Jesse managed to pry out of the skull-like face that the weather was *muy malo* at their destination. Good, at least the trip was still on.

At 6:45 a.m., the *Garífuna's* cell phone rang. After a brief conversation in a dialect Jesse couldn't understand, he clicked off and walked out, the old screen door slamming shut. In a few seconds, he came back and motioned Jesse to follow. While they walked, the man announced that the bad weather meant no flying today. They would have to drive to *Río Dulce* and take a boat to Livingston, then on to "the farm." He expertly patted Jesse down, but missed the subpoena folded in Jesse's back pocket.

"Okay," the driver grunted. "Come."

The little man hopped behind the wheel of an older, but meticulously maintained, black Mercedes sedan. Jesse was encouraged to see a statuette of the Virgin Mother on the dash with large fake pearls draped around her shoulders.

"Front seat okay," the man instructed, and off they went, tires spitting gravel, presumably headed for *Río Dulce*, a place Teo had described as a dangerous scab hanging on the wounded body of Guatemala's east coast. Jesse shivered, partly from the cold, wet morning, but mainly from his growing uneasiness.

"*¿Qué es su nombre?*" Jesse tried again, and when he got no answer decided to think of him simply as the Skull. "Nice car," he added, also in Spanish. "Love these old stick shifts."

Nothing, not even a blink of an eye.

Within an hour they were in the countryside, driving by roadside stands selling pineapples and plantains, often next to tiny shacks cobbled together from discarded scrap lumber, tree limbs, and the odd piece of corrugated scrap metal. Scrawny chickens and small herds of cattle so thin they looked like goats wandered among ancient ruins, and Mayan women balancing huge bundles on their heads trudged along the side of the road, seemingly unmindful of the speeding traffic that occasionally sprayed them with filthy water. Jesse saw a group of kids around ten to twelve years of age with blocks of cement on their heads and asked the Skull where they were going. To Jesse's surprise the Skull broke his silence. "To school," he said. "Those are their desks."

. . .

AFTER THEIR SECOND hour on the road, Jesse realized he had
seen not a single car. Even the ubiquitous Texaco, Shell, and Coca-
Cola signs—the only vestiges of Western culture outside Guatemala
City—had disappeared, but Jesse could see forests everywhere
being leveled for cattle to be eventually transmuted into American
hamburgers. The Skull followed Jesse's eyes and he said in English,
"No more tree. September come. Ground all wash away."

"Can't the government stop this?"

The *Garífuna* seemed not to hear him, but minutes later, he nodded
his head and said, "Gómez, he stop it. He stop a lot of thing."

Though spoken in almost a whisper, the words sent a chill racing
down Jesse's spine. *He hates gringos*, Julio had warned. After that, the
driver said nothing for the next two hours, leaving Jesse to anxiously
speculate on Gómez's reaction to the subpoena.

Deep into the third hour of travel, Jesse gave in to the exhaustion
that had been building since his arrival in Guatemala City and fell
asleep. When he awoke, he saw that they were paralleling a huge body
of water. *Ceiba* and palm trees guarded the shore.

"*¿Dónde estamos nosotros?*" Jesse said.

"*Eso es Lago de Izabal.*"

After nearly five hours on the road, the car stopped near a
ramshackle boat dock, next to which stood a rickety, windowless,
metal boathouse and a junked-out Ford coupe. A wooden ladder
leaned against the building, under which a pair of gaunt dogs fought
over a bleached white bone, kicking up a cloud of stifling dust.

The Skull grabbed a pistol out of the glove compartment of the
Mercedes, stuck it in his belt behind his back, and told Jesse to get
out. The heat was suffocating, and other than the scuffling dogs, utter

silence reigned. Two men waited near an outboard motorboat. One looked like an American hippie, with a shaved head, a rakish red bandana around his neck, a gold earring in his ear, and a prematurely white beard. The other one was a muscular Indian whose shoulders covered two time zones and who wore nothing above his waist but a perpetual scowl. A nine-millimeter automatic handgun hung at the end of a huge right forearm and fist.

Jesse, feeling every bit a prisoner, took a chance and spoke English to the white-bearded man. "Will I see Señor Gómez this afternoon?"

The man gave Jesse an enigmatic smile. "*Quizás,*" he said in Spanish, with an American accent much like Jesse's. The guy is from the U.S., thought Jesse. What the hell is he doing here? Doesn't Gómez hate all Anglos?

Jesse said, "Did Señor Gómez tell you that I'm an attorney for Señor Calvin Covington?"

White Beard shrugged and said, "Who the fuck is Calvin Covington?"

The Skull ordered Jesse into a small boat powered by an Evinrude outboard motor. The Indian took a seat in the bow and White Beard, wearing the same sardonic grin on his face, beckoned Jesse to sit next to him in the middle. The Skull pushed off and operated the boat from the stern. The *Garífuna's* only words to the two men consisted of a warning that Jesse spoke Spanish.

They began crossing *Lago de Izabal*, which was behaving more like an ocean. Undaunted, Skull speeded the boat up, through the whitecaps, until the bow began to pound the surf so hard it jarred Jesse's teeth.

A half hour later, when the rough water had settled down, the Indian removed some *jamón y queso* sandwiches from a plastic bag and handed them around. Jesse tried a bite, but became nauseated and gave his to the Indian.

"Look," shouted White Beard in a rare sociable gesture, "a Caribbean cow." A manatee—sleepy-eyed, ghostly grey, and the size of a small automobile—had surfaced to glare at their passing boat. Farther along, with a mangrove forest off to one side, Jesse spotted alligators, howler monkeys, and a small rock island, white with bird-shit and packed with scolding pelicans, hundreds of them jammed wing-to-wing while even more of the birds gracefully circled, looking for a spot to squeeze in.

Despite his anxiety and nausea, Jesse blinked with astonishment at such beauty in an area so notorious for its danger. They were approaching the Bay of Honduras, where cocaine and heroin from Colombia were routinely dropped from light aircraft in large plastic bags, fished out, and transported northward up the *Chocón* River toward the Yucatan and their U.S. destination.

Jesse shivered, noticing that the sun had surrendered to a giant curtain of ominous clouds that had all the makings of a squall in the Bay of Honduras.

"Push it, Ozo!" White Beard shouted, but the Skull ignored White Beard except to instruct him it was time to "hood the gringo."

"What are you talking about?" Jesse said.

"Be cool," White Beard said and gingerly moved behind Jesse. "It's routine. Orders. All visitors to the *Commandante's* farm are blindfolded for the last hour. No exceptions."

Jesse started to argue, but the big man threw a black hood over his head and pulled it down, completely covering Jesse's face. A pull-string secured the hood snug around his neck. Jesse told himself to breathe. In, out, in, out. Stay calm. At least he knew they must be getting close to Gómez's camp. The sea, however, was getting rougher, and Jesse fought off another nausea attack. A series of waves rocked the boat, bouncing him hard from side to side. He realized that the boat was going in circles and half-circles, apparently to disorient him. But once the boat straightened, Jesse could sense that waves were pushing from his right, which meant they were headed north toward Belize, rather than south in the direction of Honduras.

Within minutes, the wave action became even rougher, and Jesse felt water splashing into the boat.

"It's a squall!" shouted Ozo. "Eduardo! Help Moulas bail!"

"But the *Commandante's* orders—"

"Tape his fucking hands, you idiot. Hurry before we lose the fucking boat."

"You don't have to tape my hands," Jesse protested, his words muffled by the hood. "I *asked* to come here, remember?"

Nobody answered, and although the boat was being tossed about as if it were a toy, White Beard began to bind Jesse's hands behind his back with plastic tape.

"Don't let him tie me, Ozo!" Jesse shouted. "I can help bail!" Again, no response, but Jesse remembered that an oarlock was located on each side of the boat. He reached his hands back and found the welcome feel of cold steel. He covertly dropped his hands over the lock and began to saw the tape against the rough surface. Water had now risen well above his ankles. A wave of fear engulfed him when he realized that without a bilge pump or free ports, any water that entered the boat would stay there unless bailed by hand. He had seen neither buckets nor life preservers in the boat.

"Bail, Moulas!" Ozo shouted. "Use your hands!" By habit, Jesse took note of the men's names: Ozo the Skull, Edward White Beard the American, and Moulas the Indian. The *Tres Amigos.*

The squall was all over them now, the wind and rain relentlessly pounding. A wave exploded against the boat's frail hull, practically giving Jesse whiplash. He tried to stay calm, but vertigo and oxygen deprivation had made him light-headed and dizzy. Every time he inhaled too deeply, he sucked the inside of the wet hood against his nose or mouth, cutting off any intake of air.

"*Holy shit*, Ozo!" White Beard said. "We're going to flip over! Hold us straight into the waves!"

"I'm trying to, you fucking idiot!" Ozo yelled back.

Just when Jesse concluded things could not get much worse, the motor died, swamped by the heavy seas. No one said a word, no sound at all came from inside the boat while the men pondered their fate.

"Please, Ozo," Jesse shouted, "give me a chance." But there was no response. They would go down together, he quicker than the others. He was cold to the bone, exhausted, and terrified. His thoughts drifted to Megan, and he realized he might never see her again. He sawed all the harder against the steel oarlock.

Another wave crashed over the transom and water sloshed higher on his legs.

"We're going down!" White Beard shouted. "We better swim for it!"

Water poured into the boat and Jesse sawed even more desperately despite weakening arms and burning shoulders. The torrent of rain continued to pound against him, the water up nearly to his knees. They were sinking. A surge of adrenaline pushed him to a final effort, and he felt more strands of tape give way. How many layers could there be? With renewed hope he sawed frantically, praying his strength would hold out and he wouldn't suffocate from the sopping hood.

"Swim, Whitey!" screamed Ozo, and Jesse knew they were going down.

"Ozo!" Jesse shouted, his voice muffled by the hood. "*Cut me loose!*"

Eduardo started an apology, but the sea engulfed his words, and the boat rocked harder as they jumped. Then there was silence. He was alone in a sinking boat, his face covered, his hands bound.

More waves crashed over the transom, nearly knocking him out of the boat. The water was up over his knees now, the boat nearly submerged. But if he gave up on the oarlock and kicked free of the boat, how would he stay afloat? How would he even know where the shore was? And how long could he keep his head above water with his hands taped behind his back? His only chance was to stay with the oarlock, even if it took him down.

The water rose to his stomach, then to his neck. He took as deep a breath as he could manage and held it as his head went under. Down with the ship, he thought absurdly, and with all the strength he could muster, he jerked harder against the steel.

But the oarlock popped free of its anchorage and drifted down beneath him.

Shit, that cooked it. He was going to die here. His lungs were already starving for air. *He had to get to the surface*. He was forced to release air from his lungs, which made him sink faster, sucked downward by his lost buoyancy and his water-laden shoes and clothing. He kept kicking toward the surface, struggling not to breathe, but was soon in such agony that his body betrayed him and he instinctively gasped for air. . .and got water. White spots danced before his eyes. He was done for. Then, with his elbows still thrashing like the wings of a beheaded chicken, the last strand of tape snapped. His arms were free!

He pulled and kicked wildly, his lungs heaving. At last, amidst exploding whitecaps, his head bobbed to the surface and he ripped off the hood. He gagged up a plume of saltwater and was finally able to inhale his first burst of fresh air. Nothing had ever tasted so good.

But now what? He had no idea where he was or in which direction to go. He turned around in circles until, through sheets of falling rain, he saw the blurred outline of land. But he realized that at least a half-mile of devouring sea separated him from shore. He was freezing and exhausted and utterly alone. He rolled onto his back, stared into the merciless rain, and tried to will his leaden arms and legs to move.

25

JIM HAYDEL TOOK a seat across from Simon Bradshaw, met his eyes, and came out with it. "I've always been your guy, Simon. Supported you against Harry Reasoner when he tried to unseat you last year as the firm's chair and I'd do it again. I signed off on an SEC quarterly report yesterday that would qualify me for a Pulitzer in creative writing—or a stay in federal prison. You've got to pull the plug on CalCorp before the Justice Department pulls the plug on us."

Bradshaw listened quietly, elbows propped on the arms of his Tempur-Pedic chair, fingers steepled, choking down a touch of bile and wishing he hadn't forgotten to take his Nexium at dawn.

"We're moving way too fast, Simon. Opening a new branch office in Shanghai just because CalCorp has penetrated that market is risky. We've got too much riding on a highly questionable company."

Bradshaw stood up, turned to face his window wall, and gazed at a band of stratus clouds hanging just above his penthouse floor office. Lucy was right; he should see a specialist about his stomach. "What do you want from me, Jim? For six months, we have been one step ahead of having to shut down our branch offices in London, Paris,

Hong Kong, and Tokyo. Now they are all booming again *and* we've cracked the Chinese market. Why? Because CalCorp is dominant in all these places, providing us with instant credibility and billings, plus new client contacts. Shanghai is headquarters for Cal's Asian operations, which will soon mint money for CalCorp *and* us. Cal has brought in a business genius named Alan Cheng to run it. CalCorp stock is skyrocketing in the midst of a global recession, and we've just taken two million shares in lieu of cash as fees."

"Stock instead of cash? Shouldn't you have run this past the full partnership?"

Simon had never felt so exhausted. "Perhaps, but the stock has soared, so I'll happily take it in lieu of part of what the firm owes me if that's what they want. The point is that in a very few months, we'll be strong and independent again, at which time I will personally take great satisfaction in telling Cal Covington to go fuck himself!"

Haydel blinked. He'd never heard Bradshaw utter an expletive.

"Until then," Bradshaw continued, his tone softening, "we need Cal more than he needs us, so we'll just have to grin and bear it."

. . .

ON THE COASTLINE of the Bay of Honduras, Jesse was hurled headlong onto a rough, but welcome, solidity. He felt the grit of sand on his face and watched a sand crab skitter past his eyes. He was exhausted and hypothermic, but he had beaten them—Ozo, White Beard, even nature herself.

The rain had stopped, and the sky was clearing as quickly as it had darkened. He rolled over to face the erratic sun, but couldn't stop shaking.

Jesse took inventory. He had kicked his shoes off somewhere

during his struggle, but still had his shirt, his Dockers, and his wallet. He croaked out a laugh when he saw something else in his other back pocket, the drenched subpoena. He wouldn't need that now—he had no clue how to find Gómez's compound—but the money in his wallet could get him back to Guatemala City if he could make it to the small Livingston airfield they had originally intended to fly into. Maybe he could charter a plane there.

He coughed up some seawater, waited for the burning of the salt in his nose and sinuses to ease up. He had to get to Guatemala City for his appointment with Professor Linares Cruz the next day and then get ready for trial. With Defense Plan A shot to hell—getting his client an alibi—he'd have to go back to Plan B: proving to Teo that Linares was wrong about the land grant and Carlos V. Deal with that later. Get your bearings, get to Livingston. When the squall hit, they had been traveling north, toward Belize, so he staggered off in a generally southerly direction that he hoped would lead to the airport.

Fifty feet up the beach, walking in the shallow water to ease his bare feet, he tripped over something that was neither firm nor soft. What the hell? It was a hand, with a torso attached to it, nearly covered with sand and seaweed. He dug some sand away with his hands and exposed the top half of a head, face up. Vacant eyes stared up at him. It was all that was left of Moulas, the Indian, his face already turning the bleached-white color of death. Sharks had taken his legs. Jesse gazed out to sea in wonder that he had made it.

His moment of peace ended abruptly as, from behind, a familiar voice said, "Hello, Señor Hall."

Jesse turned to face Ozo, looking not much better off than himself, but with one important difference: he had a gun. Without another word, Ozo pulled Jesse's shirt up over his head and tied it at the top, creating a kind of blindfold, and ordered him to head back down the beach.

"Where are we going, Ozo?" His question was rewarded with a fierce jab between his shoulders with the barrel of the pistol.

"Walk!" Ozo grunted, and after a twenty-minute march on the beach, Ozo pushed Jesse into the jungle. So he was being thrown into the briar patch, and it was back to Plan A. Without shoes, Jesse winced at the pain he felt with every step, but consoled himself with the thought that Ozo wouldn't have bothered to cover his eyes just to kill him and, for better or for worse, he would soon be in Gómez's camp.

Two hours later, someone roughly pulled Jesse's shirt back down from his face, and he realized that he was inside a tent the size of a one-car garage. White Beard guarded the opening.

"You made it," Jesse said, and Eduardo nodded, offering the hint of a smile.

Jesse was given water by an old albino woman with eyes the color of Pepto-Bismol. She administered a paste of some kind to his feet, which immediately stopped the bleeding and deadened the pain. She gave him clean socks, then washed his face with warm water out of a basin. Next, she gave him a bowl of *caldo de pata*—cow's foot soup—which he hungrily devoured.

"Thank you," Jesse said, but she slowly shook her head, as if anything she might be doing for him would turn out to be, in the long run, a waste of her time as well as his.

26

SOMETHING HIT HIM in the back. Had he fallen asleep? It was a pair of canvas shoes.

"Put those on," said Ozo, "and follow me." Jesse had no idea what time it was, and the only sounds he heard were from the screeches of an *urraca*, a magpie jay common to the *Río Dulce* area. Jesse gingerly walked out of the tent in too-small shoes. As his eyes gradually became accustomed to the sunlight, he was astonished at what he saw. This was no mere hideout for a gang of traffickers, and certainly no farm, but a fully armed military base of operations, with a two-story building painted olive drab and endless rows of large tents probably housing thousands of men. A canopy of teak, loquat, *ceiba*, mango, and palm trees concealed the entire compound and camouflage netting further hampered detection by air. Rifles were stacked in neat pyramids in front and behind each tent, indicative of a discipline Jesse had seen nowhere else in Guatemala. An Apache attack helicopter bristling with guns perched like a bird of prey in a clearing on a circular cement pad.

Ozo turned Jesse over to two camouflage-uniformed guerrillas,

484 JOHN MARTEL

who rudely escorted him into the building and a reception area with walls covered by maps. A large map of Guatemala was divided into five areas by broken red lines and entitled simply, "*Familias.*" Teo had told him there were five major crime families in Guatemala, each generally respecting the territorial integrity of the others. Hung behind a small, but finely finished, oak desk was a four-by-six-foot oil portrait of a scholarly-looking man, at the bottom of which were the words: "*El Cobra.*"

"Wait," a guerrilla said, and wait Jesse did, for nearly an hour.

"Up," one of the guards finally said.

"You guys don't get paid by the word here, do you?" Jesse said.

"Quiet," said the guard.

"I rest my case."

Jesse's false bravado did little to lessen his growing anxiety, and soon the guards took him, not into the office, but back outside, through a different door. There, in a clearing among additional tents, in the center of at least forty or so uniformed men standing at ease, but clearly alert, sat a small, well-groomed man in a canvas director's chair. He wore a uniform, sunglasses, a military beret, and an attitude. Was this *El Cobra*? He resembled the portrait Jesse had seen in the barracks, but the impression created was nothing like what Jesse had expected—more like a college professor than a notorious guerrilla leader. He wore the same uniform as worn by his soldiers, plain camouflage—olive drab and dark green—and high-laced black boots. But the fully equipped warrior weighed no more than 130 pounds wringing wet. He was about five foot four, with thinning, black hair, a small beak of a nose, and a neatly trimmed beard that glistened as if oiled. His rimless, rectangular spectacles were tinted a revolutionary-pink, which conspired with the beard to overwhelm his delicate features. He held a small riding crop in his hand.

All in all, Jesse took encouragement from the man's scholarly appearance and from the obvious discipline of his soldiers. This was no rag-tag band of renegades. Perhaps this was a man he could reason with.

A soldier ordered Jesse to sit on a tiny stool directly in front of, and considerably lower than, Gómez. The same guards flanked Jesse, standing at parade rest.

"Why do you visit our humble farm?" the man asked, in English, an almost kindly smile on his face.

Jesse smiled back at him. "The guide book promised adventure and romance."

Gómez smiled again, but it was a sad, sympathetic smile. "Romance is dead in Guatemala, Señor Hall. It died with God in 1954."

Jesse knew what he was getting at. "I wasn't even born when the CIA invaded your country."

"And I am to deduce what from this?"

"I'm just hoping that is a point in my favor, because I need one from you."

He frowned. "You want a favor from me?" he asked, in an ominous tone of voice.

Jesse looked around at the guerrillas, also standing at parade rest, forming a semicircle on either side from their leader, and said, "Yes, sir. To start with, I had hoped to have a private audience with you."

Gómez smiled benignly. "Please, Mr. Hall, do not hesitate to speak freely in front of my lieutenants. We are a family here. Besides, most of them are Mayan and understand little Spanish and no English. That man over there, for example, is one of the thirteen who survived the 1982 massacre at the indigenous village of *Petanac,* where your CIA and our brave army tortured sixty-eight villagers and buried them in mass graves. Do you know what the army called these operations?"

"No, sir."

"'Taking the water from the fish.' Is that not poetic? So now, Señor, state your business."

"I am a lawyer, sir. I represent—"

"I know who you are, Señor Hall. You are an American representing another American. Spare me the charade that you have come to me as a representative of a U.S. drug merchant. I know nothing of such matters."

Jesse considered carrying the bluff through but thought better of it. "You're right. I just said that to get a meeting with you."

Gómez smiled approvingly and said to the guards, "An oddity in our midst."

"Sir?" Jesse said.

"An American who occasionally resorts to the truth," Gómez said, seemingly distracted by a large beetle that had turned over on its back in the dirt, its legs thrashing impotently. The guerrilla leader reached down and gently flipped him over with his fingernail, then watched the insect scuttle away.

"I have reason to believe, sir," Jesse said, "that my client was with you the day Marisa Andrade was murdered. I also think she was killed under orders from Victor Carano and, that without your assistance, Carano will get away with it."

Gómez shifted back to Spanish to denounce Carano and "the heartless death squads who systematically slaughter the heroes of our republic." In a lilting, guttural dialect, he translated his remarks for his Indian soldiers, then returned to Spanish, his voice breaking with emotion as he spoke of Marisa Andrade's work "on behalf of my people." Heads nodded in agreement.

Encouraged, Jesse said, "I need your help, Señor Gómez. Otherwise, the government will prevail, led by prosecutor Elena Ruiz under Carano's direction."

"Ah, Señorita Ruiz. Such a busy young woman."

"She's busy preparing to destroy me in court."

"Or maybe arranging to have you destroyed *outside* of court. She is quite capable of doing that, you know."

Jesse gave *El Cobra* a quizzical look. "I do not understand."

Gómez grinned. "Let us just say that the legacy of her father extends to more than a prestigious office in the government."

Gómez's enigmatic reply made Jesse think of Elena's equally confusing remark about using "all of the power available to her." He tried to get the guerrilla to clarify his statement, but Gómez would say nothing further.

"I was hoping, sir," Jesse said, "that you would be willing to come to Kevin's trial and tell the Court that he was here with you on the day of the murder."

Gómez burst out laughing, and when someone translated, the soldiers joined in. Jesse could feel the mood changing, the men behaving more like a gang than disciplined soldiers. Sitting on a child's stool, knees spread and nearly as high as his shoulders, Jesse felt fear and humiliation.

When the laughter died down, Jesse said, "With respect, sir, I think it would be a good chance to expose Carano. And wouldn't your followers rejoice at the opportunity for you to make your vision for Guatemala known to the world through the world press?"

El Cobra's stiff riding crop whistled through the air and struck Jesse hard across the back of his head. He felt pain all the way to his genitals. "What the hell?" Jesse gasped, struggling to maintain his balance on the stool. The hand that went to his head came back damp with blood.

Gómez's eyes were burning coals. "You dare come here and tell me what my people want?"

"Señor Gómez, I just meant—"

"Do you know who I am?"

"Yes . . . you are Arturo Gómez."

"That is my name, you idiot!" he said. "I am asking if you know who I am?"

Jesse was drenched in sweat. "I know you are a leader, sir," he said, realizing the guy was nuts and had to be placated. "The hope of many people in Guatemala."

Gómez gave his head an impatient shake, but then resumed his mild, even cordial manner. Jesse began to breathe again. "I will tell you who I am, Señor Hall. I am Mayan, but for one-quarter Toltec, or, if you prefer, Mexican. There is not a drop of Spanish blood in my body, do you understand?"

"Yes, sir."

"I was born in 1970, in Chajul, in the Western Highlands. I was only eight when the army came and burned down our village. Then, to make sure we got the point, they threw mutilated corpses into the plaza to serve as a final warning not to entertain any 'Marxist organizers.' One of those corpses was my uncle. Militia troops had already raped my mother and probably my older sister, too, although I was forbidden to ask her and she couldn't answer anyway. She has never uttered another word. Not one. She was then eleven. We were just one of four hundred villages the army destroyed during the eighties to discourage any sympathy with anyone who resisted the army."

Jesse had no idea what to say, so again said nothing.

"When I was very young, my mother told me how successfully your CIA was destroying our young democracy. You know what else my mother told me?"

Jesse shook his head.

"She said, 'Arturo, get some men in here to fuck me or your father will kill us.'"

Gómez laughed at what he had said and so did his men. "Can you believe that?" he said, still laughing mirthlessly. "It's true. I had a whore for a mother and a pimp for a father. I even helped him beat her once. He beat me all the time, too, but I never cried." The ugly smile faded and Gómez straightened his shoulders and added, "I loved my father, because he feared no man and let nobody else beat me."

Christ, thought Jesse, the man is crazier than a shithouse rat.

Gómez closed his eyes as if he were meditating. When the eyes popped open, he looked around and shouted for silence, although Jesse had heard nothing other than distant birdsong. He said, "I am contemplating this gringo's future," and closed his eyes again. In the renewed silence, Jesse wondered at the bundle of idiotic decisions—each step seemingly inevitable—that had brought him to this Guatemalan jungle.

A loud noise in the trees off to his left startled him out of his bleak reflection and he dared hope it might be rescuers. Instead, it was an incredible whirling tornado of color and sound, as a dozen or more wild parrots exploded from the trees, flushed from their hiding place.

Gómez ignored this spectacle and rose to his feet, causing all of his men to snap from parade rest to attention. "I am tired of you, Señor Hall," he said, causing Jesse's breath to catch in his dry throat. "Ozo!" he shouted. "Send this *gringo* piece of shit back to Guatemala City."

Jesse was jerked to his feet. He was home free, unless . . .

He reached in his back pocket and touched the subpoena, knowing that what he did or didn't do in the next few seconds could cost him his life. He tried to clear his head, to think. Then he simply stopped thinking and handed the wilted document to Gómez.

"What is this? I gave you no permission to hand me anything." But his curiosity made him look. Jesse waited, expecting the whip, his eyes clamped shut.

But Gómez laughed again, then read the blurred contents of the wilted subpoena to his men, who laughed, too. Then he tore the document to bits and dropped the pieces at Jesse's feet. Someone pushed him back down on his knees.

"Get down there and eat your fucking paper, *abogado*. Eat it all."

"It . . . doesn't matter," Jesse said, "you've touched it. You've . . . been served and everybody knows I've come here. They will come to find me and—"

Jesse saw the arm raise, knew it was coming, dropped his head just in time and took the whip handle across the back of his neck and shoulder. It felt like a blackjack. Someone seized his hair, pushed his head down, and shouted, "Eat dirt, *gringo!*"

Jesse could barely breathe and he struggled to remain conscious. Pain and fear had stolen his strength, his heart unable to meet the demands his adrenaline had put on it. "May I . . . speak, Señor Gómez?" said Jesse, his head still bowed submissively, hoping to avoid the whip but fully expecting it.

"Speak, then eat or die."

Jesse tried to clear his head and keep the fear out of his voice. "The chief prosecutor herself . . . told me that you are not presently charged with any crime. But if you . . . disregard this legal subpoena she knows I'm serving on you today, you will have broken the law." Jesse paused to suck air into his starved lungs. "Combine that with my disappearance . . . and the government will . . . have the excuse it needs to arrest you!"

Gómez came up off his stool, his hand on the holster hanging from his waist. "I *am* the government, you piss-ant. Judge and jury, too. Now eat!"

"You must know then," Jesse said, talking fast now, for words were his only weapons, "that the world press will report this trial. You would have the ear of the entire planet, *Commandante Cobra!*"

An aide whispered something into Gómez's ear. Was there hope?

"I am not a bully, Señor Hall, so I give you a choice. My captain thinks you have made an interesting point. But you still must eat your document or die. Your choice."

Gómez unsnapped the holster and pulled his gun free, then rested the cold end of the barrel on Jesse's forehead.

Jesse glared at his tormentor, but put the first scrap of paper in his mouth. He tried to chew, but his mouth was so dry it stuck to the roof of his mouth.

"No, no, Señor. Eat like a dog. No hands, get that pretty white face in the dirt."

Jesse watched as blood fell from the back of his head onto a piece of the subpoena. Red on white, white on red, but all Jesse saw was red.

"No," said Jesse. "I . . . I won't . . . "

Another blow from behind was followed by a flash of blinding light and the sound of his own gagging. From off in the distance, he heard their voices. "*Swallow, gringo bastard, swallow!*"

Barely conscious, Jesse realized that his throat was jammed with dirt and paper, clogging his windpipe. He tried to spit it out and gagged from the effort. His second attempt succeeded in sending a spray of dirt onto *El Cobra's* boots.

"I . . . won't . . . eat dirt for you . . . I won't . . . " Then, another blow from behind, more bright lights, then darkness. Warm, soothing darkness.

DAY TWELVE

27

JESSE HAD NO idea how long he had been out, but when he awoke, he was back in the tent with the pink-eyed woman. His headache was nearly unbearable, but he was alive. A guard stood at the opening, through which daylight shone. The woman spoke in a Mayan dialect, her voice as soothing as the substance she was applying to his wounds. She didn't seem to care that he could not understand her.

A younger Indian woman, dressed not in fatigues, but a colorful *huilpile,* entered with plantain, some *frijoles borrachos*, and a jug of water. Jesse wondered if it was drugged, but accepted the offerings. Why the benevolence? Fattening the hog for slaughter?

The food helped his headache and he was starting to feel better when Ozo and another guerrilla burst into the tent and, without a word, roughly pulled him to his feet. They pulled a new hood down over his face and secured it around his neck as before. Jesse welcomed it like an old friend. It meant they weren't going to kill him. And maybe Kevin would survive as well.

Three hours later, the sun broke through retreating clouds and blasted the windshield of Ozo's black Mercedes sedan as it pulled out of the boat harbor at *Río Dulce*. Jesse sat next to Ozo and they rode in silence. Jesse's head and shoulder ached from Gómez's whip, and he itched from the lotion the pink-eyed woman had applied to his face and arms to ward off the malaria-bearing *zancudos*.

It was two o'clock in the afternoon by the time they reached CA-9 and began the final leg back into Guatemala City, speeding past vast hillsides, badly scarred by limestone mining. To Jesse, Guatemala was like a beautiful woman marred by raw sores and lesions. The worst wound was poverty, which produced false prophets like Gómez, and those eager to follow them.

After a six-hour, two-lane rollercoaster ride, they reentered Guatemala City's more hospitable 4,500-foot climate. Back in his hotel room, he collapsed onto his bed. Why, he wondered again, had Gómez let him go? Despite his overt psychopathy, the man was intelligent and didn't seem to do anything without a reason. Was he keeping his options open? Could it be that Gómez was tempted by the opportunity to address a world audience? Another long shot at best.

He decided to call Teo, knowing he would be worried.

"Jesse!" came Teo's distressed voice. "I was about to call the police. Are you all right?"

Jesse said he was fine, then summed up the meeting with *El Cobra*. Teo could barely speak. "I cannot believe he let you go."

"I can't, either. He seems like a guy who doesn't do things without a reason."

"Well, you missed your appointment with Professor Linares Cruz."

"I'll call and reschedule."

Jesse rang off and left a message at Linares's office, apologizing and suggesting the next day, same time. Yes, time to get back to Defense Plan B, unmasking the land grant hoax and getting Carlos V back into the case. Then he unplugged his room phone, fell into bed, and slept for fifteen hours.

DAY THIRTEEN

28

THE FIRST CALL Jesse made after a cup of coffee and four Advils was to Elena.

"Where have you been, Jesse?" Elena said, her tone both relieved and angry. "There are rumors you were kidnapped. Are you all right?"

"I'm fine, especially now that I know how much you missed me."

"At least your ego still has a pulse. Listen, Jesse, we found Webster in Tikal."

Jesse smiled, almost forgot the pain in the back of his head and neck, the welts across his shins, and his nearly raw feet. "That's great news, Elena. I'd appreciate a chance to ask him some questions after you all are finished. You arrested him, right?"

"Unfortunately, he was beyond our jurisdiction."

It took only a second to sink in. "*Shit!* How long had he been dead when he was found?"

"The animals had been at him, so it's hard to tell. The pathologist thinks he died around noon on the same day Perlita was murdered. Forensics is performing ballistic tests, but he was probably killed with the same gun that was used on the girl. So tell me, where are you and are you really all right?"

"I'm fine," Jesse said, glancing at himself in a mirror over the dresser. His face was no worse than usual and nothing was broken, and whatever the old woman treated him with had worked a miracle. "I'll give you the whole story when I see you, but I—"

"Need a favor, as usual?"

"As usual. Listen, Elena, I appreciate your releasing Teo Andrade, but can you clear him, too? He's worried sick he'll be arrested again. We have a case to prepare and I need him to be fully functioning."

"Let's see what forensics finds."

"The hell with forensics, Elena. You know damn well that the same person who killed Webster killed his girlfriend, too."

"I suppose one could deduce that. So?"

"So you also know that Teo didn't have time to kill the girl, then take Carl all the way up north to Tikal, shoot him with a gun he doesn't own, and then come back down to the city in time to go to Antigua with me, find the girl's body, and be jailed!"

"That is also a possible deduction."

"No, Elena. It's a dead-on physical certainty. The girl had only been dead a few hours when we found her. You told me so yourself. Teo was in custody after that, so he *couldn't* have killed Webster."

"I told you I will consider exonerating him. Yelling at me will not advance your cause."

"Or further endear me to you?"

He could feel her smile through the phone. "Can I see you today?" he said.

"How about my annex office at noon."

The second call he made was to return two messages from Simon Bradshaw.

"Are you getting my messages, Jesse? I've been worried about you."

Jesse told him where he'd been and was greeted with a cold silence. "I thought you were going to ignore those rumors. Must I remind you that it is not our job to implicate our biggest client in a criminal conspiracy with a rumored drug lord? The same logic applies to his son."

Jesse was stunned. Was C&S still representing Cal Covington and CalCorp after the things he had told Simon three days ago? "I'm not going out of my way to do that, sir. In fact, it will be deemed legally hearsay and irrelevant at trial as to why Kevin was there or what he was talking about with Gómez; only that he was there at the time of the murder. It's a complete alibi."

"It's still too risky, Jesse. The judges could overrule your hearsay objection. Leave it alone. Cal has made it clear to both of us: stay away from Gómez."

Jesse heard the hard tone in Bradshaw's voice, but said, "So we are still representing CalCorp? I assumed that—"

"I'm starting a meeting, Jesse. Find some other line of defense for Kevin."

"That may be a problem, Simon."

"No, it's an opportunity—to show you are ready for partnership at C&S."

"But without the alibi . . ."

"Good luck, Jesse."

There was no missing the implication. Do it Cal's way, even if it means his son's life. Use the alibi, lose your partnership. Jesse felt a tightening in his chest. What had happened to his friend and mentor?

. . .

A TRIM YOUNG secretary directed Jesse into the office of Professor Linares Cruz on the beautiful campus of San Carlos University.

"Are you early, Señor?" she asked in Spanish. "The professor is not in yet."

"Actually, I'm about twenty-four hours late."

"I am sure he will arrive soon," she said.

Jesse was surprised by the unpretentiousness of the professor's quarters. The room was only large enough for a desk and chair, a bookcase, a side table buried in carefully stacked papers, and two visitor's chairs. The desk itself was clean but for a traditional inkwell and fountain pen. This was a fastidious man.

Jesse thought about the imminent confrontation, perhaps a more important examination than any he would conduct in the courtroom, not only for Kevin, but for the country. Trial lawyers liked to say that if you're going to fall off a mountain, better to fall off at the bottom than the top. Similarly, if the land grant was a hoax, better for the country to find out before the reform movement rode it up too high, only to have the hoax exposed on the eve of the election.

The professor entered, meticulously dressed in denim jeans and an open cotton shirt, canvas shoes. He wore neither glasses nor any other evidence of academia. He was about five foot ten, without a single strand of grey in either his thick mass of dark hair or his equally thick mustache. He appeared to be in his mid-forties. He looked more like a professional tennis player than a teacher of ancient history; an older, short-haired version of the top-ranked Spanish player, Juan Carlos Ferrero.

The professor introduced himself in perfect English and appraised Jesse with piercing eyes and studied confidence. Jesse felt like a bug under a microscope. Linares buzzed his secretary for coffee. Jesse thanked the professor and apologized for missing his earlier appointment, then said, "I assume you know why I'm here."

"I know why you are in Guatemala, but not why you are here in my office."

"Your support for the land grant has caused some people to assume that Marisa's last act was to affirm its authenticity rather than naming her killer. Putting it in chess terms, Professor, moving your king into the forefront has checkmated my defense strategy."

The professor's expression remained non-committal. "I see."

"So I need to know whether the *Globe* article quoted you accurately. I concede I have doubts about a five-hundred-year-old document that nobody's seen but you and the guy who wants a lot of money for it."

The professor tilted his handsome head, raised an eyebrow, and ran a hand through his lush hair. *A scoundrel, Teo had said, a scoundrel and a liar.*

"I assure you the letter exists and is authentic," Linares said, "but I understand your concerns. Does your lethargic co-counsel concur with your somewhat . . . cynical position?"

No secrets in this city, thought Jesse. "Like me, Señor Andrade just wants to do the right thing."

Linares seemed genuinely surprised. "Really? I assumed he was typically indifferent to *La Causa's* efforts and the plight of our country."

"Not at all, but since you seem critical of Professor Andrade, would you mind telling me what happened between you two?"

"A simple misunderstanding. He thought I was in love with Marisa."

"Were you?"

"Everybody was in love with Marisa."

"Then it wasn't a misunderstanding at all."

Linares's head bobbed impatiently. "We flirted, but it was harmless."

"You never slept with her?"

The man's cool eyes sparked at this. "What has this to do with a grant of land?"

"You're right, of course," Jesse said, deciding the guy was indeed a scoundrel, as Teo had said. But was he a liar, too? "I was merely trying to get some background."

Linares conspicuously looked at his watch. "What do you want to know?"

"I want to know," Jesse said, "whether you mean to put your fine reputation on the line for a letter that showed up out of nowhere after five hundred years?"

Linares shrugged. "I have already done it. The letter contains the *bona fide* seal of the Holy Roman Emperor Charles the Fifth, initially King Charles the First of Spain. In my opinion, every fact contained in the letter appears historically consistent. Moreover, the signature appears to be Charles's."

Just like that, the lines were drawn; there would be no quick knockout. Jesse took out a notebook and wielded his ballpoint pen.

Time to change direction. "Who owns the letter?"

"I never met the person or persons in possession of the letter. The copy was provided to me through a blind escrow at a bank, using a safe-deposit box. I was told when and where to go and was provided with a key."

"Your fee was paid in the same manner?"

Linares raised his eyebrows. "Yes."

"How much were you paid?"

Linares Cruz just smiled.

"I see," Jesse said, smiling back with equal insincerity. "Which bank served as the escrow?"

Linares laughed out loud and said, "That I will not tell you, either."

"What kind of material was the original written on? I assume you checked it out?"

Linares Cruz swiveled his chair around and stared out the window for a long minute, either lost in thought or wrestling with a decision. At last, he spun back and faced Jesse, his handsome features still composed. "I was not permitted to keep the original, but it appeared to be in reasonably good condition."

"Parchment?"

"No," Linares said. "Paper was introduced to Europe by the Chinese back in the eleventh century."

"Did you have the paper radiocarbon-tested for age?"

"The original of the letter could be tested with carbon-14, I suppose, but I am quite certain it will prove to be authentic."

"But you didn't bother to do that; am I right?"

"I was not asked to," Linares Cruz said, without a trace of defensiveness.

"You didn't think it was important?"

"I am not a forensic scientist, nor was I given sufficient time with the original to enlist the science."

Jesse took some time to catch up on his notes. Letting the man know he was on the record. "Exactly how did your client come by this letter, Professor?"

Linares shook his head. "That I cannot tell you. I signed a confidentiality agreement as a part of my retainer agreement."

"Are you aware of the dire political consequences to Miguel Aguilera if someone, say the Vice President, should expose a flaw in your work just before the election?"

"I am not a politician. Politicians make reality. We historians merely record it. Besides, I do not expect that anyone will succeed in casting doubt on my work."

Jesse's concern was mounting. The man was cool. "Can you at least tell me a little more about what the letter says?"

The professor nodded and offered Jesse a cigarette. Jesse declined, Linares lit his own and stared into his burning match for a few seconds, as if again uncertain how much more of his valuable time he should waste. He sighed as he exhaled smoke.

"You have undoubtedly seen the excerpts published by Marisa," he said at last. "One part of the letter indicates that everything west of longitude ninety degrees, thirty minutes west be returned to the Mayans."

Jesse smiled. He had him. "That's interesting, Professor, but I seem to recall that there was no access to longitude data back in 1530, as we have today."

Linares smiled back; the game was on. "I referred to longitude merely to facilitate a layman's understanding. Charles's letter employed only geographic features to demarcate the territory to be granted, specifically *Lago de Atitlán* and *Volcán de Agua*."

Checkmate, Jesse thought, and shifted his approach again. "But why would Charles have given away so much hard-earned land? My understanding is that emperors were not so generous to the vanquished back then."

"Charles was a guilt-ridden, dying man, under pressure from the Supreme Pontiff whom Catholics believe holds the key to eternal life."

"Your theory is that the Pope pressured the Emperor into doing the right thing?"

Linares nodded. "It is not mere theory, Mr. Hall. We historians know Pope Clement strongly influenced the Emperor and, as with many people about to face the ultimate judgment, Charles obviously did not wish to offend the Judge. Indeed, the letter mentions that a full Cardinal heard the Emperor's final confession, administered Holy Eucharist, and undoubtedly imposed the land grant as Charles's final penance."

"His ticket to Paradise? Land for peace?"

Cruz smiled. "Not just any peace, Mr. Hall, eternal peace. Remember: this Emperor convened the conference at Valladolid in 1550 to consider the morality of the force employed by Cortéz and Alvarado, an action unheard of in that day. Charles refers to Cortéz in the letter and elsewhere as 'my butcher.'"

"Okay," Jesse continued, "but why would the Pope care so much about the Maya?"

"Clement was also a reformer, both as Archbishop of Florence and as the Cardinal Medici. This attitude and action was typical of him, and since avoiding eternal damnation was high on Carlos Quinto's wish list, the stars were in perfect alignment."

The guy was showy, but damned clever, and Jesse wondered what the hell he could do if this guy ended up on the witness stand. Challenge him to a duel?

"Let's say I accept all that you've said, Professor. But we're talking about a letter written in Europe five hundred years ago. How did it get to the New World?"

Linares Cruz abruptly rose to his feet, stuck his head out the door, and shouted another request for coffee to his secretary. "When the Emperor became ill and yielded to the Pope's demands to return half the land to the Maya, he probably thought, who better to carry his instructions back to the Governor of Guatemala than the man who stole the land from the Maya in the first place? Cortéz was in Spain, facing charges of atrocities against the Indians and the murder of his second wife, Catalina Juarez. As a condition of his pardon, why not make him suffer the humiliation of personally bearing back to the New World a document that would nullify his life's work?"

"Hold on, Professor. You're saying Charles the Fifth called him all the way back to Spain for trial, then pardoned him and sent him back?"

"Exactly. Any history book will tell you that after being pardoned, Cortéz was returned to Mexico, stripped of all powers, a lonely, depressed man. Charles also no doubt realized that Cortéz's former stature would give him the credibility to deliver such a bizarre piece of mail."

Mail. Marisa's "old mail," code name for the letter she had expressed doubts about to Anastacia. But how to convince Teo of that, particularly now that Linares was in the game? His head ached again. He stood and stretched, trying to think his way around the professor's story. The coffee came at last, and the secretary poured.

When the secretary left, Jesse said, "This has all been interesting, Professor, but since the land *wasn't* split, why should anyone believe Charles the Fifth ever wrote such a letter? And what became of it after he allegedly wrote it?"

Linares sipped his coffee. "It is not so difficult to understand," he said, flashing his brilliant smile again. "Logic dictates that Cortéz was far from enthusiastic about the mission thrust upon him by the Emperor."

"So you claim that Cortéz got his revenge by concealing the letter instead of delivering it?"

"Most assuredly. I can picture the great *conquistador* sitting at sundown on his veranda, holding a glass of wine in one hand and the land grant letter in the other, gloating over it until the last day of his life."

"But once the Emperor recovered his health, wouldn't he wonder why partition never happened?"

"Bear in mind that there was no satellite in those days, no phones, no e-mail, no Twitter. Moreover, Charles's recovery was hampered by catastrophic events in Europe, painful gout, and an insane mother—Juana of Castile—all of which provoked a nervous breakdown. He renounced his throne and all worldly goods and retreated to a monastery, where he died believing he had done everything God or the Pope had asked of him."

Jesse stared down at his notepad. Linares glanced at his watch again. "The letter is real, Mr. Hall, and while there will be always be cynics, I assure you that the court of public opinion will rule quite favorably on the issue. Moreover, I hope that as a result of our conversation, there might be one less cynic roaming Guatemala City."

Jesse offered an ambivalent smile. "One more question," Jesse said. "How did the letter suddenly come to light?"

The professor gingerly placed his empty cup onto the saucer in the manner of a man who did everything cautiously—except, perhaps, where women and roulette wheels were concerned. He said, "The person who retained me said the letter was found during an archeological dig. It was tucked in the pages of an old bible that had been hermetically sealed in wax. A Mayan laborer, who had worked at the site of the dig where the book was discovered, was found murdered the next day. I suspect he had stolen the book and that if one could trace this letter all the way back to Cortéz's death, that trail would be marked in blood."

"You must have made a copy from the original while you had it. May I see it?"

Linares smiled and looked Jesse straight in the eye as he said, "Copying the original, Señor Hall, would have been unethical."

Jesse felt drained. His headache and lack of sleep was getting to him.

"I am sorry, Señor Hall, but I must go teach my class now."

"I'm finished, but tell me what you think will happen next. To the letter, I mean."

The professor stared at Jesse over clasped hands and said, "For the good of the country, money *must* be raised to purchase the original letter. Perhaps you might persuade Teo, as Marisa's widower, to throw his not-inconsiderable weight behind *La Causa* and other rights activists to launch a world-wide fund-raising effort. It is worth the five million dollar asking price as an antiquity alone!"

Interesting. For a man who knew everything, Linares Cruz was not aware that Teo had already decided to support the fund-raising drive. Jesse began to feel like he was being hustled. "Teo has already lent his name to the campaign."

Linares Cruz seemed surprised and beamed with obvious elation. "That is *wonderful* news!"

Someone knocked on the door, a secretary bearing a handful of pages for the professor's signature. "Now I *must* excuse myself," said Linares, giving Jesse one last look. "Magdalena, give Señor Hall another cup of coffee. He appears in dire need."

"I guess I look as bad as I feel. I nearly drowned in a boat in the Bay of Honduras a coupla days ago. Got caught in a squall."

"Dangerous situations are common in that area," Linares said, rapidly scanning and absently signing letters and documents. "I once nearly drowned there myself. My boat was also small and also without bilge pumps or life vests. And those waters close to Belize get extremely rough."

Jesse caught his breath. *Close to Belize . . . also small boat . . . also without bilge pumps or life vests. Also. Also.* How could Linares know all this? Unless . . .

Jesse's hand somehow remained steady on the cup, despite a heart threatening to pound through his ribs. Don't look up, he told himself. Sip your coffee. Stay cool.

"Everything turned out fine," he said, pleased he sounded calm.

The professor signed the last paper and looked at his watch. "Here you go, Magdalena, thank you. Regrettably, Señor Hall, I must go."

"I'm finished, Professor. Thanks for your time."

"My pleasure. We get fewer Americans through here these days with all the violence, and I enjoyed visiting with you."

And I with you, thought Jesse. Otherwise, I would still not know what Marisa probably discovered long before: that you were in this high-stakes con game up to your handsome mustache with none other than *El Cobra* himself, Arturo Gómez.

29

JESSE RETURNED TO his hotel parking lot. After delivering a few well-placed kicks to the trunk of the Suzuki, it popped open, and he grabbed several files fortuitously saved from the ARES raid five days earlier. He wanted to take a fresh look at Marisa's typed drafts, handwritten research notes, and published articles that had been provided by Teo.

Up in his room, he spread out the papers alongside a complete copy of the purported land grant letter Marisa had received from the anonymous holder. She had published excerpts in the *Globe,* causing a furor of excitement across the country. Jesse's lawyer's intuition was nagging him, but nothing new jumped out.

He grabbed a banana and some nuts, changed into a fresh shirt, and headed for his noon meeting with Elena. He decided not to tell her his theory that Gómez and Linares Cruz had created the hoax together and that he, Jesse, would probably be dead but for their assumption that he could influence Teo to help *La Causa* raise the money to buy it from them. Who would believe him? Nobody. So for the present, he would have to move onward to . . . what? To the

weakest strategy of all: connecting Webster and Carano without the
Carlos V clue by following the money. For this, he'd need a quicker
response from Elena and would don knee-pads and beg for it if he
had to.

He arrived right on schedule, and a secretary gave him a cup of
coffee. Christ, he was living on caffeine. Five minutes later, somewhat
energized, he entered Elena's annex office at the *Torre de Tribunales*.
She looked annoyed, beautiful in her regal petulance, but when she
took in his face, her features softened. "Oh, Jesse, what have you done
to yourself?"

Jesse thought about how nice it would be to put his arms around
her, feel her warm hands bringing blood back into his face. But she
kept her distance, so he told her about his trip instead.

Elena's annoyance returned. She slammed a pencil flat on her desk.
"What in God's name were you doing in the *Río Dulce* area?"

"Simple. I have an alibi witness. Arturo Gómez. I went out there to
try to persuade him to come in and testify."

Elena blinked, incredulous. "You intend to claim your client was
with Gómez at the time of the murder doing a *drug* deal?"

"No, only that they were together on April first."

"Gómez will never come in."

"The court issued a subpoena, but I'll admit Gómez didn't like it."

"You *subpoenaed* him?" she said, and began pacing behind her desk,
her heels clicking on the tile floor. "Didn't anybody tell you the man
is a sociopathic monster? You have done an incredibly stupid thing."

Jesse rubbed his eyes. He had expected Cal and Simon to be furious
when they learned he had gone to Livingston, but not Elena. She
began shuffling through papers on her desk. Letting him know she'd
be quite happy in his absence.

"Listen, Elena, I told you because I didn't want you to be blindsided," Jesse said, "in case Gómez does come in, which I agree is a long-shot."

Elena turned away abruptly. "On your way out the door, pick up that folder on the corner of my desk. It contains our forensic files and list of witnesses. You are entitled to them, and I'll expect the same from you tomorrow."

Jesse took the papers, but stood looking at Elena. Why was she so angry again?

"Anything else?" Elena said. "If not—"

"Just the usual question. Have your people been able to trace Carano's offshore money back into Guatemala yet?"

"I wondered when you would get to that. Yes, as a matter of fact, some of the funds did come back into Guate and into Webster's account."

"Swell," Jesse said.

"I thought you would be overjoyed."

Jesse sighed. "It turns out we won't be relying on Webster as 'Carlos V' after all. It's arguable that Marisa's final message may have had more to do with Emperor Charles the Fifth than Carl Webster the spook. At least that's what my co-counsel thinks."

"It's always difficult to reason with a convert," Elena said.

"Let's get back to the money. You said 'some of it' went into Webster's account. How much? Where did the rest go?"

"We're working on that."

"Jesus, Elena, what's taking so long? You've got all the government's resources."

She shook her head impatiently. "It's not an easy matter finding people willing to be involved in a clandestine investigation against Carano's interests."

"But you did find a way to track some of his money."

"We got a break. The commission monitoring compliance with the 1996 Peace Accords agreement has access to Interpol and banking records." She explained that the 1996 Peace Accords required that the military be reduced by a third.

"So you hinted to the Commission that Carano might be sneaking around the Accords, buying up arms off the books, using his unaudited discretionary fund."

She nodded. "They thought Carano might be dealing with a Yemeni 'charitable worker' named Yassaf Mousaffi, who is high on Interpol's list of bad guys. He delivers heavy armament to your doorstep—anything from rocket-propelled grenade launchers to Scud missiles with warheads carrying bio-agents or lethal chemicals. Hangs out in Mexico."

"Interesting. What's the sticker price these days on a Scud?"

"Mousaffi can put a complete Scud missile system in your garage for just over three point eight million U.S. dollars."

"Does that come with zero percent financing and a free toaster oven? Why doesn't someone bust this guy?"

"He's smart and fronts as a fund raiser for an agency called the Yemen Children's Fund."

"So what's his deal with Carano?"

"The Commission couldn't find one. As I told you, Carano's offshore money is coming right back into Guatemala, not to Mexico, nor to Mousaffi, nor to the Children's Fund. Moreover, the army has no new weaponry." Elena then seemed to remember she was angry with Jesse. "That's it, Counselor, enough professional civility. Goodbye."

"So where *is* the money going, and what's it going for?"

She said nothing. Why was she so upset with him?

"No hug for the ravaged warrior?" he ventured.

Elena picked up a file and began reading it.

Jesse strode over to the door and closed it. "I'd like to hold you, Elena, just for a minute."

"Please leave, Jesse."

Jesse saw that her eyes were welling up. She still cared about him.

"Okay, I'm gone, but would you mind telling me what's bugging you?"

"I can't."

Something was going on, but with Elena, something was always going on. Frustrated, he turned to go. But now it was Elena who stopped him. "Wait, Jesse. Did Gómez say why he was letting you go?"

"No, but I think I know." Jesse said. "I'll tell you when I'm sure." He took her by the shoulders. "Meanwhile . . ."

Elena stepped back from him, smoothed her ebony hair, then met his eyes. "No, Jesse. We *must* stop this."

"I know," he said, "believe me, I'm trying." But he moved toward her again and kissed her lightly on the mouth. She didn't back away. Their lips met again, then again. Small kisses at first, then deeper, searching tongues, hands pressing against each other's faces, passions reignited. But Elena backed off again and Jesse saw that her eyes were brimming with tears. "Please, Jesse. *Please.*"

"Sorry," Jesse said, hating his weakness. They stood in silence, suddenly worlds apart.

"All right," he said, "back to reality. How about Webster's murder? Any news from your forensics people?"

Elena put on her business face, too. "It has been confirmed that Webster was indeed killed at a time when Professor Andrade was in custody. I won't be charging him, but I cannot say what the police will do. Carano controls them. That is all I can say on the subject."

"And you'll keep me updated on tracking the offshore money, amounts and recipients?"

"Yes, of course." Then, without looking up, she said, "May I ask you something?"

"Of course."

"Why are you still in Guatemala? Your case has no viable defense without the Carlos V clue pointing to Webster. Gómez won't come in, and if disaster hasn't caught up with you yet, it's not because you haven't actively courted it." She looked up and Jesse saw the intensity in her gaze. He wondered whether she was truly worried about his safety or simply wanted him gone.

"I'm still trying to figure that out," he said, and walked out, closing the door quietly behind him.

30

NOW CERTAIN THE land grant was conceived as a means of funding Gómez's missile ambitions, Jesse reluctantly headed across town to tell Teo what he had learned about Linares.

Teo was drunk again and still in a somber mood. His beard was untrimmed and unruly, his eyes shot through with crimson streaks. Even the news that Elena would not file charges against him failed to cheer him.

"How little you know about our police, Jesse. Once they have you, they own you."

"What do you mean?"

"I mean that whether Ruiz charges me or not, I am under suspicion, and the PNC can show up at any hour, day or night. Whenever they want me, they will take me." He paused and squinted at Jesse. "My God, have a drink. You look terrible."

"Have you checked yourself in a mirror lately?" Jesse said, pouring himself a strong one, telling himself he was entitled to a night off.

"I would be fine if I could sleep at night. I seem to have forgotten how it works."

Jesse nodded. "I'm told coming off a single day in prison is like a trip through three time zones. Takes a while to get the body and spirit back to normal."

"True," Teo said. "So, Jesse, tell me more about your Livingston great adventure."

After hearing Jesse's story, Teo said he was surprised Gómez had let him go.

"I think he had a reason. And it has to do with you."

"Me?"

"You. I met with your pal Linares Cruz this morning. Add con artist to your list of his transgressions."

"How so?"

"When I was leaving his office, Linares Cruz got preoccupied signing letters in a rush and let out an offhand remark that revealed he knew a lot about how I nearly died."

"Such as?"

"That I had been in a 'small boat' with no life preservers or bilge pumps."

"That is all? He could simply have been making an assumption about your boat."

"It came across as fact, not assumption. He also knew I was in waters north of Livingston. Not just in the Bay of Honduras, but 'close to Belize.' I hadn't told him or anyone else where the boat was."

Teo's eyebrows rose. "I see," he said, "but what does any of this have to do with me?"

Jesse sipped his drink. "He kept saying how important it was that you inspire *La Causa* to come up with money so they could buy the letter. Don't you see? Linares was selling *me* on the letter so that I would sell *you*."

"Am I missing something?"

"I think I know the truth about the land grant letter."

Teo frowned. "I know you think it's a hoax, a trap set by Carano."

"I did, but now I think it's just a basic con job for cash, hatched by Gómez and authored by Linares Cruz."

"Gómez? Linares? Absolutely absurd."

"It makes sense. Gómez let me go because he knew I was about to sit down with Linares, who would convince me that money should be raised to acquire it."

"How would he know you were scheduled to meet with Linares?"

"I'm sure his phone records will show numerous calls between them."

Teo slowly shook his head and blew air out of an extended lower lip. "You are in fantasy land, Jesse, always reaching."

"I'm reaching for the truth. The two of them stand to split five million dollars—*if* the money can be raised. And you're the person in a position to get the job done."

Teo frowned again. "Maybe Gómez came into possession of the document and simply hired the most logical expert in Guatemala to validate it. Linares Cruz may be amoral, but he is too smart to get mixed up in an elaborate fraud. Eventually, they'd be found out."

"Look, Teo, what if Linares is in financial trouble—women, gambling, whatever? He might be desperate enough to do something as crazy as this. Sure, it would come out someday, but with that kind of money in his pocket, Linares is off to another country. As for Gómez, he doesn't care what anybody thinks."

Teo shook his head. "You are indulging in rank speculation."

Frustrated, Jesse went to the bar and poured another two fingers of *Zacapa* with a splash of soda. He was already feeling the first one, but things were piling up on him and he needed to calm down.

"You cannot prove the letter is a fake," Teo added, his voice edged, though thick with drink, his huge brow furrowed like corrugated metal, "any more than I can prove it is genuine. I suggest you do not publicize your theory. It could be dangerous."

"I'll watch myself and hold off until Gómez testifies, assuming he takes the bait and comes in to grandstand his revolutionary platform."

"It's not just Gómez. Remember that the Mayan candidate's best hope for winning is people believing in the land grant. His supporters will not allow it to be discredited."

"Aguilera's people? Aren't they the peace party?"

"Aguilera is a man of peace, but some of his people are not. I cannot protect you from . . . certain rogue elements that attach to any national candidate."

"What about you, Teo? Becoming a high-profile activist puts you into as much danger as me."

"You know nothing about my country. The more public I am, the safer I'll be."

"Really? That didn't work for Marisa, and it won't work for you."

"Marisa made a foolish mistake," Teo said, and nearly emptied his drink. A tense silence filled the room, like exhaust in a closed garage.

"Kevin?" It was the first time Teo had even tacitly acknowledged the basis for the prosecution's theory of adultery.

Teo nodded, drained his glass. "Despite her innocence, being seen in public with Kevin gave them the excuse they needed to silence her—with a young American in the wings to pin it on. I shall give them no such excuse."

Jesse exhaled with relief. "Okay, but I need you with me in court, committed to the case."

"We can't win, Jesse, and it is time to acknowledge reality."

"Dammit, Teo, we can't give up. For one thing, there are plenty of suspects with stronger motives to kill Marisa than Kevin could ever dream up. There's Carano, Webster, Gómez, maybe even her political rival, Anastacia Ramirez—"

"—and me," Teo said softly, still staring at the silent TV screen, an *I Love Lucy* rerun. His eyes glistened in the room's semi-darkness. The chirping of the *chicharsas* filled the sultry air outside, and Jesse could smell the fragrance wafting in from the *mamoncillo* tree, always in blossom at the start of the rainy season.

"Don't be silly, Teo," Jesse managing what he hoped was a convincing smile. "That's behind us."

"You are a good man, Jesse," Teo said, shaking his head sadly, "but I often wonder why you are doing this, putting yourself in harm's way for a gangster's son."

Jesse shrugged. Everyone was psychoanalyzing his motivation lately. A month ago, he would have had a one-word answer to the question: partnership.

"It's complicated, Teo, but what I do know is that an innocent man is being railroaded toward death row, and we're the only thing blocking the tracks." So there was still a one-word answer, just a different word: justice.

. . .

THE ALCOHOL HAD made Jesse wobbly, but he poured himself another drink against the wave of helplessness washing over him.

Teo walked over to the TV and turned it off.

"I am going to bed," Teo announced, but someone pounded on the front door. "Now what?" he added, careening down the hallway.

Jesse fell heavily into a chair, feeling dizzy, barely aware of the voices coming from the front door. The voices grew louder, and then the sound of something shattered—a vase? a lamp?—and men shouting.

ARES! PNC! Jesse stumbled to the front door. Teo was hunched over in the entry hall, panting like a wounded bear, blood flowing from his nose, his arms swinging wildly. His efforts to breathe sounded more like a broken calliope. A large, uniformed PNC man with a shaved head sent Teo to the floor with a punch to the back of his neck, and another man delivered a kick to the kidneys. There were two others, one also a PNC uniform and one plainclothes, undoubtedly an ARES thug.

"Stop this!" Jesse shouted in Spanish. "He's sick!"

The uniformed cop pointed a nightstick at Jesse as a warning to stand back, but Jesse leapt forward and threw himself against the man before he could deliver another kick to the fallen Teo. He and the PNC cop flew headlong out the open front door, crashing through the wire screen onto the front porch. Jesse landed on top, but was jerked to his feet from behind and dragged back into the house.

"We'll arrest you, too, if you want, Señor," said the other PNC in Spanish. "The professor resisted arrest. We had no option."

"There's . . . always an option to violence," Jesse gasped and gave his head a shake. He sucked in some air. "Show me your warrant."

"He wants to see my warrant. Show him!" he told the plainclothesman, and the ARES guy hit Jesse in the solar plexus with the butt of a nightstick. Jesse doubled over, surrendering to the shock and pain, but staying on his feet. Although starved for air, he subdued his panic and came up with an uppercut to the man's chin that missed by a mile. He spun around to confront the PNC cop he knew was behind him, but too late. In a flash of blinding light, it was over.

Minutes later, through a groggy haze, Jesse saw Anica entering from the front door.

"Where's my father?" she said, taking off her coat.

"Your father?" Jesse said, snapping out of it. "Teo! They must have taken him."

Anica angled her eyebrows. "What do you mean?"

"Oh shit," Jesse said, lurching to his feet, stumbling while he pulled his shirt down over his jeans, "the police have him again."

The girl looked stunned and deathly pale in the dim light, uncomprehending. "That's impossible. He was just released! No, this can't be. We must go get him."

Jesse steadied himself against a wall and tried to think while fighting off another wave of nausea. "Look, Anica, go heat up some coffee. I'll deal with this."

Jesse found his phone and hit Elena's speed-dial number. After ten rings, she picked up, listened to Jesse's pitch, and told him she would make some calls. "Check with me in the morning, Jesse, not before."

Jesse hung up. Anica came into the room with two cups of coffee. She had been crying. Jesse told her he thought Elena would help.

"Thank you for all you are trying to do," Anica said, suddenly looking older than her sixteen years, "but this can't go on. I won't lose my father."

Jesse tried to think of a comforting response, but he came up empty. In just two weeks in Guatemala, he had been threatened by the head of state, nearly drowned in the Bay of Honduras, been worked over by a guerrilla chieftain and ARES goons, seen his chief defense theory stripped away, been beaten up by police, and had engaged in sex with his courtroom adversary. And now, his co-counsel and only friend in Guatemala was back in jail.

DAY FOURTEEN

31

ASSURED THE NEXT day by Elena that Teo had been released, Jesse returned to Teo's home, where he found the professor in the kitchen, nursing a drink. His sparse hair looked like it had been caught in a ceiling fan, and his face was as chalky as a mime's. He sat, elbows on knees, head and shoulders hunched forward.

"Jesus, Teo, did they hurt you?"

Teo shook his head. "It was only harassment, Jesse. They didn't even question me, just locked me into a room in a holding cell at the *Torre de Tribunales* overnight. They released me after my heart acted up again. Atrial fibrillation. I think they were afraid I would die and they would be accused of torture. Then I got home, went up on my roof to relax and . . ."

Teo could speak no more. His head fell into his hands, and he issued a muffled groan, an animal-like sound.

"What's the matter, Teo? Shall I call a doctor?"

The big man looked up and stared at Jesse with blazing wet eyes that bespoke his anguish. "They *killed* them, Jesse."

"Who? Killed who?"

"My ladies. They sprayed their cage with poison . . . all dead."

"Oh, Christ, Teo. I'm sorry."

"Another warning," Teo said. He rose and paced the room, tossing his arms in despair. "My foolish Op-Ed piece in the *Globe*. The kind of thing I chastised Marisa for."

"Then you'd better back off," Jesse said. "They'll kill you next time."

"Your concern is touching."

"I'm just concerned about the case," Jesse said, smiling. "Come, let's get something to eat."

. . .

FOLLOWING AN UNEVENTFUL breakfast, Teo walked Jesse to his car. Back at the hotel, Jesse headed through the lobby toward the elevators. He glanced again at the prominently displayed mural of Pedro de Alvarado and thought about his conversation with Professor Linares Cruz, wondering if the conquistador was about to win yet another victory over the people of this wounded country.

He planned to try again to interview Anastacia Ramirez, but first, he'd check out the public library. The ARES visit and subsequent bird slaughter had convinced Jesse that his friend was in increasing danger and that the best way to save him *and* his client from Carano's government was to expose the letter as a fake—and to do it quickly.

Back in the car, Jesse drove toward the *Biblioteca Nacional*, housing Guatemala's largest collection of records and books covering the country's tumultuous history. Trials were won in the streets and in law libraries long before they ever reached the courtroom. What if he could show, for example, that Charles V never actually recalled Cortéz to Spain? Or, if Charles did recall him, that he didn't send him back to the New World a second time? Unlikely that an expert of Linares's stature would make such a mistake, but his heart quickened at the thought of how any one of these points could blow the entire scam apart.

But after two hours in the library, Jesse's eyes were burning, and he had gotten nowhere. Everything he read about King Charles and Pope Clement was consistent with Linares' claims. He felt ridiculous. There were witnesses to interview and arguments to be drafted and here he sat in a public library, reading medieval history.

Dejected, he replaced the treatises on the shelf, and left.

. . .

A LITTLE OVER 2,500 miles away, in San Francisco, an equally dismal Simon Bradshaw sat in his office across from Eric Driver and Jim Haydel. Haydel had just broken the news that Alan Cheng, head of CalCorp Asian operations in Shanghai, was about to be charged with bribing a Vietnamese official in violation of the Foreign Corrupt Practices Act. Cheng had issued a company check in the sum of $50,000 to the government's head of procurement, just one week before he awarded CalCorp a no-bid, exclusive contract to supply parts for all government vehicles.

"The shoe has finally dropped," added Haydel. "I won't say I told you so."

"What will Cheng say when the SEC questions him?" Simon asked.

"I've already handled it," Driver said, impatiently. "The payment was intended to be an advance against future taxes and the officer has already returned the money to CalCorp. Cheng has completed the charade by sending the 50K to the Shanghai tax authority, which will have no idea what the fuck to do with it. Cal will be fine and so will we."

But Haydel shook his head ruefully, and Simon said, "You disagree, Jim?"

"It made page two of the *Journal* yesterday, and the Wall Street analysts have swarmed over it like maggots on a corpse. CalCorp stock is down fifteen percent."

Bradshaw calculated that this one-day fall had knocked the value of C&S's CalCorp stock down over a million dollars. "Have either of you spoken with Cal?"

"I just finished," Haydel said. "Eric has convinced him to fight the charges all the way up to The Supremes, if necessary. Meanwhile, Cal insists we stop the Wall Street hemorrhaging by footnoting our 10-K filing to the effect that there are solid defenses to the claim and that CalCorp will likely prevail—which, of course, I told him we can't possibly do."

"What did he say to that?"

"He called me a pencil-pushing, bean-counting, chicken-shit coward and said he would hereafter deal only with Eric on this issue. Or you. He added that he would be up to see you later today. He insists that Cheng is loyal and will fall on his sword if necessary."

"If he won't," Driver added, "Cal will push him onto it. And I'll help him."

But Haydel wasn't finished. "I begged Cal to slow down weeks ago. Know what he said? He told me he'd do that when CalCorp was in the top ten of the *Forbes Global* 2000 and when the only difference between himself and Bill Gates was that Gates was 150 pounds lighter, a foot shorter, and not half as good looking."

"My lord," Simon said.

"So you agree with me, Simon?" said Jim Haydel. "We withdraw as counsel before we get sucked into the downdraft?"

"It does appear you've been right all along, Jim," Simon conceded.

Eric Driver grabbed his notes and rose to his feet. "I've had enough. I'll leave it to you two old ladies to explain to our partners and loyal staff members that you're kissing off our one hope for staying in business. Have a nice fucking day!" He turned and stormed toward the door, but then stopped, spun around, pointed a stubby finger, and added, "Oh yeah, Simon, when you meet with Cal, please tell him I'll help him find a new firm—one with balls—and that I'll be waiting there at the door to greet him."

"Calm down, Eric!" Simon said. "I haven't made a decision yet. We're simply discussing the issues."

Driver shook his head. "It's past time for 'discussing.' You've got to decide. *Now.*"

Simon's head was flashing bright colors, most of them red. He knew a migraine would soon top his insipient ulcer for attention. He wanted to rise to his feet and stand like the others but feared his legs would fail him. He wondered if his father's legs ever failed him. He seemed to be wondering a lot of things lately.

"I do feel that Jim has been right," he said at last, glad to hear a trace of residual steel in his voice, "but I also agree with Eric that we've come too far to quit."

Eric took tentative steps back into the room. Haydel's face went bone-white.

"When Cal calls, I intend to tell him that you, Eric, will footnote the 10-K as Cal has requested." Then, to Haydel, he added, "I'm sorry, Jim. We have no choice."

Haydel stared back at his friend and Simon's gaze fell away. Driver smiled.

"What the hell are you thinking, Simon?" Haydel said. "A misleading opinion like that could bring the firm down."

Eric Driver broke in, saying, "If Cal fires us, Jim, the firm is down in two months anyway."

"But at least the three of us won't be in prison!"

"That is a highly improbable scenario, Jim," Simon said, slowly rising to his feet.

"Well, you can count me out," said Haydel. "I'll clear out my desk."

Simon slowly shook his head. "No, Jim," he said, "you won't. You can't. We go way back, you and I."

Haydel stared miserably, silently at the floor. He didn't have to be reminded that he owed Simon everything he had become. He felt their eyes on him, heard Simon's clock ticking, felt a growing dampness across his back.

"All right, Simon," he finally said, "I'll see the next card, but I'll have no further involvement with CalCorp."

"As you wish, Jim. Acceptable to you, Eric?"

"More than acceptable," Driver said, glaring up at the taller Haydel. "I *insist* on it."

"All right, then . . ."

But the two men were already hurrying out of Simon's office. Simon entered his private bathroom, looked in the mirror, and splashed water on a face. His stomach ached, and his chest felt like cables were being tightened around it.

What the hell was he thinking? Jim Haydel had asked him that and he had not replied. Simon now asked the same question of his reflection—and still heard no answer.

. . .

JESSE FOUND SEÑORA Anastacia Ramirez's home in the sunny and quiet *Zona* 9, at 3 *Avenida*. The smell of honeysuckle accompanied his walk up the short cobblestone path toward the neat, white-painted cottage.

He was eager to meet the last person to speak with Marisa. He was alone, for Teo had been reluctant to return to the Ramirez house after his cold reception. Instead, Jesse asked him to try to locate and interview Webster's housekeeper—a woman who had shown up in the police investigation report Elena had given him.

With the trial starting in just two days, Jesse hoped to glean more about the final conversation Anica had overheard, and perhaps even reveal Señora Ramirez to be another plausible murder suspect. It was common knowledge, after all, that Anastacia and Marisa were at times vicious political combatants and that only by virtue of Marisa's death had Anastacia finally succeeded in taking control of *La Causa*.

The door opened a crack, revealing a fifty-something, plumpish matron with an intelligent face, wiry hair streaked with grey, and an imperious bearing. She dried her hands on a red and white towel. "Yes," the woman said warily, "I am Señora Ramirez." She did not invite Jesse inside.

"I only need a few minutes of your time, Señora," he said in Spanish, "I am Jesse Hall. I represent—"

"I am sorry, Señor Hall, but I cannot help you," she said, her lips tight with resolution. Her gaze danced nervously over his shoulder up and down the street and she began strangling the towel. Afraid of the PNC, like everybody.

"Who's watching you?" Jesse said. "ARES? PNC?"

She shook her head as if escaping hornets, tried to push the door closed.

"Would you be willing to meet me somewhere else? I have heard of your efforts on behalf of *La Causa* and I know Marisa Andrade had great confidence in you."

"Save the fancy words, Señor. I have nothing to say to you. I've told the police everything I know. Besides, Teo Andrade can go ahead and take over *La Causa* for all I care."

Jesse could hear bitter resentment in her voice and, with another glance up and down the street, she pushed the door against his foot. "It sounds to me," Jesse said, "like you are still angry about losing the election last year to Marisa."

Ramirez backed up a step, folded her arms and said, "That's a lie. Marisa and I settled our differences and I was perfectly content to remain Membership Chair."

"But when she was murdered, you became the President, am I correct?"

"That doesn't make me a suspect, and you do not scare me with your innuendo. Marisa was not my enemy. I have no enemies. I was merely urging a more conservative path. Marisa tended to be overly aggressive at times; inviting trouble. That's all. Goodbye, Señor."

Jesse shifted tactics. Bad cop wasn't working. "And you wisely preferred to put less pressure on the government?"

"I just wanted her to stop drawing criticism to the movement."

"Of course. I understand completely."

"I only urged moderation and begged her not to advocate throwing money away on a land grant that was obviously too good to be true. With children starving to death, rampant unemployment, how could we spend our precious *quetzales* on something that would further divide our country and was probably a hoax anyway?"

"I agree with everything you have said, Señora. I cannot imagine why Marisa did not see the wisdom in your advice."

Her eyebrows shot up. "But she did! She *agreed* with me in our last conversation."

"On the phone? Is that when she admitted she was having doubts about the 'old mail?'"

"*Exactamente*. We were suspicious that ARES had tapped our phones so we used code names for everything. I've told you all I know. Please leave."

Jesse felt a rush of excitement. So "old mail" *was* the land grant and Marisa *had* found a flaw in it. Would Teo accept this? "Why, Señora, did she lose confidence in it?"

"I wish I knew, because now it will probably be purchased."

"Did Marisa ever mention to you a man named Carlos Webster?"

Her eyes darted over Jesse's shoulder again. "I don't know that name and I really can't talk to you anymore. I am sorry."

Jesse kept his foot in the doorway. "Are you not interested in seeing her real killer brought to justice?"

"You are representing her real killer," she said, "and you are putting me in danger."

"Are those PNC men in the Opel parked across the street?"

"Probably," she said, pinching the bridge of her nose. "They are always watching me. And ARES at night. One of them is getting out of the car right now!"

"Okay, ma'am, you've been helpful, and I didn't come here to get you in more trouble. So what I want you to do is slap me."

"*Slap* you?"

"Hit me hard, but then answer one more question. Do that and I'll leave."

"I am not a violent . . . "

Jesse reached out and gave the appearance of trying to grab her by the shoulder. "Hit me, Señora! *Do it!*"

She hit him. Not very hard, but it probably looked good from across the street.

"Good," Jesse said, holding on to her wrist. "Now act like you're afraid of me, but tell me if Marisa mentioned money going from Carano to Carlos Webster."

Anastacia Ramirez glanced out into the street again, breathing hard from fear and the physical exertion. "All right, yes. Marisa had . . . several reliable informants, and one of them was a banker who told her Webster was getting money from Carano. Please *go!*"

"What else did the banker say? Tell me that and I'll leave you."

She hesitated, her eyes wide with fear. She tried to pull away from his grasp. "Señor! Both men are out of the Opel."

"Tell me and I'll go!"

The woman's face had turned bloodless. "He told her . . . about financial linkage between Carano and Gómez."

"You mean between Carano and Webster, not Carano and Gómez."

"No, no. Money from Carano's account went to both Webster *and* Gómez. Marisa was trying to find out why."

Carano sending money to *Gómez*? How could this be?

"Did you tell the police any of this, Señora?"

"Are you crazy? The PNC answers to Carano. Besides, I've got a family to protect. Let me close this door!"

"Is the PNC man coming toward us?" Jesse asked.

"One is still standing by his car, but the other man is in the street."

Jesse's mind reeled from what he had heard. Could Marisa have discovered a multi-sided drug syndicate, with Carano, Webster, and perhaps *La Cofradía* providing security, Gómez the product, and Cal Covington the U.S. market?

Jesse heard a screen door opening at the back of the house. Señora Ramirez glanced over her shoulder and whispered, "It is my husband. Please, you *must* leave."

Jesse still held her wrist and pulled her closer. "I will, just one more thing. I know that 'friend' was a code name for someone very important. Anica heard Marisa tell you he was connected with *La Cofradía*. Who was he?"

She shook her head.

"Tell me or I will have to subpoena you at trial."

Señora Ramirez's eyes were round with fear. *"The men are coming!"*

"Answer my question and I'll leave."

The woman's frightened eyes darted from side to side. "Anica was partly right. Marisa claimed she had learned that the one we called 'friend,' the very top person in *La Cofradía,* was high in government, but she didn't tell me who he was, I swear to you."

Ramirez pushed harder against the door and in a staged, much louder voice added, "I repeat that I have nothing against Carano or anyone else in government and I am finished with *La Causa*. I tell you *nothing."*

A stocky, scowling man of medium height came from behind Señora Ramirez and joined her in the doorway. "What's going on?" he demanded of Jesse.

Jesse said, "I am almost finished here, Señor."

"No," he said, "I am her husband and you are finished *now."* The man pushed his wife out of the way and stared around Jesse, his eyes suddenly reflecting his wife's fear. Jesse knew the goons must be close to the front door.

"I don't know who you are," Señor Ramirez said loudly, "but you must go!"

Jesse could hear the men talking right behind him, coming up the walkway, but didn't turn his head. He winked at the Ramirezes and shouted, "*Okay!* The hell with both of you if you won't speak to me!" The door slammed shut and Jesse faced the two men. The fat one with the pockmarked face and short-sleeved white shirt looked familiar. He had been at Teo's the night they took him away.

"*Buenos días*," Jesse said, and started past them.

"Hold on, Señor," the other man demanded, a narrow-shouldered beanstalk in a dark suit. "What is your business here?"

"Who wants to know?"

"We are police," said the beanstalk, "and you will answer the question."

"Oh, I'm sorry, Officer. I am a lawyer trying to interview a possible witness, but the bitch wouldn't talk to me."

"It looks like the Señora spent a lot of time not talking to you," the sweating fat one said, his face uncomfortably close to Jesse's.

"Yeah, I kept her from closing the door, even when the whore hit me. I give up. Life is too short. The hell with them."

The cops were off balance and Jesse walked to his car without resistance. He drove away, relieved to see them in his rearview mirror heading back to their car. As soon as he had time, he would report his conversation to Teo. Maybe he'd listen now, which was good, but everything else he had learned from Anastacia only led to even more perplexing questions. Gómez and Carano linked together? Impossible. And what good did it do to have identified "friend," code for the head of *La Cofradía,* as high in government, when his true name remained a secret? As for the land grant letter, Marisa had obviously learned something that put its authenticity in serious question. But what?

More questions without answers, another night without sleep.

32

ALTHOUGH IT WAS lunchtime as Jesse drove away from the Ramirez home, he had no appetite. The breeze from his open windows was hot on his face, but blew cold against a shirt uncomfortably wet across his back. He returned to the hotel for a shower and change of clothes, but first, he checked his messages at the office. None was important, except one from Megan. His heartbeat picked up and he punched in her number with suddenly unreliable fingers. Calm down, he told himself.

"It's me," he said. "I just got your message."

"I'll be quick, Jess. I just wanted you to know that I've been feeling rotten about our conversation last week. I was on a downer and didn't give you a chance to say much. I've felt bad ever since and . . . well, I've been thinking things over."

"And?"

"Oh, God, I don't know. All I'm doing lately is worrying about you down there."

"I'm fine, really great," he lied. He was encouraged, but an image of

Charlie Brown trying again to kick Lucy's football in vain restrained him from saying more.

"How's the case going?" she said.

"I'm bumbling along."

"If yesterday's AP wire is correct, you're persevering, not bumbling."

"I'm persevering in my bumbling."

"You're doing both at the moment."

"You're right as usual, Meg." He realized he was smiling for the first time in days. "That's only because I persevere."

"Seriously, Jesse, the *Chronicle* is following the Andrade story down there and says you're at risk. Are you appropriately anxious about that?"

Jesse rubbed his eyes and almost yielded to a self-indulgent need to tell her what he was going through. He settled for, "Anxious and then some."

"Good, well . . . I just wanted to apologize for being such a drama queen on our last phone conversation. I'd like to take you to dinner when you get back, and I promise to try to get through the entire meal without ragging you about your work ethic."

Jesse said nothing.

"I know our issues are still there, but . . . . look, I know you're busy. I'll let you go."

Jesse told himself to stay cool, not stick his neck out again. "Yeah, I'd better get moving."

"To do some more persevering?" He could hear her disappointment under the smile in her voice.

"I always try to fit some of that in," he said.

"I miss you, Jess."

"I miss you, too." They said goodbye, his heart incorrigibly beating with new hope. He stared at the phone, a stupid smile on his face.

But the shadow of guilt dampened his elation.

Elena. That never should have started and this time he'd see that it stopped. He owed her that.

He was drying off from his shower when his cell phone buzzed. Now what? Jesse's heart sank as he heard Cal's voice.

"Fuck's goin' on down there, Jesse? It's been nearly a week."

Jesse brought Covington up to date, skipping his trip to Gómez's encampment.

Cal was silent for a few seconds except for some disgusting chewing sounds. "Okay, Jesse," he said at last, "you've done enough. You can come on home."

Jesse gave his head a shake. "What about—"

"I've taken care of everything. Kevin should be out tomorrow or the next day."

"I . . . that's wonderful," Jesse said. "But I've heard nothing. What's happened?"

"Diplomacy, kid. Plain, old American diplomacy."

"You went through the state department?"

"Something like that," Cal said. "Your reservation home is all set. You leave at eight tomorrow morning. I'm not supposed to say anything, but there'll be a long overdue surprise waiting for you at C&S."

Jesse's initial sense of relief about returning home to his "overdue surprise" quickly gave way to unease. What was going down? An escape caper?

"The trial is scheduled to start in two days," Jesse said. "I'd better stick around. You can't trust anything Carano tells you, if that's who you're dealing with."

"Who the hell said anything about Carano? Did I say anything about Carano?"

"He's the only guy who could pull this off. He or some general in his army. It's a zoo here, Cal. Without the army to clear the mob and a police escort, Kevin wouldn't reach the airport alive."

"Fuck you smokin' down there, kid? What you talkin' about?"

"I'm saying that whoever you've paid could double-cross you, Cal—take your money, then let the mob take Kevin. So I'll stay."

"I reckon you've been speakin' the spic lingo too long, kid. You don't seem to understand plain English anymore. I'm the client, remember? You're done. Stack rifles, drop tools, whatever. Just get the hell to the airport—while you can."

Was that a warning or a threat? Jesse swallowed, measured his words carefully. "You're the client, Cal, but so is Kevin. And it's Simon Bradshaw I work for."

Silence, except for the sound of the big man's labored breathing. Then, a more conciliatory tone. "Look, kid, you've done shit about gettin' Kevin released, right? So give me a break and let me do it my way, okay? Pick up a bottle of rum at the duty free and get back to work. Don't tell Cy I blew the surprise about your new status in the firm."

"The only way out for Kevin is an acquittal, Cal," Jesse persisted. "And we've got a chance. We might be able to connect Carano to a dead CIA station chief and maybe Gómez as Carano's silent partner in the drug trade."

Cal let out a cackle. "That's rich. What the hell business do you think *I'm* in? Tradin' beads to the fuckin' Indians?"

Holy shit, there it was. Jesse could think of nothing more to say.

After a minute of tense silence, Cal said, "Understand this: I've spent years puttin' this deal together and I won't let you or anybody else screw it up."

"Does that include your own son?"

"Kevin's a good kid, but he couldn't keep his pecker in his pants and maybe can't keep his mouth from runnin' like a goose's ass neither."

Jesse's hand was cramping from squeezing down on his phone. "You're going to risk your own son's life in an escape that could backfire because you're afraid he'll blow your drug deal?"

"You best mind your own business, kid. You'll live longer."

"Kevin *is* my business," Jesse said, "and I'm going to keep on minding it."

"That would be very dangerous."

"If that's a threat, you'll have to get in line, Cal," Jesse said, with more bravado than he felt.

"I don't wait in lines."

Jesse realized he had just been given a telephonic death kiss. He had to come up with some insurance, and do it fast. "Hold on a minute, Cal. Did I mention that one of the apps of my new cell phone can record phone calls? And it's legal here." Jesse then hit "end," pleased to know his fatigued brain still had a few functioning cells.

Despite the reprieve his bluff had probably earned him, he already needed another shower. Toweling off the second time, he caught another look at his face in the medicine cabinet mirror and saw fear staring back at him. He knew he was on Carano's clock now, too, but he'd better go warn Kevin, get to him before somebody else did. When he had a minute, he'd call Simon and this time pull no punches.

He dialed Elena's number. She was still upset that he had subpoenaed Gómez, but reluctantly agreed to help him see Kevin.

"The mob out there has doubled in number, Jesse," she said. "Come around seven, when they're down to a hundred or so. Go to the back gate as before. Someone will be there. Come see me after you visit your client. I must speak with you."

"I'll be there," Jesse said. "What's up?"

"Be patient. I will be in my courthouse annex office on the second floor."

Jesse hung up, looked in the mirror again, arranged his face into a smile. "You can do this," he told the tired face looking back at him, but the face registered doubt.

He knew Cal would wait to see if he gave up on Gómez, so he probably had a day or two before anything would happen—unless Carano disappeared him first. He'd have to find a way to put this crazy puzzle together. If he did his job, maybe something close to justice would come out of it, not just for Kevin, but for the people of this God-forsaken country.

Less than two days.

· · ·

AT 7:15 P.M., Kevin shuffled into the holding cell visitor's room at the *Torre de Tribunales* as fast as his manacles would allow. Jesse went straight to it. "Have you been told your father has arranged to get you out of here?"

"I've heard nothing. How would it go down?"

Jesse rubbed his temples. "I don't think it will go down at all."

"Why not?"

"Somebody would have gotten word to you by now."

"So it won't happen tonight?"

"Look, Kevin. I don't know what Cal's up to, but it'll be dangerous, whatever it is. This isn't like the movies where you slip out in a laundry truck. Your father could easily be double-crossed."

Kevin leaned close to him. "I think I'll take my chances, Jesse. No offense."

"None taken. I'm just a lawyer here, Kevin, but in my opinion, the only safe way to the airport and out of the country is for you to first get adjudged not guilty. Until that happens, you can't trust anybody."

"Should I include you in that?"

Jesse gave him a look.

"All right," Kevin added, "sorry. So what are you so worried about?"

"I think Cal's afraid you might say something; you know, try to cut a deal?"

Kevin flared. "He knows me better than that."

"Maybe, but don't get suckered into any escape opportunity. The risk is too high."

"How about the risk of standing trial? I've *seen* those judges, plus you said we don't have the Carlos V clue left by Marisa now, right?"

"Yes, but we may have something better. An alibi. See, I had a talk with Gómez and—"

"You *what*?"

"—and I subpoenaed him."

Kevin shook his head furiously. "Dammit, Jesse, I told you I won't shoot down Dad's deal, whether I approve of what he's been doing or not. I'll take the stand and deny I was there."

Jesse stared at his client, and Kevin stared back, unflinching under his lawyer's penetrating gaze. Jesse's fevered mind flashed onto what he had risked in the service of this man who was prepared to deny his alibi to protect his father's illicit drug deal. He rose, grabbed his coat and picked up his file. "Goodbye, Kevin, and good luck."

"Where you going?" Kevin said.

"San Francisco. Eight tomorrow morning. Daddy's orders, and we always do what Daddy says, right?"

"Come on, Jesse!" A muscle on the left side of Kevin's face was jumping like a worm under his skin and Jesse could see pressure was breaking the young man down.

Jesse put on his coat.

"Please, Jesse! Believe me, this is his last drug deal. He'll be able to fund the final phase of CalCorp's expansion, and then he's out for good."

"But you won't be alive to see it. Listen to yourself: you're going to risk taking the needle for a man who's throwing you to the wolves."

Kevin's head rolled on his shoulders, as if in physical pain. Like a priest losing his faith. Jesse could see the pain of realization snaking into Kevin's eyes, now flooding with tears.

"Try . . . to understand, Jesse. He's . . . my father. He's a good man who's done some bad things, okay? He's a decent guy. He's a major donor to the Katz Cancer Center and has set up non-profit schools for deaf kids in five states."

"Praiseworthy, but probably not an offset to all the kids whose lives have been ruined by his product."

"But I'm telling you, he's getting out! He'll have CalCorp where he wants it and be able to focus more time on his schools. And if you could see the way he treats my mother. And my brothers . . ."

"Swell. So he's Father of the Year and a man who might quit trafficking." Jesse started for the door, only ten feet away, afraid he might make it through this time. Then what? Five feet. His hand on the door knob.

"*Stop!* Hold on, Jesse! Okay, I'll go along with you. I'll do my best."

Jesse turned and sighed—somewhat theatrically, he realized—and walked back. He dropped his coat over a chair and sat down across the table from his client. "Let's be clear on this, Kevin. I'll stick with you through the trial, but in return you'll promise not to get suckered into any great escape plots, you'll go with the alibi if Gómez comes in, and you'll help me put all the pieces together. Starting right now. Do we have a deal?"

Kevin reluctantly nodded his assent and managed to straighten his shoulders.

"*Say it.*"

"Yeah, sure. We have a deal."

"Fine. I think Marisa was on to some kind of a connection between Gómez and Carano. So let's start with whether Carano was involved in the new drug cartel."

"No. I'm sure Dad would have liked it, but he wasn't."

"How about Carl Webster?"

"I had never heard of him."

"Okay, who else *was* involved?"

"That's it. Dad, Gómez, and probably *La Cofradía* in the wings. And there was an Arab at the landing strip that Gómez was paying a lot of attention to, but I don't know about him."

"An Arab?"

"Looked like one, kissing Gómez on both cheeks before he gets on the plane as I'm getting off. Gómez didn't introduce us."

"This was on April first?"

"No, I arrived the evening of March thirty-first. I didn't actually meet with Gómez until the morning of the first."

"How do you know it was April first when you were there with him?"

"Gómez's men took me to a flea-bag hotel in Livingston where I spent the night. They picked me up in a jeep around ten the next morning, put me in a boat, then blindfolded me and took me to the compound. We were together through lunch. Just when I was about to head back, Gómez's radio put out the news that Marisa had been killed that morning."

"Can we prove you were there without Gómez's testimony? Did you check into the hotel under your own name?"

"You're kidding, right?"

Jesse took a seat and stared across the small, pockmarked table into the eyes of his client. "Let's get back to *La Cofradía*. While you were close to Marisa, did she ever mention someone she called 'friend?'"

"Friend? She had millions of them."

"I don't mean a real friend. 'Friend' was code for the head of *La Cofradía*. Marisa was probably closing in on his true identity. This could help us if we could I.D. him. Another guy with a motive to kill her."

Kevin shook his head, then said, "I know nothing about *La Cofradía* except it's like the Italian mafia only better because their ruling brotherhood consists of business leaders, legislators, and high government officials."

"Scary," Jesse said.

Kevin checked the guards, then said, "Look, I'm not trying to justify *La Cofradía,* but I hear that without them, the five major crime families would be at each others' throats and innocent people would get killed in the carnage."

"Gómez heads one of those families?"

"Yeah, but his is bigger than the rest combined." Kevin leaned as close as he could get to Jesse. "Gómez told me his and Dad's new syndicate would be protected by *La Cofradía*, but they'll take a hefty cut. Ironic, huh? An American mob *paying* protection?"

"Protection from who?"

"If Dad and Gómez were cutting the Colombians out of the cartel they might need the services of the whole damned Guatemalan army. *La Cofradía* would also make sure none of the other four families got in the way."

Jesse rubbed his two-day beard. "The army would answer mainly to Carano, so isn't it logical that he's the top guy at *La Cofradía?* We know it's someone high up in government."

"My father doesn't think so. First, *La Cofradía* functions outside the government and is probably much more powerful. Carano would be threatened by them. Second, Carano is known to hate drugs. He lost a brother to heroin. Third, your theory would require Carano and Gómez working together, and that could never happen. If you're right that Marisa was getting close to finding out who was at the top of *La Cofradía,* it could explain a lot about why she got killed."

Jesse watched the guards roughly escort his client away, convinced more than ever that Kevin was neither a murderer nor a gangster. Just a well-meaning young auto parts man, who got in too deep.

Not much deeper than himself, Jesse thought. Using the alibi to save Kevin could get him, Jesse, killed by either Cal or Gómez himself. Discrediting the land grant letter could get him killed by an Aguilera fanatic or, again, by Gómez. Or he might tie Carano's money to Carl Webster, which could get him killed by Carano's ARES brown shirts.

Having options was supposed to be good, but not when all of them were bad.

33

A HALF-FILLED BOTTLE and an empty glass sat on a credenza behind her desk. No ice bucket in sight. Her eyes were bloodshot and damp. Her breath was stained with the sweet stink of gin.

"You okay?" Jesse said, taking in yet another of Elena's multiple personalities.

"I'm a mess," Elena said, touching her hair. "Please, sit down. Believe it or not, I just spent ten minutes trying to make myself look better."

"You look fine, Elena, maybe a little tired. Not mad at me anymore about Gómez?"

She gave him the smile that had always knocked his socks off and fell into a chair. "You are a hard man to stay mad at, Jesse, but I hope to persuade you not to bring him in to testify."

"I have no choice, Elena, and I must say I'm puzzled by your attitude."

"We live in *detente* here, Jesse. His people hit us occasionally, he runs his drugs, the police look the other way. He mainly keeps to himself somewhere north of Livingston and sends his drugs up to Mexico and the U.S., rather than spreading the cancer to our own young people."

The words made sense, but her delivery was badly slurred. The Queen of Control was drunker than a sailor on shore leave. Why?

"So you made a deal with the devil," Jesse said. "That's why you don't prosecute him?"

Elena rose, freshened her drink, offered one to Jesse that he accepted only to avoid embarrassing her. "Our arrangement keeps the peace. Gómez has much support among the people of Guatemala City. He's a hero to most Indians. I don't want to think what would happen if he came in to testify and something went wrong. You would be upsetting a delicate balance."

"Does that mean if he comes in, you will not cross-examine him?"

"I would have to. That's the problem. I would have to. Have to."

Slurring *and* repeating herself. Jesse said, "Will you hit him with the claim that Kevin was there discussing drugs?"

"Was he?" She was drunk, but she was still the prosecutor. Elena lit a cigarette with a dancing match and tossed the pack onto her desk.

Jesse said, "You know I can't answer that."

Elena exhaled a stream of smoke. "And you know I can't ask Gómez if Kevin was there discussing drugs. If I did that, I'd be conceding Kevin *was* there."

Jesse flashed a smile. "You're a smart woman, Elena."

Elena didn't return the smile. "Once you said I was remarkable. Never mind, what I am is a realist," she said, and took another drag.

A clock chimed the half-hour. He looked around the room. His foot bounced and jiggled nervously. Something was wrong. She sipped from her glass.

"What's bothering you, Elena? I've never seen you like this."

"Nothing is wrong. I'm perfectly fine."

"If you say so. What did you want to tell me?"

"We have found where most of Carano's discretionary fund went to."

"I'm listening."

"Would you like to guess? Millions of U.S. dollars over the past two years?"

"Just tell me," Jesse said, feeling sheepish that he already knew the answer.

"They went to your genial host north of Livingston . . . Arturo Gómez."

Jesse nodded, raised his eyebrows in an effort to look surprised. It didn't fool her. Nothing ever did.

"You are not surprised? We were shocked."

"I've become immune to surprise in this country."

She reached for an envelope on her desk. "Anyway, here is your copy of the fund transfer documents, although I don't know if it helps or hurts you. I'll have more later."

So Anastacia was right. It's Carano and Gómez after all—Carano, the Vice President, and Gómez, the President of Vice. Carano must have overcome his repugnance for drugs. But why was money flowing away from Carano instead of toward him? Wouldn't he be the guy paid to look the other way? Getting his cut for providing the army for protection?

"Thanks for the information, Elena, though I can make no sense of it."

"Do not thank me. Your subpoena was broad enough to cover these documents."

Jesse scanned the bank records and supporting data. "What do *you* make of all this, Elena?"

"I produce subpoenaed documents. I am not required to interpret them."

"Fair enough. What else do you have for me?"

She sighed and picked up a larger brown folder. "Why don't I just try your case for you?" she asked, her words slurred again.

"No thanks. I need the practice. It's hard to get to trial these days in the U.S."

She smiled at that. "By the way, you can remove Anastacia Ramirez from your witness list. I am sorry to tell you she was murdered this afternoon."

Jesse heard a soft whooshing sound and realized it was his breath leaving him. "How . . . how did it happen?"

"I know nothing more at this point. Chief Inspector García is on it."

Shit. He was indirectly getting people killed down here, and with Anastacia gone, Teo would never have Marisa's doubts about the land grant confirmed. What else could go wrong? He finished his drink. Wondered if she'd offer another.

"Here is the last of what you are entitled to," she said, seemingly unaware of Jesse's torment, and handed him several pages that appeared to be Marisa's calendar. "These were confiscated by the police as evidence from her desk at home."

Jesse examined entries in January, February, and March. He noted three dates circled in the same red pen, one in February and two in March, just before her death. The last two entries next to the dates were the same. Jesse translated the underlined words and said them out loud, almost to himself, "'Mexico City again. Coincidence?'"

Jesse felt her eyes on him, but she remained silent.

"What do you make of this?" he said. "What was she talking about?"

"I was hoping you would tell me." she said. "It makes no sense to us, but you're entitled to copies under the court's order, so there they are."

"'*Mexico City again. Coincidence?*'" Jesse repeated, then gave his head a quick shake and said, "I'll run it past Teo."

"You'll tell me what he says?"

"Sure, but I doubt he'll know anything. He and Marisa led . . . separate lives. It was an unusual marriage."

She took a deep drag on her smoke. "I know about unusual marriages."

"You told me once you were 'unavailable.' Is that the reason?"

She shook her head. "After Raul's death, I willingly chose to be married to my work and my country's well-being. Can you understand that?"

He nodded. *You're married to your firm,* Megan had said.

"Are you sure the end will justify such sacrificial means?" he asked.

"I think so. We shall see."

"How will you know?"

"I will know," she said, and lurched slightly. She held up her glass in a mock toast and added, "All Guatemala will know!"

"What," said Jesse softly, made uneasy by her bizarre mood, "will they know?"

"That the end," she said, flashing a sardonic smile, "did indeed justify the means."

Jesse rose and acknowledged her clever ambiguity by touching his glass to hers. After an awkward silence, he tried to refocus her attention back to the case. "Webster told me your father had enemies other than Carano. He called them, 'unsavory former associates.' Whom did he mean?"

Her vacant eyes sparked. "Webster was well-known to be an unscrupulous CIA spook, a devious liar, and an asshole as well."

Jesse noticed she hadn't denied Webster's allegation.

"Tell me what's going on with you tonight."

She didn't answer, killed the rest of her drink in a single swallow.

Jesse persisted. "Cal Covington can be forceful at times when he's not getting his way. Has he communicated anything to you? He told me there will be no trial."

"There will be a trial, and he is not threatening me. Let's not go there again."

"Then what's going on with you?"

"I'm just tired," she snapped, and then her voice softened. "Tired, that's all."

"Is the responsibility getting to you?"

She managed a doleful smile. "Responsibility?" she said, her voice breaking. "You cannot *begin* to know." Her eyes teared-up and her hands fell lifelessly to her side. "God knows I'm trying hard to change things," she added, "to make lemonade out of the lemons he has handed me. Really trying."

Jesse's brow knitted in confusion. "Lemons he handed you? Are you talking about your father? What are you saying—"

"Shhh," she said, moving close and touching a finger to his lips. The intimacy of the gesture both silenced and excited him. Watch yourself, boy. "Any more case-related questions?" she said, abruptly breaking the mood. The woman was on a rollercoaster.

"No, that's all I have. Kevin is safe? There are rumors of an escape attempt."

"Under double guard," she said. "I assure you he will not be leaving us."

"Until after I win the case," Jesse said, offering a smile. She was standing so close he again smelled the gin on her breath. "Elena, what's with all the boozing?"

She turned away from him, walked over to the makeshift bar. "Freshen yours?"

"All right," he said, ignoring his cautionary instincts, giving her his glass.

She made drinks and handed one to him. They touched glasses again and she tilted her head up towards him, her lips parted, the invitation clear. He felt awkward and uneasy, but undeniably excited. She put a hand around his neck and pulled his lips to hers. She ground her hips into his sudden hardness.

Jesse looked into her large eyes and the urgency he saw there wasn't born of love or even desire, but something dark he couldn't name. She led him toward her conference table and backed seductively against it. When he hesitated, she glanced at the door and shrugged. "I agree, it is not ideal, but . . ."

Jesse stopped her, stood back, hands on her shoulders. "That door has no lock on it, Elena, plus you're not a drinker, and you've had way too much."

She looked down, embarrassed, but did not move away.

"Besides, the last time you rejected me you've pointed out that I'll be leaving here in a week, and you were right. I care too much about you to . . ."

". . . take advantage of another moment of weakness?" she said through tightened lips. She hurried past him, smoothing her skirt down with both hands. "Please don't patronize me. I've humiliated myself enough already. Please leave."

"And you'll 'see me in court,' right? Come on, Elena, I'm just saying let's not do something we might both regret."

"*Leave!*" she shouted, and this time he did.

. . .

JESSE WALKED BACK to the Hotel Conquistador Ramada, never more lonely, his mood slipping lower with each block covered. He was already second-guessing himself about what had happened. He had humiliated Elena, someone he really cared for. Didn't she realize that her career would have been ruined if someone had come through the door in the middle of things? He had done the right thing on several levels, but still felt like shit.

He took the elevator to his room and opened the door. Before he could flip the light switch, he felt the force of air in the darkness, something coming hard at him. He ducked, and the main energy of the blow was taken on his shoulder, the same one he had hurt escaping the boat. He saw the man's form in the semi-darkness and fearing a knife or a gun, went for his legs. With surprising ease, he took the man down, then pinned his forearm into the assailant's throat.

"Stop, Señor Hall," the man grunted in Spanish, "you're . . . choking me."

Jesse recognized the voice from earlier that morning. It was Anastacia Ramirez's husband. Jesse pulled the older man to his feet and switched on the lights.

"What the hell?" An eighteen-inch billy club was on the floor next to them.

"She is *dead,* you bastard!" Ramirez gasped, sobbing into both hands. "My wife is dead because of you."

A searing pain stabbed Jesse's head. "Señor, I . . . I am so sorry. I was . . . just trying to do my job and—"

"Your *job?*" Ramirez gasped, tears streaming down his face.

"I told them you both refused to talk to me," Jesse said, hearing the torment in his own voice. "I did the best I could."

"You idiot! You think the best you can do is sufficient to defeat the corruption we live with here? Do you understand *anything* about the nature of the evil we endure here?"

Grim-faced, Jesse nodded. He *was* beginning to understand.

The older man wiped away tears. "The PNC thought she was cooperating with you, and they must have forced her to tell them everything Marisa had told her."

Jesse's shoulders sagged under the weight of the accusation. "*Lo siento, Señor.*"

Ramirez grunted, and kicked the nightstick into the bathroom. It clattered loudly as it skittered across the tile floor.

"I doubt the police killed her, Señor Ramirez. I think it was someone who wants *La Causa* to acquire the land grant and considered your wife an obstacle."

Ramirez shrugged. "What does any of that matter? My wife is gone."

. . .

JESSE INSPECTED THE door after Ramirez left. The lock was unbroken. He wondered if the entire population of Guatemala City had a passkey to his room. With housemaids considered lucky to have a weekly salary of 150 *quetzales*—about nineteen U.S. dollars—even a five-dollar bill would prove irresistible.

He tried to calm down, but guilt and frustration had pumped too much adrenaline into his bloodstream. He considered going downstairs for a beer, but switched on the TV to catch the nightly news at the top of the hour. Elena Ruiz's press secretary was on, saying that the CP was calling a press conference for noon the next day. Jesse grabbed his phone and caught Elena still in her office.

"I just saw the news. What's this about a press conference?"

"Relax, Counselor, it's not about Kevin Covington." Her voice was cold, strained. Jesse knew she had called him "Counselor" to signal a renewed formality.

"Is it about the Webster or Ramirez murders? Is there a break in the cases?"

"No," she said, "and I cannot say more."

To keep her on the phone, he told her about his visit from Anastacia Ramirez's husband.

"Do you want a restraining order against Señor Ramirez?" she asked.

"No. He's the least of my worries. You're my biggest at the moment. Sure you won't give me a preview?"

"You will have to tune in like everybody else. Don't worry, Counselor. What I say tomorrow might actually help your case."

Jesse heard something more than coldness in her voice, a tension he had picked up early in the evening. The woman was afraid of someone or something.

"Why didn't you tell me you were calling a press conference?"

"Three reasons. Number one, when last I checked, you were not my press secretary."

"Meaning, it's none of my business."

"To the head of the class. Two, I wasn't sure I was going to do it. Three, I was too busy humiliating myself. But I must go. Goodnight."

"Hold on, Elena. You didn't humiliate yourself. You were just—"

But she had hung up. He'd hurt her all right, and calling her hadn't helped. Jesse looked at the clock. Midnight. He turned out the lights, but knew sleep would not come easily.

DAY FIFTEEN

34

JESSE AWOKE EARLY the next morning with a badly bruised shoulder. So it hadn't been a dream. Somebody had killed Anastacia Ramirez, and her husband had earnestly, if inexpertly, tried to kill him. Who would come at him next? He'd bet on Gómez, who had only spared him temporarily so that he could motivate Teo to sponsor fund raising. Now that Teo was fully engaged in the process, Jesse was every bit as expendable as Anastacia.

The realization snapped him out of his morning lethargy. That, along with the fact that the most important trial of his life was starting in less than twenty-four hours. Would Gómez show up to testify? If not, could he somehow turn Carano's implausible financial records into a plausible defense?

He wondered if Elena knew why money could possibly be flowing from Carano to Gómez. He hadn't had the heart to bug her more about it the night before, but tomorrow he'd try to convince her that the money trail might be a chance for her to kill two vultures with one stone. Meanwhile, Simon had failed to return any of his calls. It was time to see what was happening at C&S.

He caught Simon at home reading the Sunday paper, sounding friendly and at ease. "Hello, Jesse. Are you back in town?"

The words and their casual delivery hit Jesse in the gut. "Why would I be in San Francisco, Simon," he said, trying to match the partner's relaxed tone, "when I've got a trial about to start in Guatemala?"

"You *what?* Good God, Jesse, the client told you to come home and that's what you must do." His tone had hardened.

"I told the client I take my marching orders from you, Simon, not him."

"I'm glad you haven't forgotten that," Bradshaw said, "so here it is from me: pack your bags, get on an airplane, today if possible, and come home. The Cristal is on ice, awaiting your return."

The sickening irony, the naked absurdity of his situation, hit Jesse like a collapsing building. He almost laughed out loud, though he felt more like crying.

"And our client, Kevin Covington?" Jesse heard the coldness in his voice. "Remember him? The innocent young guy, fighting for his life here in Guatemala City?"

"Our client is Cal Covington, who is arranging for his son's release. You need no longer concern yourself with that . . . inconvenience."

Jesse paced. "The prosecutor knows nothing about any release and an attempted escape in this setting would be suicidal—exactly what Carano would like to see."

"What Carano would like to see is you bringing in Arturo Gómez so he can arrest and expose him."

"I see Cal Covington is keeping you up to speed."

"It's my job to stay up to speed, Jesse. I'm also aware that should Cal's release efforts fail, he will simply retain other counsel. In either event, you're finished there."

"We've already been the 'other counsel' route. Nobody will step in given the—"

"*Jesse!* I want you to stop concerning yourself with details and get out of there!"

There it was: Simon Bradshaw, Jesse's mentor, champion, and friend, willing to let an innocent man die to protect the firm's balance sheet. "Details, sir? I think it's the details that the press will be most interested in. I've been following the *Chronicle's* coverage online and note that C&S is scoring high points with the public for its noble effort down here."

"You're following the local reporting here in San Francisco?"

"It's my job to stay up to speed, too, Simon. And try as I might, I can't think how I'd explain to the *Chronicle* why we left our client to die down here. So I'm thinking I'd better hang in with Kevin a while longer."

Silence. Had Simon hung up? Then came the senior partner's measured words again, each one wrapped in velvet, but the meaning clear. "Your colorful history of *pro bono* overkill and commitment to various lost causes has created problems for you in the past, Jesse. You know how much I admire you, but you're on very thin ice down there. Wrap it up soon—*very, very* soon."

"Soon as I can, Simon," Jesse said without hesitation. "Meanwhile, you might consider also 'wrapping' things up with Kevin's father, a known international drug trafficker. Surely the *Chronicle* would be interested in *his* colorful history."

Another beat of silence, the click of a cigarette lighter. "Okay, Jesse, simmer down. Certainly if you feel so strongly about it, finish the damned case. I'll deal with Cal."

Jesse's eyes widened. Nobody faced down Simon Bradshaw. Had he just done it?

"But please do your best, Jesse, to . . . keep things simple. You follow?"

Jesse followed. *Stay clear of Arturo Gómez*, but he said nothing.

Simon added, "We've got problems enough here *north* of the border."

"I've heard," Jesse said. "My secretary told me about Cal's Shanghai problem with the SEC. Will the firm be defending him?" As if Jesse didn't know.

"The Shanghai matter has been way overblown, and yes, Jesse, we will represent CalCorp, but only for a few more weeks. Trust me on that."

Jesse said nothing, for he had now lost trust in Simon. He also knew he would stay in Guate and continue to protect Kevin as best he could—Cal, Simon, Carano, Gómez be damned.

Jesse went down the elevator to meet Teo for breakfast and a final planning session and paused at the news stand on the way to the hotel's restaurant. The murder of Anastacia Ramirez had made the front pages of both *La Prensa* and the *Globe,* but blaring bold type on page two of the *Globe* also caught his attention:

NEW HOPE FOR A BLOODLESS REVOLUTION

Jesse scanned the story. It reiterated Professor Linares Cruz's opinion that the rumored land grant letter had, in fact, been written by Carlos Quinto. The journalist reported that *La Causa* was resuming efforts to acquire the document, sending out an international appeal for funds. "Money is pouring in," the article said.

Jesse saw that Teo was the first signatory on the plea for funds.

The big man was the only person seated in the hotel restaurant, a huge, open area behind the Ramada registration desk boasting at least thirty linen-covered tables and place settings on each. He was drinking coffee and smoking. "*Buenos días, mi amigo,*" he said, smiling broadly at Jesse and jamming his cigarette into an ashtray that contained no fewer than a half-dozen butts.

"*Y tu,*" Jesse said, then added, in English, "You've been here a while, Teo."

Teo followed Jesse's gaze to the ashtray, then raised both hands in the air in mock surrender. "Ah, unmasked again by the clever Detective Hall. All right, I confess. I came early to get out of the house, where Anica will not let me smoke in peace."

A waiter took their order, and Jesse held up the Anastacia headline, saying, "I take it you've seen this?"

Teo's smile faded. "Murderous bastards."

"Death is close on all our heels, Teo," Jesse said, though he knew the warning would go unheeded. "I'm sorry to have brought this down on you."

"Do not punish yourself, Jesse. It is the way of life in Guate."

"I don't know how you live with it."

Teo smiled sadly. "We love our country and don't want to leave. We persuade ourselves that we will not be the next victim."

"Anastacia Ramirez probably thought that," Jesse said, and Teo merely shrugged and sipped from his coffee cup. Jesse brought out Marisa's calendar pages that Elena had given him. He showed them to Teo. "What do you make of the reference to Mexico City?"

"I have never seen this calendar." Teo said, "but it is her handwriting."

"Do the notes or the dates mean anything to you?"

Teo studied the copies of the calendar pages. "Nothing, but back to Anastacia. What do you think happened?"

"I think she was killed by someone who wanted the land grant financing to proceed, the same person who killed Marisa because she was changing her position about its validity."

Teo put a second teaspoon of sugar into his half-filled cup of coffee, then a third one. "Do not start with me again, Jesse."

"Anastacia Ramirez confirmed to me that Marisa had voiced doubts about the authenticity of the land grant letter on the day she was killed. The same thing Anica overheard."

"Bah!" Teo said. "Of course Anastacia would say that. She *never* believed in it."

Jesse shot him a mocking smile. "Neither did you, until you fell off your horse on the road to Damascus and hit the ground as a human-rights activist. Dammit, Teo, go ahead and ignore reality, but recognize that there are powerful, competing forces at work here, and you could be their next victim."

Teo shrugged, and showed his palms. Jesse realized he had hit a wall. People on a crusade were moved by emotion, not logic, and Teo, perhaps for the first time in his life, had a cause, one he was willing to die for.

"Linares has received a communication from the seller, extending the time to buy," Teo said. "This is perfect, as the trial will be very public with the world press here."

Jesse felt anger rising. "You want to turn a murder trial into a fund-raising opportunity? *Jesus*, Teo, a man's life is at stake!"

Teo was unmoved. "What is at stake is the resurrection of a democracy your CIA destroyed in 1954. The land grant will restore hope and justice to the people of Guatemala. Do you really expect me to favor one man's life over the future wellbeing and greater good of twelve million citizens?"

Jesse slammed his coffee cup down and glowered at his friend. Teo looked away and Jesse leaned close to him. "*The greater good?* That's playing God, Teo, a common rationalization for injustice—whether it's one man killed or the genocide of six million."

Teo mockingly clapped his hands together three times. "A *lovely* polemic, young Jesse," he said. A waiter arrived with their food, and the men fell silent. A vein pounded in Jesse's temple. If Teo had found out the truth about Kevin and Marisa, Kevin would always be guilty, whether he killed her or not, and Teo could rationalize his revenge as for the "greater good" of Guatemala.

"This just isn't you, Teo. We've got a case to try, and we're still on the same side."

"I'm on Marisa's side. Belatedly, I grant you." He attacked his ham and eggs with knife and fork, then abruptly pushed the plate away and added, "You say I am turning Marisa's heroic effort into a fund-raising opportunity. Well, I cannot allow you to twist her dying message into a mere defense exhibit. Her voice in support of the land grant must be heard all over the world. I owe her that!"

The waiter approached them again, breaking the tension. "*Más café, Señores?*"

"*Gracias,*" they said in unison while glaring at each other. Jesse realized he was getting nowhere, and after taking a minute to calm down, he reported on his conversation with Bradshaw.

"Has your senior partner joined the drug syndicate with Cal Covington?"

"Of course not," Jesse said, too quickly, then added, "I'm not sure."

They finished breakfast in silence, except for Jesse telling Teo to keep his radio on, because Elena would soon be conducting a press conference that could affect the case. Then Teo paid the check and Jesse walked Teo to his car, trying to think of a way out of their stalemate. Teo squeezed into the seat of his car. The driver's-side window was down, and Jesse rested his hands on the door. "You're lead counsel," Jesse said, "so I have no choice but to play it your way. But I won't stop trying to persuade you that the letter is a hoax."

Teo nodded and gunned the engine so that Jesse had to raise his voice. "One more thing, Teo. You said you would interview Webster's housekeeper, remember? She's mentioned in the police report."

Teo furrowed his brow. "No, I don't remember that."

"What?" Jesse said. "We talked about it a couple of times. She moved to *Chimaltenango*, remember? You told me you'd go see her."

Teo stared through the windshield, his huge hands clenching the steering wheel as if the vehicle were skidding out of control. "I did?"

"What's going on, Teo?"

Teo rubbed his temples, then stroked the sides of his bearded face with both hands. A blast was heard in the distance, then sirens. Jesse waited.

Teo said. "I will go to *Chimaltenango*."

"Maybe you should see your doc first, Teo."

"There will be time for that after the trial and fund raising is behind me."

Jesse realized that his doubts about Teo—his health and emotional stability, even the residual suspicion that he'd murdered Marisa—were intensifying.

"All right," Jesse said. "I've got to prepare some motions and run some errands."

"I will leave a message at your hotel when I return from *Chimaltenango*."

"One more request, Teo. I want you to ride shotgun with me while I have another go at Linares Cruz. You can stay out of it, just watch and listen. All I ask is that you keep an open mind and be willing to reconsider your stand on Carlos V if I can convince you Linares is lying."

"I will accompany you, of course, but I make no promises."

Jesse nodded, and then wearily watched the twin swirls of exhaust as Teo sped away.

Jesse headed back to his hotel room and retrieved his copy of the *Globe* article in which Marisa had quoted parts of the land grant letter. He scanned the text, trying to find something he had missed on his trip to the library, something he could use against Linares Cruz.

Ironically, even as he scanned the excerpts for flaws, he found a part of himself wishing the damned letter were authentic. He had always been a zealot for justice, and what could be more just than granting land back to the descendants of those from whom it had been stolen? Yet he was convinced the letter was a lie and that it would be best for everyone if he were somehow able to expose it as early as possible.

Unable to find any discrepancies, he turned to the final lines of the Holy Roman Emperor's purported letter to the Governor of the New World, which had created almost as much public furor as had the grant itself when it was published *verbatim* by Marisa in the *Globe* article.

Alas, my Dear Governor, we have rid these people of their nakedness, their innocence, their land, and their gold and have justified their enslavement as compensation for having saved their immortal souls.

I hereby repent for encouraging the conduct of men like Cortéz and Alvarado, and I beg the forgiveness of the Maya. I pray that those in the newly divided lands may live in peace.

And now I, too, shall rest in peace, with God's grace, amen.

The Holy Roman Emperor, Charles V.

Jesse had to admit it was persuasive, and if it were not valid, wouldn't the government's expert historians be all over it? Not necessarily. If Carano were somehow also involved in the hoax, he'd wait to expose it until just before the election for maximum impact in discrediting Aguilera, as Elena had hinted.

He walked downtown to buy snacks and office supplies, and while heading back to his hotel, noticed a crowd of ten or so locals blocking the sidewalk. They were standing in front of an appliance store, staring through the window at a television set. At over six feet, Jesse had no trouble seeing images of the remnants of an office that had been torn apart by an explosive blast. He froze, felt blood begin to pound in his ears.

The office was Elena's.

The windows of her second floor office lay in shards on the Plaza below. The next image was her picture, framed in black. The caption read:

CHIEF PROSECUTOR ELENA RUIZ ASSASSINATED

Jesse's legs buckled under him, and he heard his own voice shouting an anguished denial. Questioning faces turn toward him, but he didn't notice. He felt the blood drain out of his face and sat down on the curb. He buried his head in his hands. A barefoot kid in shorts and a faded U2 T-shirt asked him if he was all right.

Who could have done this?

He lost track of time, but eventually made his way back to his hotel and called Teo.

"Have you heard?"

"Yes, and I am sorry. I know you . . . admired her greatly."

Jesse hung up and let the tears come.

35

HOURS LATER, STILL shaken by Elena's death, Jesse stumbled into the hotel lobby. Sitting there, slumped in a chair, was Teo, bloodhound eyes scarlet with despair.

"Come on up," Jesse said, and led him to his room.

"I am truly sorry, my friend," Teo said on the elevator. "I had my doubts about Chief Prosecutor Ruiz, but this is unthinkable. And I know you valued her greatly."

Jesse nodded and motioned him into his room. Teo sat on Jesse's bed, his head in his hands. "Carano is eliminating his detractors, one-by-one. Did you see him on TV, wringing his hands about Elena and making a big show of doubling her father's protection? Did you see the hypocrite trying to fake tears?"

Jesse said, "We can't be sure it was Carano . . ."

"Who else?"

"Are they certain it was Elena?"

"Yes. Confirmed by dental records and fingerprints. Why do you think Carano killed her?"

"I don't know who killed her. All I know is that she was ready to blow the whistle on somebody at a press conference and that same 'somebody' stopped her. I should have seen it coming."

"What do you think she was going to say?"

"I'd give a lot to know the answer to that one. So what brings you here, Teo? I thought you were on your way to see the housekeeper in *Chimaltenango.*"

Teo started to rise, but fell back onto the bed. "I was, but it is obviously hunting season and I must lie low for awhile," he said. "Marisa, Webster, Anastacia, now Elena Ruiz. I'm probably next on his hit list—right after you, of course. The bastard is going to kill me before my heart, brain, and prostate get around to it." Teo tossed his hands into the air. "My life is worth little, Jesse, but I cannot risk that Anica will become collateral damage when a bomb comes through our window. *La Causa* is providing us an apartment in Mexico where she will be safe."

Jesse rose and began to pace as far as the small room would allow. He could not replace Teo and the Tribunal would never permit him to defend Kevin alone. Yet the case had brought nothing but grief to Teo and Anica, and Jesse knew he had to let them go.

"I would ask Julio to take Anica to Mexico so that I might stay with you, Jesse," Teo said, staring into his hands, "but Julio has gone to join his uncle in Livingston."

"*What?* Julio has joined the insurgents?"

Teo seemed not to hear him. "My hope is that the Tribunal will continue to allow you to handle the defense, like when I was in prison. The presence of the world press might help. In any case, Elena's death will require a continuance, and you'll have ample time to try to replace me. I have prepared a new list of lawyers to serve merely as local figureheads. They are admittedly incompetent, but will probably be willing."

Jesse nodded.

"There are two other reasons for my departure," Teo continued. "The governing board of *La Causa* has insisted that I go into seclusion as a safety precaution, although I told them I could raise more money as a dead martyr or by returning to prison than by hiding."

Jesse said nothing.

"There is another reason. I have had . . . problems again. My doctor insists that I rest for a few days under medical care or I might . . . well, please know that I feel terrible about this."

Jesse nodded. "It'll be fine, Teo. I understand. It'll be fine. Really."

The sing-song wail of a siren blared from below, then faded into the distance. *It'll be fine*—reassuring words that gained no credibility with repetition. Did they ever?

Teo hauled himself off the bed, took Jesse's hand in his, wished him well, and lunged through the door. Jesse stared after him, feeling like a deep-sea diver whose air hose had been cut.

Señor Ramirez was right when he told Jesse he was in over his head. He was back to square one and people were dying. Elena's death would haunt him the most. With nobody to talk with but her demented father and no one to trust, she had reached out to him. And self-righteous prig that he was, he had rejected her extended hand.

DAY SIXTEEN

36

THE NEXT MORNING at 8:55, Jesse sat alone at counsel table in Department 16 on the sixth floor of the courthouse. He kept looking back at the crowded gallery, absurdly hoping to see Teo careening through the door. He had tried to talk to someone in the prosecutor's office earlier, but had only reached a secretary, who told him that the judges would delay the trial.

The courtroom was already filling up, including the press corps, carrying laptop computers, notepads, and cell phones. Jesse recognized two of them as reporters for the *L.A. Times* and the *Washington Post*. He had declined interview requests, not wanting to further antagonize the panel of judges. He heard correspondents in back conversing in French and another pair speaking in a language he couldn't make out. Elena's death had ratcheted up the news frenzy another notch. Good. They were his best protection against Carano and Kevin's best hope for justice.

The door to the courtroom swung open just after nine and a lean man who looked to be in his early forties powered through. He was handsome, despite a swarthy, acne-scarred face. He casually slammed his briefcase down on the table, and then turned his dark eyes on Jesse.

"My name is Enrique Amaya," he said in accented English. "I am the new prosecutor on this case. I take it you are Mr. Hall?" He extended his hand, a grip firm and dry, sure of itself.

"Call me Jesse, and I'm pleased to make your acquaintance. Though I wish the circumstances were different."

Amaya stared at him disdainfully. "Where is counsel?"

"He may be indisposed today." Jesse keeping his options open.

Amaya grunted and turned away. Jesse had run into lawyers like this one before, fighters made for the courtroom, the love of battle deep in their bones. He figured Amaya for the kind of guy who could play tennis in a tuxedo and whip your ass without breaking a sweat.

The doors swung open again, and it was Kevin, handcuffed to a chain looped around his waist and ankle manacles as well, with a pair of guards in front and two more in back. All wore side-arms and were frighteningly young, with cold, smart-ass expressions on their faces. One of them stopped momentarily to chat with a girlfriend in the front row.

Jesse broke the news to Kevin as soon as he reached counsel table.

"He's gone? What the—"

"Don't worry," Jesse said, not hearing much certainty in his voice. "We'll be okay for now."

A side door opened, and the three judges walked in. After the gallery was seated, the senior judge looked at Jesse and said, "Where is counsel for the defense?"

Jesse felt his face redden. "I was hoping to be it, Judge Chavez. My co-counsel is . . . ill . . . and I request that I be permitted to speak in behalf of the defendant, at least today."

Judge Chavez shook her head. "You know that we rarely waive

Section 187 without the express consent of the prosecution and even then it would be most unusual. Does the prosecutor consent?"

Amaya rose and said curtly, "No, Your Honor, and any past implied waivers by my predecessor are hereby rescinded." Jesse's face tightened with anger. This cold-nosed bastard hoped to drive the final spike into Kevin's coffin.

"Then we cannot proceed?" the judge said.

Amaya rose again. "We cannot, for two reasons. As the court knows, I was just assigned this case last night. Because of this, I must request a four-day delay, during which the defendant can find new local counsel and I can familiarize myself with the case."

"New local counsel?" said the senior judge. "Will that be necessary, Señor Hall?"

"It might be, Your Honors," Jesse said, "but—"

"All right. The government's motion for continuance is granted," she said, and closed her notebook. "This will also allow ample time for the defense to replace Professor Andrade if it becomes necessary. We are adjourned."

"Pardon me, Your Honors," Jesse said, as the judges started to rise. "I would like the record to show I have made diligent efforts to find counsel in the past, and nobody will even meet with me."

Judge Chavez smiled indulgently, but said, "This is a problem of your own making, Señor," and she was gone, followed by the two male judges. Within seconds, the gallery was empty. One of the guards saved himself the trouble of asking Kevin to rise by slapping him hard across the back of the head. Yielding to frustration, Jesse seized the guard by the hand and twisted it until the man dropped to his knees.

"Don't, Jesse!" Kevin shouted, "Get off him!"

Other guards rushed toward him, but Jesse raised both hands in submission and the procession started toward the elevators. Jesse tagged along, exchanging venomous looks with the offending guard. An internal voice of reason warned Jesse to get himself under control.

"Jesse," Kevin shouted, "you won't leave, will you?"

"Not until you do," Jesse said, starting to back away. "Don't worry."

Kevin reached out and seized Jesse by his sleeve, fixing him with bloodshot and imploring eyes. "A guard told me this was my last day here, that I'd be gone—"

The guards grabbed Kevin roughly by both arms and pushed him into the elevator.

"Who told you that?" Jesse shouted, but the doors began to close, Kevin shuffling toward the middle to keep Jesse in view as long as possible.

"The guard. He said I was gonna be gone—"

But the doors slammed shut. Jesse shuddered and walked slowly back to the courtroom, giving his heart-rate time to settle. He had to get protection for Kevin, but first he had to deal with his new adversary. He approached Amaya, who was snapping his briefcase shut, about to leave. He looked up and flashed Jesse a ridiculing smile that suggested the *gringo's* fuse was too short for this line of work.

Jesse ignored the unspoken insult. "I wish you would reconsider letting me try this case, sir. Elena was willing to—"

"What Señorita Ruiz was willing to do is irrelevant, and you will not mention her name to me again."

. . .

PACKING UP HIS files, Jesse fought off fingers of anxiety clutching at his heart. Was tonight the scheduled "release" of his client? If it were State Department intervention, he would have been notified. More likely, Cal had fashioned an escape plan in which Kevin might die, and Jesse was helpless to stop it. People would think a lawyer was crazy for reporting that his client was about to escape.

He realized he was alone in the courtroom, save for the court attachés and a woman who had entered so quietly he hadn't heard her. It was Elena's tiny secretary, Rosa Lemus. She looked frightened, continually glancing behind her as if she thought she was being followed.

"Señor Hall, it is I—"

"I know who you are, Señora," said Jesse, in a gentle voice, "and you have my sympathy."

"And you mine," she said. "I know that although you were opponents, you and Elena . . . well, she was like a daughter to me, Señor, and I know that she cared for you. I know, too, that she trusted you."

"Thank you, Señora Lemus," Jesse said, then pulled a chair out for her. "Come sit down for a minute. Are you all right?"

The nervous little woman took the proffered seat. "Who will ever feel right after this? Señorita Ruiz sent me home on Saturday. She said, 'You go home and be with your grandchildren.' She said she didn't want anyone in her office while she prepared for her press conference. She knew something could happen to her, Señor Hall."

"I think you're right about that, Señora. Did she say anything to you about who she was worried about?"

"No," said Rosa Lemus, glancing furtively toward the door, pulling her sweater close around her throat, "but she told me that if anything should befall her, she would no longer have any need for secrets from you."

"Secrets from me? She mentioned me by name?"

She nodded again. "Yes, yes, Señor Hall, many times."

The words stabbed at Jesse's heart. The woman opened her purse.

"Right after the bombing, the PNC asked me for the key to her desk drawer at her main office in *Zona* 2. I said I did not have one but that I would find it. They broke the lock later, but not before I had removed these notes."

Señora Lemus handed him a sealed envelope containing two memos. One was written in Elena's own hand to herself. The other was unsigned.

The first note read as follows:

"Some of the money from Carano's discretionary fund has been going to Webster, but most of it goes to Gómez! Why!? Was the whole thing a façade?"

Elena had already given him money-trail documents, but what did she mean about the whole thing being a façade? What whole thing? A clicking sound spun his head to the side. Rosa Lemus had snapped her purse shut. Calm down, son, he told himself and picked up the other note, which was typed out, undated and unsigned.

"I think," Rosa said, "one of her father's loyalists may have intercepted this one and passed it on to our office."

"Friend: Forgive my boldness, but you are wrong about my dealings with Yassaf Mousaffi. This is not a 'complication,' as you insist, but an opportunity, good for the people, good for you and number one. Rest assured of your safety and wellbeing. I know that you least of all will miss the dog Carano. May God be with us and our noble cause. G."

Jesse quickly noticed two things. First, another reference to "friend." Second, he figured the G must stand for Gómez, suggesting that a double-cross of Carano might be imminent. A long shot, but maybe he could exploit the possibility.

"Thank you, Rosa," Jesse said.

The secretary made the sign of the cross. "I hope I have done the right thing and will be forgiven if I have erred."

Jesse nodded. "You did the right thing, but do you know what any of this means?"

"No, Señor, it is beyond my understanding," she said, and rose and scurried toward the door of the courtroom. "It is up to you, young man. There is no one else now."

. . .

WITH FOUR DAYS to accomplish the impossible task of finding a new lawyer, Jesse picked up a sandwich and headed back to his hotel to make some calls. The desk clerk handed him a sealed envelope. Inside was a typed message:

> *Señor Hall:*
> *Regarding the matter and timing of your departure, we are prepared to suggest a compromise we think you will agree is more than fair. Meet me for lunch today at Portal del Angel. Ask for me.*
> *Your servant,*
> *Antonio Vargas*
> *Special Counsel to the Vice President.*

"Yesss," Jesse murmured. A safe, public restaurant, one of my favorites. Perfect. He checked his watch—nearly noon—gave his sandwich to the desk clerk, and raced to the parking lot. The Suzuki's battery was dead, and after administering a therapeutic kick to the car's left front tire, he waived to a battered Chevy taxi parked at the curb near Jesse's car.

"*Sí, sí, Señor*," shouted the driver, a wiry local in his thirties, with a shaved head, Fu Manchu mustache, gold-ringed ears, and tattoos covering his neck. Jesse barked out the address and slid into the cracked Naugahyde-covered rear seat. The sharp tang of air freshener assailing his nostrils, he grabbed onto the side of the car as Fu Manchu attacked the chaotic roadway like a NASCAR driver about to lose his sponsorship. Still preoccupied with the meaning of Elena's two notes, it took Jesse several minutes to realize they had passed through *Zona* 1 and were heading away from the center of town.

"Where are you going?" Jesse demanded.

"Shortcut. Okay?"

"Not okay. You're lost, and I don't have time for this. Stop the car."

The driver hit the accelerator and cranked up a plexiglass shield between the front and rear seats. The cab speeded up to sixty kph, wildly zigzagging around vehicles and pedestrians. Jesse tried to roll down a window, but the handle came off in his hand. Ditto the other one. Remote back door locks snapped into place with a loud click. Trapped like a fish in a bowl, Jesse shouted and waved his arms at pedestrians and drivers, but this was Guatemala City, where stoplights were uniformly ignored and law enforcement nonexistent. His gut seized up with fear. Now he knew why his car wouldn't start. It had been a carefully planned kidnapping, and the hotel message was part of it.

Was Carano about to disappear him? Jesse knew he had to act, and when the driver slowed to around fifty to execute a sharp turn, Jesse put his full weight behind a kick that propelled his foot through the plexiglass shield and slammed a part of it into the kidnapper's head. The force drove the man's face into the steering wheel, and the suddenly driverless vehicle fish-tailed, careened out of control, and crashed into a concrete lamppost. Jesse's own head banged into a remaining slab of plexiglass, resulting in a brilliant starburst of orange-white light, followed by an instant of black silence.

Seconds later, Jesse was jolted back to consciousness by the pungent smell of steam billowing from a corroded radiator. Fu Manchu remained slumped against the wheel. The force of the collision had sprung a back door open and Jesse pulled himself out and into an alley lined with trash. He limped toward a main street, but glanced back and saw that Fu Manchu had miraculously made it out of the car and was gaining on him fast. Jesse knew he wouldn't make the main street, so he entered a doorway into a small bar packed with locals and shoved his way through men smelling of booze and perspiration toward the rear. A back door might provide a shortcut to the main street.

But when he got there, he found no back door, not even a window, just a cluttered hallway leading off to his left. He glanced back and saw his pursuer coming toward him, scattering patrons like bowling pins. A stubby bartender looked away, occupying himself drying glasses as Fu Manchu strode toward Jesse, his right hand behind his back. Jesse raced down the hallway, where light from a flickering bulb hanging at the end of a frayed electrical cord revealed a bathroom door. Jesse flung open the door and saw . . . no window, not even a washbasin, just a grimy toilet facing the open door. Dead end.

Sweat stung Jessie's eyes, and when he opened them and turned, there was the cabbie, closing in on him with what looked to be a hunting knife in his hand.

So was this how it all ended? Trapped in a crummy bar with a knife-wielding assassin on a drab Monday afternoon, thousands of miles from home? The thought filled him with an anger nearly equal to his fear—anger at Eric Driver and Cal Covington for conning him into coming down here, and anger at himself for having always been the kid who couldn't say no.

Manchu smiled and moved forward in a slight crouch. Jesse stripped off his shirt and wrapped it around his right forearm, keeping his eye on the knife as Manchu tossed it casually from hand to hand. Then the smile faded and he struck. Jesse tried to block the attack with his wrapped arm, but the knife slashed through the shirt and through Jesse's skin and the cloth bloomed red. Jesse somehow got in a hard left to the attacker's jaw and the man stumbled off balance, then tripped on a cardboard box Jesse pushed in his way. But Manchu recovered and struck again, this time slicing a thin crimson line across Jesse's stomach. Jesse yelped and jumped back through the bathroom's open door and Manchu was on him again, knife raised high, ready for a final deadly thrust.

The instant the weapon came down toward Jesse's unprotected chest, he grabbed the side edge of the bathroom door and swung it hard against the descending blade, blocking the thrust. The knife penetrated the wood by six inches and Jesse, too shocked to move, gazed at the bloody point, halted just short of piercing his chest. He reached down and absurdly pushed the frail knob, locking the door, though he realized the futility of the gesture.

He felt light-headed and saw blood from his arm pooling on the filthy floor. As he waited for the door to come crashing into him, he heard the assailant on the other side of the door—the fucker was *humming!*—then another sound, eerie and high-pitched, like fingernails on a chalkboard, the sound of the steel blade grating against wood. The goon was slowly rocking the knife out of the door. Then he would kick his way through the door and finish the job. Jesse had run out of ideas and hope.

I don't want to die.

Then it hit him, an idea so ridiculous it might work. He grabbed the doorknob with his good hand and jerked it open with all his strength. With the assailant's hand gripped tight on the knife handle, the door's momentum pulled him straight into the tiny room and

Jesse's clenched left fist. Manchu staggered from surprise and the blow, but didn't go down. Jesse tried to make it around him to the door, but Manchu punched him in the solar plexus. Jesse again yelped with pain as he staggered backwards and ignominiously plopped onto the stinking toilet seat. Dark spots, like blobs of ink, marred his vision. His strength was ebbing fast, but he staggered back to his feet.

Behind Manchu, Jesse's blurring eyes saw the knife blade still protruding through the door, and as the assailant grabbed him by the throat, Jesse managed to kick the door shut behind him. Though lighter and shorter than Jesse, the assailant was strong, and Jesse's arms felt like concrete blocks. He found himself pinned against the rear wall, his legs awkwardly straddling the toilet, the killer's powerful tattooed forearm pushing against Jesse's throat, slowly crushing his carotid artery. He could smell the assailant's rank breath, feel the assailant's sweat on him.

"I've killed this way before," the man said. "Cleaner than a knife. Slower, too."

It was now or never. Jesse marshaled his dwindling energy and brought a knee hard into the assailant's groin, followed by a savage head butt that brought a satisfying crunching sound as the man's nose flattened. The thug staggered back a step or two, though he seemed more surprised than hurt. Jesse threw his weight against the killer, shoving the smaller man sumo-style toward the door, foot-by-foot, closer to the protruding blade.

Manchu smiled, showing his amusement at Jesse's clumsy effort. "Second wind?" he said, having fun with Jesse now, despite the blood streaming from his broken nose, which reddened his crooked teeth. Then he stopped. "This dance is boring me, *gringo,* so I kill you now. Okay?"

"Not really," Jesse grunted, and with the last of his strength, grabbed Fu Manchu's jacket lapels and thrust him up and against the door.

"Whaaaat?" the man gasped, then began swatting behind his head like a man in a phone booth filled with hornets, trying in vain to reach the place where at least four inches of blade had pierced his back. "*Jesus, man,*" the assailant said in a tone that suggested something unthinkable and terribly unfair was happening. "You've fucking killed me!"

Jesse gasped for air and clamped his eyes shut, unable to look at his victim, but leaning all of his weight against him, keeping the man's struggling body secured to the killing door like an insect on the end of a pin. He felt Manchu's life slowly bleeding out of him, his body jerking spasmodically, but more slowly now, a puppet dancing on uneven strings.

Finally, the thrashing stopped, and as gravity took over, Jesse knew the blade was carving the man's back open. At last, he let the assailant's body slump to the floor. Struggling to catch his breath, he took the taxi's keys out of Manchu's pocket, stepped around the man's lifeless body, and headed back down the hallway toward the bar. He staggered shirtless and bleeding past the bums, bar flies, and regulars, ignoring their open-mouthed stares. The bartender was now standing by the door, but quickly got out of Jesse's way.

"Better get a vent fan in that bathroom," Jesse gasped. ". . . Code violation . . ."

Back into the narrow alley, Jesse stared down at a blurry pavement filigreed with large cracks crammed with bright green weeds struggling for sunlight. He ignored staring onlookers, kept putting one foot in front of the other. Two kids kicking a soccer ball gave him a wide berth.

The cab was right where the assailant had left it. Jesse was woozy, but fell into the driver's seat. He opened the glove compartment and searched the sun visor for some clue as to Fu Manchu's name or affiliation. Nothing.

On the third try, he got the key into the ignition, and miraculously the engine turned over. He backed the rattletrap away from the crumpled lamppost and made it three blocks before passing out and crashing into a construction barricade.

DAY SEVENTEEN

37

LIGHT. HAZY LIGHT. Blurred figures, distant voices, calling his name. He wanted to answer, but he was dead, so what the hell did they expect from him?

"Jesse, you *gringo* faker, talk to me."

Familiar voice. Brain to eyelids: open up.

Won't open.

Cold on eyes, stinging. Alcohol?

One eye open.

"Teo?" he whispered. "Leave me alone. I may be dead."

"You are quite alive, my friend. You merely suffered some lacerations, blood-loss and a mild concussion. You are going to be fine."

"Bullshit," Jesse managed to say, certain somebody had put coffee grounds in his eyes and socks on his teeth before wrapping his brain in burlap. Yet despite his gauzy semi-consciousness, he felt a warm glow of relief upon recognizing his friend's voice.

"You American lawyers will do anything to delay the start of a trial," Teo said. "Seriously, how do you feel?"

A nurse came into view, put a warm hand on Jesse's forehead. "The gentleman is heavily sedated. I do not think he's ready to talk just yet."

Teo kept looking at Jesse. "Well?"

"What she said," Jesse murmured, and fell back asleep.

DAY EIGHTEEN

38

ON WEDNESDAY, AFTER nearly two days in the *Hospital Centro Médico* on 6 *Avenida,* Jesse was released into Teo's care. Teo explained that he and Anica had temporarily moved to a local safe house north of the city, having delayed their trip to Mexico.

"I see," Jesse said, his fingers cautiously probing his scalp. Cuts had been sutured, and the top of his head felt like a relief map of Guatemala's Western Highlands. He was pain-free, however, as long as he stayed on his meds, and eager to get back to work. "I appreciate you guys staying over, but I'm fine," he lied. "How did you learn what happened to me?"

Teo explained that he had heard about the attack just as he and Anica were about to drive to Mexico City. It was easy finding out where the ambulance had taken him. The name of Jesse's assailant remained unknown. The police had accepted Jesse's statement while semi-conscious that the man had run from the cab after attacking Jesse, who then was trying to drive himself to a hospital when he crashed. The police suspected a recent deportee. Deportees from L.A.

prisons routinely flocked to Salvador and Guatemala without money or jobs and were swept into gangs.

Carano's office denied having a Special Counsel named Antonio Vargas and also denied having sent a message to Jesse's hotel. Nevertheless, Jesse suspected that on the day after Carano's one-week grace period had expired, Carano had tried to expire Jesse. It was time to surround himself with some protection, if he hoped to see the trial through to conclusion.

．．．

INSIDE THE RUSTIC adobe safe house, Teo and Jesse sipped coffee in a brightly lit, colorful kitchen. "By the way, while I was tracking you down," Teo said, "Julio called to tell me Gómez is going to come in and testify after all, though for his own reasons."

"That's terrific news!" Jesse said. "I'm feeling better already. Did you put Gómez's name on the witness list in case he actually decides to testify?"

"Yes, and Carano's name, too, in case you have to call him on the financials." Teo paused and stared bleakly at the tip of his cigarette.

"What's the matter, Teo? This is fantastic news!"

"Perhaps, but your elation may be misplaced. *El Cobra* is quite unhappy with you."

"Did Julio say why?"

"Julio heard from several of Gómez's soldiers that you humiliated him."

"That's a good one, Teo. I seem to recollect that I was the one with my face in the dirt."

"Julio says you spit some of it on *El Cobra's* boots. That is not a good thing."

Jesse's lips curled inward. "What changed his mind about coming in?"

"Julio says he wants to show the people of Guatemala his high regard for the rule of law," Teo said. Jesse started to laugh, but his head hurt. "In the abstract, of course."

"Whatever," Jesse said. "So I may have an alibi witness, now all I need is a lawyer."

Teo lowered his eyes. "You have one—if you still want me."

Jesse's eyes popped wide open. "What about Anica? And your ill health?"

"With Julio back to look after Anica, I am free to finish the trial. We will stay here, and nobody will know our location but you. Regarding my health, my doctor was not overjoyed, but he is resigned to my early demise. My one condition remains: no defense base on Carlos V. I will feel less guilty about that, now that we have the alibi defense."

Jesse scowled, trying to fight off that old nagging suspicion that continued to flit around his mind like a bat in a cave—that Teo may have learned about Marisa and Kevin. If so, what better way to avenge himself on his wife's seducer than to block the clue most likely to save him?

"And if you give me any trouble," Teo added, smiling and handing him a copy of *La Prensa,* "I will inform the *Policía Nacional Civil* who killed this poor unfortunate."

Unlike the *Globe,* page two of *La Prensa* featured a crime scene photo of a body in a fetal position near a blood-smeared door in a seedy bar in *Zona* 1.

"I don't recognize the gentleman," Jesse said, feeling a wave of nausea.

"Too bad. The police would like to give a medal to the guilty party.

According to the article, this so-called 'victim' was a notorious M-18 gang member, a professional assassin."

"The paper say who he was working for?"

Teo raised an eyebrow. "Why didn't you ask him?"

"He wasn't much of a talker," Jesse said. "Let's go to the courthouse and see if our client is still with us."

Teo shook his head. "Because of the trial delay, he is back in *Purgatorio*."

· · ·

AS THEY DROVE toward the prison, Jesse explained that Cal Covington might have orchestrated an escape plan.

"Even if he got out," Teo said, "he would never make the airport."

"Just what I told him."

"By the way, while you were catching your beauty sleep, I confirmed Webster's housekeeper's address in *Chimaltenango*. I'll go there tomorrow. Finally."

"Be sure to ask her if she ever overheard Webster talking to Carano or Gómez. Find out if either Webster or his girlfriend was acting strange or had any unusual visitors during the previous few days."

They discussed trial strategy. "We have some new facts." Jesse handed Teo copies of the notes from Elena's secretary.

"What in God's name are these about?"

"The first one, in her handwriting, confirms what we knew: that money flowed from Carano to Gómez as well as to Webster. But what do you make of the part where she asks herself whether the 'whole thing' was a 'façade?'"

Teo shrugged. "I have no idea, but the only thing that would bring those two within ten meters of each other would be a duel to the death. Perhaps Carano was paying some kind of ransom or blackmail."

"That theory could tie in with the second note." Jesse read part of it out loud. *"This is not a 'complication,' as you insist, but an opportunity, good for the people, good for you and number one. Rest assured of your safety and wellbeing. I know that you least of all will miss the dog Carano. G. "*

Teo put an index finger to his eyebrow. "I do not understand this, either."

Jesse said, "What about the reference to 'the dog Carano?' If Carano and Gómez are mortal enemies as you say, doesn't this support the notion that it came from Gómez? And that Gómez was planning to get rid of Carano?"

"Guatemala is full of people who think Carano is a 'dog,' including two people in this room. Am I right? This could have been written by someone in *La Cofradía*. It could have been written by a sixteen-year-old on speed, masturbating on the Internet. I tell you, Jesse, this is the worst kind of hearsay."

"Stop being a law professor for a minute and think about what it means and how we can use it."

"All right, I will exercise my common sense, but you won't like it."

"Try me," Jesse said.

"What if a Presidential loyalist did not 'intercept' that note? What if it was sent to Elena? Does it not clearly reference 'number one?' Who else could that be but her father, who, as titular president, is the number one man in Guatemala?"

"You're suggesting that Elena was in a conspiracy with Gómez?"

"It is possible that she was planning a coup with Gómez against Carano."

"Elena? Working with Gómez?" Jesse said, as if he hadn't been wondering about the "number one" reference himself. He knew

Elena feared Carano's intentions toward her father probably even more than she feared Gómez, and Jesse remembered her enigmatic assurance that she would use her "power" to make "lemonade out of lemons." Had she meant that she would cooperate with Gómez against Carano, figuring she could dump Gómez after Miguel Aguilera was elected? But what if she had found out that Gómez was in league with terrorists such as Yassaf Mousaffi? And that maybe he was planning something more ambitious, say, a violent revolution? She would have objected, of course, and Gómez would have written this note in an attempt to pacify her. Elena, dear Elena—what were you onto? Or, more accurately, what were you *into*?

Jesse said, "Impossible to imagine the chief prosecutor dealing with the country's chief drug lord."

Teo smiled. "You remain enamored, but this is wasting time. These notes do not support our case."

"I disagree," Jesse said. "We've only got to find the connection between Carano and Gómez before they become convinced we know there is one."

"I suggest that they already know. Didn't I just pull you out of a hospital?"

"True," Jesse replied, but something else was nagging him, trying to work its way through the haze of his pain-killing drugs, like the distant glow of a miner's lamp in a collapsed tunnel. It was important, but it darted just beyond his mind's grasp. "Let's go visit our client."

. . .

AT 10:30 A.M., two new guards escorted Kevin into the dimly lit visitors' area at *Purgatorio*. Both were short. One had an eye so clouded with cataract he reminded Jesse of a Picasso painting. The other one was young, with a short beard. The bearded guard sat Kevin on a wooden chair facing Jesse and Teo, his hands cuffed behind his back. Jesse demanded they be removed, and was surprised when the younger guard relented.

"You haven't had any medical attention?" Jesse said.

Kevin's head slowly rotated, and he strained to focus his eyes on his lawyers. "Wrong HMO I guess. A guy who spoke English told me that since my 'guardian angel' was dead, I was lucky not to be dead, too, and to stop bitching."

"Guardian angel?" Teo said.

"Was he referring to Elena Ruiz?"

"I guess. Didn't she seem to be helping us when she could? Anyway, I begged them to call you, at least get me some pain pills. They said you didn't answer your phone."

"I've been in a hospital ward myself the past couple days."

"You? What happened?"

"Fell off a bar stool," Jesse said. "Let's stick with you. Will you be okay? I'm afraid there won't be any escape other than by a favorable judgment."

Kevin slowly shook his head again, glanced over at a pudgy guard, and managed an unconvincing smile. "They're gonna get me, Jesse," he said. "And when they do, tell my folks I was innocent and that I loved . . . that I loved them. Tell Mom not to be hard on Dad . . ." Kevin's voice broke again, and he went silent.

"I'll get you out of here," was all Jesse could manage, but Kevin gave him a strange, sweet smile and shook his head again. Jesse was learning that hope didn't die all at once in a place like this, but rather atrophied a day at a time, withering like leaves on a dying vine. He steadied himself and moved close to his client. "The trial starts Friday morning, Kevin. You've got to hold on. You'll be moved back to a holding cell downtown before the day is out. I'll see to it, and I'll have medical help waiting for you."

"Sure, Jesse," Kevin said, but in tone that seemed intended only to make Jesse feel better. "Oh, and by the way," he added, "one of the guards said Dad was here."

"*Cal?* In Guatemala City?" Jesse's throat tightened.

"Here at the prison," Kevin said, "but they told him I was in protective security."

Good, Jesse thought. "It's almost over, Kevin. Hang with us a few more days."

Kevin nodded and managed a smile toward Teo. "Glad you're back, Professor," he said, and then started scratching himself so violently his filthy fingernails left stripes on his face and arms. He had also developed a facial tic in his left eye and upper cheek that was hard to ignore. "Sorry I stink," he muttered. "I can't remember when I had my last shower. I can't even stand to be alone with myself." He paused and started counting on his fingers. "How long have I been in prison?"

"About a month, Kevin," Teo said.

They sat in silence for a moment. Jesse was looking at a young man living in quiet desperation, trying to summon the strength to stay alive one more day; to see one more card played in a game he knew he was losing.

"You know what I don't get?" Kevin said. "Elena Ruiz. She was pretty decent to us, right? Then this new guy comes in and he's a hard case. What's going on?"

Jesse had no answer. He had wondered from the very beginning about Elena's casual approach to the case that at times looked like she was taking a dive. And now the guards had referred to her as Kevin's "guardian angel." Had she so resented Carano's intrusion into her prosecutorial domain that she would tank Kevin's case to spite the Vice President? Or could it be that . . .

"So," Kevin persisted, "what do you think is going on?"

Jesse's gut was churning, because there it was, right where it always had been, the nagging suspicion that had suddenly taken form and was breaking through his denial. He raked his hair with trembling fingertips, clamped his eyes shut.

"Are you all right, Jesse?" Teo said. "You look ill."

Jesse took in some deep breaths of the stale air, then, mindful of the guards on both sides of the plexiglass panel that separated prisoner from counsel, leaned in close to Teo. "Tell me, Teo," he said in a hoarse whisper, "what one thing jumped out at you in Elena's notes?"

"Good Lord, I have no idea. The word 'façade?' The reference to Yassaf Mousaffi? Hell, Jesse, it's all a puzzle to me."

"Remember Marisa's conversation with Anastacia that Anica overheard? The part where Marisa said she'd discovered who 'friend' was? Well, I just remembered that Anastacia told me 'friend' was code for the person running *La Cofradía,* someone in government even Gómez reports to."

"All right, Jesse, but where does that take us?'"

The words fought their way past Jesse's clenched teeth. "Who was Gómez's note addressed to?"

"'Friend,'" Teo said. "That's how it started."

"And who have you been saying the letter was written to?"

Teo stared at Jesse, then blinked and gave his head a quick shake, as if warding off a fly. "*Elena?* You are suggesting she headed *La Cofradía?*"

Jesse nodded, felt a stabbing pain in his chest. Kevin looked from Jesse to Teo and back. "Will somebody tell me what you're talking about?"

"The lady had even more faces than we suspected," Teo said.

Jesse glowered at his friend. "Whatever she was doing, she had her reasons."

"I am sure she did," Teo said, "and they were all preceded by dollar signs."

Jesse fought to control his emotions. *Jesus, Elena, what were you thinking?*

I'm trying so hard to change things, Jesse, to make lemonade out of the lemons he handed me.

Jesse tried to clear his head. "I think Gómez was trying to assuage Elena's concern about a major attack he was planning. Maybe he's the one who's been getting firearms and ammunition from Yassaf Mousaffi."

"The Yemeni," Teo said.

"The guy I saw with Gómez at the airport!" Kevin added.

"Elena must have gotten wind of new weapon supplies from Mousaffi," Jesse said, "and figured out that Gómez was negotiating for a missile system. He was trying to reassure her that she and her father would be okay, but not the 'dog Carano.'"

Teo looked skeptical. "But what about the money? It makes no sense for Carano to send money to someone intending to attack him."

"Making sense is not a prerequisite for this course, Professor."

"Agreed, but what triggered your notion that Elena was the head of *La Cofradía?*"

Jesse rubbed his red-streaked eyes. "Remember how we kept wondering why Elena was often so helpful to us? I think as head of *La Cofradía* she'd be pressured to protect its cut in the drug deal and make sure Gómez's drug conduit to the U.S.A. could continue to function in Cal Covington's behalf. She didn't realize Kevin was nothing but a reluctant messenger boy."

"Messenger boy? Thanks a lot, Jesse," Kevin said, with sarcasm, but no malice.

Teo stared up toward the yellow, water-stained acoustic ceiling. "You could be right, Jesse," he said, "but the real puzzle continues to be the money Carano sent to Gómez. If they thought Kevin was part of their drug deal, why would Carano push to prosecute him in the first place?"

"No more whispering!" the young, bearded guard repeated in Spanish.

Jesse shrugged. "I haven't figured that out yet."

"Take your time," Teo said. "The trial doesn't start for forty-eight hours. And when you get that worked out, tell me why they killed Elena."

"That's easier. Elena found out about Gómez's larger ambitions. When his note failed to pacify her, she decided she had to go public, blow the whistle on his intentions at a press conference. He learned what she was planning to do and had to stop her."

"*Gómez* killed her?" Kevin said, as if snapping out of a deep slumber.

"That's what I think," Jesse said, "and maybe he also had Webster kill Marisa."

Kevin said, "Will somebody tell me how any of this helps to win my case?"

"Score a point for the client," Teo said.

Jesse nodded and whispered. "We can't use Carlos V, so we'll keep our focus on Carano paying Webster to silence Marisa, and pray that Gómez will come through on the alibi."

"That's enough," the bearded guard said in Spanish. "I warned you."

He and the older guard roughly seized Kevin and took him away.

. . .

JESSE RETURNED TO his own safe house, a new hotel called
The Centenario, which he had checked into under a pseudonym. He
would be not only safer there, but closer to the *Torre de Tribunales*.
It was cheaper, too, important now that he was under tight scrutiny
from San Francisco. The tradeoff was that the second-floor room was
pitifully small. Its pictureless walls featured water-stained and peeling
grey wallpaper. The one small window had to stay closed because of
the smells of garbage and human excrement drifting up from the alley
and the cacophony of cars, crowds, and musicians from the street just
fifteen feet below his narrow bed. Not that he expected chocolates
on his pillow, but this could get old fast.

In his loneliness, he felt like calling Megan, but feared he'd end up
whining. Instead, he put his various and sundry problems, enigmas,
and questions without answers into the will-call part of his fatigued
brain, turned out the light, and fell asleep fully dressed.

DAY NINETEEN

39

JESSE SLEPT FOR eleven hours, awakened by a dream in which a huge black dog with eyes like red-hot coals was nipping at his heels. At around ten in the morning, Teo checked in by phone from *Chimaltenango*, about to meet with Webster's housekeeper. Jesse stayed in his hotel room, still groggy from the concussion and pain pills, but determined to get his strength back. He was hungry, but too tired to go out for food.

He sank back into a narrow bed that felt like a broken trampoline, not expecting to sleep again despite his exhaustion and new anonymity. Too much street noise and too many questions haunting him, like what if Amaya not only destroyed Gómez's credibility as a witness, but justified arresting him on drug conspiracy charges? Although Jesse didn't like Amaya, he saw him as a zealot for justice like himself and ambitious enough to gamble on a single career-making move. And if Jesse's use of Gómez blew Cal's drug deal, Kevin would not be Cal's only victim.

At 4:30 p.m., he awoke again and thought about eating, but fell back asleep. He finally got up at seven, feeling good, but hungry. He wanted to avoid restaurants, so he decided to find a store and pick up supplies from the four major food groups—crackers, cheese, ham, and beer.

He entered the dimly lit parking area and was too close to his new Suzuki rental to back off when he realized that a man had filled up the passenger seat. Another man was in the back, pointing a .45 at him through an open window. Pinpricks of heat shot up Jesse's spine. So much for the safety of safe houses. Were there no secrets in this city?

"Get in and drive," said the man in the passenger seat.

"Hello, Cal," Jesse said, his voice reedy, but clear. "Need a lift somewhere?"

"Still cool, ain't you, kid? That's somethin' I used to like about you. Never let 'em see you sweat, right?"

Jesse glanced uneasily at the man in the backseat, a huge, menacing presence.

"That's Felix," Cal said, "a local guy who does odd jobs for me." Cal took in Jesse's bruised face. "You look like shit. Been shavin' with a machete?"

"I'm due for my weekly facial."

"And still the funny man. Not too fucked up to drive are you?"

"I'm fine," Jesse said, and headed the Suzuki north toward *Tikal* as instructed.

"You seem to have a knack for throwin' shit into the nearest window fan, kid."

"I've been told," Jesse said, fighting off fear and nausea from the smell of Cal's cigar. "Any chance your bozo could take the gun away from my head?"

"Hey, kid, relax, okay? We just need to talk."

"All right, let's talk. Were you at *El Centro Preventivo* yesterday?"

"Yeah, and I see why they call it purgatory," Cal said, eyes peering straight ahead into the dull glow of the headlights. "I've traveled all over East Jesus to find my own goddam kid, and the pricks wouldn't let me see him. They say he's in some kind of special lockdown I couldn't buy my way into. I bet *you* can't even get in to see him."

Jesse looked out at dense, moonlit *ceiba* trees on each side of the road. He rolled the window down to clear out the cigar smoke, and cool air hit his damp shirt. He wondered if Cal knew that it was he, Jesse, who had requested the court-supervised security lockdown.

"What happened to your famous escape plan, Cal? Change your mind?"

"Didn't change my mind. They changed the guards on me and threw in the lockdown. Had things all set up, too. Can't get anything done in this fuckin' town anymore."

"Tell me one thing, Cal. Is Bradshaw a part of your syndicate now?"

"Naah, he's only tryin' to save his own ass and C&S; anything for the firm. Just like you, kid."

Just like I was, Jesse thought.

After five miles of tense silence, Cal told Jesse to turn the car around and pull into a turnout on the west side of the road. Jesse complied and killed the engine, wondering if the black dog with red eyes had caught him.

"All right, Jesse Boy, here's what I wanna know. Let's say I let this case go to trial. Can you win it and, if so, how?"

"Simple," Jesse said. "Gómez gives him an alibi."

Cal grunted out an I-figured-as-much. "You don't listen, do you? Didn't I tell you in plain English I don't want Gómez involved? See, you may know why Kevin was down here, but the judges don't. The D.A. don't. I wanna keep it that way. I'm bettin' Kevin does, too."

"I'm representing Kevin in a murder case, Cal, not trying to involve him in a drug beef. I have no dog in that fight, believe me. But we need Gómez, and I can do it in a way that won't reveal anything about your . . . business dealings."

"This I wanna hear," he said in Felix's direction. Felix apparently spoke English.

"All that's going to come out is that Gómez and Kevin were together the day of the murder. Anything else is hearsay and irrelevant under the rules of evidence here, just as in the U.S.A."

"Bullshit, the prosecutor would be all over the drug deal like a dog on a bone."

Jesse explained the law, trying to ignore the noxious stream of smoke blowing past his face. He left out the part about his fear that Amaya might think outside the evidentiary box.

"It's still too risky," Cal said.

"You're wrong, Cal. Even if Amaya *was* stupid enough to get into your deal, Gómez would never admit he was into drugs. If the government could tie him to drugs, they would have done it years ago. Okay? With Gómez, I can save your son!"

Cal shook his head. "Won't work. Besides, Gómez plans to kill you if he comes in. Seems to me you've got plenty of motivation to cancel that subpoena."

Jesse swallowed hard. "I won't do that."

Cal glanced in back and Jesse felt Felix's claws attach to either side of his head.

"Don't move a muscle, Jesse. I'd hate to see Felix snap your spine like a pretzel."

Jesse didn't move a muscle.

After a few seconds, the hands dropped away. "Then start payin' attention," Cal said. "I don't like it when people ain't listenin' to me."

"I'm listening."

"Good. With my escape plan in the toilet, I'm gonna let you win your fuckin' case. But do it without Gómez or things could get very bad for you. *Comprende?*"

"Are you saying you would kill me, Cal?"

"Jesse, Jesse. Where do you get such ideas? Did you hear me say that, Felix?"

Predictably, Felix shook his head. "I don't hear that."

Questions ripped through Jesse's head like tracer bullets, leaving comet tails of fear: Will it be done here in Guate? Will Cal do it himself? But he settled on a question he might get answered: "Were Elena Ruiz and *La Cofradía* involved in your deal with Gómez?"

"*La Cofradía* will wet its beak, but no, they're not directly involved."

"Is that straight, Cal? Because we were doing fine with Elena Ruiz, and now I've got this Enrique Amaya, who is a giant pain in the ass."

"Why didn't you say somethin'? You want him whacked?"

"Jesus, Cal."

DAY TWENTY

40

THE NEXT MORNING, Jesse approached the *Torre de Tribunales*, relieved that, for better or for worse, the trial was finally starting. He was eager to get inside the building, to avoid both the crowds and the sweltering climate. The air was sticky, packed with humidity and tension. Two hundred special members of the *Policía Nacional Civil* in full riot gear created a passage for him through screaming protestors. The noise was deafening, and as Jesse ran the gauntlet, he had to dodge flying objects, everything from hurled fruit and stones to shoes and baseballs. A rock shattered a large window near the front door.

Jesse took the elevator to the sixth floor, where he showed his credentials and entered the packed courtroom. A camera zoomed in so closely that the lens smacked him on the forehead.

"Is the Elena Ruiz murder connected to this trial?" someone shouted.

"Is it true you subpoenaed Arturo Gómez?" a reporter bellowed in Spanish.

"Will your client testify?" demanded another.

Jesse kept repeating "no comment" and pushing his way through the crowd, but the questions kept coming. "What's your defense strategy going to be, Mr. Hall?" a reporter asked in English.

Jesse smiled at that, wishing he had one that didn't depend on a psychopathic guerilla showing up and doing the right thing. "Faith in a fair and independent judiciary," he said, and headed to the defense table against the far wall.

The courtroom teemed with reporters, curiosity seekers, a frenzy of news junkies, gossip mongers, members of *La Causa,* and various officials, many lured by the rumor that Arturo Gómez might appear. Jesse scanned the gallery and was chagrined, but not surprised, to see Cal in back between Felix and another bodyguard. A row ahead, Jesse met the stern gaze of Señor Ramirez. And off to the right, Juan Domínguez. His enemy roster was nearly complete.

Teo was already at counsel table and Jesse was relieved at the absence of alcohol on his breath. He had even gotten a haircut and trimmed his beard.

Jesse said, "You look elegant, Professor. You've practically lost the beard."

Teo blushed. "I never really liked it. I put up with it because Marisa thought some facial hair lent me what she called a 'Leninesque mystique.'"

"So, how did your mystique fare with Webster's housekeeper?"

"I charmed her into admitting that she returned to the house and took a coat for herself and a laptop for her son that Webster kept hidden in a partition behind a closet. But guilt forced her to the confessional and she was ready to return her ill-gotten loot. I insisted, however, that Webster's girlfriend would have wanted her to have the coat."

Jesse grabbed his arm. "And the laptop?"

"I told her to say three Hail Marys and I would turn it over to the appropriate authorities."

Jesse smiled for the first time in days. "Which would be me?"

Teo smiled and said, "Precisely. The bad news is that there appears to be nothing important on it."

"Okay, but I want to see it after court today."

After a twenty-minute delay, Kevin was escorted into the courtroom. Jesse shuddered at the sight of the prisoner. He wore the same clothes—a sport coat, open-collared shirt, and slacks—as when arrested more than a month before. They had taken his belt so that he had to hold his pants up, no small feat with manacles connecting his hands and ankles. He wore no socks. His clothing appeared to have been washed, and hung from his gaunt frame like crepe paper. The shrunken sleeves of his jacket seemed stuck to arms shriveled into broomsticks.

Guards roughly pushed Kevin into a seat between his two *abogados*. He gave Jesse a quivering smile. Jesse put a hand on Kevin's bony shoulder and nodded reassuringly.

The Tribunal entered the room two minutes later. Judge Manuela Chavez, looking hostile as usual, was first through the doorway leading from chambers, followed by Judge Renaldo López, whose generous stomach and red-veined nose preceded him. Young Judge Bernardo Guzmán, nearly as tall as Judge Chavez, was last. Appearing indifferent, they took their seats behind the raised dais and began talking quietly among themselves, as if unaware of the expectant world press and restless, overflowing gallery.

Judge Chavez granted the gallery a cursory glance, slammed her gavel down, and called for order. The courtroom fell remarkably silent and the clerk, a narrow-shouldered, thin-faced man with a look of profound solemnity, embarked on a routine and seemingly endless reading of the court record, to which no one seemed to pay any attention. Kevin tried to look around when Jesse whispered to him that his father was in the rear of the courtroom.

"He agrees that we should see the trial through, Kevin."

Kevin's eyes bulged. "You met with him?"

"He took me for a ride last night."

"I doubt that."

"Why?"

"You're still alive." Kevin added, "Gangster joke, get it?"

Jesse smiled, encouraged by Kevin's attempt at dark humor. Jesse helped him rotate his chair so he could look behind him. Kevin's eyes lit up at the sight of his father. "I told you I could count on him."

Jesse realized it would be useless to try to persuade him of the truth about his father. Most fathers—excluding his own—had a hold on their sons, and that was that.

Kevin said, "He gave me a thumbs up, Jesse. Means he's got another plan."

"He has no plan, Kevin. Pray that Gómez comes in. That's the only plan we've got, and your father is fine with that." What the hell. Criminal clients lie to their lawyers all the time, so what's sauce for the goose . . .

But Kevin didn't buy it. "Find another plan, Jesse. Sorry, but I just can't do it."

"We had a deal, Kevin—"

Teo leaned forward. "The judges are ready, Jesse."

Jesse caught a deep breath and reached across Kevin to give Teo a reassuring squeeze on his forearm. "It's time to feed the bulldog, big guy."

"All right," Teo said, "but as usual, I have no idea what you are talking about."

The senior judge hit her gavel again and ordered the parties to make their opening statements. Amaya rose from his table to the right of the gallery.

"Inspector García led the investigation in this case," he began in Spanish. "He will testify that the defendant is reputed to be a member of an American gang involved in trafficking, and that Señora Andrade—"

Teo rose to his feet and shouted, "*Impertinente!*"

"Why?" asked Judge Chavez.

"Your Honors," Teo said, "I am most reluctant to interrupt my esteemed colleague—and former student—but I object to his assertion of guilt by association. There is no evidence of trafficking by my client."

Judge Chavez raised her eyebrows and seemed to be considering a smile. "Come now, Professor. You do not expect us to leave our common sense at the door?"

"That is exactly what I expect," Teo said, "and more important, it is what the law expects."

Jesse could barely suppress a smile. Teo was in good form.

"Very well, Professor, we will consider your objection when Inspector García testifies. But please take your seat and allow Señor Amaya to make his statement."

Amaya glanced disdainfully at his former professor and continued, "Because of his personal contacts, the evidence will show that the defendant was approached by Señora Marisa Andrade, who was interviewing people with access to a certain local drug-lord chieftain."

Teo objected again, but got nowhere.

Amaya continued. "The defendant, however, denied all knowledge of Marisa Andrade in his statement to the police, a blatant lie. I will also prove that he was seen leaving the house he claims never to have entered, and when was this? During the time frame the government's pathologist has established as the time of death.

"But the defendant's problems do not end there. A glass found in the bathroom revealed a fingerprint belonging to the defendant."

Teo's head shot up as if he'd been asleep.

"Only eight points, I grant Your Honors, but sufficient, as we will show."

Jesse studied his friend's reaction. Teo seemed surprised, though he must have known that Marisa sometimes interviewed people at home.

"That is not all," continued Amaya. "DNA tests have established that hairs found in the Andrade home present a perfect match with hairs taken from the head of Kevin Covington."

DNA! What the fuck? While Teo was looking more concerned than surprised, Jesse overcame his own shock and leapt to his feet. "Objection, Your Honors, we've been told nothing of any DNA evidence!"

"DNA testing is notoriously slow, Your Honors," Amaya responded. "We only obtained the results late last night."

"We will consider the evidence," said Judge Manuela Chavez, "and the defense will be given ample opportunity to study it and cross-examine the experts."

"These hairs, incidentally," Amaya continued, his lips curled into an imperious smile, "*were found on the floor of the Andrade's master bedroom.*"

This declaration triggered a collective gasp from the gallery and caused Teo's head to snap around toward Kevin. Jesse could not meet Teo's eyes. He felt Kevin's hand gripping his arm and turned to translate for him.

Teo stood as if awakening from a nightmare and shouted, "*I object!*" drawing a curious look from Judge Chavez. She gaveled the courtroom back to order and gently reminded him that Jesse had already objected and been overruled. She used a sympathetic tone, as if soothing a roadside accident victim.

Jesse had hoped that both Teo and the Court would accept the home interview explanation for the fingerprints. But now everything was changed.

Fucking Amaya. This was not merely goading your adversary. Everybody did that. This was a serrated blade twisted in Teo's gut. Jesse urged Teo to sit down, noting that his eyes lacked focus and that his face was a dangerous crimson. *"Easy,* Teo," he said, and then said it again.

Kevin leaned close to Jesse, giving himself as much distance as possible from Teo. Jesse could hear Teo's labored breathing, could only guess at what he must be going through. For weeks his friend had wrestled with his suspicions, had drowned his doubt in rum, had endured night sweats and cuckold imaginings. But denial had ceased to be a viable option; his wife's betrayal was no longer a rumor, but a scientific reality.

Too late, Jesse realized his error in not coming clean with Teo, once he had himself learned the truth. Meanwhile, the gallery had gone silent again, leaning forward with prurient attentiveness while Amaya continued. "Your Honors, as important as these facts are in terms of putting the defendant at the murder scene, what is equally damning is that he lied about ever having been in the house! Why, we must ask, would a man lie about being at the scene of the murder, even *knowing* the victim, other than to conceal his guilt?"

Jesse realized that Teo was no longer watching Amaya, but was staring at Kevin with murderous eyes. When those eyes suddenly converged with his own, Jesse could see anger directed at him as well.

Jesse met Teo's gaze and gave his head a warning shake, mouthing the words, "Stay cool, friend. Stay cool."

Amaya advanced toward the judges. "This defendant is a man incapable of truth, Your Honors. He is a gangster and a *murderer!*"

With this final flourish, the prosecutor took his seat. Jesse was not surprised that Amaya had made no mention of the Carlos V clue. It led nowhere the prosecution wanted to go. Fine, but now what? It was time for Teo to deliver his opening statement, and Jesse knew the only thing Teo Andrade wished to deliver was a blow to the windpipe of his client. Jesse rose to his feet.

"Your Honor, in light of certain new allegations in counsel's opening remarks, may we have a brief recess?"

Without consulting either of the other members of the Tribunal, Judge Chavez refused. "Your opening statement please, Professor Andrade."

Jesse glanced at Teo, who glared straight ahead, perspiration gleaming on his forehead. Jesse grabbed a piece of paper, scribbled a note, and thrust it in front of his friend. It read, "No lawyer has been more tested, Teo. Be faithful to your oath." Jesse knew these were pompous, high-sounding words, but all he could hope to do at this point was challenge Teo's sense of professionalism.

Teo silently studied the message, then clamped his eyes shut and crushed the paper in his fist. He picked up the outline Jesse had drafted for his opening, and Jesse feared he was going to crumple that up, too.

"Señor Professor?" Judge Chavez said. "Your opening *please.*"

Teo rose and glared once more at his client. Then he faced the judges, rubbed a hand across his forehead, and took a deep breath. There was not a sound in the courtroom. He stared down at the floor, Jesse's outline still clutched in his hand. His lips began to move, but produced no audible sound.

"Professor?" urged the senior judge.

Teo's raised his head. "May it . . . may it please the Court . . ." Then, a word at a time, one following upon the other, Teo stammered his way into his opening statement. He kept his back to Kevin and kept glancing at the outline, slowly gaining momentum.

"I ask Your Honors," he continued in a rote monotone, "to withhold judgment on this case . . . until all the evidence has been submitted. The PNC, you see, did not exercise such restraint. They rushed to judgment, based on nothing more than prejudice against the defendant's father's perceived mob involvement, including irrelevant and wholly unproven suggestions of drug trafficking, none of which apply to the defendant."

Jesse winced. A criminal defense lawyer never refers to his client as "the defendant," but rather by his given name. But at least the big man was on his feet and putting words together. Teo paused, licked his lips, and then said, "I can think of nothing that would do more violence to the image of Guatemala's new democracy than to honor the universally rejected notion of guilt by association."

He started to pick up a glass of water, but his hand was trembling badly and he put it back on the table with a resounding *clunk*. He licked his lips again, and muddled on in a hoarse voice, promising to produce the electric company's meter reader whom the witness had mistakenly identified as the defendant. Next, he cited the absence of a murder weapon and the unreliability of circumstantial evidence and DNA junk science, "which, I submit, Your Honors, is all the prosecution will be left with after their so-called 'eyewitness' is discredited."

Not surprisingly, Teo did not address the matter of adultery. Nor did he mention the Carlos V clue left by Marisa, obviously baffling Amaya, who probably assumed it would be their primary defense.

Teo closed by asserting that the evidence would point to enemies of the victim with far stronger motives to kill Marisa than those attributed to Kevin by the prosecution.

"These enemies include a high-ranking official," he said, "who wished to silence the victim before she could expose the entirety of his corruption."

This dramatic finish, with its blatant insinuation pointing at Carano, created a buzz in the gallery. Jesse's face went hot, for this attack had not been in his outline, and he did not like the reaction he saw on Judge Chavez's face. Still, he was relieved and awed by Teo's demeanor, knowing that the man's weak heart had been shattered yet again, and that he would have liked nothing so much as to strangle his client in open court rather than to stand and defend him.

. . .

THE PROSECUTION CONSUMED the balance of the day with the testimony of several lesser members of the *Policía Nacional Civil*. Teo's cross-examinations were more than adequate, though his every word seemed burdened by the weight of grief. If the judges were persuaded one way or the other by Teo's courageous effort, however, their indifferent expressions did nothing to reveal it. Indeed, they seemed to have already made up their minds, just as most jurors do after hearing opening statements.

And the worst evidence lay ahead: Kevin's lies, combined with his hair and fingerprints in the house.

. . .

BACK AT THE Andrade safe house, Jesse sipped a beer, nervously awaiting an overdue explosion from Teo, who had yet to react to the day's revelation. It wouldn't be a small blast either, more like a roadside bomb, filled with nails and shrapnel so that nobody in the vicinity would escape injury.

The professor had driven them home after the day's recess, staring straight ahead over the steering wheel, like a ship's captain snaking through icebergs, not uttering a word. Now he sat pensively gazing into his second rum, looking as pale and wretched as a beached whale.

"So, Jesse," Teo said at last, "how long have you known our client was fucking my wife?" His tone was as cold as the ice he rattled in his suddenly empty glass.

Dread assailed Jesse, but he met Teo's eyes. "I didn't know about the DNA, but Kevin did admit the affair to me. You didn't want the truth, so I didn't give it to you."

"You preferred to let me continue to make a fool of myself?"

"I'm sorry, Teo, and I'm ashamed of the way I handled this. I was afraid you would quit on us. I'd do it differently if I had it to do over. I know you must hate him, maybe her, too, and, of course, me. But please consider that we've still got a case to try."

"*We?* So you have a mouse in your pocket? Your case can go to hell, and your client, too."

"I understand your feelings, Teo, but take a little time and—"

"I assure you, Jesse, I am the very last lawyer in Guatemala you want defending this particular client."

"You *are* the very last lawyer in Guatemala, Teo! No one else will come aboard and you know it. If you don't continue, you have effectively killed Kevin. Is that what you want? An eye for an eye?"

Teo's eyes locked onto Jesse's. Was that a slight nod of his head? "Save your rhetoric for the courtroom, Jesse. You're going to need it."

"No. They won't let me proceed without you and you know that, too. They'll appoint some local Carano toady to take our place, and he'll sleepwalk through the rest of the trial. Is this the kind of justice system you advocated when you were at the university? I don't think so. I'm guessing you taught your students they couldn't hope to have a working democracy without a functional justice system."

Teo lumbered over to the bar and prepared another drink. He took a sip and smiled wistfully into the dark liquor. "You are talking theory to a man who is no longer a theoretician. Yes, I taught justice as a foundation for democracy, taught it three times a week, mouthing idealistic tautologies from my ivory tower that were scattered into dust by the time they hit the ground."

"So, no longer a theoretician; what are you now, an ostrich?"

"I am a pragmatist."

"Fine, Teo, you want to talk pragmatics? Look outside. People don't even stop for a stop sign anymore because nobody else is stopping and there's no cop to arrest them. You stop for a stop sign or a pedestrian in *Zona* 1 and you get rear-ended. And even if you do get busted, you pay the cop, he lets you go. If he won't let you go, you pay the judge and *he* lets you go. If the judge won't take the money, you pay the prison guard and just walk away! If you hope to achieve a democracy here, you've got to have a justice system people have confidence in! *That's* being a pragmatist. *That's* reality."

Teo made no response, and Jesse thought he might be gaining ground. "Look, Teo. I feel terrible about what I did, but I beg you to stay with the case. Help me nail Webster, then tie him back to Carano with the money trail. And if *El Cobra* comes in, we might even have an alibi. If it's vengeance you want, direct it toward the corrupt tyrant who *killed* Marisa! In the process, help finish her work, and show the people of your country an adversary system capable of producing justice."

Teo said nothing for a full five minutes, just stared out the window and smoked. Finally, he turned back to Jesse. "I don't think the alibi will work."

Jesse exhaled with relief. Teo would stay, and maybe this thing could still end well. The *Globe* showed CalCorp stock was up again, and that would be good for C&S, too. The Golden Fleece, badly tattered and assumed lost, might be salvageable if Simon would soon be in a position to dump Cal and C&S returned to normal. And if C&S's new partner candidate made it home alive.

"The alibi could work," Jesse said, "unless our own client screws it up. I'll grant you that Kevin is so enamored of his father he might stand up and deny he was at Gómez's camp."

"Such filial loyalty. One almost has to admire it. But without the cooperation of both Gómez and the client, the government wins regardless of what I do or not do."

A heavy silence fell like a curtain between them. Jesse knew that even if Teo stayed with the case, he might view Kevin's ultimate conviction as a kind of rough justice. By his stubborn support of the land grant, Teo could rid himself of both Carano *and* Kevin.

The big man suddenly lurched to his feet. "I will continue to do what I can. Now, do you want to see Webster's laptop or not?"

The first thing Jesse checked was Webster's C-drive. Teo was right; there was nothing of interest. A dozen or so recipes—Perlita's—a list of Christmas card addresses, personal letters written by both Webster and the girl, and Perlita's poetic reflections on life.

"I am no computer whiz," Teo said, "but why is there so little on it?"

"I think it's the household computer," Jesse said. "I'm guessing Webster knew he was in danger and got rid of anything marginally important. For CIA stuff, I'm sure he had his own encrypted computer and he probably took that one with him. Anyway, it won't hurt to check the recycling bin on this one. You never know."

"The what?"

"The recycle bin holds things that are dumped until you dump the bin itself."

Teo's face was a blank. Jesse added, "Things you dump, but can retrieve. Let's have a look," he added, and double-clicked on the recycle bin icon.

A host of entries showed up on the deleted file documents screen and Jesse restored all of them. He then opened a document called "To Do," and up popped a list, obviously Webster's. Items 1–5 referred to mundane things like dental appointments and construction project reminders, but Jesse's breath caught in his throat when he read item 6:

"Hit G up for another five percent or maybe C, but first write insurance letter to Post."

Jesse said, "Look at this."

"So what? An insurance agent named Post?" Teo asked.

"It's an if-anything-should-happen-to-me letter, like the one I sent you when I went off to see Gómez. 'Post' probably refers to the *Washington Post*," Jesse said, "the logical recipient of such a letter."

"Webster might have left the letter for his lover to send if he was taken."

"Possibly, but when he was taken," Jesse said, "the killers must have assumed he was bluffing and killed him anyway. Or maybe they tortured the truth out of him about the girlfriend having the letter, then killed her before she could mail it. Or maybe she just gave it to them, hoping to save her own life."

Teo stroked his beard and said, "Whichever of your disjunctives is the correct one, it would have been a nice letter to have."

"You have a way of understating things, Teo. That whistle would have blown all the way to Washington D.C."

"But it is gone, so we have wasted our time."

"Not completely. At least this confirms that Carano was indeed passing money to both Webster and Gómez."

"And that Webster was trying to extort more out of Carano or Gómez or both."

"Right," Jesse said. "And that one or both of them didn't much like the idea."

Jesse stared at all the recycle bin items with growing frustration. The insurance letter could have been the evidence they needed to blow this thing wide open.

"The letter might be in here somewhere and we've got to try to retrieve it. Where can we get a computer text retrieval expert in this city?"

"A what?"

DAY TWENTY-ONE

41

SIMON BRADSHAW'S DAY began as usual, at precisely six a.m., at his Woodside mansion thirty-two miles south of San Francisco. He sat at his breakfast table and appraised two perfectly-steamed poached eggs atop a single piece of unbuttered wheat toast cut into six equal sections by his wife Lucy. The day's *Wall Street Journal* surrounded him like a tent, discouraging conversation.

He smiled. The news was good. His portfolio was performing tolerably, despite the recession. Caldwell and Shaw's favorable imprimatur on CalCorp's 10-K had calmed Wall Street jitters about the current SEC investigation in Shanghai, and Cal Covington was "as pleased as punch" with the firm's performance.

The phone rang. Irritated, he tried to ignore it. He heard Lucy's muffled voice in the den and she entered a minute later.

"It's Eric Driver," she whispered, handing him the phone and hurrying out of the room. Bradshaw's face morphed into a mask of worry. At this hour on a Saturday, this could only be bad news.

"Yes, Eric, what is it?"

"Alan Cheng has turned. He'll testify for the government in the SEC's Shanghai investigation of CalCorp."

Before Bradshaw could react, Driver continued. "I put together a quick amendment to the 10-K that will minimize the impact. I just wanted you to know what's happening."

Bradshaw scowled. "Eric, our firm's due diligence is on the line here and I think we've gone too far already. Nevertheless, I'll come in right away and take a look at what you've drafted. My gut reaction, however, is not to—"

"Actually, Simon, it's already been filed."

"You *filed* the amendment without talking to me?"

"Now don't go off on me, Simon. You weren't in yesterday, and Cal insisted I file it immediately to prevent CalCorp stock from plummeting when the markets open on Monday."

"I was at the *dentist*, for God's sake. I didn't leave the office till nearly four!"

"Calm down, Simon. We're fine. Cheng's just covering his own ass and cutting a deal with the SEC at the expense of the company. It's obvious to anyone what he's up to. Anyway, I'm at the airport and gotta run."

Driver clicked off and Bradshaw stared at his phone for five full seconds, then pushed his tea aside and hurried over to the kitchen sink, where he vomited up his perfectly steamed poached eggs and unbuttered toast.

. . .

AN HOUR LATER, Simon chugged a third dose of Pepto-Bismol, wishing it were Scotch whisky, and called Cal Covington. "'Morning, Counselor," came Covington's cheery voice at the other end. "I reckon I know why you're calling."

"I'm confident you do," Bradshaw said, his tone icy. "May I ask how long you have known that Alan Cheng was intending to turn state's evidence?"

"Just learned it myself, Cy," Cal said, "and don't get your feathers ruffled. I'm all over it like ticks on a yellow dog. Trust me, this will *not* be a problem."

"Dammit, it's already a problem. That's *our* name on that 10-K and I hear Cheng will probably be giving the Feds a statement in Shanghai tomorrow, which it soon will be given the time difference."

"As usual, Cy, you're tellin' Noah about the flood. It's 10:00 p.m. there to be exact about it, fifteen hours difference, San Francisco time."

"And where are you, Cal?"

"Out laborin' in the fields of the Lord is where I am, Cy. I'll deal with Alan Cheng, and I'll do a better job of it than you've done with your pretty boy lawyer here in Guate. Did you know he's been recording my phone conversations? The stubborn prick refuses to leave town, no matter how many times we've both told him, and now he's pressured me into lettin' him finish the damned trial. On top of that, I think he's still hopin' to get Gómez to testify."

How, Simon wondered, does this hayseed always put me on the defensive? "I *am* dealing with Jesse, Cal, but the presence of the press there gives him powerful leverage. And it *is* your son he's trying to protect, after all."

"Yeah," Cal sighed, "which he never misses a chance to remind me about. All right, Cy, looks like we've got fires in two different ends of the world, so I've got my fireman's hat on. Don't you fret. Be assured that I'll by God take care of our Mr. Cheng in Shanghai *and* your hotshot lawyer here in Guatemala if he brings Gómez to within fifty miles of the courtroom."

The line went dead in time for Bradshaw to make it back to the kitchen sink.

.   .   .

With the trial finally underway, Jesse stayed in his room all day Saturday to catch up on loose ends. He spoke only with Teo, who called Jesse's room to report that he had delivered the computer to a retrieval expert. By day's end he had reconstructed most of his stolen files and locked them in the trunk of his car along with Marisa's notes. He then outlined Teo's cross of the first prosecution witness and fell into bed.

DAY TWENTY-TWO

42

JESSE SLEPT WELL and rose early Sunday morning. He walked through the narrow, noisy streets of his new neighborhood to a local favorite called Lila's that served *jamón y huevos* the way he liked them. None of that hot-sauce *rancheros* crap. He lingered for a second cup of coffee and read *La Prensa* from front to back. He was now reading, speaking, and thinking in Spanish. He might even be dreaming in Spanish as well, except he was too tired to remember dreams.

Returning from breakfast, he saw a news stand and bought a copy of *The Sunday Globe.* Across the street, a dozen young Sunday school kids roughhoused in a loose-knit queue near an ancient bus, with no driver in sight. A flustered nun struggled to maintain control. The bearded old man behind the news counter was fishing change out of a cigar box, when a scream from the nun jolted Jesse. He turned and spotted a thick-wasted, dark-complexioned man trying to pry a briefcase from her determined grasp.

Jesse ran across the street, but not toward the thief. Jesse had noticed that while the thief was distracting the nun, another smaller, tattooed man, with shoulder-length hair, a backwards ball cap, and rings protruding from various body parts, was pulling one of the young boys toward a beat-up Chevy.

Jesse, mindful of Guatemala's rampant kidnapping and child-export racket, shouted and threaded his way through speeding traffic, recklessly dodging vehicles coming from both directions. *"Alto!"* he shouted, grabbing the kid and wrestling him away from the thug. Jesse and the youngster tumbled to the ground, and the thug hopped into the Chevy. The car sped away, and the diversionary mugger fled on foot in the opposite direction without the nun's briefcase.

"Are you okay?" Jesse asked the boy.

"*Sí, Señor*," was all the kid could manage. He was holding his arm, which the kidnapper had obviously twisted, if not broken, and tears of pain and embarrassment streaked his cheeks. Jesse called the PNC and the nun called the boy's parents. They then waited to give the PNC their statements.

Eventually, a police officer driving an Opel appeared, followed minutes later by the boy's anxious father, who profusely thanked Jesse, introduced himself as Geraldo Maldonado, and presented a card that stated he was a government immigration officer. He then led his son to an old, but well-maintained Toyota, and they sped off to the hospital.

Jesse resumed his trip toward the hotel, conscious that some of the children were giving him a shy thumbs-up through the bus windows, but unaware that without breaking a sweat, he had just altered the course of his destiny in Guatemala.

DAY TWENTY-THREE

43

MONDAY MORNING. READY or not, the trial was about to resume in the stale, crowded courtroom. Jesse noted with disappointment that Cal Covington and Felix were in their usual seats in the rear of the courtroom.

The first witness was PNC officer Oscar Morales. With small, black eyes, and a forehead that sloped on nearly a straight line to the tip of his nose, the man bore an alarming resemblance to a ferret.

Morales worked in the subversive elements division and, to Jesse's astonishment, testified that Kevin had been under surveillance by the division for nine days, from March 27, six days before the victim's murder, to three days after. *Jesus,* Jesse thought, exchanging an anxious look with Teo. Morales's name was on the prosecution's Article 347 witness list, but Amaya had given no hint that the cop might be an eyewitness to Kevin leaving the scene!

"We may be fucked," Jesse whispered to Teo. Kevin looked stricken.

"Why were you trailing the defendant and monitoring his activities?" Amaya asked after the formalities were completed.

"Objection," Teo said. "The reasons for the invasion of Mr.

Covington's privacy are irrelevant to the charge under consideration and are being offered for the sole purpose of prejudicing the defendant."

Jesse was not surprised when the objection was overruled or when the officer cited an Interpol file linking Kevin's father to organized crime.

"We also learned," continued Officer Morales, "that the defendant was to be interviewed by Marisa Andrade owing to rumors he had met with Arturo Gómez, a self-styled revolutionary and crime family head, probably planning a major cocaine—"

"Objection!" shouted Teo, but the panel was interested. Judge Chavez overruled the objection and glowered at Kevin. The judges had abandoned their masks of indifference.

"Everyone knows," the Ferret continued, "that Gómez is an active trafficker, although we have not yet been able to prove it."

"Hearsay, irrelevant, prejudicial, and conjecture," Teo said, but was ignored.

"Very well," Amaya said. "Did you have occasion to observe the victim and the defendant together while you were trailing him?"

"Yes. Three times over the course of the five days before her death."

"And were they intimate on some of these occasions?"

Teo leapt to his feet. "I object to this . . . this travesty!"

Oh shit, thought Jesse, here we go again.

"On what grounds do you object, Señor Professor?" said Judge Chavez.

Teo seemed surprised at the question, as if his consternation and the mere intensity of his objection should be sufficient. Chavez waited, and Teo gazed dumbly back at the judge, veins bulging in this neck. Jesse wondered how much emotional trauma the man's heart could handle.

"Sugestiva y conclusiva," Teo managed at last, and then collapsed into his seat.

"Sustained," said Judge Chavez, but it was clear the technical objection served only to highlight the importance of the proffered testimony and delay the inevitable. "Please rephrase your question, Señor Prosecutor."

"All right, Officer, did you or did you not see them engaging in acts of intimacy?"

Christ, thought Jesse, do they have a video in full color? He glanced at Teo, whose huge hands seemed bent on strangling each other.

"Yes."

"Please tell the Tribunal what you saw."

"I climbed a fire escape and observed them through a second floor window of a motel. Through a small opening in the drapes, I was able to see him remove Marisa Andrade's clothing and—"

"I *object!*" Teo jumped to his feet as if shot from a cannon. His current leap upended the entire table, files and papers flying everywhere, but Teo seemed not to notice. He glared at the prosecutor and shouted, "I object most strenuously to this assassination of my wife's reputation! Not another word! *Do you understand?*"

"Teo!" Jesse said, seizing the big man by the arm, but Teo had spent himself and was already falling back into his chair. He covered his face with trembling hands. Amaya indifferently raised his eyebrows and indicated he was finished with the witness. Guards hurriedly righted the table, and Jesse picked up the scattered papers. "May we have a recess, Your Honors?" Jesse shouted above the tumult in the gallery. "I urge the Tribunal to take into consideration the unusual circumstances."

Jesse expected Judge Chavez to censure Teo, but she was vainly trying to control a noisy gallery now ignoring her gavel. Giving up, she motioned for the *Policía de Presidios* to remove anybody who was not instantly silent. The first spectator forcibly ejected from the courtroom served to subdue the rest.

Jesse put a hand on one of the big man's shoulders and whispered, "Stay cool, Teo, or it's over for us."

Teo nodded and slowly rose to his feet. Kevin cowered in his chair. "My apologies, Your Honors," Teo said in a quiet voice thick with despair. "It won't happen again. Perhaps my co-counsel would be permitted to cross-exam . . . "

"Please say no more, Professor," the senior judge said. "Out of respect for your years of sterling work at the University, the Court accepts your apology and grants your request. Señor Hall may complete the examination of this witness following a five-minute recess."

The five minutes stretched into ten, which was fine with Jesse, who needed time to study Morales's report and try to figure out what the hell he would do with this dangerous witness. Often, Jesse knew, able trial lawyers like Amaya will leave crucial things unsaid so that they will come across with even greater force when the hapless cross-examiner walks into the trap. Like leaving verbal land mines just below the surface.

Jesse also wondered how he might console Teo, who was wandering up and down the elevator lobby talking to himself. Jesse hated Amaya for his emotional mugging of the fragile professor.

"I have been a fool," Teo told Jesse, who wasn't sure if he was talking about his faith in Marisa or his display in court. "A crew was shadowing Kevin around the clock."

A *Policía de Presidio* signaled from the doorway and Jesse began guiding Teo back into the courtroom when it hit him: *Around the clock! Yes,* maybe it would work. It could be a land mine, but he would have to risk it.

"I might be able to get him," Jesse told Teo.

"How?"

"Occam's razor."

Teo nodded. "*Entia non sunt multiplicanda praeter necessitatem.*"

"Roughly," Jesse agreed, "the simplest explanation is often the best one. It was right in front of us, Teo. I might be getting suckered-in, but I've got to risk it."

. . .

CHAVEZ CALLED THE courtroom to order and Jesse approached the witness. He towered over him, for Guatemala City courtrooms have no elevated witness stands. Jesse noticed that Officer Morales's hair, clearly the unfortunate-looking man's best feature, appeared to have been cut by its owner, even the back.

Jesse smiled at the witness and said, "I have reviewed your report with interest, Officer Morales. You were assigned to trail Señor Covington starting on March the twenty seventh, were you not?"

"Yes."

"Your job was to stay close to him, note his activities?"

"Yes."

"And to make a written report of those activities, which you did, right?"

"Yes."

"How many days did you follow him altogether?"

Officer Morales's gaze cut toward Amaya, but Jesse had blocked his view.

"I personally? Over a period of nine days."

"What was your shift? What hours?"

"From four a.m. to noon."

"So you were on duty those hours on April first?"

"Yes."

Morales blanched, and Jesse's heart pounded. It was one of those moments where you had your hand around the balls of an adverse witness and you looked unswervingly into his eyes so that he knew that you knew. Then you squeezed.

"And the report you wrote is the one you have been looking at, is that correct?"

"Yes."

"I think you know what's confusing me, Officer Morales. I've looked everywhere on this report and can't find a single mention of Señor Covington being anywhere near the Andrade premises at the time of the alleged murder, which occurred during the time you were, as you said, 'staying close to him.'"

Jesse heard clicking and scratching sounds behind him from the press area, comforting sounds. Fingers on key pads, pens raking paper.

"He was observed leaving the premises by another witness—"

"Move to strike," Jesse said. "Your Honors, may I have the witness ordered to answer the question?"

"The answer will be stricken," said Judge Chavez. "Answer the question, Officer. Did you see him?"

"No."

Jesse moved in a step closer. "And you are, I take it, a trained observer?"

"Well . . . "

"They teach you observation skills during your training, do they not? They don't just point a finger and say 'go follow that guy?'"

"We are taught the basics of trailing a subject, yes."

"So here you are, a trained observer, assigned to observe this particular subject—the man I'm pointing to—and yet you didn't observe him leaving the scene of the murder between the hours of ten and twelve in the morning of April first, which is when Mr. Amaya has told us the murder took place. Am I right about that?"

"Well, no."

"No, I'm wrong, or no, you didn't see him?"

"No, I didn't see him."

"I guess that makes me right?"

"You are right."

"You have been very helpful, Officer," Jesse said with a glance at the engrossed judges. "That's all I have for the present."

On redirect, Amaya had no choice but to elicit from the officer that he had lost sight of Kevin around 10:00 a.m. on March 31, while he was getting himself a cup of coffee, and that the subject had not been picked up again until another officer spotted him returning to his hotel around 7:00 p.m. on April 1, the day of the murder. Officer Morales then picked him up again on his usual watch, four o'clock in the morning of April 2. Jesse assumed they had cooked up the coffee explanation in case it might be needed, yet knew it was probably true, as that was when Kevin had gone to Livingston.

Amaya forced a smile and thanked Morales for his testimony. The policeman rose and bolted toward the rail. Just as quickly, Jesse rose and blocked his way. "Hold on, Officer. A couple of more questions, if you don't mind." The officer looked up at the judges as if to plead double jeopardy, but his appeal was ignored.

Jesse bore in. "You are not suggesting that Señor Covington intentionally tried to evade your invasion of his privacy, are you?"

"Would you repeat that?"

"You lost Mr. Covington because you needed some coffee, right?"

"That's true."

"Is it really?" Jesse said, smiling humorlessly. "Sounds convenient, doesn't it?"

"What does?"

"Your story. Tell me, Officer, how many times did you manage to lose sight of the subject during the nine days you followed him?" Jesse turned toward the gallery as he spoke and caught a knowing smile from Teo. "Three times? Five times? More than that?"

"Oh, no, no, no, sir. Only that once, I swear it!"

Jesse smiled back at Teo. The witness had taken the bait. "Ahh, I see. Just once. So you want these judges to believe that you got yourself a cup of coffee and lost sight of the witness only *once* during those nine days, and this one single time just *happened* to be during the two to three hours when somebody murdered Marisa Andrade?"

The witness looked confused, and Amaya jumped up.

"Objection! This is an argumentative—"

"By the way, Officer Morales, I'm looking at your reports, *and I also see in your report no mention of you ever once losing sight of Kevin Covington.*"

"Objection!"

"I'm through with this witness," Jesse told the Tribunal. "Go back to whatever you were doing, Officer. Grab a cup of coffee on your way out of the building."

.   .   .

THE NEXT WITNESS was a forensic witness specializing in fingerprint and DNA analysis, who testified that the hairs found in the Andrade master bedroom perfectly matched the DNA of those taken from the prisoner's bed at the *El Centro Preventivo*. After three hours of tedious technical testimony on direct, Jesse asked only one question on cross.

"Are you aware, sir, that Marisa Andrade sometimes conducted interviews in her home?" The witness said no and Jesse said thank you and abruptly sat down, relieved that the expert didn't laugh at the notion of bedroom interviews.

Kevin looked disappointed and whispered, "Couldn't you do something?"

"I did do something. I kept my mouth shut and didn't make a bad thing worse. A little known fact is that sometimes saying nothing is what trial lawyers do best. Consider yourself lucky they didn't find semen."

"I always used a—"

"Never mind," Jesse said as Amaya rose to call his next witness, a tall, impeccably-dressed police inspector to whom Kevin had claimed he did not know Marisa, had never been in the Andrade house, and certainly had never had sexual relations with her.

After covering these points, Amaya said, "Tell us what the prisoner told you when you asked him his whereabouts on the morning of April the first?"

"He said he was sleeping in his hotel room. Alone, of course."

This touch of sarcasm brought chuckles from the gallery and a stern rebuke from Bernard Guzmán, the tall judge seated to Jesse's right.

"Thank you, Inspector. Your witness."

"All right," Jesse said, approaching the witness. "Tell me, Inspector, do you consider yourself a gentleman?"

Amaya half-rose, then with a bemused expression stayed seated.

"I do. Yes."

"All right then. Please do not take this personally, sir, because I'm being entirely hypothetical here. Let us say rumors got around that you were having an affair with a highly respected woman. Would you boast about it? Or would you try to protect the reputation of the woman by denying it, even if it meant telling a white lie or two?"

Amaya shot to his feet. "Objection, Your Honors."

"I'll withdraw the question, Your Honors. The inspector has already answered it."

"He has done no such thing!" Amaya said.

"Oh, but he did, Señor," said Jesse, "by telling us that he considers himself a gentleman."

Several reporters laughed. Renaldo López, the phlegmatic judge to the left of Judge Chavez, proved he had been listening by smiling broadly for the first time. Amaya appeared to be thrown off balance by the exchange and said nothing. The inspector left the courtroom with Jesse's thanks.

"Well done, Jesse," Teo said.

"We need Gómez," Jesse said, cutting his eyes toward Kevin.

. . .

AT THE END of the noon recess, Teo reminded Jessed to expect a call from the expert who had Webster's laptop computer. "The man is busy, but he promised me an answer within twenty-four hours. I gave him your cell number and the phone number at your new hotel in case he cannot reach me."

The Tribunal returned to the packed courtroom, which seemed to Jesse to have risen in temperature by twenty degrees. He knew his shirt would be soaked by day's end. The windows were open, but people sat on the ledges, blocking any airflow.

Enrique Amaya called his eyewitness to the stand, a woman in her mid-fifties, who had allegedly observed Kevin leaving the premises at or about the time of the murder. Jesse was relieved to see she wore thick glasses, not that it suggested poor eyesight to him, but because it often did to young jurors or judges the age of Judge Guzmán.

After the preliminaries, Amaya requested the Court to order Kevin to stand and face the witness. Jesse rose and objected. "Leading, Your Honors."

"Leading?" said Amaya, looking somewhere between perplexed and annoyed. "I haven't even asked a question."

Judge Chavez appeared to share Amaya's bewilderment, so Jesse added, "Mr. Amaya is essentially conducting a lineup with only one man. The witness is being asked to select one out of one." Jesse turned to the gallery, focusing on the press, and added, "Let's all take a guess which one she'll pick." He then turned back to the panel. "Furthermore, Your Honors, the police report indicates that identity was made from the back, not the front."

Jesse's remarks again budged Judge Renaldo López from his torpor. He smiled at Jesse's objection, and uttered his first words of the trial. "That appears to be what the police report contends, Señor Amaya. She did not see his face."

Amaya's impatience was obvious, but he flashed Judge López an oily smile and requested that Kevin be ordered to walk away from the witness toward the windows.

"I'll allow that," Judge López said, and ordered the guards to free Kevin of his manacles. He then allowed his dark eyes to slip back under their hooded lids and added, "For what it is worth."

The last five words lit a small candle of hope among Jesse's numerous dark forebodings. Kevin walked. The witness stared hard. Amaya spoke. "Is that the man you saw leaving the Andrade house just before noon on the first day of April?"

"That's him," said the woman, obviously enjoying her fifteen minutes. "The only difference is that he wore a green jacket that day."

On cross, Teo pursued the usual eyewitness gambits—estimated distance from suspect, use of corrective lenses, sun in eyes, no frontal view—then acted as if he were trying to shake her testimony about the color of the jacket. The more Teo pressed her, the greener the jacket got.

Teo then opened a large box under counsel table and removed a black jacket.

"May Señor Covington be allowed to don this jacket?"

"Yes."

Kevin donned the jacket and walked away from her again.

"No," she said, losing patience, "I told you it was green!"

Teo removed another jacket from the box and asked Kevin to put it on. Teo smiled at the witness and said, "You're not saying it was this green, are you?"

"I most certainly am. That's the man and that's the jacket he wore that day."

"Thank you, Señora," Teo said. "Your Honors, the witness has just identified a jacket routinely worn by meter checkers for *Empresa Eléctrica de Guatemala*." Teo entered the jacket into evidence amidst murmurings of surprise from the gallery.

So far, so good, Jesse told himself. And Judge López's awakening was encouraging, but to bring the other two around, they would still need an alibi.

. . .

COURT WAS RECESSED and the courtroom cleared. Cal
Covington came forward, along with Felix and another goon. Cal
grabbed Jesse's arm and said, "This guy Amaya looks like the type
who'll open up a can of worms if you bring Gómez in. I'll say it once
more: no Gómez."

"We've been through this, Cal. If Gómez comes in, Amaya knows
that to ask what was said at Gómez's camp on April first would tacitly
admit Kevin was with him on the day of the murder."

"I think you're wrong. I think he'd rather bust Gómez than convict
Kevin."

Jesse gave Cal a look usually reserved for the cockroaches in his
hotel room. "Most fathers would be on their knees praying for that.
You're one of a kind, Cal."

"The hell with you, kid. Do I have to repeat the consequences to
both of us if you screw up my business here?"

"No," Jesse said, walking away. "You've done everything but put a
horse's head in my bed."

44

PACING IN HIS room at The Centenario, Jesse knew that though his cross-examinations had gone well, his toolbox was nearly empty. Teo would refuse to allow the use of Marisa's dying clue at trial and Cal Covington would probably persuade Gómez to ignore the subpoena.

On an impulse, Jesse called Simon Bradshaw.

"Cal is causing me problems down here, Simon. I need your help."

"Look, Jesse, if Cal seems a little erratic, it's because he's had a serious reversal. The SEC is all over him and CalCorp's Shanghai CFO is about to plea bargain and testify against the company. We've taken steps, but CalCorp stock will take a serious hit."

Which is why Cal needs his drug deal more than ever, even if it costs him the life of his son. "That may explain his actions, but it doesn't excuse them. I know you're pissed at me, Simon, but if you've got any leverage with him, please use it. I think the crazy bastard might try to kill me." Jesse heard his own voice break.

Silence, then, "That's absurd, Jesse, but I'll call him."

Jesse thanked him and hung up. He then turned his thoughts back to finding a flaw in Linares Cruz's analysis, his best hope of possibly freeing Kevin without bringing down the wrath of Cal Covington. But what could Jesse Hall—world history retard—bring to the table that *bona fide* sixteenth-century experts hadn't already considered?

He started pacing again. Maybe he'd been approaching the problem the wrong way. He was a lawyer, not a historian, and one thing lawyers were good at was attacking sham evidence. So he would envision the land grant letter as an exhibit and Teo as the judge he had to persuade. He would research the letter as a lawyer would, using evidence, investigation, imagination, wit, and guile. He'd get into Marisa's head and glean the doubts she had expressed to Anastacia. But how, with both of them dead?

He retrieved Marisa's resource materials she had used in writing her land grant articles for the *Guatemala Globe*. Might be something there worth a second look. Flicking a silverfish off the large envelope, he spread the contents on his bed. He picked up the transmittal letter written to Marisa from the grant letter's anonymous holder. It was signed, "A Fellow Warrior For Democracy." As "good faith proof of the validity" of the proffered original, the sender had attached a list of excerpts from the original letter.

He placed this page of excerpts beside Marisa's *Globe* article breaking the land grant story and realized that in the interest of journalistic brevity, she had referred to only a few of them, presumably the most telling. He applied Post-its to the selections she had *not* published, and his heart leapt as he realized he was looking at excerpts from the original land grant letter that had not been seen by anybody other than Marisa, Linares Cruz, and the possessor of the document.

One of last ones jumped out at him:

"Alas, Dear Governor Hernandez, it is almost finished for me, and

may the merciful Lord God Almighty have pity on my unworthy soul. The doctor has left, as has my confessor. Neither displayed optimism concerning my future.

"I pray that those who read this letter will forgive the sad insufficiency *of my words, for I am an Emperor, not a* literati. *I am grateful to Pope Clement VII for dispatching his personal aide, Cardinal Adriano Vespucci, to administer the Holy Eucharist, assign my penance as set forth above, and comfort me as time for my ultimate judgment draws closer."*

Jesse paused. This was the first time he had seen a Red Hat identified by name. Vespucci. What if there was no such Cardinal? Or no Governor Hernandez? He would check every single person named in the document and make sure they not only existed, but existed when Cortéz was in Spain, before his return to the New World.

Excited, he swept the letter and list of excerpts into a folder, and returned to the *Biblioteca Nacional.* But his enthusiasm was short-lived; everything he read supported Linares Cruz's claim of authenticity. Carlos Quinto had not only, in fact, pardoned Cortéz, but had indeed returned him to Mexico as a *hidalgo*—a mere landowner—just as Linares had said. Jesse was still hopeful, however, because so far, Cardinal Vespucci was not mentioned.

Jesse turned to his last reference book, one on the culture and religion at the time of the reign of Emperor Carlos Quinto. It not only confirmed the Emperor's devout Catholicism and the Pope's powerful influence on him, but also mentioned Charles's nervous breakdown, even how he renounced all earthly goods and retired to a monastery two years before his death. Linares Cruz either had every base covered or the damned letter was real after all. Jesse clung to his one hope: he still had found no mention of a Cardinal Vespucci.

The library lights began blinking on and off. Closing time.

Jesse found another treatise on New World history and scanned the index. No Vespucci. Jesse could barely sit in his chair. More than one prizefight had been turned around in the fifteenth round with a single lucky punch. But he had to be sure.

The overhead lights blinked a final warning and chairs scraped against wooden floors as people rose to leave. Shit, here came the bouncer, an elderly librarian.

"I am sorry, sir," she said in English, "but we are closing."

"Just another ten minutes?" he pleaded, holding up a book by Vicente Danielle on *Medieval Catholic Hierarchy,* and flashing the lop-sided smile that Megan once admitted had shattered her resistance.

She hesitated, then, "All right. Ten minutes only, while I lock up the back."

He quickly thumbed to the V's in the index and . . . *oh shit*, there he was: Cardinal Adriano Vespucci, formerly Archbishop of Florence, awarded his red hat and sash in A.D. 1517.

He thumbed back to Vespucci's brief bio and found to his further dismay that Vespucci was a favored member of Papal royalty who often stood in for Clement VII when the Pontiff was indisposed. In other words, he was the guy most logically positioned to deliver the Pope's prescribed penance to Carlos V. Jesse's heart sank.

He heard the librarian returning and quickly scanned the final paragraph of the bio. Then he felt her hand on his shoulder. Also a sudden electrical charge that surged up his spine and into the back of his head, but it wasn't from her hand.

Holy shit, he said aloud, there it was, what he had been hoping for, though in an entirely different form than he had imagined. Time to find a copy machine.

DAY TWENTY-FOUR

45

JESSE AWOKE THE next morning to light streaming through his small window. He looked out and saw a blazing red-orange sun rising between two majestic volcanoes. Yes, he thought, it's Tuesday. I'm still in Guatemala. I'm still alive.

He showered, dressed, and grabbed a quick breakfast downstairs. Eyes followed him everywhere now, his anonymity gone. He might as well have stayed at the more comfortable Ramada. By the time he reached his car outside, the sun had been swallowed up by fast moving cumulonimbus clouds now blanketing *Volcán de Fuego*. But if things broke right, this could be his best and brightest day since leaving home.

Jesse met Teo as agreed at Linares Cruz's office at seven. By 7:20, they were working on second cups of coffee, waiting for their promised "five minutes" with the celebrity professor.

"He is keeping us waiting to humiliate me," Teo told Jesse. "He also wants me to have ample time to observe that his office has a better view than mine did."

"He has a right to be pissed. We had no appointment, Teo. Cut him some slack."

"This is all a waste of time. You will not change his mind *or* mine."

"Bear with me, Teo. I hope to be able to open your eyes."

"And how do you expect to do that? By catching Guatemala's leading medieval historian in an error? Once again, my young friend, you have exalted hope over logic."

Jesse shrugged. "He may be your leading medieval historian, but is he an expert in Catholic dogma and Papal succession?"

"No, but you are not, either. So what are you suggesting?"

"Last night, I—"

The door opened and the handsome professor strolled in holding a mug of coffee. He offered neither handshake nor smile.

"So, gentlemen," he said, beckoning them to chairs, "to what do I owe the pleasure?" His tone suggested that their presence prompted no pleasure whatsoever.

Jesse engaged in misdirection, harmless questions about Linares's research, until Linares glanced impatiently at his watch. "Señor Hall, I have already discussed all of this in detail with you. Forgive me, but I have an early class this morning and—"

"Of course," Jesse said. "You're aware Teo's wife published some of the paragraphs that had been anonymously sent to her."

Linares agreed that he had seen them, too, in both the *Globe* and *La Prensa*.

Jesse continued. "One excerpt included a reference to the Cardinal who assisted Pope Clement VII when everybody thought Charles was dying. Do you recall that?"

Professor José Linares Cruz smiled, displaying his even chalk-white teeth, set beneath a black knife blade of a mustache. "Yes, Clement sent his eminence, Cardinal Adriano Vespucci, to assign the Emperor his penance and administer last rites."

Linares rose, looked at his watch again, and put his empty cup down with a purposeful thud. "I hope I have been helpful, Teo, and that you and *La Causa* will be able to obtain funding for the letter with all deliberate speed. I really must go—"

"Just one more question and we'll leave, Professor," Jesse said. "Please explain to Teo how Cardinal Adriano Vespucci administered the last rites to Emperor Charles when, according to Danielle's definitive work on the ecclesiastical hierarchy, the Cardinal died two weeks before Charles recalled Cortéz to Spain, at which time the Emperor was still very much alive."

46

ANXIETY STIFLED THE air as Jesse and Teo drove away from the University, headed for Court. Linares's response to Jesse's query had been to look like a deer staring into his very last headlight. Teo's reaction had been a cold silence.

Teo's cell phone rang, breaking the brittle tension. It was the court clerk, advising that Judge Chavez had an emergency hearing and that the trial would not resume until 1:30 p.m. Teo made a sudden left turn and headed for Jesse's hotel.

"Why a recess?" Jesse said, but Teo continued to drive in silence, his bloodless lips pressed together as if suppressing words that could kill.

After another ten minutes of silence, Jesse could stand it no more. "It would have all come out eventually, Teo."

Teo pounded the flat of his hand against the steering wheel. "Perhaps," he said, "but you were able to do it now only because of unpublished excerpts you found in Marisa's papers. *Papers I entrusted to you in confidence!*"

A cloud exploded overhead and sent a sheet of rain hydroplaning along the roadway toward them. The Volvo's windshield wipers were powerless to keep up with the torrent. Teo did not slow the car.

"Nothing this important could have survived exposure," Jesse said, squinting nervously through the windshield as rain pounded the roof of the car, "and you've admitted there were serious legal doubts concerning its enforceability anyway."

Teo gave Jesse a chilling look.

"Look, Teo, I was just the messenger. Once I figured it out, I couldn't ignore it."

"Would you ignore it now if I asked you to?"

"*What?*"

"You heard me."

"Why would you want me to?" Jesse said. "It was a hoax, Teo, just a dream!"

Teo pulled the car into The Centenario's parking lot and they sat in silence for a full minute. "'Following darkness like a dream,'" he said at last, his expression softened with resignation. "'For that we're after.'"

"I'm afraid you've lost me, Teo."

"Pedro Calderon de la Barca, a Spanish poet. His most famous work is *Life is a Dream,* the theme of which is that our perceptions are merely shadows, that true reality is found in that which is invisible and eternal."

"Maybe you could try this on me in Spanish."

Teo looked tired, more tired than Jesse had ever seen him. "I am saying, young Jesse, that real or false, what you call a 'dream' might still become a symbol around which a new reality might be created, a myth fulfilled, a democratic renaissance in a country facing anarchy and despair."

"You still want *La Causa* to *buy* the damned thing, knowing it's a fake?"

Teo stared straight ahead through the windshield of the parked car. The rain stopped as abruptly as it had started. A bird perched on the front of the car, playing the role of a hood ornament.

"I don't know what I am going to recommend," he said, reaching across and opening Jesse's passenger door. "I will tell you when I know."

Jesse stepped out of the car. He had run out of arguments.

"Will I see you before court resumes at 1:30?" Jesse said.

Teo nodded and sped away. At least it looked like a nod.

. . .

JESSE CHECKED FOR messages at the hotel's front desk. Geraldo Maldonado, the immigration officer whose son he had rescued, wanted him to call. The other message was from a man named Domingo Caníz from Computer Mania, presumably the computer specialist to whom Teo had entrusted Webster's laptop.

"Your computer is ready. You can pick it up at ten-thirty this morning." An address was included, but no mention of whether the expert had been successful.

Daring to hope, Jesse headed for his car. While walking, he returned Maldonado's call on his cell. Maldonado explained he had obtained his hotel residence from the police report. "I only wanted to thank you again for saving our son," he said, "and to ask if there is anything my wife and I can do to repay your courage and kindness."

Jesse told him he was a little busy at the moment and thanked him for thanking him again. He hung up and started his car, pleased to see the rain had stopped. Webster's "insurance letter"—if Caníz had retrieved it—would surely implicate his co-conspirator, presumably Carano. It might even mention Marisa's murder and, since it was to be read only in the event of his death, might even include a confession.

Jesse arrived in the general area of 15 *Vista* in *Zona* 3 well before 10:30. It was a seedy neighborhood wrapped around a giant *barranca,* a ravine that spanned a quarter of a mile across at the widest point. Jesse's Suzuki bumped and heaved its way over deep ruts in the dirt road. Shacks the size of one-car garages clung to the hillsides on both sides of the canyon, most of them made of scrap lumber and corrugated metal patched together with mud and scavenged baling wire. One homeowner had repaired a broken window with part of a "Salem Cigarettes" carton on one side and a "Huggies" patch on the other. Latin music poured from many of the openings, though only a few people, mostly Indians, were visible. Clothing hung everywhere from wire and string. The odor of decaying garbage penetrated Jesse's nostrils. What kind of computer expert lived in a neighborhood like this?

Jesse wondered if he was lost. He saw a young boy perched behind the steering wheel of a Chevy stripped of wheels, doors, and engine. A few feet away, a scrawny goat foraged in the rubble. Yet surprisingly well-kept cars were parked bumper to bumper along the edge of the pitted streets. Signs of capitalism in Guatemala had stubbornly emerged in the most unlikely places, like a worm out of a rotten apple.

He checked the house numbers and saw he was getting close to 15-42. Kids off to one side of the narrow street, seemingly unmindful of their poverty, laughed loudly, playing a game involving nothing but a partially deflated soccer ball and sticks. A pack of mongrels, heads hanging between boney shoulders, stared hungrily toward Jesse, but none summoned up a decent bark.

The road improved when Jesse approached a dead end, as did the quality of the dwellings. Jesse found the address of the computer analyst, one of the better hovels on the street, but still not what you'd expect. He spotted some parking places three houses back down the hill, made a U-turn, swung downhill back past the house, and parked across the street.

Trudging back up the hill toward 42, he took in the shiny black Mercedes sedan parked in front. Maybe he had been wrong about this guy and his clientele. Two hard-looking kids, no more than eight or nine, glared at him.

He approached the house, noticing the blinds were drawn. A small, emaciated dog, the stub of his tail in perpetual motion, barked at him, breaking an unnatural silence. He checked the address for the third time. No mistake, but his instincts flashed caution.

Heading up the walkway, he realized that the Mercedes looked exactly like the one that had carried him to *Río Dulce*. Coincidence? Sure, there must be hundreds of black Mercedes sedans in Guatemala City.

But did they all have a statuette of the Virgin Mother on the dash, draped with a string of beads exactly like the one in Ozo's car?

Fucking Gómez!

As he spun around, a bullet whistled past his ear, then another. He knew he'd never make it back to the Suzuki, so he hurried for the Mercedes as a third shot missed and ricocheted off the vehicle's roof. Jesse raced around to the rear of the car and hunkered down behind the driver's door. Bullets from inside the house smacked against the car.

Then someone began shooting rounds under the car and bullets bounced off the asphalt. They were aiming for his legs, and one slug whistled close, clipping his cuff. He couldn't stay there and he couldn't leave. The kids were gone. So was the dog. Neither kids nor dog were likely to have phoned the PNC. He was on his own.

He cowered behind the front wheel. Bullets from the automatic pounded the entire car, slugs whizzing by dangerously close, generating sparks on both sides of the wheel. A noxious blend of scorched asphalt and burnt rubber assailed his nose. Another gun—it sounded like a twelve or sixteen gauge shotgun—opened fire, blasting away at the car with enough force to rock the vehicle on the pitted asphalt roadway. They were slowly taking the car apart. During a moment's pause—probably reloading—he heard whimpering from beneath the car. It was the tiny mutt, trembling, but miraculously unhurt. Jesse reached down and grabbed the pooch by the scuff of his neck and tossed it through a blown-open back window into the rear passenger seat, temporarily out of harm's way.

His arm and the flying dog prompted a resumption of gunfire. How long would it take them to realize he was armed with nothing but a felt-tipped pen, car keys, and some Kleenex?

Car keys. He had his car keys, but the Suzuki was at least twenty-five yards down the hill and on the other side of the street. He'd never make it. Unless . . .

Jesse reached up and jerked the driver's side door open. He released the hand brake and shoved the gear shift into neutral.

"Stay down, pardner," he said to the mutt, who needed no urging. The Mercedes slowly lumbered down the steep grade, a moving shield, heading for his Suzuki across the street, gathering momentum with an agonizing slowness owing to its partially blown tires.

One of the men burst out of the front door, his gun spitting more fire into the shell of the Mercedes. "Stay down!" Jesse warned the mutt.

Jesse was getting close to the Suzuki, but realized the car was veering off to the right with no curb to stop it—heading straight toward a neighboring house! Jesse reached in and tried to turn the wheel, but the damned thing was ignition-locked. *Shit.* He could see that the runaway car would take out the house and its inhabitants if it continued on its present course. The dog whimpered.

Jesse made a quick decision. Instead of racing toward his Suzuki, he leapt into the battered Mercedes and hit the emergency brake, the sudden stop throwing his head forward into the steering wheel and the dog onto the floor in back. He saw dark spots through the windshield. No, they were inside the car. No, they were inside his head. He fought dizziness.

"Good luck, pard," he said to the dog, and staggered toward his car, now thirty feet away. A new barrage of shots issued from the house and Jesse nearly tripped over the mutt. "*Jesus*, dog, *go!*" he shouted. He reached the Suzuki's door and frantically yanked on the handle. It didn't budge. He'd locked it.

The two men started down the front steps of the house, guns sparking wildly, coming into effective range. Jesse fumbled with his keys, but couldn't get his ten thumbs around the one elusive key that would open the door. Two hoodlums were on the street now, only fifty feet away. One of them reloaded the automatic while the other blasted away wildly with another handgun.

Jesse found the right key and was inside at last, but the goons had moved into handgun range, and slugs peppered his car, one of them shattering the rear window. Getting the key into the ignition with jittery fingers was like threading a needle while riding a bike, but the engine fired, and Jesse managed to steer the vehicle downhill. He heard another shot or two, then saw his pursuers in his rearview mirror, racing back up the hill for the Mercedes. Jesse smiled at the irony; they had shot out all four tires of their own car.

He jumped as something cold was pressed against the back of his neck. *Now what?* It was a nose, approximately eighteen inches away from a wagging stub of a tail. "Okay," he said to his canine stowaway, "But you're Bonnie; I get to be Clyde."

· · ·

ALTHOUGH BACK IN urban Guatemala City with no danger in the rearview, Jesse's hands would not stop shaking. It had been Ozo's Mercedes in front of the house, which pointed to Gómez. Or maybe Ozo was a private contractor, hired by Cal Covington. Or by one of Aguilera's fanatics, weary of Jesse's attacks on the credibility of the letter. Or by Carano.

Worse questions haunted him. Who, other than Teo, knew that Jesse might bite on a message from someone posing as the computer expert? Who, other than Teo, even knew they had hired one? And who knew Jesse was in recess for the morning and free to sucker into the trap? Only Teo Andrade knew all three of those things, plus he had two good motives for dropping the dime on Jesse: payback against Kevin by insuring his conviction, and putting an end to Jesse's threat to expose the land grant hoax.

No. Impossible. Sure, Teo was angry, but . . . *could it be?*

Jesse heard a whimper from his stowaway and saw blood on the back seat of the Suzuki. The dog had been hit, but it looked to be just a flesh wound, a nick in his left hindquarter.

"You sure are complicating things, little guy," Jesse said. The tiny mutt was so dirty that Jesse feared an infection could move into the wound, so he pulled into a gas station, got a phone book, and found the nearest veterinarian. He dropped off the dog, promising he'd be back soon to check on him and was rewarded by grateful licks on his cheek.

He headed for Teo's safe house, still tense from his brush with death at the *barranca*. The professor was standing in the doorway. "Your car is a mess," he said, shaking his head. "What in God's name happened to it?"

"I went out to see our 'computer expert,' Teo. A bunch of guys opened fire on me with automatics from his address out on the *barranca*, so I put their car in neutral, jumped in, and ran it downhill while they shot at me until I was close to my car. A heroic little dog gets an assist for distracting the shooters and drawing fire."

Teo shrugged and said, "All right. If you do not want to tell me what you've been doing this morning, it is perfectly fine with me."

"I'm not making this up, Teo!" Jesse said, and as Jesse told him more, Teo appeared genuinely shocked. But Jesse persisted. He had to know the truth.

"Who else knew you had hired a computer expert, Teo?"

"Nobody I can think of."

"How could the guys who set me up have known you hired an expert? How could they know we were in recess this morning? Help me out here, Teo. What's going on?" If Teo knew he was being cross examined, he didn't act like it.

"Maybe somebody has bugged your phone, room, or car. I will have them checked by Michael Cooper, my Israeli friend. My phones, too." Teo's gaze was unwavering, and Jesse had to concede that with his own problems with Carano, plus Marisa's past and Teo's current targeting by the PNC and ARES, phone monitoring of all of them was a distinct possibility.

Teo put a hand on Jesse's shoulder. "I insist that we hire men to protect you. I should have seen to this sooner. I will call."

"I'm much obliged, Teo," Jesse said, "but—"

"Here is Michael's card. He is the best, like Blackwater in Iraq, only better. Tell them you want two men, twenty-four hours a day. Give them the address you went to; maybe they can trace your attackers somehow. Have their bills sent to me if your office will not pay for it."

Jesse was touched and felt better about Teo. Still, he would heed Sun Tzu—*Keep your friends close, your enemies closer*—and asked Teo to accompany him to talk to Kevin.

Teo shrugged. "Of course. Have you had your car radio on?"

Jesse said no.

"Professor Linares Cruz killed himself this morning only hours after we left."

"*What?*"

"He shot himself with a thirty-eight revolver. The reports cite massive gambling debts and a threatened divorce. I suspect it was fear of exposure—or another murder."

Jesse didn't believe it was suicide, but what did it matter? What mattered is that there was no hope for a public recantation by Linares now. Teo would stand firm on the letter's validity and insist that Jesse keep his promise to do the same. The Carlos V clue pointing toward Webster was as dead as Webster himself.

. . .

JESSE AND TEO found Kevin highly anxious, his grimy face streaked with tears.

"How are you holding up?" Jesse said, looking around at the scarred yellow walls of the courthouse holding-cell.

Kevin's eye twitched. "Not so good," he said.

Silence filled the room, broken by an argument next door between some other doomed prisoner and his lawyer. A car horn sounded on the street below.

"I've given you guys the truth," Kevin said at last, "and now I want some truth from you. Do we have a chance?"

Jesse started to speak, but Kevin turned toward Teo. "What do you think, Professor?"

Teo said, "I fear I have little to contribute."

"Well, I'd like to hear it from you, sir," Kevin said.

"What would you like to hear, my confession?"

"*Your* confession? About what?"

Teo gazed into his hands as if waiting for them to speak for him. Finally, in a low voice, he said, "About how I've wanted you dead, Señor Covington, since the day the DNA evidence came out about you and my . . ."

Teo's voice broke. Jesse and Kevin stared at him in stunned silence, then at each other. Nobody spoke for several seconds.

"If it's any consolation, Professor," Kevin said, "I don't see myself getting out of this, and if I were in your shoes, I guess I'd hate me, too. So I don't blame you. Not a bit."

Teo seemed surprised and put off balance by Kevin's candor. He grimaced painfully, as if wrestling with internal demons. Finally, he managed an anemic smile and said, "Rest assured young sir, that I deserve blame nevertheless. I have been both unprofessional and immoral. You have not been the been the beneficiary of my . . . best effort."

The three men sat in silence again before Teo exhaled loudly and added in a hoarse voice, "It would appear, Señor Covington, that we both have much to forgive."

Kevin nodded and Jesse sensed—hoped—that some kind of catharsis had occurred. "Kevin asked you a question, Teo. What are his chances?"

Teo gave Jesse a glance that said he knew where Jesse was going with the question.

"Yes, well, I suppose there's always the possibility of prevailing," Teo said. "We have the utility man and the offshore money."

"Anything else, Teo?" Jesse said, his eyes holding Teo's until the big man pressed the palms of his hands into his face as if to shut out the world. He clearly knew what Jesse was asking him, asking *of* him. He dropped his hands, stared at Kevin's bruised and bloody face, and breathed in so powerfully it straightened his posture.

"Well, Kevin," he said at last, using the defendant's given name for the first time, "I suppose there would be Marisa's dying message . . . pointing to Webster as her killer."

Jesse felt a rush of gratitude for his friend and nodded his thanks. Then he turned to his client. "Don't give up yet, Kevin. With Carlos V and a possible shot at an alibi, we might both get out of this alive."

. . .

"IT CAN'T BE," Simon Bradshaw shouted into his office phone. "Cheng is *dead?*" He felt relief, followed by instant guilt, then a profound apprehension. "How did he die?"

"Hard to say," said Cal Covington. "Just got the text on my Blackberry. Wife says he went outside at nine last night to check a lawn sprinkler that had come on by itself and never returned. She called the cops at ten and a trawler came across him this morning."

"In the water?"

"A floater. The police say he had burns on his throat suggesting foul play."

Suggesting foul play? The fucking Chinaman is strangled on the eve of his testifying against CalCorp? Bradshaw tried to speak, but the words choked in the barren desert his throat had become.

"We're in the clear, Cy. They got nothing on us now."

Us. Bradshaw closed his eyes as a new wave of nausea swept through him.

47

JESSE WAS SURPRISED to find a message from Simon Bradshaw on his cell. He returned the call and was doubly surprised at how amiable the senior partner seemed as they exchanged greetings.

"I know you and Cal are pissed that I'm still down here," Jesse said, "but for what it's worth, I've now got a real shot at winning."

"That's *wonderful,* Jesse! I'm delighted to hear it."

What? Jesse felt an irresistible tug of new hope. Had he been wrong about Simon caving to Cal? Had Simon dumped CalCorp?

"I know my behavior may have seemed . . . somewhat confusing lately," the senior partner continued, "but that's in the past. I have good news, Jesse. You were elected to partnership last night!"

Jesse didn't know what to say. He had dreamed so long of this moment, yet felt . . . nothing. Neither joy, nor gratitude, nor pride of accomplishment.

"We're back to full strength here, Jesse," Bradshaw continued. "Our line of credit has been increased, and we've brought in a group of I.P. lawyers."

Why did good news lately always foreshadow bad news? "Oh, and I just got a call from the SEC. They're dropping their attack on CalCorp in Shanghai, and assuming you can keep Cal happy in Guatemala, we're golden."

"Why did the SEC drop their investigation?"

"They lost their key witness. Alan Cheng. It seems he was . . . killed."

"Killed? How?"

"He was apparently . . . strangled. At night."

Heat spread through Jesse's body. "Doesn't that strike you as a bit convenient?"

"What are you getting at, Jesse?"

"I'm trying to get at the truth, Simon. The one guy who could sink CalCorp just happens to be murdered before he can testify against the company?"

Simon said nothing. What was there to say? The truth was obvious. So was the fact that the *quid pro quo* for his partnership was to keep Cal happy. Abandon the alibi. His heart felt punctured. C&S had been an essential first step in Jesse's career strategy—but it was not to be.

"You want me to cancel the Gómez subpoena, right?"

Jesse heard the click of the Simon's lighter and could picture the glasses being pushed up his nose, the senior partner tilting back in his chair. "He *is* the client, Jesse. As a partner now, you must internalize the primacy of the bottom line. The fact is, Cal *is* our bottom line."

Jesse wished things could be different, but knew it was over. "Is the bottom line more important than an innocent man's life, Simon?"

"Don't turn this into a morality play, Jesse. In the eyes of the partnership *and* the law, Kevin Covington is not our client. *Cal* is."

"Simon says, 'Whose bread I eat, his song I sing.'"

When at last Simon Bradshaw spoke, his tone was predictably cold. "The election is not final until you accept it, Jesse. It's up to you."

"Goodbye, Simon."

"You're playing a dangerous game, Jesse, and I can't protect you."

"I can't protect you either," Jesse said, and clicked off.

. . .

AT 1:25 P.M., Jesse met Teo at the courtroom for the third day of trial. Jesse had inhaled three espressos during lunch to little effect. His confrontations with Bradshaw had depleted most of his adrenalin, and he was running on empty again.

"Bad news?" asked Teo. "You look glum."

"I'm where bad news goes when it's in a bad mood," Jesse said, and started to reveal his conversation with Simon, but just then the guards escorted Kevin in. Cal Covington was in the rear of the courtroom again, his predatory eyes fixed on Jesse. Teo nodded toward the electric utility man who would testify that he, and his green uniform jacket, were at the Andrade house at the time that the prosecutor's eyewitness had mistaken him for Kevin. The man nervously smiled back. The air felt jittery.

Noisy press reps were everywhere. A probable murder conviction of an American in a foreign court was always a big story, particularly when the defendant was the son of a U.S. billionaire and rumored drug trafficker. Jesse was glad see CNN on the scene; the more public this thing got, the better.

A door at the front of the courtroom opened and the judges entered. After the clerk's preliminaries, Amaya told the Court that his remaining witness, Chief Inspector Antonio García, was finishing an assignment in the Highlands and would arrive any moment. In the meantime, the defense was instructed to call the utility man out of order.

"I object to this witness," Amaya said, when Teo beckoned the man forward.

"One moment," Judge Chavez said, and then allowed the utility man to give his name, take the oath, and describe his meter reading duties. Puzzled by Amaya's objection, Jesse was pleased to see that the witness's height and build were similar to Kevin's.

"All right, Señor Amaya," Chavez said, "what is your objection to this witness?"

"I was not notified of his intended appearance, a clear violation of the local rule you have promulgated, Judge Chavez."

Teo rose. "We filed our witness list with the court under Article 347, Your Honor. Moreover, Señor Hall and I informed the former prosecutor on the case, Señorita Ruiz, both orally and in writing, of our intention to call Pablo Rodriguez. If necessary, I will testify to it."

Amaya took a step toward the bench and said, "*I* am the prosecutor on this case and *I* received no such notice as required. If necessary, I will testify to *that*. Moreover, if the defense did not think it was necessary to notify *me* personally, why did they give me the names of Señor Carano and Gómez last week?"

"Because," said Teo, obviously struggling to contain his anger, "you are now, regrettably, the trial prosecutor. We had previously given notice to your *superior*." There was no missing the double entendre intended by Teo, but before Amaya could take offense, Judge Chavez ruled that they would hear the testimony subject to a motion to strike thereafter. Teo fumed, and Jesse felt a sense of foreboding, but shrugged his shoulders and nodded to Teo, who approached the witness.

The examination proceeded without a hitch, the witness testifying that he'd read the Andrade's meter at 11:45 a.m. and Teo producing the green jackets for comparison. There were both the same dark green; the only difference being that the uniform jacket was a waist-cut jacket, while Kevin's was a standard sport coat. The Court granted permission to have the meter reader and the prisoner walk away from the Tribunal side by side. After the demonstration was completed,

Judge Chavez said, "Do you wish to cross-examine, Señor Amaya?"

"I do not think that will be necessary, Your Honor. I renew my former objection and move to strike the testimony. Moreover, I point out that the witness bears little resemblance to the defendant in that the jackets are different styles, the defendant's jacket is somewhat darker, and the witness's hair is much longer. Finally, the previous witness for the prosecution testified that she saw the defendant at 'approximately 11:45,' allowing ample time for the two men to have missed one another. Accordingly, the testimony not only violates the rules, but proves little if anything at all."

Teo rose and pointed out that Amaya's points were questions of fact for the Court's ultimate determination, not grounds for striking the testimony. The judges consulted with one another—a full minute of wrangling, during which López, the short and usually taciturn judge, appeared ready to explode. A recess was called.

When the judges returned, López was scowling, not a good sign. Judge Chavez said, "The issue before us is whether the trial prosecutor, Señor Amaya, was notified. We rule that failure to notify the prosecutor currently responsible for trying the case violated my department's rule. I also note for the record that the evidence presented is weak at best, thus ruling out any prejudice to the defense."

Jesse leapt to his feet. "You can't be serious. Notice to the chief prosecutor is obviously notice to all prosecutors under her supervision."

"Sit down, Señor Hall," Judge Chavez said. "Must I remind you that this is not a U.S. courtroom and that you are permitted to speak only at our sufferance?"

Jesse felt Teo's firm hand on his shoulder and took his seat. Teo moved the Court for reconsideration, but to no avail.

Jesse rose. "May I address the court once more on this issue?"

"Briefly."

"I'll be more than brief," Jesse said. He could hear the contempt in his voice and made no effort to mask it. "You said this wasn't a U.S. courtroom, and you just proved it. We gave up lynching in America a long time ago."

The reporters and a handful of others applauded, as Jesse sat back down. The senior judge glared at them, then at Jesse. "You insult this court and our justice system. Any repetition will be dealt with summarily and harshly. Señor Amaya, I see your witness has entered the courtroom."

. . .

IN SAN FRANCISCO, Eric Driver waddled solemnly into Simon Bradshaw's office, Jim Haydel close behind. Driver said, "As you know, Simon, the SEC has formally dismissed its complaint against CalCorp."

"I know that," Bradshaw said impatiently, "and it's hardly cause for your long faces."

"*But they've filed against C&S,*" said Haydel, "claiming our footnotes were 'false and misleading!' Having lost Alan Cheng as a witness, they are getting at CalCorp through *us*. The complaint also names Eric and you, Simon, as Chair of the firm."

Bradshaw's eyebrows shot up above a face turned chalk-white. He wanted to reach across his desk, seize Driver by his hideous necktie and bang his head onto the oak surface. All three knew that the firm's vulnerability largely derived from Driver's 10-K footnote, filed without consulting Bradshaw. But that was history.

"Can they do that?" Simon asked Haydel. "Doesn't their dismissal against CalCorp imply that our footnotes were indeed fair and accurate?"

Almost in unison, the two securities specialists said, "They can do anything they want." Driver added, "We'll fight the bastards, of course."

Simon pushed an intercom button and instructed his lead secretary to get Cal Covington on his cell phone. He noticed that his fingers were trembling.

. . .

JESSE WATCHED CHIEF Inspector Antonio García march to the stand as if walking barefoot on broken glass with a broomstick up his ass. He was dressed exactly as he had been at the scene of the murder of Webster's girlfriend—a navy blue suit and tie, a starched white shirt, and thick-soled black shoes, shining with a military luster.

He glared at Teo with palpable disdain, their mutual enmity obvious to all. Jesse knew that Guatemala courtroom procedure allowed a witness to testify in narrative form as distinguished from the question and answer method to which he was accustomed, so he prepared himself to listen patiently as the pockmarked PNC chief cleared his throat loudly, as if even the taking of the standard oath heralded an act of signal importance.

Amaya started by showing García colored photos of Marisa's mutilated body. He then had the chief inspector recreate the attack in excruciating detail, indicative, he opined, of a passion slaying. One photo depicted defensive stab wounds to Marisa's right hand, while a morgue shot revealed several gaping wounds across her torso.

Teo cradled his face in his hands and slowly shook his head. Even Judges Chavez and Guzmán averted their eyes.

Over objection, García next reviewed Cal Covington's history as the kingpin of an East Coast U.S. racketeering organization and his son's rumored association with Arturo Gómez. Amaya then elicited from the chief investigator the discovery of Kevin's partial fingerprints on a bathroom glass, as well as his hair samples in the bedroom.

"Did you ask the defendant if he had been a guest in the victim's house?"

Jesse saw Teo wince at the question and felt a dark foreboding. The judges had removed all doubt as to their bias by blocking the testimony of the meter reader. Now García would drive in the final nail.

García cleared his throat. "I did, Señor Prosecutor, and he denied it. The only thing he has not lied about is his alibi, because, of course, he has none."

Inspector García then detailed the incriminating DNA evidence and reported on the witness who had seen Kevin leaving the scene at the approximate time of the murder. He finished with a flourish by naming Officer Morales, who had observed the victim and the defendant behaving romantically, "a fact also denied by the defendant under oath."

"Cross-examination, Professor Andrade?" Amaya said.

Teo had obviously been shaken by the photos and references to his wife's affair. Even rising to his feet seemed a nearly insurmountable effort.

"So you are the top man at the PNC?" Teo said, in a tone suggesting that if this guy was the best, he'd hate to see the rest.

"Yes," said García, his head and shoulders erect. "I am Chief Inspector."

Teo produced a close-up photo of Marisa's dying scrawl. "Well, Chief Inspector, what did you first think of these letters scrawled in blood and ink when you saw them?"

"They appeared to be her attempt to write something."

Teo glanced at Jesse, then turned back to the witness. "Did not the formation of the letters give you a clue as to the victim's possible murderer?"

Jesse felt a rush of love for Teo. He was indeed going for Webster as Carlos V and would make García look bad in the process.

But Teo suddenly staggered and grabbed counsel table for support. "Your Honors," he gasped through purple lips, "may I have a moment?"

Judge Chavez, without hesitation, called the afternoon recess.

Teo sprawled in his chair, his fingers pulling his collar loose, his face pallid and glistening with perspiration. The guards held the gallery back and Jesse leaned in close to his friend.

"Teo, what is it?" Jesse said.

Teo forced a weak smile and popped a tablet under his tongue. "Nothing, Jesse, really. It's just a bit . . . warm in here."

"Level with me. Was that nitroglycerine? The heart?"

"It has been acting up on me again. I thought I could make it for these few days."

"Who's your doctor? I'll call him."

"I do not want a doctor. I am already feeling better."

"You're finished for the day, Teo," Jesse said. "With all this press present, they'll have to allow me to take over. Can you sit at counsel table?"

"I tell you, I am fine!"

Kevin touched Jesse's arm. "What do you make of the court's striking the utility guy's testimony from the record?"

"Tell him, Jesse," Teo said in Spanish, his voice a hoarse whisper. "Tell him the judges are under Carano's thumb. Tell him we have no chance."

. . .

WHEN COURT RESUMED, the court grudgingly permitted
Jesse to function as counsel, if Teo remained at counsel table. Judge
Chavez ordered the chief inspector back into the witness chair.

"I believe," Jesse began, "that you and Professor Andrade were
talking about those letters that the victim wrote on the floor in ink
and her own blood, sir."

"Yes."

"You are a highly experienced homicide inspector, sir. Isn't it true
that victims often try to leave a clue to the identity of their killers, if
they can?"

"I've observed this, yes."

"And did those letters appear to form the beginning of a person's
name?"

"Possibly."

"Carlos, correct?"

"Yes, and there is a V after it."

"Would it be a logical deduction for a trained investigator such as
you are, sir, that she was spelling the name Carlos? Writing the name
of her killer?"

"It might have been Carlos, Carlotta, Carl, Charles, any number of
names. The woman was dying and presumably not thinking clearly."

"Would you agree that Carlos is most logical, since that's what she
spelled?"

"Carlos would be a possible conclusion," García conceded, with
a furtive glance at Amaya. "I observe, however, that your co-counsel
prior to today has publicly insisted that 'Carlos V' referred to *Carlos
Quinto*, a former King of Spain."

"But *you* didn't think that, Inspector, did you?" Jesse said. "In fact, at one point in your investigation you inferred that the 'V' was the beginning of a 'W' she had been unable to complete. Am I correct so far?"

"That also was one hypothesis."

"One that led you to suspect that Carl Webster, a rumored station chief for the CIA for Guatemala, known to Marisa as 'Carlos,' might have murdered Marisa Andrade, right?"

A low murmur rose from the gallery. García shifted in his seat.

"Objection," said Amaya. "This is not a case about rumors."

"That part may go out," said the Chief Judge. "Answer the question."

"Señor Webster was one of many early suspects," he said, stirring uncomfortably.

"And you brought him in and questioned him, didn't you?"

"Yes."

"And since then, he has also been murdered, true?"

"He is deceased, yes."

"He had multiple bullet wounds in the back of his head and shoulders, right?"

"That is how he passed away."

"You keep using words like 'deceased' and 'passed away.' Are you suggesting that Webster died of natural causes, or by shooting himself three times in the back of his head, then twice more between his shoulder blades? The man was *murdered*, wasn't he?"

Amaya rose. "Is this the sort of sarcasm we can expect if Señor Hall is allowed to question witnesses?"

Judge Chavez gave Jesse a hard look. "You will show respect to the chief inspector."

"That's a challenge, Your Honor, but I'll do my best." He turned back to the witness. "Are you aware, Inspector García, that Mr. Webster was receiving substantial sums of money from Vice President Carano's discretionary account?"

"Objection! Irrelevant! No foundation!" Amaya shouted.

"Your Honors," Jesse said. "I have already shown proof of this fact to Señor Amaya and will prove it through official bank documents I offer into evidence."

"But that is not the point," said young Judge Gúzman on Jesse's right. "The payments could have been for anything."

"I concur," said Judge Chavez. "Objection sustained, although the documents may be marked for identification only."

Jesse was tired of swimming upstream with these judges. Next thing, they'd be making objections for Amaya, then sustaining them. The trial was a sham. Surely everybody must be thinking that.

Jesse turned around and gazed out over the room, trying to calm himself. Something was circling his mind, looking for a place to land. What was it? Well, while awaiting inspiration, he had to do something, so why not just stir things up a little? The press always liked a circus, so what the fuck? Maybe it was time to give them one.

"Let me make my intentions clear to the witness and everyone in the courtroom, Your Honors. Our defense theory is that Vice President Carano, who bore the brunt of the victim's journalistic criticism, paid Carl Webster to kill Marisa Andrade and . . ."

The explosion of sound from Amaya and the gallery nearly drowned out Judge Chavez's gavel. "Señor Hall!" she shouted. "You must . . ."

". . . and then he had Webster killed in order to silence him!"

The noise level was unabated as nearly half the gallery seemed to be on cell phones, phoning in tomorrow's headline.

"Order! Order!" shouted Judge Chavez. "Bailiffs, seize those cell phones!"

It took Judge Chavez twenty minutes to restore order. "Señor Hall, you are not permitted to defame high-ranking officials. Do you understand me?"

"Perfectly, Your Honor," Jesse said, "and I am through with this witness."

"Very well. Are you finished with the prosecution's case, Señor Amaya?"

"The prosecution rests."

"Good. Does the defense have any witnesses other than the utility man?"

Jesse took a deep breath, because he knew the next seven words he uttered would start the craziness all over again.

"The defense calls Vice President Victor Carano."

48

CARANO HAD BEEN subpoenaed, but it was not the Vice President, rather his legal representative, an attractive forty-something woman, who rose immediately from her seat in the first row. "We are reviewing the statutes on executive privilege, Your Honors. We will get back to the Court by tomorrow morning."

Jesse felt it all slipping away. How naive he had been to think Carano would honor a valid subpoena or that his lackey judges would require it.

"Hold on, Counsel," came a voice from the bench. Jesse was stunned to see that Judge Renaldo López had stirred, blinked his glazed eyes twice, and was about to open his abundant mouth for the second time since the case began.

"Is it your position that the Constitution gives a Vice President the power to flout the judiciary? That he cannot be legally subpoenaed to testify in a case as a witness involving the murder of a respected citizen of this country?"

"No, Your Honor," the woman sputtered, "we are merely—"

"I suggest that you tell *Vice* President Carano to be here himself tomorrow morning at nine. If not, I will hold him in contempt." Apparently exhausted by the outburst, Judge López's eyes hooded back over and he relapsed into his typically dormant state.

Stunned, Jesse looked across Kevin at Teo, whose wide eyes mirrored his own. Judge Chavez's mouth hung open as if she were about to speak, but nothing came out.

The court adjourned for the day, and the six o'clock television news featured a courtroom artist's rendering of Carano in caricature, wearing a black robe and wielding a giant gavel. The caption, paraphrasing Shakespeare, read, "Let's kill all the judges!"

Later, Jesse and Teo drove to the veterinary hospital to pick up Jesse's tiny mutt. Teo smiled in amusement at the small canine and said, "He appears to be ready for show."

Jesse said, "He is a fine looking beast, isn't he? Aren't you glad he's on our side?"

"A formidable animal indeed. And healthy again, I see."

"Healthier than you, I'm afraid. How are you feeling, my friend?"

"Ready for a marathon. Tip top."

Jesse raised an eyebrow. "I'm sure. Tell me, do you think Carano will show?"

"Yes," Teo said, scratching the dog's head. "The media is blasting him, and he needs the public's support with elections looming."

"We'll see. Look, Teo, the vet says I can take my dog home now, but he needs a pill twice a day. Could Carmen keep him at the safe house during the day?"

"I'll ask. What do you suppose the lad's lineage might be?"

"I'd guess somewhere between a Jack Russell terrier and junkyard mini-mutt."

"Have you given him a name?"

Jesse gazed lovingly at the tiny pooch, busily engaged in attacking a flea.

"I think I'll call him Rex the Killer Dog."

. . .

THEY RETURNED TO the safe house so Jesse could review the findings of Teo's computer expert. Teo assured Jesse the report was from a real expert, not thugs posing as one.

"He told me he was able to restore the hard drive," Teo said. "On a related note, here is a written report from my Israeli investigator, who found that my cell phone has been bugged. He thinks that is how the goons were able to set you up out at that phony address. The bastards have been monitoring our every move."

Jesse was relieved to be free at last from his latest suspicions about Teo and turned his attention to the computer files, which first appeared to be nothing but a mix of construction memos and Perlita's correspondence. Then he spotted an entry that sent tiny needles up his back: a list of rockets, mortars, RPG launchers, rocket-propelled grenades, small arms, ammunition—a sufficient quantity of each to fight a *bona fide* war.

Teo looked at the list. "This confirms that Webster was CIA," he said, "probably arranging legitimate U.S. arms sales to the Carano government. But how does it help?"

"Maybe it doesn't," said Jesse, "except that Elena told me it was illegal for the government to be building up its army under the terms of the 1996 Peace Accords."

"All right, but with Gómez's guerrillas around, I doubt anybody is complaining."

Jesse continued studying the screen. "Here's a page that looks like a rough draft of a CIA report Webster prepared for Langley."

"Probably incorporating the army's request for weaponry," Teo said.

Jesse shook his head. "Then why does he seem worried? Look at this paragraph: 'The subject mobile-launch delivery system of concern is a derivative of the German V-2 adapted by the Russians and North Koreans. . . . The subject system follows the old Soviet Scud-B design, but aspires to a longer range, possibly as high as three hundred to five hundred km, just the range he needs for delivery of the warhead. Inject that warhead with explosives, or a chemical or biological agent, and we could have an apocalypse.'"

"Who do you think is the 'he' referred to there?" interrupted Teo.

Jesse shrugged and kept reading. "'The price included the launcher, a vehicle based on a MAZ-543 wheeled chassis and 7,000 kg of IRFNA (oxidizer) and fuel sufficient for two launches, which is all he would require.'"

"Require for what?" Teo said. "And there is that reference to 'he' again."

Jesse kept staring at the monitor, remembering the Yemeni Elena told him about.

"It could be Carano," Teo said. "That 'range' mentioned there would be about the right distance to take out Gómez's camp in the *Río Dulce* area."

"With lethal agents in the warhead?"

"So it seems," Teo said, "but how do we use this information?"

"I don't think we use it at all. This memo would allow Carano to claim he was laundering payments offshore not to pay an assassin, but to get around the Peace Accords restrictions on rearmament, further endearing him to the right wing that runs the country."

Teo nodded. "All right, but I've been wondering about something else. What will you do if Gómez shows up, makes his self-serving speeches, and then denies Kevin was with him on April first?"

"We act as if we knew what he'd say," Jesse said, "and move on."

"Always cool."

"Always."

"After you finish acting cool, the witness will still be sitting there. What then?"

Jesse warmed his hands on his coffee cup. "I dunno. Maybe I'll ask him how he'd feel about being blown up by one of these missiles Carano might have purchased."

Teo scowled. "Seriously, Jesse, you need a plan, a defense strategy. You can't keep making it up as you go along."

"Hell, Teo, you play a lot of stuff by ear in this business. When I was growing up, there was a mean old guy in our neighborhood with two dogs. When one of them did some damage and he wasn't sure which one to punish, he set them to punishing each other."

"Cruel," Teo said, "but perhaps effective with animals."

"That's exactly what we're dealing with here. If we have nothing better, we'll put Carano and Gómez at each other's throats, then sit back and see what comes of it. Thanks to Judge López, we're going to get a shot at one of our dogs tomorrow morning, and I'm hoping his testimony might force the other one to come in."

Teo frowned. "I know little about dogs, but I do know how they breed cheetahs."

Jesse shook his head impatiently. "I'll bite. How?"

"Before bringing in the female," Teo said, "they put two males in a cage together. It's the struggle that arouses them."

"Hell, Teo, that's exactly what we want to happen."

"But sometimes the handler gets badly mauled."

"Okay, I hear you." Jesse knew Teo was right, but the idea that had been eluding him was slowly boring its way into his consciousness. "By the way, have you been able to come up with anything on those dates from Marisa's calendar?"

"Something about trips to Mexico, right?"

The bulb lit up at last, only sixty watts, but it was something. "Yesss," Jesse said, "and I happen to know a guy in Guatemala Immigration who thinks he owes me a favor."

. . .

BY EIGHT O'CLOCK, Jesse was sitting with Geraldo Maldonado in a cramped carrel at the *Oficina de Immigration.* "I thank you for seeing me, Señor Maldonado. Do you always work nights?"

"Every three weeks, Señor Hall. I should thank you for disrupting the boredom. Besides, my wife and I will never forget what you did for us, Señor, and for little boy. What can I do for you?"

Jesse handed him a copy of Marisa's calendar. "I need to know if you can tie these dates of travel in or out of the country to any of these three men."

While Maldonado scanned the calendar, Jesse slid a paper with three names on it a across the desk. Smiling, Maldonado reached for the paper, but the smile faded when he read the names. He slapped the fluttering piece of paper face down on his desk and glanced over his shoulder.

"I . . . I don't know, Señor Hall," he whispered, "you are asking about *Victor Carano? Arturo Gómez?* I don't know . . ."

"Look Geraldo, I know I'm asking a lot, but it's important. Not just to my client, but to your country. You won't even have to testify, just get me the information. Nobody will know where it came from."

Maldonado averted his eyes and wiped both hands on his trousers.

"You do ask a great deal, Señor. These men . . ." He exhaled sharply. "Who is this third man, this Yassaf Mousaffi?"

· · ·

THAT NIGHT, BACK in his room, Jesse yearned to hear Megan's voice, maybe tell her how C&S was forever out of his life. But then she'd assume he was on his way home and invite him to dinner to have that talk she had suggested, and he'd have to say he was a little busy with a case right now which wouldn't surprise her, because she knew that the more things change, the more they stay the same, and then he'd be standing there staring at his phone like a total asshole and would probably blurt out how much he still loved her, and she wouldn't know what to say, and there'd be this awkward silence, this awkward silence, this . . .

Instead, he picked up a legal tablet and wrote her a letter, telling her things he had learned about himself, about his runaway ambition, his audacity, his well-meaning but crazed grandiosity.

"*I realize I didn't just want to make a difference,*" he wrote, "*I wanted to be the difference.*"

He told her he was leaving C&S and planned to join a small firm doing public service work when he got home, and to live a normal life. He closed with the hope that he could spend that normal life with her and Melissa. He'd call when he got home and maybe they could go off somewhere romantic together—on a lark, maybe even to Paris, as she had always wanted. He told her he loved her and hoped it was not too late.

Jesse stared at what he had written and then hurried downstairs before he could change his mind and handed the letter to the night clerk for faxing.

DAY TWENTY-FIVE

49

AT 8:50 THE next morning, Vice President Victor Carano, his thin black hair carefully arranged and sprayed hard as baling wire, appeared outside the courthouse before a hand-picked television crew and a dozen reporters. Accompanied by bodyguards and his legal representative from the day before, he was the picture of a man in full command, cool and dapper despite the high humidity and a temperature that had been steadily rising every day. Standing before the camera, he smiled and awaited his cue from the producer before solemnly expressing his profound commitment to his country's new democracy and an independent judiciary.

"It is an honor," he concluded, "to show the gathered world press that we Guatemalans are as committed to the rule of law as other modern democracies."

"Then why," queried a press representative from a German newspaper, "did you fail to appear yesterday?"

"The result of an unfortunate scheduling conflict," Carano said, with a hard glance at the woman to his right who had spoken up in court the day before.

. . .

COURT RESUMED AT nine sharp with the Vice President on the stand, his melon face a picture of reasonableness and cooperation.

"Thank you for coming, Señor Vice President," said Jesse, who, owing to Teo's weakened state, was allowed to continue as temporary lead counsel.

"I'll get right to it, sir. I'm sure the prosecution has shown you these documents that demonstrate money flowing from your discretionary account to an offshore account, then back and into the personal account of Señor Carl Webster, a former CIA station chief residing in Guatemala City?"

"Objection," Amaya said. "There is no evidence that Señor Webster was a CIA operative."

"We can prove that, Your Honors, if it becomes necessary. For the present, I'll withdraw that part of the question."

"My fund," began Carano, looking cool and unruffled, "is used for many purposes, all for the good of Guatemala, of course. I understood Señor Webster to have been in construction, and I presume any payments to him were in connection with potential government projects."

"Did you always use an offshore account to pay for government projects or was this a method of laundering the funds so that—"

"Objection!" Amaya shouted, nearly tipping over his chair as he leapt to his feet.

"Sustained!" Chavez said, then added, "Watch yourself, Señor Hall."

Jesse kept his eyes on Carano's. "Please tell the Court how many projects you have done with Webster's firm."

"I don't know."

"Well, sir, I do. The people at his construction company tell me they've never done a deal with the Guatemalan government. I've got a witness willing to come say it."

Carano smoothed his mustache with a trace of a tremor in his fingers. Hadn't Carano and the prosecution assumed Jesse would check this?

"So, Señor Vice President, maybe you could explain payments of nearly half a million U.S. dollars from your account that ended up in Carl Webster's personal account? Would you like to see the backup documents from the bank that have been marked for identification?"

Carano reddened. "I deal with hundreds of requests for funding every day. I cannot be expected to keep track of all these foreign company requirements."

But the gallery was murmuring and Carano's forehead had begun to glisten. Time to lower the hammer on the payments to Gómez, thought Jesse, though he wasn't sure whether the hammer would fall on Carano's head or his own. The case was forcing him to take risks trial lawyers work hard to avoid.

"Let's look at another recipient of your generosity. Here is a document that shows several million dollars transferred to the same offshore account, but this money was forwarded back into Guatemala to an account at the Livingston branch of *Banco de Comercio*. Can you guess whose account that went into?"

Amaya rose. "Your Honors, I most strenuously . . ."

"Then let me tell you," Jesse said. "The records show an average annual payment of two and a half million for the past two years—"

"Objection! *Objection!*"

"—to the account of *Arturo Gómez!*"

An audible gasp issued from the gallery, and Amaya continued to shout, "Irrelevant and hearsay!" After order was restored, Jesse offered to bring in the bank representatives.

"Your Honors, I have never seen these documents," Amaya protested, "and even if I had, what possible relevance could they have to this case?"

"You haven't seen them? They were provided to me by your boss, Señorita Elena Ruiz, which is confirmed by the stamp of the prosecutor's office on each one of them. And Señorita Ruiz must have thought they were 'relevant' or she wouldn't have given them to me."

This silenced Amaya, and Jesse could see that Judge Chavez was trapped. Judge López leaned forward, glaring at Amaya, his stubby arms resting on the dais. Then he turned and whispered something to Judge Chavez, probably reminding her they were sitting in a journalistic fish bowl. She frowned, but slowly nodded agreement.

"In addition," Jesse continued, directing his remarks to Judge Chavez, but with a quick glance toward the gallery, "the victim in this case had publicly accused Carano of corruption and possible involvement in drugs. The relevance of these suspect payments is crystal clear."

"All right," Judge Chavez said at last, her reluctance obvious, "subject to being stricken later on grounds of irrelevance or document inauthenticity."

Jesse uneasily approached the Vice President, knowing he was about to violate the time-honored trial lawyers' principle: never ask a question of a hostile witness when the answer isn't known in advance.

"Please explain why you sent money to the head of a suspected drug family."

Amaya rose again, his voice trembling with urgency. "There is no evidence before this court that Gómez is the head of a 'suspected drug family.'"

Before Judge Chavez could sustain the objection, Jesse said, "I might be inclined to agree with you, Señor, except that your Inspector García testified yesterday, over my objection, that Kevin Covington had been seen in the company of 'the head of a suspected drug family,' Arturo Gómez. Remember? You said the same thing yourself in your opening statement. Do you wish to have García's testimony and your own opening statement stricken from the record as unreliable?"

Red-faced and fuming, Amaya took his seat. Jesse knew he was taking control of the courtroom, and moved in to press his advantage.

"So how do you explain all this, Vice President Carano?" Open-ended questions of a hostile witness are also taboo, but Jesse saw that Carano's confidence had wilted; even his mustache seemed to droop. He stared pleadingly at Amaya, but saw only the top of the prosecutor's head. He turned his gaze toward his personal lawyer, but she was studiously gazing at her long, squared-off, coral-colored fingernails.

"What I did," Carano said at last, in a barely audible voice, "I did for the people of Guatemala. It had nothing to do with drugs or with Marisa Andrade. You have my word on it."

"Thank you, Señor Vice President, but please tell us what it *did* have to do with."

After Carano again looked for help and got none, he began speaking in a monotone that had everyone in the courtroom leaning forward so as not to miss a word. "Very well. Our democracy had been challenged since the Peace Accords, but under my leadership as head of security, Guatemala had, by 2001, effectively stifled guerrilla activity and drug production."

Ignoring a sprinkling of hushed laughter from the gallery, Carano paused to request a drink of water and failed to conceal a tremor while sipping from the plastic cup. "That is, as they say, the good news. The bad news is that the U.S.A. began to pay less attention to us, bogged down in their Iraq and Afghanistan adventures. I began to realize that America's support for a poor country was inversely related to that country's success in its battle against drugs and left-wing uprisings. My worst fears were realized in 2009, when the U.S. Consulate told us to anticipate massive reductions in U.S. aid. We had become victims of our own success."

Carano drank more water and seemed to drift into a meditative state. Was he stalling, searching for plausibility? Hoping for a hurricane, a new volcanic eruption?

Jesse stepped in closer. "So you are telling us that to improve the economy, you sent taxpayers' money to a drug lord?"

"Without ongoing aid from the U.S., my people would have starved," Carano said, shaking his head. Then his small hands suddenly balled into fists. He glared defiantly at Jesse and said, "Your country wanted to see a left wing menace like Cuba used to be, Señor Hall, *so I gave them one.*"

Judge Chavez leaned forward, looking perplexed. Jesse was looking worried. Elena's first note about the whole thing being "a façade" finally made sense. When she discovered that Carano was transferring large sums of money to Gómez, she was asking herself whether Gómez's incipient revolution was being staged; a mere façade.

"You are saying that the government was financing the hostile incursions in Guatemala City? You were paying Arturo Gómez to attack your own people?"

"Yes, Señor Hall. For my country, I made a compact with the devil. We created the appearance of a potential revolution to ensure the flow of aid from your country. I had no choice. So yes, I paid him."

From behind Jesse came a loud *whooosh,* a gasp of astonishment from the gallery. Television crews scrambled toward the door to set up cameras and microphones to catch Carano when he left the courtroom. Most of the journalists remained seated, frantically typing on laptops or scribbling on pads—U.S. reporters from *The New York Times*, the *Associated Press*, the *Washington Post*, and *Vanity Fair*—visions of a Pulitzer for the reporter who would best dramatize this incredible con job, with Uncle Sam the patsy.

The usually calm Judge Chavez seemed too stunned by what she had heard to pound her gavel. Carano glanced around him at the excitement, obviously wondering how the people would react to this revelation.

The gallery slowly quieted, and Jesse turned his gaze back to Carano who returned the look without a blink or a trace of guile. So now what? Jesse knew that he could only press on. But to what end, now that he had single-handedly shot down his Webster-as-paid-assassin defense?

"Please proceed, Señor Hall," Judge Chavez said, dabbing her inflamed cheeks with a lace-embroidered handkerchief.

"Didn't your arrangement with Gómez result in the death of innocent civilians?"

Carano's voice faltered and he theatrically lowered his head. "That was *not* supposed to happen. It was never part of . . . our arrangement. But yes, there was occasional . . . collateral damage. My government was exceedingly generous in compensating victims and their families."

"You paid Carl Webster, too, did you not?"

"He found out what I was doing and extorted a cut in exchange for his silence."

Shit, thought Jesse, but figuring it couldn't get much worse, he plodded onward.

"So you lied a minute ago, Señor Vice President, when I asked you why you paid money to Webster."

"I was less than truthful. Gómez was also paying him some percentage out of his fee. I don't know how much."

"Why was Gómez paying him?"

"The same reason I was. Not only for his silence, but also to exaggerate the extent of Gómez's insurgencies in his reports to Washington D.C. He probably generated much more aid money than we paid him. So it worked out well for everyone."

Except, Jesse thought, for victims of Gómez's violence and the U.S. taxpayers.

"Until Webster got greedy?"

"Not with us. I think he got greedy with Gómez."

"Who do you mean by us?"

"My people. The people of Guatemala."

A few people in the gallery who started to applaud were quickly silenced by Chavez's gavel. The pendulum of popularity was amazingly swinging back Carano's way. He had been caught red-handed in a con game with a drug lord and was turning it into a political pep rally. You could almost feel the man's impatience to get out where the cameras were.

"I say for the record that I have no regrets about what I did. By the close of business tomorrow, I will open all my books and show to the satisfaction of my legislature and the public that every cent paid to Webster and the mercenary Gómez was returned one hundred fold to my people in the form of health and welfare programs funded by U.S. aid."

"Your books will show that *all* aid money was turned over to the people?"

"Yes, except for a small percentage of aid money that was returned to my discretionary fund that had made payments to Señor Gómez and to Señor Webster."

"Your discretionary fund," Jesse said, feeling Kevin's main defense theory slipping deeper into the quicksand of the sleazy Vice President's narrative. "Did you use some of that fund to pay Webster to acquire weaponry for your army?"

"What do you mean?"

Jesse picked up the list from Webster's computer. "Things like TNT, mortars and fuses, RPG launchers, and grenades?"

"Our army is minimal under the terms of the Peace Accords. We purchased nothing from Webster. I do not know what an RPG is, but any army representative can tell you we certainly have no rockets."

Jesse's intuition told him Carano was resorting to the truth again, and he decided to shift gears before he screwed things up even more. "You disliked the critical things Marisa Andrade was writing about you, did you not?"

"It is the role of a leader to lead, not to be loved. Particularly by journalists."

"You were a constant target of her criticism, were you not?"

Carano smiled beatifically. "Again, such is the destiny of all who aspire to serve their fellow man. Are you suggesting that I discourage free speech?"

"I'm suggesting that some of the money you gave Carl Webster was for the purpose of permanently discouraging free speech in the case of Señora Marisa Andrade."

A low murmur of voices from the gallery greeted this pronouncement, but Carano did not flinch. "You are a desperate man, Señor Hall, but it should be obvious that the best evidence of my tolerance for free speech is that you remain alive to publicly engage in such absurd innuendo." Casting his eyes toward Judge Chavez, he added, "I will say no more. Good day."

Jesse was relieved when Judge Chavez looked at the clock on the wall and stopped the hemorrhaging. "We are in early recess," she announced. "Judge López has a hearing this afternoon. We will resume at nine o'clock tomorrow and I want this trial ended." She banged her gavel and the reporters streamed from the courtroom.

Teo, who obviously realized their best defense had been shattered by Carano's amazing revelation, put a consoling hand on Jesse's shoulder. "Sorry, Jesse."

"My shining hour," Jesse said. "Will your citizenry let Carano get away with this stunt?"

Teo nodded sadly. "The Guatemalans will love him for having pulled the wool over Uncle Sam's eyes. You must understand that Carano's party controls the legislature as well as our version of your justice department. He will appoint a commission to check his books, and they will find nothing. Actually, the bastard might even be telling the truth about his finances. So we've lost our paid-assassin defense, but at least we'll surely get the other dog into court."

Jesse nodded. "I agree. Gómez will have to come in now to deny Carano's claim that he's just a common mercenary." But what if he didn't? Jesse knew he would have Kevin's blood on his hands, his soul forever stained by his bungling of Carano's examination. *Why hadn't he seen this coming?*

Teo, Elena, and Megan had all asked him what he was doing in Guatemala and now he knew. He had come to fuck up an innocent man's trial. He had seen himself riding into this poverty-ridden city on a white horse wielding the sword of justice. But the truth? The truth was that after first trying to talk his way out of coming to

Guatemala, he had agreed to the assignment mainly to further his own aspiration to achieve partnership.

How many times in his life, he wondered, had he wrapped his personal ambitions so tightly in the banner of noble endeavor that he had blinded himself to his true motivations? And now, his blind ambition had obscured facts he should have anticipated.

. . .

JESSE LOOKED UP to see Cal Covington charging through the rail, Felix and another thug trailing behind. Teo lurched to his feet and stopped Cal's progress with a huge hand against his chest.

"All right, back off," Cal said, his hands up in mock surrender to Teo. "Jesse, call off this refrigerator with feet. I just want a private word with you, okay?"

"It's fine, Teo," Jesse said, and followed Cal to one side, Felix close behind.

"Jesse, Jesse, Jesse," Cal began. "It's just what I warned you about. According to my translator, you've put Gómez in a position this morning where he'll have to come into court. And once he's here, Amaya will expose his trafficking."

"That's possible," Jesse said, "but unlikely, for the reasons I've told you."

"I don't deal in 'unlikely.' Cancel the subpoena. Today. *Now!*"

"Can't do it," Jesse said, meeting Cal's laser gaze. "Besides, have you considered that Gómez is the only person now who might be able to save your son's life?"

Cal shook his head impatiently. "Kevin knew what he was takin' on when he came here, and if it wasn't for the short-circuit between his prick and his brain, none of us would be in this fix. So you better pray I can stop Gómez from coming in, because *nobody's* gonna blow this deal—not you, not my cunt-crazy son, *nobody!*"

Neither Cal nor Jesse realized Kevin was standing right behind them.

"Dad?" he said, his face full of pain, his voice shaky and barely audible.

Cal spun around, obviously embarrassed. "Things are . . . complicated here in Spicsville, Kevin. I'm doin' what I can, but meanwhile you just hang tough."

Kevin slowly shook his head. "I . . . heard what you said. Is that what you think of me? Haven't I always done everything you asked of me? Haven't I—"

"Come on, kid, I didn't mean nothin' personal."

"Nothing *personal?* Christ, I'm your *son!* I did this for *you!* I risked everything for . . ." His words drifted off in a strangled lament.

Throughout the weeks of abuse Kevin had suffered, Jesse had never seen him so desolate. His face was florid with agony and his manacles clattered loudly as his hands attacked each other like writhing snakes. He continued to stare at his father through cavernous eyes. Cal's giant head bobbed from side to side as if ducking blows.

"Listen, kid," he said, "you may have come here for me, but when you started porkin' that married gal, that was all about *you,* okay? Trouble with you young people nowadays, you're too damned busy chasin' earthly pleasures to get a goddam job done right." He paused and then started out into the gallery, but turned and added, "You betrayed my trust, son, but Jesse's fixin' to get you out of this anyways. So just relax and keep your damned trap shut."

Cal turned his fierce gaze back on Jesse. "You *will* get him out of this, Hall, and you'll do it without Gómez or I swear I'll put your fancy-ass firm into bankruptcy."

"I can't do it without Gómez, Cal. Besides, it's not my firm anymore. It never was."

"Yeah, then how 'bout Felix here giving you a more *personal* motivation for not bringin' in Gómez?" He nodded at Felix, who walked over to the rail and shocked everyone by effortlessly ripping out one of the two-inch-thick pieces of vertical oak railing, causing a loud crack that echoed through the courtroom. An immobilized guard watched as Felix, his extended forearms trembling from the exertion, snapped the solid member in two pieces. He handed one half to Jesse, the other to Teo.

"Don't stick your neck out, Jesse," said Cal through smiling lips, "*comprende?*"

50

BACK IN THE safe house's living room, Teo, having refused a medical house call, poured himself a tumbler of rum, "for the stomach's sake."

When Jesse gave him a hard look, Teo said, "You're not familiar with the New Testament admonition? Paul's Epistle to Timothy, I believe."

Rex the Killer Dog snuggled into Jesse's lap and began to doze off.

"I know the passage," Jesse said. "But in my recollection, the reference was to a modest portion of wine, not six ounces of straight ninety-proof rum."

"I am *not* drinking straight rum. It will be supplemented by ice and a slice of lime."

The men sat together with nothing but the sound of an occasional match striking, the hallway clock ticking, the odd tinkling of ice. Teo broke the silence, expressing his frustration at Carano's manipulation of the media. Jesse's heart was too heavy to reply, for he knew that by blowing their defense theory that Carano had paid Webster to kill

Marisa, he had also wasted Teo's gracious forfeiture of the *La Causa* interpretation of Marisa's dying clue.

Rex snuffled in his sleep, probably pursuing a rabbit—a small one.

"You realize," Teo said, "that if Gómez comes in, he *will* kill you. He has lost face and will seek vengeance, a matter of honor."

"The things that are done in the name of honor sometimes puzzle me," Jesse said lightly, concealing the fear chewing at his guts.

. . .

WHEN JESSE RETURNED to his hotel, the barely-awake night-shift desk clerk called out to him. "You received a fax from a Señorita Megan Harris at nine-fifteen tonight, Señor Hall."

He handed the transmittal to Jesse:

> *Dear Jesse: Message received. Don't beat yourself up. Sometimes searching for something we thought we wanted awakens us to what we needed all along.*
> *Always, Megan*

Jesse's heart sank. Typically insightful words, but *"Always,* Megan?" What was that about? Always *what? Always* your old pal? *Always* the one you never listened to? *Always* the gal that got away?

And not a word about his suggestion that they might go off together. He crumpled up the note and mentally kicked himself in the ass. She was right, of course. Not for the first time, he had stopped pursuing what he thought he wanted too late to get what he really needed.

. . .

LATE THAT SAME day in San Francisco, Simon Bradshaw sat in a private booth at Sam's Grill on Pine Street facing his partner, Jim Haydel.

"This better be good," Bradshaw said, fighting a growing apprehension, "and it better be fast. I have a meeting."

"It will be fast," his downcast partner said, "but it will not be good."

A pale, elderly waiter appeared, but was dismissed by a wave of Bradshaw's hand.

"CalCorp dumped us," Haydel said. "We just got a fax ordering us to transfer all files, cases, and documents to Farell and Brown."

Bradshaw eased his glasses up on his nose and stared at his partner, looking for the punch line he began to fear would not be coming. "It's a mistake," he whispered, sliding out of his seat. "It's got to be. I'll call Cal and get it straightened out. Don't sign anything or hand over any files. It's some kind of simple mistake."

. . .

SIMON STUMBLED OUT of Sam's like a drunk leaving a building on fire, unmindful of people's curious looks. *Think, think, think,* he ordered himself. *What am I missing?* He stopped, leaned against a building wall for support, loosened his tie, and caught his breath. He had to *act*.

He grabbed his cell, called his secretary. "Book a night flight to Guatemala. I need to get there by mid-morning." He listened to the authority in his voice—yes, his father's voice. "Wait a minute. Charter a jet instead. Then set up a lunch meeting with Cal Covington in a hotel office suite close to the courthouse. Got it? And don't let

Cal stonewall you. Tell him I've learned something too important to discuss by phone. If he presses you, tell him a critical issue has arisen regarding his charities. Tell him anything, *but book an office suite and get Cal into it!"*

Fuck Cal Covington, fuck Eric Driver, and fuck my father, too. I can pull this off. Cal just needs his hand held. Or maybe a threat. Or a blow job. Whatever it is, by God, I'll give it to him. *This firm will not go down on my watch.*

DAY TWENTY-SIX

51

CITIZENS WERE AGAIN lining up early in the *Centro Cívico* plaza, hoping to get a cherished seat in the courtroom and a peek at Gómez, rumored to be making an appearance.

Back in his room, Jesse answered the phone.

"Julio? Where are you?"

"I just arrived in town and am with my uncle. Anica came, too; she's visiting her father at the safe house."

"Will Señor Gómez testify?"

"That's why he is here."

Jesse felt a rush. "Thank you, Julio, that's great news for Kevin."

"But not for you, Señor Jesse. I am sorry. He is very angry with you and wants Teo to conduct his examination."

"Too risky. Teo is sick, and the Tribunal is allowing me to question witnesses."

"You must know by now that only Gómez decides what Gómez will do."

"The stress could kill Teo. His heart is acting up again."

"I am sorry, Jesse, but Teo has already agreed to do it. In fact, he suddenly seems eager to meet with my uncle."

To try to save me, Jesse thought. "Will Gómez alibi Kevin Covington?"

"He will not say. I think he's coming in primarily because of the way Carano maligned him yesterday."

Well, at least the dogs would be at it.

"And also," Julio added, "to . . . deal with you. *Lo siento.*"

"Not as sorry as I am," Jesse said. Earlier in the morning, he had received a call from Teo's security guy, who said Teo had ordered two additional bodyguards and an armored sedan to escort him directly to the airport when the trial was finished. Jesse considered leaking this to Julio, but decided against it. Indirectly passing this information to a man like *El Cobra* would constitute a challenge, not a deterrence.

"Will your uncle be represented by independent counsel?" Jesse asked.

"Hah! A couple thousand of them, Jesse, all trained and heavily armed."

"Jesus, Julio, this isn't a video game. Real people are getting killed here. Are you saying he has brought his army to Guatemala City with him?"

"I'm just suggesting that you warn the prosecutor that any attempt to cast *El Cobra* as a drug trafficker would provoke dire consequences."

"Julio, I am not in a position to control Señor Amaya."

"Well, nobody can control *El Cobra* . . . especially lately. At least try to help Teo restrain the prosecutor when he cross-examines my uncle."

"I'll do what I can," Jesse said. "How is Anica?"

Julio laughed boisterously. "She is wonderful and . . . we are married, Jesse!"

"Married? That's . . . great, Julio. Does Teo know?"

"Not yet. My uncle performed the service himself as *de facto* head of state."

Head of state?

"I know," Julio said. "I'm afraid he's, well . . . anyway, we will tell Teo the good news after court this afternoon, but we will say it was performed by a priest, okay?"

"Sure. Fine."

"And Jesse, all I can do about my uncle is warn you of his intentions. He does not listen to me at all. If I could do more, I would."

"I know, and thanks for the heads-up."

. . .

JESSE WAS ESCORTED into the courthouse by a phalanx of PNC cops attired in full riot gear, their shirts dark with sweat. The temperature was already in the eighties, and army troops had been brought in to deal with thousands of onlookers.

Streets were closed to vehicular traffic for three blocks surrounding the *Centro Cívico.* Beggars, musicians, and food and souvenir vendors moved through the colorfully-dressed crowd. The scene seemed more festive than threatening.

Jesse met Teo just before nine inside the courtroom, and even there they could hear the street crowd chanting: "Gó-mez! Gó-mez! Gó-mez!" The courtroom attachés, usually blasé, chatted nervously, unable to sit still. Teo fell into a chair, exhausted from pushing through the crowd both inside and out. His breathing was alarmingly quick, noisy, and shallow.

"You okay, Teo?" Jesse said. "You've gone an even whiter shade of pale."

"I'll be fine," he said. "Anica will stay with me until the trial is over. She'll make sure I do not overtax myself."

Teo excused himself and headed for the men's room. When he returned, he reeked of rum and spearmint. Jesse looked at him with mingled anger and concern. "Putting Gómez on direct could finish you, Teo. He's totally unpredictable."

Teo straightened his tie and his shoulders. "I said I would put him on and I shall."

"All right," Jesse said, "but stay seated and keep it short, okay? Just the questions I've drafted."

Bodies jammed the courtroom, people again sitting on the sills of open windows, sixty feet above the ground, hanging onto the casements with their fingers. The wide entry door was left open to allow people in the crowded elevator lobby to listen to the proceedings, but air was in short supply.

A bailiff pointed out a section of seating blocked off for Gómez and his anticipated entourage, and Jesse saw that Cal and his two thugs were in their usual places in the rear of the courtroom. Another half-dozen seats were reserved on the opposite side of the aisle. Jesse asked Amaya who else was coming.

"Our Vice President will be here to testify in rebuttal."

"Rebuttal to what?" Jesse asked Amaya.

"To Gómez's anticipated denial that he is a drug trafficker and to rebut any slander."

"Jesus, Enrique, tell me you aren't going to get into the drug thing with Gómez. You'd be throwing a match into a gasoline spill."

Amaya's eyes sparked. "You're getting just what you asked for, and if you and your client get burned, you have only yourself to blame."

Jesse looked around and saw a half dozen men in business suits and expensive-looking shoes inside the rail—usually the sacrosanct preserve of lawyers and attachés only—taking seats in yellow plastic chairs.

"Who the hell are those guys, and how'd they get in here?" Jesse asked Teo.

Teo rubbed his thumb and two fingers together. "Money. Our little trial has become the hottest ticket in Central America this year. They are wealthy business leaders, retired military, and politicos. Some are probably members of *La Cofradía.*"

Jesse spotted ten uniformed *Policías de Presidios,* four near the single entry door and six posted along the opposite wall, and wondered how many plainclothes PNC and ARES goons were in the crowd. After trying in vain to I.D. his own bodyguards, he eyed the chambers door, maybe the only refuge if the defense won. He reflected on the ineffectual metal detector and guessed there were dozens of handguns in the courtroom, at least two in the possession of Cal's thugs, probably under orders to kill him if Amaya exposed his drug consortium.

At 9:30, still no judges. At 9:50, Jesse heard a racket in the elevator lobby. Surrounded by bailiffs, the manacled prisoner shuffled into the courtroom. He seemed to be sleepwalking, oblivious to the uproar. He wore socks and his clothes had been ironed, but the disarray on his face could not be hidden.

"Welcome to the asylum," Jesse said. Kevin dumbly nodded, and when Jesse told him that Gómez was coming in, he merely nodded again.

"When we lose," he whispered, breaking his silence. "I want you to kill me or have my father do it. I won't go back to *Purgatorio.*"

It was then that six men in olive and black camouflage jumpsuits, high-laced black boots, and black berets roughly pushed through the crowd and entered the courtroom, followed closely by a half-dozen toughs in jeans and jackets, plus Julio, Anica, and two other women.

In their midst was Gómez, in an elegantly tailored dark suit. Only one of the women was shorter than he, and with his conservative attire, his thinning hair, a neatly trimmed beard and glasses, he looked more like a professor than Teo did. Gómez's entourage took their seats in a blocked-off area. Teo walked out through the rail and was introduced to Gómez by Julio.

"You have a delightful daughter," Gómez said, and Teo nodded with reserve. Just hearing Gómez's voice sent a shiver through Jesse and his nod to *El Cobra* was rigidly formal. Gómez arranged his mouth into an imperious smile, but his eyes sparked with danger. Neither man offered his hand.

With Gómez's entrance, hardly anyone noticed the judges enter. Judge Chavez did not call the room to order, but instead sat silently, occasionally glancing at the clock. Judge Renaldo López looked miserable and rubbed his temples. Judge Gúzman, youthful, yet stately, scribbled on a notepad without looking up.

After five minutes of this, Teo rose and said, "Should I commence my questioning, Judge Chavez?"

"No, Señor Andrade," she said, but offered no explanation.

Just before ten, another rumble of excitement began to build outside, and then burst loose in the elevator lobby. The crowd at the door parted as Victor Carano and three civilians, including his anxious-looking legal adviser, entered among four large uniformed PNC's. He sat down in the front row on the opposite side of the courtroom from Gómez. The two men did not exchange looks, but the tension was so palpable that Jesse felt that a mere spark could set the room ablaze.

At 10:15, Judge Chavez called the courtroom to order at last and nodded at Teo, who was sweating profusely, all color drained from his face and lips. "The defense calls Arturo Gómez," Teo said, lurching as he rose.

Gómez took the stand as calmly as if walking to lunch.

"You appear here pursuant to a subpoena, Señor Gómez," Teo said, his voice ragged, "is that correct?"

"Yes." Gómez shot a sardonic smile at Jesse. "I believe I did briefly see a subpoena. I must say, however, that had I known of the perjury this court was to suffer yesterday, I would gladly have volunteered to testify without one."

Both Amaya and Judge Chavez opened their mouths as if to object to the characterization of Carano's testimony, but neither did.

"I am here, Your Honors," *El Cobra* continued, "because I believe that the foundation of our new democracy must be a new and truly effective judicial system." Although Gómez was looking at the judges, it was clear he was speaking to the reporters. Here we go, thought Jesse, another speech.

"There can be no justice," he said, "without a reliable means for discerning truth. Why? Because truth is the mother of justice. I am saddened to say, however, that today our beloved country enjoys neither truth *nor* justice. This condition *shall not stand.*"

Except for occasional audible grunts from Carano the gallery was silent, seemingly mesmerized. Even Judge Chavez was silent, probably afraid of pissing off this scary nutcase, who probably had his own small army in civilian attire inside the courtroom—and God knows what sort of devil's cadre outside.

Amaya, however, rose and quietly said, "We are straying off point, Your Honor. May the witness be asked to limit his response to the question asked?"

Gómez gave Amaya an indulgent smile and clicked his tongue, like a father about to correct a misguided son. "Ah, but you see, Señor Prosecutor, that's exactly what I have done. I was asked why I am here, was I not? So, I will tell you again.

"I have come to tell the people of Guatemala that a legal system must also inspire *trust* in those whom it serves, or it will most surely fail." He paused to glare at the three judges, who busied themselves scribbling on legal pads. He then looked back at Amaya and said darkly, "This trust will soon be restored, Señor, I assure you. *Quite soon.* Ask your next question, Professor Andrade." Letting everyone know who was running the show. For his part, Jesse found it hard to disagree with Gómez's rambling diatribe, but he gave Teo a look that urged him to steer the witness to the alibi testimony.

Nervously, Teo complied. "Señor Gómez, do you know the defendant, Kevin Covington?"

"I do."

"And would you tell the court where you last saw him?"

"Yes, it was at one of my farming headquarters, in an area north of Livingston."

"And the date?"

The entire courtroom seemed to lean forward and hold its breath.

"It was," Gómez said, looking directly at Judge Chavez, "on April first."

The courtroom exhaled. Jesse and Teo exchanged a look of relief. *Gómez was coming through!*

"During what hours on April first was Señor Kevin Covington in your company?"

"All morning. He arrived the previous night and stayed at my farm north of Livingston. He returned to Guatemala City in the afternoon."

Teo mopped his face with his handkerchief and leaned against counsel table. His voice was weakening by the minute and Jesse feared he would not be able to finish.

"How . . . do you have occasion to remember it was on the first day of April?"

Gómez winked at Jesse and said, "To paraphrase your great President, Franklin Roosevelt, April first is a day that for us will live in infamy. As you know better than any of us, Professor, a great patriot was murdered on that day."

"Yes," Teo agreed and looked down at his notes, trying to control his emotions. "But how do you connect the day of the murder to the presence in your midst of the prisoner on April first?"

"Ah. One of my farm workers happened to be an American who, upon hearing the tragic news, said he thought it must be an April fool's prank. We agreed with him."

Edward White Beard, a farm worker, Jesse mused. Sure.

"Thank you, Señor Gómez. You may cross-examine, Señor Amaya."

Jesse gave Teo a reassuring nod, and the big man collapsed into his chair. Jesse translated the testimony for Kevin, whose face flooded with relief.

Amaya rose, and, in a quiet voice, said, "Señor Gómez, may I ask what the defendant was doing at your headquarters?"

Jessed noticed that the prosecutor was uncharacteristically diffident. In fact, everyone seemed intimidated in the presence of Gómez, except for Carano, who eagerly leaned forward as Amaya began his questioning. Jesse glanced at Teo, waiting for his objection, but Teo's head was lowered, his eyes shut, his hands flat on the table before him as if for support.

"Objection," Jesse said. "The reason why Señor Covington was out of town in Livingston on April the first is irrelevant and calls for an opinion and hearsay. The only thing that is relevant to this case is that Kevin Covington *was* out of town."

Teo's eyes popped open and he gave Jesse a weak smile of gratitude.

Judge Chavez waved off the objection and said, "Are you ill, Professor Andrade?"

Teo tried to rise, but fell back into his chair. "I am indeed unwell, Your Honor. If the Court would be so kind . . . to again allow Señor Hall to be my voice . . ."

He slumped in his chair, too weak to say more.

Judge Chavez seemed greatly annoyed by this development, but acceded.

"My thanks, Your Honor," Teo said without rising.

Amaya glowered at Jesse and said. "Answer the question, please, Señor Gómez."

"I renew our objection," Jesse said.

"Overruled," Judge Chavez said. "You may answer the question, Señor Gómez."

Carano beamed, but Gómez seemed untroubled. "I will be pleased to do so. You see, I am currently drafting a ten-point recovery plan for Guatemala. Señor Kevin Covington and I were discussing how the infrastructure of Guatemala could be improved. He is an expert in construction, having worked with rebuilding projects in the flood-ravaged regions of New Orleans."

This straight-faced declaration brought some chuckles from the gallery and derisive sniggering from Carano and his attachés, but Jesse and Teo exchanged looks of relief. This might work.

Amaya cleared his throat. "You are aware, Señor, that the defendant's father is a member of an organized racketeering organization?"

Jesse didn't bother to object. That horse was long out of the barn.

"No. I met with the son and we discussed construction."

"Well," Amaya said, obviously piqued, "you are aware, are you not, that your *Río Dulce* and Livingston areas are known corridors for drug trafficking?"

Jesse had to try again. "I repeat, this is patently irrelevant, Your

Honors. Kevin Covington is not being tried for drug trafficking, nor is Señor Gómez."

Amaya said, "That may be true at the moment, but I am entitled to test the credibility of the witness by demonstrating what everybody here already knows—that Señor Covington did not fly all the way from the United States to Guatemala's premier drug trafficking area to discuss construction techniques."

Jesse remained standing. "Señor Amaya is asking improper questions and now he's answering them, too. We called this witness for the sole purpose of establishing that Señor Covington was present at a location halfway across the country at the time Marisa Andrade was murdered. That he has done."

"State your objection, Señor Hall," Judge Chavez said, glancing at Carano.

Jesse said, "Irrelevant, hearsay, argumentative, lacking in foundation, and exceeding the scope of the direct examination."

"Thank you. Overruled. Please sit down."

"*Your Honors,*" shouted Jesse, glaring at the Tribunal, "this is crazy!"

"Professor Andrade, you will control Señor Hall, or I will have him removed."

"My apologies, Judge Chavez," Jesse said quickly.

"Proceed, Señor Prosecutor."

Amaya nodded. "Are you not aware," he continued, "that there is heavy drug trafficking in the *Río Dulce* area as well as in the Bay of Honduras?"

"I have seen no such activity in my area," Gómez said, "and I intend to ensure that *any* unlawful agriculture, including marijuana and poppies, are plowed under and that corn and coffee are planted in their place."

Many in the gallery loudly voiced their approval. Judge Chavez warned that she would clear the courtroom, if necessary, to maintain order. Jesse marveled at Gómez's ability to lie so convincingly and dared again to hope it might work.

"And just how," said Amaya, moving closer, "do you intend to bring this about?"

Jesse objected again and was pleased to hear Judge Chavez sustain the objection, adding, "We are getting a bit off point, Señor Amaya." Jesse saw that Chavez was taking her cues from Carano, who didn't like the way the gallery was responding to Gómez.

"Move on, Counsel," Judge Chavez said, and Amaya turned back to the witness.

"It has been suggested in this trial, that you and Vice President Carano are in some kind of drug conspiracy. That is not true, is it?"

"I am not in a 'drug conspiracy' with Carano or anyone else."

Amaya smiled. "Thank you, Señor. But it is true, is it not, that the Vice President paid you to create the impression that a Cuba-type revolution was about to take place so that U.S. aid would continue?"

"That is correct, for the benefit of my people."

Here we go again, Jesse thought. The "people" of Guate must wonder at having such diametrically opposed leaders. Carano looked furious, but Amaya was smiling, seemingly confident.

"I submit," Amaya said, "that the money you accepted from the government was for your burgeoning drug empire, not for 'your people.'"

Gómez's eyes narrowed. "I assure you that every *quetzal* I received has gone into building a new culture and a socialistic revolution. Men like you, incidentally, will not be a part of it."

Jesse groaned inwardly as mixed applause broke out in the gallery.

Amaya just smiled, seemingly back in control. He said, "Have you just threatened me, Señor? Threatened the entire government?"

Gómez smiled back with equal insincerity and glanced impatiently at his watch. "You heard what I said, *Señor Prosecutor.*" He spat out the last two words as if they were snake venom, then added, "Make of it what you will."

Amaya held his ground, winning Jesse's grudging admiration. "Then let me see if I have understood you, Señor Gómez. Is it fair to say that you consider yourself not only a revolutionary, but an anarchist?"

Oh shit. Just as victory for Kevin seemed within reach, Gómez was discrediting himself as a witness. If Amaya kept goading him, then hit him with his rap sheet of convictions during the thirty-six year war, the judges would have ample reason to disregard his testimony, maybe even put him under arrest.

"I am a *patriot,*" Gómez said in a restrained voice.

Amaya lowered the boom. "You are also a convicted felon, are you not?"

"Not unless you consider death squads to be duly appointed judges. I had neither a trial nor a lawyer." He held up his left hand that was missing an index and a ring finger. "I confessed to my alleged crimes to save my other three fingers."

Nervous tittering from the gallery broke the tension as it appeared that Gómez was giving Amaya the finger. But Gómez wasn't laughing, so the courtroom went silent.

"This was in the mid-1980s," he continued, "so I suppose I should be grateful to have only been imprisoned and mutilated, not summarily shot like many of my friends and family who, like me, were guilty of nothing but the crime of trying to build a nation of democracy and equality."

The silence of the crowd, awed by Gómez's words, made the sound of Teo's head hitting the table seem magnified. Jesse rushed over and bent down close to his friend's face. The eyes were glazed, half-opened, and staring blankly. His breathing was shallow. "Teo?"

Teo pointed to his vest pocket, from which Jesse extracted a tablet. "Nitroglycerin?"

Judge Chavez leaned forward. "What is wrong with the professor?"

Jesse placed a capsule on Teo's tongue with trembling fingers. A minute later, Teo's eyes popped open and he managed a weak smile. "Did I miss anything?"

"No, Teo, just the end of civilization as we know it. I'm calling a doctor."

"Absolutely not," Teo said. "Call a recess instead. I can finish the session, if I may just have a minute. And some water please."

"A recess, Your Honors?" Jesse said.

"No objection," Amaya said. "We are finished with this witness." Carano and Amaya apparently realized that Gómez was turning every question into a political harangue and felt they had done sufficient damage to his credibility and, with it, the alibi.

"A recess, then, of course," said Judge López without even looking at Judge Chavez. "Shall we call an ambulance?"

Teo shook his head and said, "I am perfectly all right, and I apologize to all."

Jesse leaned close to his friend. "All right, Teo, but so much as a wince, and we're off to the hospital."

Although the court was in recess and the judges had left the dais, spectators did not move, as there was nowhere to go, the hall outside being packed. Gómez joined his retinue in the first row.

"I am sorry, Jesse," Teo said, "we did not need more drama."

"You have a flair," Jesse said, as Teo's frantic, pale daughter leaned over the rail and hugged her father. "Oh, Papa," Anica exclaimed, "let us take you to the hospital."

"Hello, Sweetheart," Teo said, reaching up with one arm to return her embrace, whispering reassurance in her ear.

Julio pushed his way up to the rail behind Anica and motioned Jesse closer. "I have news. My uncle just told me he liked the way you handled Amaya. He's provisionally removed the death warrant from your head."

"Death warrant? *Provisionally?*" Jesse could see that Julio was troubled.

"Just do your best to ensure that Amaya does not anger him further. Everything could get worse if he is angered or embarrassed. He's been weird lately. I am afraid my uncle is . . . well, not the person I thought him to be."

"Amaya is finished with him, Julio, but thanks anyway. We can hope that he got by, but see if you can calm him down. Tell him I must try to rehabilitate him by asking what he meant by 'revolution.' See if you can get him to say something soothing like, 'an army of volunteer reformers,' you know, like a Guatemalen peace corps?"

"I understand what you need," he said, and returned to the Gómez contingent.

Kevin asked, "Where does all this leave us?"

"We have our alibi," Jesse said, "but it's hard to know how much he hurt himself with his anarchist tirade." Seeing Kevin's downcast eyes, he added, "We may be okay." Sure, he thought to himself, we'll be swell. With a biased court and a guerrilla lunatic for a key witness?

"Can't you rehabilitate him or whatever you call it?" Kevin asked.

"I've got to try, but it's hard to rehab a witness who doesn't want to be rehabbed. Saving you was not the main reason he came here,

Kevin. But I may be able to restore his credibility on redirect—if he'll go along with me."

Teo nodded agreement. "He may listen to Julio."

Jesse felt a tap on his shoulder. He turned, expecting Julio, but it was Geraldo Maldonado, the immigration officer, a shirtsleeve ripped, his lip swollen.

"Geraldo? What the hell happened to you?"

"The people outside were not happy about me pushing my way in," Maldonado said, wincing in pain while trying to smile, "but I made it!" The little *Ladino* shoved a manila folder toward Jesse. "I think I found what you wanted."

Jesse opened the folder and saw Marisa's calendar and several log sheets, none of which made sense.

Maldonado said, "See the circled dates there? Those are the ones you asked me to check."

Jesse's thoughts were spinning, his brain unable to focus. "I remember, but what do they show?"

"Look at the next sheet. Arturo Gómez made a trip to Mexico City on each of those dates."

"All right, Geraldo," Jesse said impatiently, "but so what?"

"An hour ago," continued Maldonado, "my Mexican counterpart in immigration got back to me with logs showing trips into Mexico by one of the other guys you asked me to check on. Both men were in Mexico on those same three dates, and neither was there without the other *or* at any other time."

"Okay," Jesse said, his interest growing. "Who's the other guy?"

"Look at the last sheet."

Jesse shuffled through the papers until he came to log sheets from Mexican immigration. Goose bumps spread up his spine and across his back. He read the name: Yassaf Mousaffi.

Teo stirred in his chair. "The Yemeni?"

"It gets better, Señor Hall." Maldonado leaned across the rail and pulled out one of the other sheets. "These are hotel records. Gómez and Mousaffi were not only in Mexico City on all three dates, but in the same hotel, and always on the same floor. I also checked with Interpol and you were right about Mousaffi. He is a fund raiser all right, but for *al-Qaeda.*"

"Are these documents certified, Geraldo?"

"Mine are, but not the Mexican logs. I assure you, however, they are all accurate."

"Are you willing to testify to this? They have to be authenticated to get into evidence."

Geraldo shook his head violently. "I hope you will consider my debt to you paid, Señor. I have a family, and must ask that you do not contact me again. Good luck, *amigo.*" Maldonado turned and disappeared into the crowd.

So Marisa had been right. It was no "coincidence" that these birds were together in Mexico City. And when she publicly demanded that the government explain rumors about a Yemeni posing as a charitable worker traveling in Guatemala, Gómez had to shut her down.

Someone was buying arms from Mousaffi, all right, and negotiating for a Scud missile, but it was Arturo Gómez, not Carano. Jesse remembered the note signed "G" to Elena Ruiz that started, "You are wrong about Yassaf Mousaffi. This is not a 'complication' . . ."

The pieces were coming together like scattered metal filings drawn together by a magnet. Elena had mentioned that Mousaffi could deliver a Scud missile system for under four million dollars, the approximate asking price for the phony land grant letter, with a million left over for Linares's share. The bastards had been trying to get Guatemalans to pay for a weapon Gómez would then turn on them.

The "complication" was so potentially disastrous that Elena felt obliged to go public to stop it. Carl Webster, as Gómez's hatchet man, probably had also learned that *El Cobra* was trying to acquire a Scud missile system from Mousaffi—with the potential to reach U.S. gulf states with a WMD warhead! This, together with the Yemeni's ties to *al Qaeda,* had been too much even for Webster. He probably drafted the report to Langley they had found on his laptop and threatened to send it if Gómez didn't back off. So Webster also had to die.

Jesse wondered if Gómez had Webster kill Marisa because she was onto Gómez's weapons dealings with Mousaffi in Mexico City or to stop her from revealing that the "old mail" was a hoax, thus killing the source of funding for his missile system. Or was it because she had figured out Gómez's crazy conspiracy with Carano? Or all three things? Gómez could not allow any one of these truths to be exposed. Jesse's suspicions of Carano's complicity in Marisa's murder had been wrong. He was corrupt, but not Marisa's killer.

Teo interrupted his reflections. "Gómez has wounded himself, Jesse, but not fatally. Rehabilitate him as a witness and Kevin will have the alibi that should save his life." *And mine, too,* thought Jesse.

He closed his eyes. So now what? Rehabilitate a witness with global mayhem on his mind? Make Gómez look like a credible, solid citizen, win the case, and fly away home, knowing he had fulfilled his professional obligation to his client? Why not? It was Legal Ethics 101. He had an oath to uphold, and his sole duty was to his client, not to thousands of people he didn't even know. He would leave the "greater good" balancing act to politicians and philosophers. This was not a dilemma, it was a no-brainer.

Then why did he feel so bad?

The clerk returned to his position, signaling the imminent return of the judges. Jesse sipped some water, steadying the glass with both hands. He was aware of a curious, almost ravenous murmuring behind him in the gallery—like a horde of locusts advancing on a wheat field—waiting to see what the kid from America would do, the kid whose heart was a wild horse threatening to kick out the rails of his chest. He felt the reporters watching him, too, and resented them now as much as he had counted on them before. This was all just too much, but he managed to croak out words in the affirmative and the two judges nodded, and then sat silently, awaiting Guzmán.

"What is it, Jesse?" Teo said. "You look like you are ready to explode."

"*I could get him,*" Jesse said quietly. "I think I could expose Arturo Gómez."

"Lovely," Teo hissed sarcastically. "Dog catches car!"

"What's up?" said Kevin.

Jesse explained how Maldonado's documents showed that Gómez had planned to buy a Scud missile system from a broker connected with al-Qaeda.

"*A missile system?*" Kevin asked.

"With a WMD warhead capable of hitting, not only Guatemala City, but the U.S.A." Jesse's head was reeling as the potential consequences of Maldonado's revelation sunk in. Gómez's intentions had been too much for even Webster to swallow. Little wonder the revelation was tearing at the linings of Jesse's stomach.

Kevin said, "Hell, then why *not* show what the man's up to?"

Teo shook his head furiously. "We cannot lose focus here, gentlemen—not if either of you hope to get out of Guatemala alive. Rehabilitate the witness, Jesse! You can still win."

Kevin looked troubled. "Why *not* expose him and try to win the case, too?"

Jesse turned to Kevin. "I can't do both. We've got to choose. Teo is right. If I show Gómez is a monster planning an attack on Guatemala City or even beyond, the judges will throw out his testimony and your alibi goes with it."

Kevin nodded, but still looked troubled. Teo said, "So we're all agreed? Jesse will try to rehabilitate the witness?"

Kevin shrugged, still obviously troubled. "How bad is this guy, Jesse? Could he really launch an attack on one of the Gulf states?"

Jesse felt like his head was on fire. "Gómez is as bad as you can get, Kevin, and the Yemenis he's getting involved with are even worse."

"So where," Kevin said, seeing the torment in Jesse's eyes, "does this put me?"

Jesse started to speak, but Teo grabbed his shoulder. "I know what you are thinking, young friend, and I will not let you do it. I have developed a certain affection for you and will not permit you to commit forensic suicide. You are too young to die so far from home."

Jesse's eyes were red and watery as he turned them on the professor. "I'm sorry, Teo, but this is our decision, Kevin's and mine."

Kevin said, "Decision? What about?"

"Here's the thing, Kevin," Jesse said. "If I expose Gómez's plans, I think we'll save lives, maybe thousands of lives—but probably not our own."

As Kevin solemnly took in Jesse's words, the air seemed to grow heavy, and the men were blanketed in silence. Finally, the prisoner batted his eyes several times and spoke in a quavering voice. "We're gonna lose, Jesse? You don't want to rehab him?"

Jesse couldn't meet Kevin's red-rimmed eyes as he said, "I wish I could go that route, Kevin, but no, I'd prefer not to. The stakes are too damned high."

Kevin stared at him, but then slowly nodded his head and forced a smile. "Well, what the hell, Jesse. Even if you rehab'd him, it's one in a hundred Carano's judges would let me walk out of here. Am I right? And even if I did walk, that would mean Gómez would be walking, too, wouldn't he?" Kevin straightened his shoulders and added, "Besides, I didn't go through all this shit to see Marisa's killer go free."

"The young man makes a point," Teo said.

"I'm just saying," Kevin said, "that Marisa deserves that the truth be told."

Jesse nodded. "I agree, but just to be clear, I think I can tie Gómez to the Yemeni and expose their plans. As for proving Gómez ordered the kill on Marisa, I doubt I can pull that off."

"But you believe he did, and you'll try, right?" Kevin said. He then leaned in close to Jesse, manacles clanking together noisily. He grabbed his lawyer's arm with surprising strength and whispered in his ear, out of Teo's hearing. "I need you to understand that my time with Marisa was not a casual flop, okay? I loved her, and I always will." He squeezed Jesse's arm tighter and added, "*So I want you to get the bastard!*"

"You understand, Kevin, we're giving up our main defense—"

"Just open your eyes, Jesse. These judges hate me, hate Gómez, and hate you, too. I appreciate your bullshit efforts to give me hope, but the odds of you turning Gómez into a witness they will credit are roughly zero."

Jesse nodded and smiled sadly at his client, and they exchanged looks that said that for whatever time they had left to live, they would be bonded as brothers, not just lawyer and client. They took each other's hands.

The buzz in the gallery went quiet as the clerk handed Judge

Chavez a note. She scanned it, frowned, and then apologized for the delay, explaining that Judge López had been called to an emergency and that they would take the noon recess. Jesse glanced over at Gómez, who was looking at the back of Cal Covington, making his way out of the courtroom.

52

EL HOTEL SELECTO was a new, seven-story, brown stucco building on the northeast corner adjacent to the *Centro Cívico*. Simon Bradshaw waited there in a third floor office suite, red-streaked, sleepless eyes squinting through a shuttered west window toward the front entrance of the *Torre de Tribunales*. His heart rate quickened as people began pouring out the main entrance, signaling the noon recess. A minute later, the unmistakable figure of Calvin Covington emerged, two heads taller than the human sea surrounding him, impatiently pushing and shoving his way through the crowd.

"*I can do this,*" Simon repeated aloud to himself. He would save his firm. True, he wasn't the charismatic, creative genius his father had been, never had his father's magic, couldn't make handfuls of gun powder explode to beguile, confuse, and mesmerize the illiterate savages in the jury box. Simon's edge was a good mind combined with a dogged diligence. His father had raised him to always look over his shoulder and to be aware that no matter how hard he worked, there was somebody out there working harder. The lesson had stuck, so it had been second nature for him to stay awake the entire flight to Guatemala, preparing for anything the CEO could throw at him.

A few minutes later, Simon faced Cal Covington across an ornate and formidable desk, which gave the senior partner the advantage of looking down at Covington. The CEO appeared unaffected by the gambit, however, and sat in his usual relaxed pose, one arm looped over the back of a large swivel chair, his long legs casually crossed at the knee.

"So, what's this about, Cy? Your secretary's got me curious."

Simon told him about the fax that purported to fire C&S. Cal listened, said nothing, picked a piece of lint off the lapel of his lightweight tan sport coat. Simon waited, could bear the awkward silence no longer, and said, "So I, well . . . thought I'd come down to clarify any . . . confusion in the communication."

Cal slapped his thighs, and, for a second, Simon feared the man was going to stand and walk out. But then he knitted his brow, gave his head a little shake, and said, "Wasn't no confusion, Cy. I've hired Farell and Brown to replace you. Fact is, I figured by this time you'd have signed off. Is there a problem?"

Simon was dumbstruck. *Was there a problem?* Other than ending the life of Montgomery Street's most venerated law firm and putting hundreds of employees out of work? Other than . . .

"Cal," he managed, "you can't be serious. What about the Shanghai office C&S opened solely to accommodate you? And the risks we've taken on your 10-Ks? And the fact that the SEC has come after *us* now, because of those risks we took for *you*?"

Covington listened with the calm of a Buddha, and when Simon had finished making his points, Cal slowly shook his bald head. "Yeah, well, it's that SEC thing that was sorta the last straw, Cy. See, I can't have my company represented by a firm with a shadow on its reputation."

Bradshaw blinked in utter disbelief. Then he was on his feet, sending his swivel chair crashing into the back wall, storming around the ornate desk, fists clenched, his eyes on the fleshy folds of the big man's face, shouting like a maniac. "That 'shadow' on my firm's reputation, you *cocksucker?* We picked up that 'shadow' in the process of protecting your ungrateful ass. And now you would turn your back on us?"

"Ironic, ain't it?" Cal smirked.

Bradshaw advanced another step. Cal didn't flinch. "You gonna hit me, Cy? You flew your skinny ass all the way down here just to bitch slap a former client? Well, go right ahead, and I'll have Joe Jamail slap you with a lawsuit for assault and battery. Ten minutes in a deposition with that man, he'll have you calling him Daddy."

Lawsuit! The word slashed through the twisted maze of Simon Bradshaw's torched brain. He leaned back against the desk for support, his body suddenly gone weak and rubbery.

"Let's be honest, Cy," Cal continued. "I got hit with that SEC complaint on *your* watch, plus you never did get rid of Jesse Hall, who you know has been a bone in my throat all along. And if the top dog can't control a goddamn kid-associate in his firm, how can I trust him to handle the SEC and all the other jackals tryin' to piss on CalCorp's territory? So watch and learn, Cy. I'm gonna show you how to handle a problem like Jesse Hall."

Covington headed for the door, adding, "Doug Young and some of his people from the Farell firm will be at your office this afternoon to pick up all my files. He'll have a check covering my current outstanding balance of six-point-two million dollars along with mutual releases, confidentiality agreements, and substitutions of attorneys. Sign 'em, Cy—if you can use the money. And no hard feelings, okay? It's just business."

53

WITH COURT RESUMED, the clerk handed Jesse a note delivered during the noon recess by an "older American gentleman." Jesse tore open the envelope and saw it was from Simon Bradshaw.

"Dear Jesse. I was here briefly and had hoped to see you, but circumstances require my immediate presence in SF. I regret to tell you that the firm no longer represents CalCorp and that C&S will be dissolving. Worse, Cal has gone off the rails and threatened your life in my presence. I would take you back with me, but I know you too well to expect that you would leave before the trial is finished. I have, however, taken some steps for your protection to aid your departure at the close of the proceedings. I am sorry, Jesse. Sorry about everything. Please be careful. Your Friend, Simon."

The air in the courtroom had suddenly gone dead. Jesse carefully folded the note and put it in his briefcase. He turned and scanned the courtroom, but didn't really expect to see the senior partner there.

"Please proceed, Señor Hall," said Judge Chavez, moments later.

"Yes, Your Honor," Jesse said, rising on unstable legs. He wondered if any trial had ever come down to such a single, telling moment.

When you shoved all your chips onto a single number and spun the wheel. Surely, no serious gambler would take these odds. And if he failed, it wasn't just chips. *El Cobra* would find new sources of funding his ambitions, probably through his new *al-Qaeda* contact. And he wouldn't stop once he controlled Guatemala, nor would *al-Qaeda* allow him to stop, not with New Orleans, Miami, and other parts of the U.S. in easy range of ballistic missiles armed with chemical or biological warheads.

"Then please proceed, Señor Hall," Judge Chavez said.

Jesse tried to deepen his breathing, slow his heart, but nothing helped. He glanced at the reporters in the gallery, glad again they were there.

Gómez had resumed his seat in the witness chair and Jesse turned to face him. "A few more questions, Señor Gómez," he said, and handed Gómez a telephone bill Teo's investigators had obtained. Jesse hated that Gómez could see the page shaking in his hand, hated him knowing he was afraid. "Is that your phone number at the top?"

Gómez perused the sheet and glowered. "My phone bill? How did you get this?"

"Please answer the question." Jesse expected no objections and got none.

"Yes, that is my telephone number. What of it?"

"Recognize that other number there with the eight or nine marks beside it?"

"How do you expect me to—"

"Let me refresh your memory. The telephone company confirms that is the private residence number of the late Professor José Linares Cruz. Are they right about that?"

Amaya sat as motionless as a lizard watching flies. Carano smiled.

"What has that to do with anything?"

"Just this, sir. You and Linares have been talking together two or three times weekly for nearly three months. The records show that you talked together twice the day I was your prisoner north of Livingston on May second. That was when you learned from Linares that I was scheduled to meet with him, and probably when you two decided I was more valuable alive than dead, am I right? That Linares could influence me to influence Teo Andrade to throw his weight behind fund-raising to acquire the land grant letter?"

Gómez fiddled with his glasses. "That is absurd, although there would be nothing wrong with influencing Professor Andrade to do the right and proper thing."

"The records also show Linares called you the morning that Professor Andrade and I met with him. I'm guessing he called to tell you that I had figured out the land grant was false—a hoax probably conceived by you and drafted by him."

The allegation rocked the courtroom. Amaya sat silent. This was news to nearly everyone. A bizarre blend of groaning and cheering temporarily overruled they judge's gavel.

When order was restored, Jesse continued. "Within hours of Linares admitting his fatal error to you, he became a fatality himself, a bullet in his head. Do you expect us to believe that was a coincidence?"

Amaya remained silent, as Jesse expected. The press was wide-eyed. An uneasy commotion stirred in the gallery, and spectators looked at each other in confusion. Gómez glanced at his watch, and his jaw muscles were jumping, but his voice remained calm. "The timing of his suicide was indeed pure coincidence. My contacts with the professor merely involved our mutual interest in the history of our country. I was thinking of having him write a history of the sixteenth-century Maya."

"That's interesting, sir, but as it happens, he had already written the definitive book on that very subject. So what we would all like to know, Señor Gómez, is what you were going to do with that five million dollars if *La Causa* had raised it for you?"

Amaya, seeing Carano's pleasure at Gómez's discomfiture, continued to make no objection. Gómez reddened and said, "I am losing patience with your impudence."

"Permission to treat the witness as hostile, Your Honor?"

"Granted," Chavez said, seeing the smile on Carano's face, "but move along."

"Let's change the subject, Señor Gómez. In answer to an earlier question, you said that you and Vice President Carano were not involved in a drug conspiracy. Is that true?" Time to get the two big dogs riled up at each other again. "He testified that you were a mercenary, and that he was forced to make a 'deal with the devil.' That would be you, Señor."

"*Carano* is the devil, not I! Why would I work with a man who pockets most of the U.S. aid money himself instead of sharing it with my people?"

"Objection!" shouted Amaya.

"Sustained!" said Judge Chavez.

"That's a lie," Carano shouted and leapt to his feet, "and I have already said I will prove it!"

"Move to strike the witness's answer!" yelled Amaya.

"Yes," said Judge Chavez. "The answer will be stricken from the record. And please, Señor Vice President, if you would be so good as to resume your seat?"

While Judge Chavez and the *Policía de Presidio* tried to restore order, Teo motioned Jesse over to counsel table. "You're creating a potentially explosive situation here, Jesse."

"I know," Jesse said, hearing the anxiety in his own voice and wincing at a bead of stinging perspiration in his eye, "and I have no choice but to light a match."

The crowd went quiet in anticipation of what might happen next. Gómez appeared calm and Jesse wondered how many of *El Cobra's* soldiers in civilian clothes were embedded in the gallery and in the hallway outside. Too many guns on both sides, he thought.

"Please complete your examination, Señor Hall," Judge Chavez said, dabbing at her face with her handkerchief. "You have five minutes, and then we will have closing arguments. Understood?"

"Yes, Your Honor." Jesse turned back to the witness. "Did you ever meet the victim in this case? Marisa Andrade?"

"No," Gómez said, "but I had great admiration for her work on behalf of the people's movement."

"You mentioned that the defendant was with you at the time Señora Andrade was murdered. Would you happen to know who killed her?"

Gómez sniffed. "Everybody does. Señora Andrade was exposing the corruption of the putative Carano administration. It was Carano who paid the CIA *gringo*—Carl Webster—to kill her."

"*Objection!*" shouted Amaya over an even more explosive tumult from the spectators. "Opinion, hearsay, invading the province of the Court! Move to strike!"

"What could be more relevant," Jesse asked Judge Chavez, "than—"

"*Sustained and granted!*" said Judge Chavez, pounding her gavel for order. "That is enough, Señor Hall. If I have to—"

Carano interrupted Chavez's lecture, saying, "Judge Chavez, this proceeding is ended, and I demand that you arrest the witness and hold him for questioning."

Nobody moved. Carano's face looked like a red balloon with too much air in it. "All right, then!" he shouted. "*I* will arrest him in the name of the government, for inciting a riot and encouraging seditious conduct."

But hoots, whistles, and catcalls drowned out Carano's words. The guards stood motionless, staring nervously at their sergeant, whose eyes darted back and forth between the grimly smiling Gómez and the crimson-faced Vice President.

Carano advanced toward the railing. "For the last time, Judge Chavez, I insist that you order your *Policía de Presidio* to take Señor Gómez into custody."

Jesse said, "And the defense insists that the Court enforce order in this courtroom. Vice President Carano is not a witness, whereas Señor Gómez is testifying under oath and pursuant to a duly served subpoena. Is that not correct, Señor Gómez?"

Gómez smiled grimly and said, "By your own hand, as I recall, Señor Hall."

The judges exchanged questioning looks, as if hoping someone would come up with legal precedent for this sort of thing. Judge Chavez met Carano's angry eyes and shrugged her shoulders.

Jesse was relieved to see that the reporters behind him were feverishly writing. The rest of the gallery muttered among themselves and shuffled about. The PNC and *Policía de Presidio* watched, hands on holsters. Carano retreated into his chair. At the rear of the room, Jesse spotted Cal Covington, who turned his fingers into a gun and pointed it at him. Everybody else's eyes were on Gómez, who smiled beneficently at Judge Chavez and then extended his right hand to silence the crowd.

Jesse swallowed hard. "Señor Gómez, you have pointed out that

Marisa Andrade was critical of the Carano administration. Is it your practice to read the local newspapers?"

"Of course, I read them every day."

"So you saw her article criticizing the Vice President for not arresting a Yemeni suspected of being a black-market arms dealer, perhaps a member of *al-Qaeda?*"

"I did read that, yes." Jesse noticed more movement in Gómez's jaw muscles. "And, of course, Carano did nothing."

"And you know Yassaf Mousaffi, don't you?" It was more an assertion than a question. "In fact, you met with him?"

Gómez glared. "Why would I do that?"

"You deny it?"

"Of course."

"Allow me to show you the dates of those meetings, Señor Gómez," Jesse said, and handed Marisa's calendar to the witness. Amaya rose, but said nothing.

Gómez held the calendar close to his thick, tinted spectacles. After a half minute, he grunted disdainfully and threw it back at Jesse, who could almost see the wheels turning behind his eyes. *He doesn't know what I've got. More important, he doesn't know what I haven't got.*

Jesse reached for Geraldo's file. "I also have official records from both Guatemala immigration and the Mexican government that show you met with Mousaffi in Mexico City." His heart pounded, and his mouth was dry, for he knew Amaya could block this line of questioning on several grounds. Jesse didn't like Amaya, but trusted his desire for justice and in that, at least, they were alike. So he risked a subtle nod toward Amaya, hoping to convey that Gómez was the target, not Carano. Amaya read the message and sat down. For now, at least, he would give his adversary some rope.

"Impossible," Gómez said, and checked his watch again. Was this a nervous mechanism or something on *El Cobra's* schedule Jesse didn't want to think about?

"Really?" Jesse made a show of scanning the notes Geraldo had given him. "These documents clearly establish that you and Mousaffi met three times at the Hotel Mirador, each time staying on the same floor. Your room number on the last visit was 1208. That was on the nineteenth of March. Do you still deny it?"

While Gómez warily contemplated his response, Jesse glanced at Carano, whose brow was corrugated with amazement from watching the other big dog begin to bleed. A mounting murmur of protest rose from the spectators, and Jesse knew the word about the meetings in Mexico City was being passed back to the crowd in the elevator lobby. For the first time, *El Cobra* seemed immobilized, stunned into silence.

"So, Señor Gómez," Jesse continued, "what were you discussing on those dates?"

"That is . . . " *El Cobra* stammered, "what you lawyers call 'irrelevant.' Move on."

But Jesse took a step closer. "In the absence of any objection," he said, "it *is* relevant. This is how the 'strong legal system' you advocated a while ago really works."

Gómez looked up at the judges, then at Amaya, and seeing no help anywhere, put a hand to his forehead and said, "Ahhh yes, I recall. The Yemeni! But an arms dealer? No, no, no. He was a humble charity worker. Perhaps I had been considering a donation. I try to assist people in need everywhere."

"Isn't it a fact that you were negotiating the acquisition of a Scud missile system with which you planned to threaten or attack

Guatemala City?" The crowd's astonished murmur grew louder, and Jessed had to raise his voice to add, "And wasn't the money you needed for the missile system, $3,800,000, *about the same price you wanted the people of Guatemala to pay you for the fake ancient letter?*"

Bedlam erupted, first in the gallery, then spread like a breaking wave as the allegation passed into the elevator lobby and eventually to the huge crowd outside in the *Plaza Cívico*. People began shoving each other again, until they remembered there was nowhere to go. Jesse saw confusion in the eyes of many, anger in others.

Amaya continued to sit quietly. Carano appeared genuinely stunned by what he was hearing, and Cal Covington seemed shocked as well, leaning forward, nearly out of his seat. Teo's eyes were wide open in astonishment.

When Judge Chavez finally restored order, Jesse saw that Gómez's face was a crimson mask of anger. "That is an absurd statement," he said, "and I have nothing more to offer this Tribunal." He uncrossed his legs as if to rise from the witness chair, but several uniformed PNC officers moved up to the rail. Encouraged, Jesse also moved in front of Gómez, determined to swing once more for the fences. He stared into Gómez's hard eyes, ignoring the beads of sweat snaking down his forehead. So many bodies crammed into the same room seemed to have used up all the oxygen.

Jesse grabbed another document off counsel table and said, "Mousaffi had previously provided you with illegal arms and weaponry during the past year, had he not?" He shoved the list of conventional weaponry retrieved from Webster's computer into Gómez's hand.

"How did you . . . " Gómez's scowling face was suddenly flushed. Jesse had seen the man betray anger today, but never surprise.

"Let's just say your former partner Carl Webster was very helpful."

El Cobra said nothing, so Jesse added, "You remember Carl Webster, don't you? The man you paid to kill Marisa Andrade when she was about to expose your relationship with Yassaf Mousaffi?"

The gallery issued a communal gasp that sounded like a hundred tires blowing out at once. Gómez said nothing for a minute, listening to the hostility building among the people. He shot Jesse a look that told him he would never get out of Guatemala alive. Then, just as suddenly, there was the imperious smile again. He casually crossed his legs.

"You have no proof of this," Gómez said. "And I will speak no more about it."

"Is that so? I suggest, Señor, that after Carl Webster killed Marisa at your behest, he learned you intended to purchase a missile delivery system from the Yemeni, and he told you to back off or he'd have to tell Washington. Am I right?"

Gómez said nothing, but the gallery continued to hum with excitement, like a swarm of bees, creating a constant white-noise background. Judge Chavez ineffectually struck her gavel, then gave up.

"So you had to kill him, too, am I right?"

Gómez folded his arms and said nothing. For the first time, he seemed afflicted with indecision. "That is all I have to say on this matter."

"All right, Señor, then let's talk about why you killed Elena Ruiz, head of *La Cofradía*."

The courtroom erupted again in shocked amazement, perhaps more at the assertion about Elena than the accusation of her murder, but Gómez let out a laugh that came out a mirthless hack. The judges seemed immobilized, apparently realizing they had lost control of the courtroom, but the gallery silenced itself, curious as to how the guerrilla leader would respond to Jesse's latest brazen allegation.

"*La Cofradía?* Never heard of it. You have been reading too many American crime novels."

"No, Señor, I've been reading the confidential files of the former chief prosecutor. I know that her code name was 'friend,' and I know that you and other crime families reported to her. I know that when she objected to your plan to bring the country to its knees with a missile, she threatened to go public in a press conference and you had her office bombed!"

Gómez betrayed his surprise, but not his cool detachment. The bluff wasn't working. *Why was he so cool?*

"I have," he said, "no idea what you're talking about."

Jesse had one bluff left, and it was time to play it. He walked over to the counsel table and picked up the note from Elena's file.

"Have you forgotten," asked Jesse, "the note you wrote her?"

"*Note?* What note?" Gómez stole yet another look at his watch and seemed to take comfort from what it told him. Why this preoccupation with the time? Gómez had something scheduled, and it wasn't a golf date. Whatever it was, Jesse knew the clock was ticking and that he'd better get into a hurry-up offense.

Jesse passed copies of the note to the three stunned judges and to Amaya, who handed it back and quietly sat back down in his chair. Again, he had numerous grounds for objecting, but Jesse knew Carano would not want his prosecutor to object. Not now.

"I'll read it out loud, Señor Gómez." Jesse began, in a hoarse, but loud, voice, to read the note into the record. "*'Friend, forgive my boldness, but you are wrong about Yassaf. This is not a 'complication,' as you insist, but an opportunity, good for the people, good for you and number one.'*"

Jesse knew he was speaking too loudly, trying to force the tremor out of his voice through sheer volume. He felt like he had a bird inside his chest, wings flapping against his ribs, pecking at his flesh to get out.

"Sound familiar, Señor Gómez? I'll continue: '*Rest assured of your safety and well being. I know that you, least of all, will miss the dog Carano. May God be with us and our noble cause.*' Signed, 'G.' You do remember signing that note to Elena Ruiz with a 'G', do you not?"

The people in the gallery and hallway were silent, mouths open in amazement. The battle-tested reporters held to their seats, wielding their pens. Victor Carano, recovered from his shock, leapt to his feet, shouting and pointing a trembling finger at Gómez. "*You bastard!* You lying, double-crossing *bastard!* I'll send you to hell myself!"

A woman screamed, and that's when Jesse saw that Carano wasn't pointing a finger at Gómez. It was a small automatic handgun.

A *Policía de Presidio* grabbed Carano's wrist and the gun went off with an almost comic popping sound. In the crowd's sudden silence of the moment, the bullet hit the acoustic ceiling with a loud *thwappp*.

The Vice President was disarmed, but not before he had everyone's attention. He faced the gallery, the constituency that mattered most at the moment. "*I* know who Yassaf Mousaffi is," Carano quavered loudly. "Webster warned me about Mousaffi, just before he was killed. Our PNC is in pursuit of the Yemeni at this very moment! The *gringo* lawyer speaks the truth."

"Shut up, you idiot!" Gómez shouted. "You are an utter stranger to truth."

The dogs were at it now, Jesse thought, but he was concerned about Gómez's relatively unruffled demeanor. *The bastard has a plan.*

"*Order!*" shouted Judge Chavez, pounding her gavel.

Jesse's eyes locked on Gómez, who surprised everyone by rising and moving toward the rail, where he brazenly faced down the PNC officers and the suddenly hostile gallery.

"*Admit it, Señor!*" Jesse shouted at his back. "*Admit that after you sent Carl Webster to kill Marisa Andrade, you killed him, too, then Anastacia Ramirez, because she intended to stop La Causa from purchasing your phony land grant letter, and then Elena Ruiz, because she learned what you intended to do with the money!*"

Gómez froze, his hand on the rail. He raised his chin abruptly, and Jesse saw that it was a signal to his men, several of whom were already surrounding him.

Teo said, "Don't worry, Jesse, his men are far outnumbered here by PNC."

"This is not about his men inside, Teo," Jesse said, noting that Cal and Felix were hurrying toward the door. "It's something worse."

"Order! *Order!*" shouted Judge Chavez, to no avail.

Jesse moved right up behind Gómez and shouted, so that everyone could hear him: "Tell me, Señor Gómez. *Where am I wrong?*"

Gómez turned around, gave Jesse a murderous look, and raised his hand. Jesse saw a glint of metal pointing toward him. "You were wrong," he told Jesse, sounding almost casual, "to come to my country in the first place. I appeared here today in peace, to persuade my people of my good intentions. You have ruined everything, and what is about to be done is on your head and yours alone."

Jesse backed up a step and raised his own hand defensively, somehow managing to feel stupid in the process. Why did people always put a hand in front of their face as if it could stop a bullet? But no bullet pierced his hand, no explosion filled his ear, and he realized that Gómez did not have a pistol, but a cell phone. "It's outside!" Jesse shouted. "*It's something outside!*"

Jesse heard the table skidding against the floor behind him and turned to see Teo struggling with the men who restrained him.

"Answer his question, Arturo Gómez!" Teo shouted at Gómez.

"Did you kill my wife?"

Gómez rose to his feet and a dozen of his men shoved the PNC cops aside and prepared to escort him into the gallery. "Not with my own hand, Professor. Despair not, for she would be the first to tell you that sometimes good people must die . . . for the greater good."

Despite everything, Jesse could see that the irony of Gómez's "greater good" comment was not lost on Teo. Without warning, the professor charged at *El Cobra,* but Gómez's soldiers wrestled him to the floor. Jesse felt hands pinning his own arms to his sides as women screamed and people stampeded toward the courtroom's only public door. The PNC and *Policía de Presidio* seemed immobilized, apparently trying to decide which side to be on in the face of all the Gómez militiamen surrounding them.

Jesse turned to make sure the judges, crouching behind the dais, had heard Gómez's implicit admission of culpability in Marisa's murder.

Gómez opened the gate to join his entourage in the gallery, but turned back to face Jesse once more. "You are a foolish young man, Jesse Hall. You and that old sack of shit will be tried by the People's Court and found guilty of crimes against the people—spying and treason—and you will be *shot.*"

Jesse struggled against the hands restraining him and Gómez strode into the gallery, the trapped spectators backing away as if the guerrilla leader were a suicide bomber wrapped in explosives. Gómez's bodyguards surrounded their leader and pushed through the crowd, but there was nowhere to go, for the crush of people blocked the exit. Seeing this, Carano was finally able to urge several of his PNC into the fray, but the loud report of a gun froze everyone. One of Gómez's men was shooting an automatic weapon into the ceiling. The jostling and screaming stopped, and *El Cobra* climbed up on a chair. He raised his hands, commanding silence. The room went instantly quiet, except for moaning sounds from people injured in the charge through the doorway.

"My friends," Gómez intoned, "we are at *war,* a war against this administration's corruption and American imperialism! Those who resist will die."

Gómez took a final look at his watch, hit a button on his cell phone, and spoke into it. Within seconds, explosions and the rat-tat-tat of automatic weapons could be heard outside. Gómez shouted, "I had hoped for a more peaceful people's revolution, but those of you by the windows may wish to look outside. My men have surrounded all government buildings. The country is mine!"

Gómez's words cut like an icicle into Jesse's heart. *What have I done?* He cursed his hubris. Another thing he should have seen coming.

Unnoticed in the confusion, Teo suddenly broke free of his captors and stormed toward Gómez, Gulliver unbound. *"Teo!"* Jesse shouted, reaching out to restrain him, but it was too late. Teo snatched a gun from a PNC cop's holster, and with a surge of superhuman strength, crashed through Gómez's guards like a bowling ball through pins. Gómez, trapped by the circular wall of people surrounding him, struggled in vain to get down from his chair and escape the onrushing giant.

Then the popping sound again, louder this time, and Gómez's tinted glasses flew off his head, revealing a small dark hole over his right eye. A lucky shot, was all Jesse could think; Teo had probably never fired a gun before in his life. Now more guns fired and people screamed, shoving against each other, trying to get out of the line of fire. Gómez toppled from his chair, and Teo fell, too, disappearing into the sea of people. Jesse frantically pushed his way toward his friend.

By the time Jesse reached Teo's side, all color had drained from his face and blood oozed from his chest and stomach. Ten feet away, a spectator who appeared to be a doctor stood over Gómez's inert body, shaking his head.

Slowly the tumult dissipated, and spectators, PNC, and guerrillas alike stood in shocked disbelief, arms at their sides, staring at the corpse of the guerrilla leader. Scattered gunfire continued outside, but seemed to be dissipating. Jesse bent down over Teo, saw that he was still breathing, and shouted at the doctor, apparently penned in by the crowd.

Jesse held one of Teo's cold hands; his friend's breath was coming in short gasps. Jesse screamed again at the doctor.

"I . . . think I . . . warned you," Teo whispered, managing a smile, "that you would be . . . starting trouble, did I not?"

"'Unimaginable trouble,' I believe were your words. And yes, I started it, but you finished it."

"I got him?"

"Through the head. A lucky shot. Lucky for all of us. Lucky for your country."

Another smile appeared at a corner of his mouth. "I actually got something right?"

Jesse's throat was so tight he could hardly speak. "There's a first time for everything, old man."

"Yes, and I fear . . . it will be my last time for anything. Can . . . you find Anica? And . . . a priest?"

Jesse told him Julio was trying to doing that. The dark stain spread across Teo's belt-line like wine from a broken bottle.

"Doctor!" Jesse shouted. "*Get the hell over here!*"

The professor smiled up at Jesse. "Maybe things will be better now."

Jesse was no longer able to feel his friend's pulse. "Marisa . . . would be very proud of you, Teo."

The doctor arrived, and Jesse saw Anica frantically pushing her way toward them, then glanced toward Gómez, a coat pulled over his face. Within minutes, an outside loudspeaker broadcast the news that Gómez was dead and urged the rebels to put down their arms. The news broke the spirits of the rebels, who retreated in disarray before the government's army. The courtroom remained in chaos. Jesse could not see Cal or Felix, but knew he'd see them again soon enough for he, Jesse—and the luckiest shot in the history of firearms—had blown away Cal's deal of a lifetime.

Beyond *El Cobra's* body, in the elevator lobby, Jesse could see the bright lights of the television crews. Victor Carano—who had escaped through chambers in the melee—was talking to reporters. Someone had handed him a bullhorn.

"The terrorist conspirator is dead," Carano bellowed, "and I have just been informed that his rebel army has been dispersed. I urge you all to stay inside until we take the last traitor into custody. Arturo Gómez is dead at the hands of a hero of our new democracy. We were tested, my friends, but we will now be stronger than ever."

Inside the courtroom, Jesse urged Teo to hold on, hoping he couldn't hear the tireless politician at work in the elevator lobby, exploiting the courage of a man who despised him, turning Teo's sacrifice into a campaign speech. Anica was finally able to push her way through the crowd and gasped when she saw her father's face.

"My Anica," Teo whispered. "My dove."

"Oh, Papa," she cried, pressing one of Teo's huge hands to her face as the doctor bent over him. Jesse could see it was a losing battle. The priest arrived and Jesse, his heart broken, backed away to make room.

The last words Jesse would hear from his friend were, "Forgive me Father . . . for I have sinned . . . " The big man's eyes closed, and his lids fluttered, but he apparently completed his confession and received absolution. His face was as serene as Jesse had ever seen it, and he was still smiling as death took him.

DAY TWENTY-SEVEN

54

AS A FORMERLY successful real estate broker, Lucy Bradshaw had seen a wide variety of reactions from people as they were confronted by disappointed expectations. Still, she was astonished by her husband's serene manner as he told her that the firm was finished.

She could think of nothing to say, so she simply put her arms around him. He surprised her by the strength of his return embrace. It was as if he needed her again, like when they were young.

She was upstairs, getting him a sedative, when she heard the shot.

"Simon!"

His head lay sideways on his antique desk, a dark Rorschach-like stain blooming on the leather-framed beige blotter, thin arms hanging straight down from his narrow shoulders, the fallen gun on the floor near his right hand. Later, a paramedic noticed two sets of documents and a note—his only note—instructing that one set of documents be directed to the Drug Enforcement Agency, the other to the SEC.

Nobody fucked with Simon Bradshaw, even in death. He'd take the hillbilly bastard down with him.

TWO DAYS LATER

55

AFTER ARTURO GÓMEZ'S clear insinuation that he had ordered Marisa's death, the Tribunal's "not guilty" rendering the day after the trial ended was a mere five-minute formality. Jesse didn't expect that Cal Covington would be in the courtroom for the *denouement,* but saw two of Michael Cooper's security men sitting on either side of the courtroom, a posthumous gift from Teo. Maybe some others were out there, courtesy of Simon, but it wouldn't be enough. If Cal wanted to be rid of him, he wouldn't skimp on manpower.

Newspapers around the world trumpeted the news of a Central American murder trial that had been interrupted by a courtroom gunfight and a failed guerrilla coup, but not before a young American lawyer had exposed an international U.S. aid scam and a thwarted missile sale.

The U.S. Consulate was interviewed regarding the foreign-aid conspiracy and offered only an indignant, "We are looking into the claims which, based on our preliminary review, appear to be utterly without substance." It was clear to Jesse that the U.S. position would be "the less said the better." Within Guatemala, however, Carano's gambit had cast him as a hero and the polls had him running ahead of Miguel Aguilera.

Teo's memorial service was scheduled for Wednesday, which Carano had designated as a day of national mourning, the final irony. Jesse packed his bags and checked out of his hotel. He had offered to stay for Teo's service, but Anica had sent word through Julio that he would not be welcome.

"She blames me," Jesse told Julio at lunch at the Europa, "and understandably so. If I had not come down here . . . if I had picked someone else to help me . . . "

"If, if, if," chided Julio. "In time, she will realize that but for his involvement in the case, all the good that has happened would not have happened. Moreover, Teo would soon have died of sclerosis or heart failure instead of dying a hero, advancing Marisa's cause."

Jesse nodded, though he felt no better. Rex the Killer Dog snoozed quietly at Jesse's feet while Jesse kept a surreptitious lookout for Cal's goons.

"Anica and I together," Julio added, "will try to continue her parents' work."

Jesse felt a rush, thinking about how redeemed Teo would feel to hear himself given equal billing with the work Marisa had begun.

"Teo loved you, Jesse," he added. "You were the son he always wanted."

Jesse nodded, although he heard the trace of envy in Julio's words. "He was the father I wish I'd had."

"When are you flying home?" Julio said.

"Later today," Jesse said. *If I live long enough to get on the plane.* "First, I've got to go out and make sure Kevin's been properly released."

"From what Teo said about his father," Julio said, "that would be very dangerous. Insane, actually. He might be waiting for you there."

Jesse shrugged, though his mouth went dry. "The job's not done till the client is free," he said. "Especially here."

Lunch arrived, and Jesse slipped some chicken down to Rex.

"Have they caught the Yemeni?" Julio asked.

"No, but they will. They think he's holed up in Mexico."

"What's the story with Elena Ruiz?" Julio asked. "If she was really head of *La Cofradía,* why couldn't she control Gómez?"

Jesse shook his head. "In my experience, nobody is ever fully in control, no matter who you are. Sometimes the higher you get, the more people you have to keep happy. She was always walking a tightrope, like when Carano made her bring charges against Kevin, whom she knew to be innocent. That's one of the reasons she let me win a few motions."

"So it wasn't your good looks after all," Julio teased.

"No."

"Nor your professional skill." Julio was smiling again.

Jesse smiled back. "Certainly neither of those."

Julio said, "But Elena turned out to be a wolf in pretty sheep's clothing."

"I can't judge that," Jesse said. "Her father was probably the head guy at *La Cofradía* until he was no longer the sharpest knife in the drawer. I suspect she took on his job as the only way to protect him from Carano."

"But nobody forced her to take it on," Julio said. "She could have said no."

Jesse gazed out a window, off into the distance. "She told me once that some inheritances were more a curse than a blessing. At the time, I thought she was talking about her job as chief prosecutor, but now I see she meant taking over *La Cofradía* from her father. She probably emerged as the logical person to prevent civil conflict between families that could have blown Guatemala apart. Maybe she hoped to reform the whole damned system—make lemonade out of lemons, she once told me—but found herself on a fast-moving train she couldn't get off."

Julio said, "Yeah, but a lot of power went with that fast-moving train."

"Sure," Jesse said, "but when it threatened to derail and wreck the whole country, she had the courage to jump off and got herself killed doing it. I just wish I'd been there to try to catch her."

Julio gave him a rueful look. "Sounds like you were hot for her. There are rumors."

"I'll never forget her," Jesse said, "but I left my heart in San Francisco."

They were finished, and Jesse paid the check.

"I'll take you to the airport," Julio said.

"Thanks anyway, but I've got a car to check in there. I do have a favor though."

"Anything," Julio said, "just name it."

"I'd appreciate it if you'd help get my dog back to San Francisco, you know, the immigration shots and red tape?" Julio nodded, and Jesse added, "I've got things started. Here's his ticket and some money."

Jesse nuzzled Rex and handed him over. "See you soon, Killer," Jesse said. The men shook hands, and Rex let out a final bark of protest.

Jesse drove off, his neck on a swivel, waiting, wondering when Cal would come at him and how. A car was following him—probably Michael Cooper's men or maybe his golden parachute from Simon—but he took little comfort from them.

. . .

CUMULUS CLOUDS FLOATED across the asphalt-colored sky outside *Purgatorio*, thick enough to blur the distant hills at the foot of *Fuego*. Jesse's heart accelerated at the sight of the drab yellow prison looming above the tenements. He turned in to the narrow prison entry road and parked halfway to the front gate, from where he could spot Kevin coming out. He turned his Suzuki around in case a quick exit was required and trained the rearview mirror on the front gate. The car driven by Teo's men was parked off to his right 100 yards away. Another car—Simon's guys?—moved in behind them.

A light rain started to fall as a black Jaguar sedan turned in to the gate road. The windows were dark-tinted, but Jesse knew who was behind them. The car pulled up and stopped alongside his car and Jesse stared into the opaque windows, heart pounding in his temples, bracing himself. But as he waited for a gun to appear, the Jag started moving again and stopped between Jesse and the gate. Then a Lincoln Town Car pulled up between Jesse's Suzuki and Jesse's bodyguards' car, neutralizing them.

A sad-faced young woman, probably on her way to visit her husband, stopped at one of the nearby stands and purchased burritos for herself and her child. Two screeching feral cats leapt out of nowhere and fought over a scrap of meat that fell from the child's burrito. A man jumped out of the Lincoln and quickly ushered her and her child away from the cars toward the main gate. The area again silently seethed with insipient danger.

Time passed—five, ten, then fifteen minutes—and no Kevin. The windows of Jesse's rental were fogging up and he leaned back and wiped the rear glass with his sleeve so he could better see the entrance and keep an eye on the Jaguar. His heart jumped as Felix, the Jag driver, came out of the car, opening a back door. Cal Covington stepped out, hitched his massive shoulders, and began to stride toward Jesse's car. Felix and another man fell in behind Cal, and two of Michael Cooper's men quickly stepped out of their car in response.

But Cal quickly dismissed his men with an imperious wave, and they returned to the Jag. Just as quickly, Cooper's men stopped, seemingly confused as to what to do next, while Cal continued his casual stroll toward Jesse's car. Jesse's pulse quickened. Was Cal going to do it himself?

Jesse reflected on the absurdity of it all. Having come so far, the job nearly done, his return airline ticket in his pocket, and now this? He thought about Megan, and then took a deep breath and rolled down his window. He knew he should get out of the car, but didn't trust his legs. "Hello, Cal."

"Hello, kid. Convenient, you bein' here."

"Everybody's gotta be somewhere."

"Yeah, well, you royally fucked up when you were in court a couple days ago."

"I fucked up a lot of people."

"I warned you not to do that."

"So you did."

Cal stared at him. A rooster crowed. The rain had already eased into a drizzle.

"I warned Cy, too. Are all lawyers deaf?"

"We hear what we want, like everybody else."

"Whatever. The fucker had the last word. CalCorp's been put into federal receivership, and the Feds wanna visit with me. I can't ever go back to the U.S." He spat on the ground. "No matter, one more deal and I'll have more money than God. Anyways, goodbye, kid, and good riddance."

Cal's hand went inside his coat. Jesse said, "So, you're gonna do it yourself?"

"Do what? Kill you? Hell, no." He pulled out a cigar and bit off the end. "My deal's back on with a Columbian I'll meet with tomorrow. It's riskier, but my cut will be much bigger without Gómez's beak in it. Turns out you did me a big favor, kid."

"Accidents happen," Jesse said, beginning to breathe again.

"I'm just here to pick up Kevin," Covington said. "We'll meet in Livingston tonight with Gómez's second-in-command. Life goes on."

Jesse froze. "Kevin's in on the new deal?"

"He wasn't before, but after all he's been through, I'm cuttin' him in, plus he'll have to be my clone in the U.S. now, thanks to that fuckin' Cy."

Jesse shook his head. "Christ, Cal, you must have money stashed everywhere. Mind telling me why the hell you're messing with the Columbians? They're more dangerous than Gómez."

"Same reason a dog licks his balls," Cal said. "Because he can."

A loud clanging drew their attention to the front gate and Kevin emerged, heading toward them at a fast, but unsteady, pace. His father turned from Jesse and approached Kevin, stopping in the middle of the road, a full smile on his face, arms extended, palms up, elbows tucked into his sides, smug as ever. A typical Cal pose that said come to me, prodigal son, all is forgiven.

But Kevin walked right past him without a word, his eyes straight ahead.

Jesse had never seen Cal look confused before.

"Kevin!" Cal shouted to his son's back. "The deal's back on, and you're gonna be in with me. It'll be sweeter than ever!"

Kevin kept walking.

Cal's smile vanished. "You hear me, kid? It's back on, even better now!"

Jesse saw a half-smile form on Kevin's lips as the distance grew between himself and his father. The huge man took a funny little hop toward Kevin's retreating back and jabbed a finger at him. "Reject your father after all I've done for you?" he shouted. "That's how you wanna play it? Well, fuck you, Kevin, okay? You hear me? *Fuck the both of you!*"

Kevin kept walking until he was beside Jesse's car.

"Hey, Kevin."

"Can I catch a lift to the airport, Jesse?"

"Sounds like you're in a hurry."

Kevin nodded. "Got to get home, Jesse. Start putting a new life together."

Jesse smiled. "Now there's a coincidence. Hop in."

Kevin grinned and ran around the front of the car and jumped in.

. . .

ON THE ROAD to *La Aurora* International Airport, they listened to Victor Carano's radio address, assuring the people of Guatemala that his program for the reform of Guatemala would continue. Aguilera still had a chance, Jesse assumed, but wondered if things would be better even if he won.

Jesse looked to the west and saw the sun heading that way, just as it always had. Maybe most things did stay the same, as Teo had said.

But not everything. And not everyone.

He flicked the radio off, and the lawyer and his client rode toward the airport in silence, staring straight ahead.

EPILOGUE

THREE WEEKS LATER, Jesse read that Cal's huge hacked-up body had been found on the side of a muddy road near the Livingston airport. The corpse was picked clean, his passport and wallet, even his shoes and his coat had been taken.

A shudder passed through him. Not a good way to go, but at least Cal wouldn't have to deal with the subpoenas that were flying out of the SEC and Justice Department. Simon Bradshaw's final act had forced Cal Covington to take the biggest risk of his life—a gamble that had resulted in his brutal murder over 2,500 miles away.

Jesse put down the *International Herald Tribune*, ordered a créme caramel and another espresso from the *garcón*, and smiled at the woman across the table from him.

It was misting outside the Paris *bistro*—not unusual in June—but Megan Harris smiled back at him and a warm white light filled the room.

VERBATIM EXCERPTS FROM THE 2012 U.S. STATE DEPARTMENT ADVISORY ON GUATEMALA

GUATEMALA HAS ONE of the highest violent crime rates in Latin America. In 2011, an average of 40 murders a week were reported in Guatemala City alone, and an average of 109 murders a week were reported countrywide . . . local officials, who are often inexperienced and underpaid, are unable to cope with the problem. Rule of law is lacking as the judicial system is weak, overworked, and inefficient. Criminals know there is little chance they will be caught or punished, as the rate of convictions/resolution are very low.

The number of violent crimes reported by U.S. citizens and other foreigners has remained high and incidents have included, but are not limited to, assault, theft, armed robbery, carjacking, rape, kidnapping, and murder, even in areas once considered safe such as Zones 10, 14, and 15 in the capital. Since December 2008, 31 murders of U.S. citizens have been reported in Guatemala, including six in 2011 and three in 2012. Victims have been killed when they resisted attack or refused to give up their money or other valuables. Assailants are often armed with guns and do not hesitate to use them if you resist.

Emboldened armed robbers have attacked vehicles on main roads in broad daylight. Travel on rural roads increases the risk of being stopped by a criminal roadblock or ambush.[1] Widespread narcotics and alien-smuggling activities make remote areas especially dangerous. A number of travelers have experienced carjackings and armed robberies after just having arrived on international flights, most frequently in the evening. In the most common scenario, tourists or business travelers who land at the airport after dark are held up by armed men as their vehicle departs the airport, but similar incidents have occurred at other times of the day. Recently, there have been numerous reports of violent criminal activity along Guatemala's main highways… Carjacking persists as a problem . . . Leaving cars unattended in parking lots of fast food franchises can also invite break-ins in spite of the presence of armed guards. Make sure you leave the car just long enough to complete the meal and not any more—the armed guards are for decoration only.

Women should be especially careful when traveling alone and avoid staying out late without an escort. A U.S. citizen teenager attending a party was raped by four teens in June 2010 in Jutiapa. In August 2010 a U.S. citizen woman was raped on the beach in Monterrico by a person claiming to be hotel security who offered to escort her to her hotel. In March 2011 a U.S. citizen student was accosted by two men on a street in Panajachel and raped by one when she left a bar late in the evening. In August 2011 two U.S. citizen tourists traveling from El Salvador were raped by five armed men when their vehicle was hijacked on the Carretera a El Salvador (CA-2), 16 miles away from Guatemala City.

Kidnapping gangs, who are often connected to narco-traffickers, are a concern in both Guatemala City and rural Guatemala.[2] Gang members are often well armed with sophisticated weaponry and they sometimes use massive amounts of force to extort, kidnap, and kill. Some kidnapping gangs are known to kill their victims whether or not the ransom is paid. In January 2012, a U.S. citizen was kidnapped in Santa Rosa and was reportedly killed when kidnappers did not get the ransom they had demanded.

1   The author and his wife were saved from an attempted kidnapping by a single courageous armed escort.
2   Within a week of the author's visit to the main courthouse, a judge was kidnapped from the main entry and another judge was assassinated in the same area.

CPSIA information can be obtained at www.ICGtesting.com
Printed in the USA
BVOW072113051112

304724BV00001B/14/P